P9-CLJ-110

In a
BOOK CLUB
Far Away

Center Point
Large Print

Also by Tif Marcelo and available from
Center Point Large Print:

Once Upon a Sunset

**This Large Print Book carries the
Seal of Approval of N.A.V.H.**

In a
BOOK CLUB
Far Away

Tif Marcelo

CENTER POINT LARGE PRINT
THORNDIKE, MAINE

This Center Point Large Print edition
is published in the year 2021 by arrangement with
Gallery Books, a division of Simon & Schuster, Inc.

Copyright © 2021 by Tiffany Johnson.

All rights reserved.

This book is a work of fiction.
Any references to historical events, real people, or real
places are used fictitiously. Other names, characters, places,
and events are products of the author's imagination, and
any resemblance to actual events or places or persons,
living or dead, is entirely coincidental.

The text of this Large Print edition is unabridged.
In other aspects, this book may vary
from the original edition.
Printed in the United States of America
on permanent paper.
Set in 16-point Times New Roman type.

ISBN: 978-1-64358-897-1

The Library of Congress has cataloged this record
under Library of Congress Control Number: 2021930285

For my Army spouse siblings
and book club ladies

PART ONE

I volunteer as tribute.

—*The Hunger Games* by Suzanne Collins

CHAPTER ONE
Regina

Present Day, Saturday

In a commercial kitchen far, far away, in a military town in the middle of Georgia, a caterer named Regina Castro had an online crush. It was ridiculous, really, how often she thought of Henry Just, but when one was a single mom and an entrepreneur who didn't have the time and the energy to date, an online flirtation was absolutely and positively enough. A heart on a post from Henry sent her spirits soaring. She preened whenever he commented on a photo, which, these days, was often. On the day over a year ago she received her first direct message from Henry—an innocuous note on how to properly grease and flour a cake pan, because he was a baker (and how sexy was that?)—she rushed through the kitchen, arms extended like Fräulein Maria singing "The Hills Are Alive." Through the screen, Henry Just was sexy and sweet, and safe.

But now, looking down at an open package atop her work desk addressed to her from Henry, she wasn't sure whether to scream with glee or to pack up and run to the next state.

"Earth to Regina? Hello?"

Regina snapped her gaze up to her catering manager, Alexis McCartney, who had a hand on her hip at the office doorway. "Excuse me?"

"I said that I need to head out to do another round of shopping. We underestimated the flour for the Food for the Gods." Alexis's gaze traveled from Regina to the package, and her expression switched from the usual stoic, don't-give-a-damn nature to mischief. "But it looks like someone got a package."

Regina shut the flaps, face burning. "It's nothing."

"Uh-huh." Alexis entered the office, dimming the room. The office was closet-sized, and not even the walk-in type. With the two of them, it was a shoebox.

The sleeve of Alexis's black chef's jacket brushed against Regina as she flipped one of the box's flaps. "From Henry Just of Just Cakes in Alexandria, Virginia? Huh. *The* Henry? The one you've been canoodling with online?"

Regina looked up then, shocked, to see Alexis's raised eyebrow. She gasped. "I'm *not* canoodling. That's not even possible."

"Mm-hmm." Alexis rolled her eyes. "With the way you've been writing each other? You're practically making out. You can't deny it—we share the same social media account, and I see all the details and the DMs. But obviously he hasn't gotten the memo that the way to your heart is through movies, not books."

"Hey!" Regina objected, though she was partly feigning her defensiveness. There was truth to Alexis's words. Regina could recite movie lines like some people did the lyrics of their favorite songs but couldn't remember the plots of many literary classics. But Alexis's implication was reminiscent of something Regina's ex-husband had said so long ago and was a poke in the tender parts of her heart. "What about all the bedtime books Miko insisted I read a million times? Not to mention culinary-school textbooks. And cookbooks."

"That's all for work or part of parenting. But for fun?" She gestured to the book nestled in the box. "May I?"

"Be my guest."

Regina thought back to the very last "fun" book she'd undertaken. It hadn't been for fun at all but for a book club—the only book club she'd ever been a part of—in upstate New York when she was still on active duty in the Army.

"*The Sky Is Everywhere.* That was the last book I read for fun." She half smiled at the memory of the chaotic circle of hens—and a couple of roosters—that had comprised the Millersville Book Club, and a pang of regret sliced through her heart. She heaved a breath. "But anyway. Henry and I were DMing about books chefs should read, and I guess he took our conversation to heart."

Alexis nodded in approval. *"Blood, Bones, and Butter: The Inadvertent Education of a Reluctant Chef.* Looks older."

"He said he found it at his local used bookstore."

"So thoughtful." Alexis flipped the pages. "And now the pressure's on. Time to get reading—he might ask at some point if you enjoyed it."

Regina pressed her lips together. In truth, she didn't have time to read. Heck, she didn't have time to stand around to even talk about reading, if she was being honest, because every minute not earning money meant she was losing it. "Or maybe, because we're so far away, I don't have to. Two whole states separate Georgia from Virginia. He won't ever know."

"Well, I think it's sweet. Though at some point, maybe you *should* speak. Like on the phone or video chat. It's ridiculous how much you've flirted without actually communicating in real life."

"We're just friends," Regina said.

"Uh-huh. Online friends with imaginary benefits." Alexis cackled.

"Funny har-har."

She pretend-flipped an imaginary shirt collar. "That was pretty good, if I say so myself."

Regina busted out with a laugh; she couldn't help it.

From behind them, a crash sounded, followed immediately by the clatter of dishes. Regina winced at what she imagined had found its way to the floor, perhaps the tray of vegetables from Pickett Farms, which she had driven two hours for.

But she didn't move.

"What the hell are you guys doing over there?" Alexis pressed her hand against her blond hair, which was pulled taut into a bun, and went to the doorway. With her back to Regina, Alexis took command of the chaos that had erupted. Both former military, Regina and Alexis had divided up the labor so that it ran like an Army unit, like a chain of command.

Their system had worked, thus far. Regina found comfort in using the rules that had been ground into her since becoming a soldier, and she thought it the right way to do business. Regina was the good cop, and Alexis, the scarier one despite being the smaller of the two, was the bad cop. They both abided by standard operating procedures, by lists, by following orders. Finally, she and Alexis believed in BLUF, bottom line up front, with the overall business mission taking precedence over feelings and emotions.

All truly the Army way, despite Regina having left the Army more than seven years ago.

When Alexis turned back to her, she said, "Okay, back to our business. As I was saying,

I'm stepping out for about an hour. Are you due anywhere?"

"Nope. I'm here all afternoon."

"Great. Because . . ." Alexis's shoulders slumped. "We need to do another monthly roundup." She gestured toward the local Boy Scout troop calendar on the wall, open to the month of March. The picture was of two Scouts whittling down pieces of wood. One of these Scouts, fair-skinned and freckled but with dark brown eyes and hair, was Regina's son, Miko.

Regina dropped her eyes, and the last bit of warmth she'd felt from her receiving the package shriveled up. *The talk.* The talk of business finances, and whether The Perfect Day Catering would survive. She stood quickly to walk Alexis out. "Yes, of course."

Alexis nodded and led the way to the kitchen.

Regina's eyes swept across the humble starter kitchen, cozy even for her staff of five part-time employees. One hundred percent of her employees had other jobs elsewhere, which made for, sometimes, a hodgepodge of a skeleton crew whose employment loyalties were challenged by their steadier paychecks. Despite its three-year anniversary coming up, The Perfect Day Catering still clamored for purchase in their military town, where there was a limited amount of clientele.

Currently, two employees rolled lumpia, and

one skewered marinated pork onto sticks. One was off to the side making batter for Food for the Gods. And their last and newest employee, the culprit of the crash, was at the sink washing vegetables he had, indeed, dropped, now flanked by Alexis.

Soon, all of these parts would come together like an orchestra. The next night was the biggest catering job they'd had yet, an eighteenth-birthday party. The Filipino debutante party, wedding-like in scale, was a departure from their usual promotion party and Army-unit event. The event would boast a coordinated dance, a princess dress worn by the celebrant, and a horse-drawn carriage that would sit in front of the VFW for picture taking.

The event had been a risk to undertake, but it was time to level up. Not only was it the rare occasion that Regina could fix the recipes she'd learned from her own mother—because there weren't a ton of Filipino cultural events happening in their tiny town—but the company had nothing in the books scheduled for another month. The profit from this debutante party was already earmarked for rent and utilities, leaving little for much else.

Regina's tummy soured at the thought.

"What are you thinking about?" a voice whispered from behind her, which made Regina jump and spin around.

"Ma! Geesh. I swear you're always in my shadow."

Gloria Castro gave Regina a mischievous smile.

Her mother seemed to be everywhere Regina turned, in both good times and in bad, and at the most critical junctures in her life. Much like right then, when Regina's mind was in a vortex of doubt.

And like a shadow, Gloria was wearing all black, though not as part of the catering staff. This was her perpetual mourning attire. Regina's lola, the Castro matriarch, had died almost five years ago, but Gloria had never kicked the habit of wearing black to honor her mother. On her most whimsical days, Gloria wore shades of gray and, depending on her mood, might surprise everyone with a pop of color in a statement necklace, a fancy bangle, or pointed, impractical shoes. And despite this outward appearance of gloom, Gloria was as cheerful as ever.

"So?" Gloria asked.

"So, what?"

Gloria's eyes widened.

"I'm not thinking about anything. But wait . . ." Regina looked at her watch. "Miko's supposed to be at baseball in fifteen minutes. Is everything okay? And speaking of, you didn't forget to bring oranges did you?" She ran through the never-ending list in her head. Today was her son's baseball clinic, and she was the team mom but occasionally delegated her responsibilities to her mother at business crunch times.

"Dios, I know what time it is! Don't worry, Miko's outside with Alexis. But the mailman caught me at the door on the way out and this looked important. You know, that Mr. Leong is such a handsome man. Fit, too, carrying that bag and driving his car. So good at parking."

"I'm ignoring you, Ma."

Gloria presented her the stack of mail. "Maria Regina. You're really not allowed to ignore me since I'm your mother. Life cannot just be about work."

"It's not just about work. It's about Miko, our future."

"That's still work. You volunteer for everything; you don't ever take a day off. And I asked Mr. Leong—he doesn't work Sundays." She blinked repeatedly, her flirtatious look. "So maybe you shouldn't work one Sunday so you can have a good time? I already talked to him."

"You did *not*."

"I did. Since you're so type A about everything except your social life, I thought I would take the initiative."

"I don't even know what to say."

Gloria was right, of course. Regina approached parenting like her business, completely hands-on. Team mom, room mom, PTA mom. All of it. Still, she pretended like she didn't hear her mother, and instead, flipped through the mail: Credit card bills. A notice for her to re-up her commercial kitchen lease. A note from her accountant to remind her that quarterly taxes were coming up.

"I mean, you could have just saved all this for me to look at later," Regina said, properly deflated.

"There's an express envelope in there."

Regina fished out the official envelope marked for two-day delivery. She tore it open to reveal a kraft envelope with her name and address handwritten in a fancy scrawl in blue ink, complete with curlicues on the first letter of her first and last names. And while the top-left corner of the envelope didn't bear a return address, Regina knew who it was from. No one had a love for kraft and calligraphy more than her longtime friend Adelaide, who also had an obsession with burlap, lanterns, wreaths, and antiques. While Regina could wax poetic on wine and menu pairings, Adelaide was equally as passionate about interior design. Adelaide was a woman who embraced her Southern roots despite not having lived in the South for years, with a homey and modern style that had preceded Joanna Gaines and the Magnolia empire.

"Adelaide," she whispered.

"I could tell it was important," Gloria noted.

Adelaide had only mailed Regina three times: once, to invite her to a book club at her home

18

all those years ago; second, to apologize over their biggest fight; and third, to announce her pregnancy and Regina's new role as godmother. Even more, Adelaide had her number. There was no reason why she couldn't have called with news. They followed each other on social media and could have easily DMed.

Regina thought back to the last time they had touched base. It was a random text about six months ago when Adelaide let her know that she and her daughter were PCS'ing, or moving, to the DC area from South Korea. *I'm on your side of the world, finally!* it had said, though after a couple of back-and-forth texts, their communication had trailed away.

"Thanks for bringing it over." Regina absentmindedly sidestepped to a barstool in the corner of the kitchen and popped up onto it. Around her, sounds prattled on. She slid a nail under the flap to lift the envelope's seal.

Under her breath, she read aloud, " 'To my dearest Reggie. I know it's been a hot second, but I need you . . .' "

"What is it, iha?" Gloria said, sensing Regina's rise in panic as she skimmed the rest of the note. Regina didn't catalog every word or all the details, but the message came through loud and clear.

"Sounds like I'm going to get the vacation you say I need." She looked up at Gloria. "It's an SOS."

CHAPTER TWO
Adelaide

Present Day, Thursday

"Lord, help me," Adelaide Wilson-Chang groaned at the kitchen sink. She let go of the vintage Corelle plate, grateful that it was indestructible as it clattered into the porcelain, and gripped the sink's apron front with her left hand. She pressed with the heel of her right hand against the sharp pain in her abdomen.

She counted backward from ten and focused her eyes on the sponge sitting in the sink. These days, she'd resorted to her labor breathing to cope, and while for the most part it worked, the pain was getting worse. Last week, she could have walked through the pain; two weeks before then, she'd been able to fake her way through her mommy meetups and her neighborhood La Leche League meetings. But now, God, she couldn't even do the dishes without her gallbladder acting up.

Five . . . four . . . three . . .

The pain ebbed, and Adelaide straightened tentatively. Her vision expanded to include the entire room; sounds returned. The laughter of her

daughter, Genevieve, reached her ears—a salve—
and with that, the rest of the pain subsided.

Two . . . one.

And with one final deep breath, Adelaide's
body relaxed into its normal stance, and her
breathing returned to normal. Her gaze lingered
on the open window that provided a view of the
postage-stamp–sized backyard of her town house,
and she pressed a hand against her forehead, now
damp with sweat.

"It's fine, everything's fine," she said aloud to
the empty kitchen, echoing what her mama would
say when the poop started to hit the fan. The
mantra acted like a reset button, her declaration
to the world. If she said it, it would happen. After
all, everything *was* fine. She had pain, sure, but
that would be fixed soon. Her family was safe,
albeit not all present, and best of all, one of her
best friends, Sophie, was here, and the other,
Regina, was on the way.

Currently, Sophie was play-chasing and pretending to lose a game of tag to Genevieve in
the small area of grass. Sophie cackled, and
her laugh traveled through the air like skipping
stones. At almost two years old, Genevieve was
quick on her feet, and as she ran, her arms flailed
in uninhibited joy. Her innocence was both
beautiful and bittersweet, and Adelaide wished
for the hundredth time that her husband was
home to witness it.

"Hey, Adelaide, what time is it? I don't have my phone with me." Sophie's voice knocked Adelaide out of her thoughts. Sophie was gazing at her through the open kitchen window. "I have to call Jasper. I completely forgot to check in when I landed."

For a beat Adelaide was transported back to when Sophie had played with her own kids in their shared backyard years ago, because it was as if she hadn't aged at all. Sophie's dark skin was smooth and free of wrinkles; the only clue that time had passed were the occasional silver strands of hair in her tight ponytail. She and her partner, Jasper, currently lived in Tampa. They were newly retired from the Army and starting the next chapter of their lives.

"It's just shy of three," Adelaide answered, voice croaking, after glancing at the hanging grandfather clock. "What *did* Jasper say when you left? Was he upset I asked you out here?"

"No, c'mon." Sophie's voice grew louder as she came in through the French doors, carrying Genevieve on a hip. She snorted through her sardonic smile. "You know how many trips away from home he's made, some of them last-minute. He can handle a long weekend on his own."

Adelaide worried her bottom lip. It had been a little more than a week since she sent the SOS in a fit of panic and pain, and she hadn't really

23

understood what kind of corner she'd backed her friends into. Sophie was a pediatric nurse, and for her to ask for days off after recently being hired . . .

"Hey." Sophie tugged on Adelaide's arm as they migrated to the living room. "Don't worry about it. I want to be here. You can't have surgery without help. And what's the point of me becoming a nurse if I can't be there for the people I love? It's your damn gallbladder, Ad. And your husband's in another country. Anyway, I've been wanting to spend some time with my goddaughter. If I waited any longer to meet her, it would have taken her days instead of an hour to get used to me."

Sophie snuggled Genevieve. In response, Adelaide's baby girl giggled, cheeks reddening with joy. "And SOS or not, honestly, I needed some time away, even if it is twenty degrees colder here." She shivered. "I almost need a coat, and I don't think I've put one on since moving to Tampa."

"You can borrow any one of mine. I grew quite a collection in Seoul. Though, I might have to declutter since I admittedly went overboard shopping over there."

"You're preaching to the choir. I actually took a trip to the post thrift shop a week ago to donate all of mine," Sophie said, nonchalant.

With every duty station came a different way

of life, dependent on location and on the job their spouses, as active-duty soldiers, held. Duty stations were also how Adelaide marked time, both as an Army brat and an Army wife. Two years here, one year there, and sometimes a midyear switch that threw everyone into a tizzy. It had been a little over six years since she and Sophie had lived in the same location—they'd been lucky to have ended up together twice in the last ten years—but it was as if no time had passed.

It would only be made better by Regina's arrival. "I'm thankful you're here, Soph. As much as I can't wait to get rid of my lemon of a gallbladder, selfishly, I needed adult company. This place feels too big even with just the two of us."

"It doesn't feel too big to me. It feels lived in, like you've been settled in for years instead of months." Sophie gestured a hand toward the dining room, at Adelaide's nine-foot buffet, smiling. "And it looks like everything's intact."

"We got lucky with movers this time. But you know how it is. We gotta make it a home or else we'll never feel like we're home," Adelaide said, ready to launch into a diatribe about her predicament of having to lease a storage unit, since the town house didn't have an attic or a basement for all of her memorabilia, but her phone buzzed in her pocket. Her eyes shot to the front windows that looked out onto the narrow cobblestone street, and she approached the foyer. A shadow of a person crossed the window next to the front door, and Adelaide stepped back, gasping. "Jesus, I'm still not used to being this close to the sidewalk. People are literally on the other side of this wall."

Sophie joined her. "That's what you get for wanting to live in a historic town. I'm actually surprised that you didn't choose the suburbs. What happened to your 'colonial house with a wraparound porch'? You hated apartment living in Millersville."

At the mention of the military town where they'd met, Adelaide turned her attention to the empty parking spot in front of her town house. Millersville was a decade ago, and what she was back then, idealistic and somewhat naive—she no longer was. With a softer voice she said, "I guess I changed my mind."

"That car . . ." Sophie peered as a tan Mercedes-Benz rolled up.

The car in question parallel parked with ease, on the first try. It was a behemoth, a vintage coupe. There weren't many like it on the road, because it was the Euro version five hundred series that had been converted to American road standards. The car's name was Baby.

Adelaide knew all of this because the owner had once told her so.

"You didn't." Sophie's voice was tight, strangled. "No, Ad."

Adelaide giggled, because what else was she to do? Despite the drama that would soon engulf them, her best friends were about to be in the same vicinity for the first time in ten years. The occasion was momentous—a feat only Adelaide could coordinate.

Because this SOS wasn't just about her. Adelaide's gallbladder might've turned her life upside down, but her upcoming surgery had given her the opportunity to make lemons out of lemonade. She had a plan—to reunite her estranged best friends with an SOS after The Fight a decade ago had broken their three-pack apart.

CHAPTER THREE
Sophie

Sophie Walden wasn't the kind of woman who minced words. It came from years of being in the nursing field, where directness was an asset. Sure, empathy and compassion were key to a caregiver's success—she herself didn't appreciate hardened nurses who'd forgotten the plight of the sick—but there was no substitution for the straightforward truth.

But Sophie also believed truth could be told with grace. Her mother had excelled at this sleight of hand, with hidden messages behind her words, often peppering her constructive criticisms with the sweet addition of an endearing nickname to ease the sting. This belief also came from dealing with a partner—a husband in the eyes of the law—for twenty years who lived and died by her opinions. It came from her children's reactions to her mood.

And despite the avalanche of conflicting emotions at seeing Regina Castro unload her car, Sophie remembered that Adelaide had been and was in pain. So instead of launching into a tirade, Sophie simply asked, "What is *she* doing here?"

Adelaide mumbled something indecipherable, brushed past her, and rushed to the oak door, throwing it open. Light spilled across the threshold. The moment was straight out of the past, when once upon a time, Adelaide opened her home for get-togethers with Sophie and Regina. It was a moment of déjà vu so vivid that Sophie had to remind herself that it was 2021, not 2011.

With Regina's appearance, The Fight rushed back in full clarity, as if time simply picked up where it had left off. Then again, The Fight was never resolved. It wasn't resolved because she and Regina had simply walked away from each other, and life had gone on. Despite Sophie's multiple attempts at reconciliation with Regina, they'd both moved on and somehow were able to each negotiate, over time, a friendship with Adelaide, but not with each other.

Regina appeared at the door, a vision of color, dragging a green hard-shell suitcase with her. Her long brown hair was highlighted, some strands red against the sun. She wore a sunny yellow flowered shirt and white jeans, complementing her light brown skin. Divorce and civilian life looked good on her.

"Oh my God, first of all, Northern Virginia is so pretty. And this town! I'm seriously packing up my business to bring it here. Your foyer, so beautiful! I recognize so many things! And you!

I missed your face!" Regina, the epitome of a chatterbox, threw herself at Adelaide.

Sophie winced at Regina's insensitivity to Adelaide's pain.

Then, Regina's attention migrated to one of Adelaide's decorations on the wall and she commented on it, too. "How do you make everything look so good?" Her eyes scanned the rest of the room. And when she turned, her gaze landed squarely on Sophie.

Sophie met her eyes and willed herself to smile.

Or at least, grit her teeth together. In truth, Sophie's insides were a furnace lit by a decade-old ember.

Regina's eyes widened, and she stepped back. She side-eyed Adelaide, whose entire face had flushed pink. "Um, what's going on? And what's *she* doing here? You sent *me* an SOS."

"Well, at least we got the same story for this trick," Sophie added. Somehow, though, she'd had a tiny inkling that something like this was going to happen, eventually. Adelaide had occasionally brought up Regina in their conversations, as if testing the waters, admittedly smoothing some of the jagged edges of their past. But there had been no lead-up to this moment, no hints dropped. Sure, Sophie thrived on the unexpected—hospitals were a hotbed for it—but this, from Adelaide?

This trip was supposed to be Sophie's getaway.

Besides her primary mission to help Adelaide, her plan was to relax.

Sophie shook her head. "I left Jasper and my girls, Adelaide. I took days off without pay. This is wrong."

"I know, you guys . . ." Adelaide looked at them with those doe eyes, a hand reached out to each. "So I tricked you both, sort of. But I didn't lie. Reggie, I said I needed help with Gen, because you are the most fun person I know, and Soph, I said I needed a nurse because you're the best caregiver I know. All of these things are the God's honest truth, pinky swear."

Ah, those eyes. Sophie always fell for those eyes. Her twins had the same look—and they also knew when to wield it. She shook her head, undecided on what to do. This was not ideal, but Sophie refused to be the one to leave. Ten years ago, it was she who had quietly slinked away, but she was here first, quite frankly. And she couldn't go back to Tampa. Not yet.

Not until she figured out herself and her relationship with Jasper.

Regina dipped her chin. Then, she started to laugh.

The woman was laughing. Of course she would laugh—she laughed at the most inopportune times.

"What's so funny?" Sophie asked.

"I just . . . I can't believe this. I mean, thank

goodness I didn't have to cancel a catering client. And that I have my mom and Logan to take care of Miko. Not cool, Ad."

Adelaide sidestepped so she blocked the front door. "Please, don't go, either of you. My gallbladder needs to come out. I'm in a lot of pain. Matt's family is in Taiwan, and they're too old to travel here. My mom's caring for my dad full-time now. And yes, there are folks I know in the area who could make me meals, who could check in on me." Fear flashed in Adelaide's eyes. "But I don't trust anyone else with Genevieve, or to come into my home and really know my business. You are the only two I trust in this whole wide world besides my husband. When I go under the knife tomorrow, I won't be worried at all if I know you're both here." The last of her words echoed through the house, and it was answered by Genevieve's faint cry. The little girl had been so quiet, Sophie had forgotten she was in her arms.

Genevieve wiggled and reached out to her mother, like she knew Mama needed a hug.

Adelaide slung her daughter on her hip, wincing a little, and Genevieve buried her face into her mother's neck. All at once, Sophie's heart relented. There were only a few family members left in her life, and Adelaide was family by choice. Reggie had been, too, once upon a time. For family, Sophie would have spared no expense or time to ensure they were okay. Old beef or no old beef.

She wasn't the kind of woman who walked away.

Or am I?

Her own words speared her.

No, no, she wasn't.

CHAPTER FOUR
Regina

"This is . . . I can't do this." A swirl of anger swept Regina up like the beginnings of a tornado, and it threatened to upend her. Grappling with the handle of her suitcase, she leaned against the wall to get her bearings.

When a military spouse called for an SOS, the answer was always yes. The reason was clear and undeniable: milspouses didn't rally the troops for the small things. They'd endured too much, forged by over two decades of conflict, stemming from 9/11, when lives had been divided into *before* and *after*. Before, in the post–Desert Storm calm, the most inconvenient duty station for families had been a tour in South Korea. But in the after, everything changed. In the after, deployments were a given. In the after, families had to bend in new ways.

What rose from the constant ash of a long war were families who learned to survive. It meant single-parent families; it meant children displaced from their parents. It meant bolstering oneself for the worst-case scenario despite maintaining positive thinking. It also meant saving your help tokens until you needed to cash them in.

Once upon a time, Regina, Sophie, and Adelaide had agreed to always show up when an SOS was called. And Regina, despite having left the milspouse life via divorce, still held fast to this rule. In fact, being an Army veteran was part of her identity, and she was proud that she'd been a part of something bigger than herself.

But she hadn't anticipated Adelaide taking advantage of her loyalty by bringing in Sophie, too.

Sophie, a woman she hadn't seen in a decade. The only other woman in the world who had made as good a friend as Adelaide, close enough to be sisters.

No, this wasn't part of the agreement.

"I'm leaving." Regina's gaze darted between them, and she turned toward the front door. Twelve hours she'd been on the road, and her body was bone-tired, but she'd endure another twelve rather than face Adelaide's attempt at playing peacemaker.

Adelaide's face fell. "No, please."

"Excuse me," Regina said firmly, quietly.

Seconds passed, and finally, Adelaide moved away from the door.

Regina stepped across the threshold. She didn't look back. Although she felt the heat of Adelaide's pleading stare, she put one foot in front of the other.

Outside, she allowed the anger to well up

within her. She loaded her suitcase forcefully—she knew she would be mad at herself later on if either the car or the suitcase ended up with a scratch—but she didn't care at the moment. Then she rounded the vehicle and slipped into the driver's seat, where she struggled to fit the key into the ignition. The keys fumbled in her hand as she frustratedly banged and pushed the key against the ignition, but everything seemed to work against her. "Damn it."

The sharp echo of her voice startled her, and it gave her pause. She put her hand against her chest, feeling the familiar pound of her heart, of it breaking, again.

Regina took a deep breath and methodically stuck the correct key into the ignition. She turned it with a click, and Baby growled to life.

How foolish she had been to so easily have jumped into the car just days after that debutante party, without asking Adelaide any pertinent questions. She'd scrambled and made plans with Logan and her mother for Miko's care, which had been a cobweb of coordination.

With shaking hands, she set the map of her phone back to Columbus, Georgia, 550 miles.

The phone buzzed, and a text flew in.

Henry
You're prob stuck on I95 but just wanted to say welcome to VA!

Disappointment added to Regina's anger. Meeting Henry was supposed to be a bonus. She'd imagined a *You've Got Mail* scenario but without the power imbalance and the drama. A romantic first meeting.

She texted slowly, unsure what to say:

Thanks. I'm here actually. But

A knock sounded at the passenger-side window, interrupting her. Regina looked over; it was her nemesis.

Sophie pointed down at the seat.

"You want to come in here?" Regina asked aloud.

Sophie nodded.

Regina put away the phone and unlocked the door. She sat up in the bucket seat as Sophie entered the car, though unfortunately, Regina was still shorter than Sophie's seated form. "What do you want?"

"Look. You can't leave," Sophie said. "Adelaide needs you."

So Sophie was going to play the role of a martyr. Regina rolled her eyes. Immature, yes, but they were in *her* car, and she could do what she damn well pleased. "Looks to me you have that covered."

"I'm mad at her, too, you know. I didn't know you were coming. But we're here now, and you heard what she said about needing the both of us."

Regina snorted. "C'mon. You don't believe that entirely, do you? One of us would have sufficed. She's trying to get us to make up."

"I thought of that. But she's also one of the strongest women we know—we have to trust that she knows what she needs."

"*We* don't have to do anything."

Sophie clasped her hands in her lap. "I tried. Stay or go. It's your conscience."

"Yeah, okay, thanks, Mom." Regina looked away, toward the front windshield. Her actual mother would kill her for how rude she was being, but Sophie and her righteousness was the last thing she had expected or wanted today. Or any day of the last decade.

After seconds of silence in the car, she heard Sophie open the passenger-side door, slide out of her seat, and shut the door.

Without thinking, Regina placed Baby in drive.

Coming around the corner onto Burg Street, the main street of Old Town, the traffic was heavy. Cars cruised down the road at a snail's pace, much slower than the tourists' gaits on the sidewalk. The street bustled with a kind of optimism, the vibe quite the contrast to her sleepy military town, and a feeling bloomed in her belly. It might have been because DC was just a stone's throw away that Old Town absorbed this energy.

Or maybe because the old buildings carried their own history, inspiring a wish that her catering business could take up residence behind one of these shop windows.

It was only when she passed a bar called the Whistling Pig, written in a calligraphy font on a hanging wooden sign, that it dawned on her why her nostalgia had reared its ugly head: this place reminded her of Millersville's Main Street.

She shook her head to derail her meandering thoughts and looked at the map on her phone. The freeway was up ahead about five miles. Five more miles, and she could put all of this behind her.

At a stoplight, a herd of people meandered past in the crosswalk. On the right, Regina spotted a shop's purple-and-white awning. The front window, decorated with colorful vinyl lettering that spelled out *Just Cakes*, featured a white, four-tiered model cake on a stand. Two small children milled in front of the window, hands against the glass, peeking in, no doubt hoping to catch sight of more cakes inside.

Regina stilled. Just Cakes.

Henry Just of Just Cakes.

Her brain flipped to a new page.

He's in there.

At that moment, those children at the front window were possibly watching Henry work. In real life.

Would it be weird for her to just show up unannounced?

What was there to lose, now that she'd walked out of her friend's house?

Regina growled at her ping-pong of emotions and at the next street turned into an open parking space.

She swallowed her nervousness and sorted through her cluttered thoughts. She and Henry had had a revealing and intimate online friendship, DMs constantly flowing. They'd discussed everything business related; Regina had found solace writing to Henry's beautiful face. There was a freedom in their veiled anonymity; the computer screen was like a confessional, and Henry had responded reliably and thoughtfully. He'd remembered the things she told him. He'd checked in on her on event days. Such small gestures, but gestures she'd wished her ex would've picked up on when they had been married.

But seeing Henry in real life . . . this was opening Pandora's box, and especially now, in her grim mood. Would he be as gracious as he was online? Would he be as kind? What if he smelled or had bad breath?

A woman across the street called the children from the window, who bounded away, exposing the shadows of movement inside.

Don't be a fraidy-cat, Regina. You're friends.

She heaved a breath and straightened her posture.

Oh God, am I really doing this?

She stepped out of the car.

Yes, yes, I am.

With faux confidence, she jaywalked across the street, and upon reaching the door of Just Cakes, she opened it with much more strength than she'd anticipated and it flew inside with a bang.

The heads of the crowd inside swiveled toward her, and silence fell over the shop. Had she not been so consumed with the stares of the individuals, then she would have been able to adequately take in the bright room, the hanging star lights that added whimsy, and the high round tables where groups congregated for samples of cake. How quaint it all was.

She also didn't fully grasp that the man she wanted to see was approaching her, not until he was two feet away. Henry Just, in all of his baker glory and then some. He wore an apron over an oxford shirt, with one of its collars caught in the apron's neckline. His hair, curly up top and cropped on the sides, had bits of blond woven in with red, which hadn't shown in his photographs.

This was the man who'd sent her that book package last week, a book that—while she hadn't read it yet—she had placed on her bedside table, where only precious things like Miko's framed picture resided.

"Hi, name, please?" Henry held a clipboard and hadn't glanced up to look at her.

"Um, excuse me?"

The tip of his pen was poised on the list of names on the clipboard. "Last name of either party."

"Oh, I'm sorry, I don't . . . actually have an appointment." Regina's tongue tied at the tip. She gazed at the top of his head. Surely, any second now, he was going to look up.

Except, he didn't. "Ah, I apologize, but all of our tastings are by appointment only. I hope you understand. I think that . . . hm . . . that we might have availability tomorrow." He looked through the papers on his clipboard.

All around her, people focused in on their conversation. Regina's face burned with the beginning of embarrassment.

"I'm actually here because . . ." She cleared her throat. "Hello, Henry."

Henry stilled. Then, slowly, he looked up. Up close now, she took him in. Her mind cataloged the differences between Instagram Henry and For Real Henry. His eyes were a much clearer hazel in person, but the smile, the generous smile that appeared on his face, was definitely spot-on.

"Regina?"

"Hi. It's me."

Months. Months, they had been corresponding, almost every day, and this was all she could say? He was her pen pal. She had been looking forward to this. But instead of joy, what she felt seeing him this first time was *relief.* Relief that there was someone here in Old Town to turn to in the middle of her dysfunctional friendship-triangle with Adelaide and Sophie.

"Hey! Are . . . are you okay?" His expression changed from excitement to worry. He stepped into her, tentative, as she felt her face crumble.

She shook her head as a decade's worth of memories and drama rushed toward her.

"Can I . . . Is this?" he asked, arms out, an awkward gesture.

He was asking her if she needed a hug. And in fact, she did.

She stepped into his body, crowd be damned.

CHAPTER FIVE
Regina

July 2011—About Ten Years Ago

"No, no, no. This is not okay."

Regina paused at the door of apartment E of 2100 Bell Street at the sound of her husband's muffled voice. With a letter in her hand, she took a deep breath and turned the doorknob, popping it open a crack. She peeked inside.

The hard bass guitar of rock music blared from the living room on the right, and the exhaust fan whirred from behind the wall on her left. And in the middle of the hallway was her cat, Shadow, nestled next to Logan's boots, atop his discarded socks and uniform top. Shadow eyed her, in warning.

"He's cooking again, isn't he?" Regina asked Shadow.

The cat meowed.

Regina entered and bent down and rubbed the back of Shadow's ear, then stepped over the pile of dirty clothes.

"Hey! Hey, I thought I heard you come in." Logan stuck his head out from their galley kitchen and yelled above the exhaust. Behind him was a plume of smoke.

For a beat, Regina lost her train of thought. Her nose tickled at the scent of burnt cheese, a sure sign that Logan had somehow fried the boxed mac and cheese he had insisted on buying in bulk from the commissary. It was supposedly one of the only things he knew how to cook. Supposedly.

"Babe?" he said, with an expectant look and a frozen smile. A smile that said that he was trying. They were on the heels of a fight from the night before, this time about him taking the reins as a true partner in their home—since her role seemed to have evolved to a full-blown housekeeper and cook. The fight had ended with him doing exactly what he did each time they disagreed: leaving.

Regina wasn't sure how to respond. Or which version of Logan this one was. So she shook a smile onto her face and pretended that she couldn't hear the sizzle in the background. She lifted the letter in her hand. "I got invited to book club."

The man cackled, ducking back into the kitchen.

"What's so funny about that?" She unlaced her combat boots and propped them next to the front door and, in stocking feet, unbuttoned and hung her camouflaged shirt in the hallway closet. Their apartment was tiny, not quite what

46

she had envisioned for their first home together, and had almost zero storage space. Their uniform tops were relegated to the hallway closet, where they'd become accustomed to dressing and undressing.

"You don't like to read," he said.

She gasped and went to their bedroom. "I take offense. Yes, I do." She changed into her college sweatshirt and leggings, then stood at the kitchen's entryway. She slung her arms across her chest to watch this man—her husband—attempt to cook. He was still in his brown T-shirt and camo pants and barefoot, and she couldn't help but just look. Logan Hardin was handsome. Shy of six feet, he had these captivating light brown eyes and was built like a tank, muscle everywhere. They had married right after his graduation from West Point and hers from Villanova; after a short two months of Officer Basic Course, they'd transferred to Upstate New York's Army post, Fort Fairfax, and there they were, almost two years married. Though, sometimes, like the night before, when their conversations ignited into a forest fire, it felt like they were still strangers.

"In fact, I have a book on my nightstand," she pointed out.

He snorted. "The Bible is not, technically, a book."

"Don't let my mother hear you say that. It's a family heirloom."

47

Logan stretched out a hand, a signal for her to come close, to snuggle in. This was another routine step in their silent apologies to each other. Because he wasn't the type to say sorry—and, well, she, she was always right, so why should she?—she stepped forward and buried her face in his chest while he kissed the top of her head.

"Lemme see that invite," he said.

Regina placed the invitation in his hand and grabbed a soda from the fridge. She plopped down in one of the chairs of their two-person dining room set and brought her knees to her chest.

His eyes gleamed. "Oh, fancy."

She popped the can open. "Hand-lettered. You know it's serious."

An eyebrow rose. He slipped the marbled paper from the envelope. "From Captain Chang's wife? I didn't realize they decided to live off post. Oh, and printed fancy paper, too. 'Hello, neighbors! Since we're all connected to Fort Fairfax but live off post, I thought I'd start a book club. For our first meeting, I picked the book just so we can get it started. It's called *The Hunger Games*. It was just published a few years ago, but I hear it is a page-turner. Now, don't be wary that it's teen fiction! I know most of us have read *Twilight*— don't pretend you haven't! Book club will be four weeks from today, August 28, at my house: 2110 Bell Street Apartment A, Millersville Heights

Apartments. Can't wait to meet all of you.' " He snickered. "Book club. You're more of a movie club kind of person, don't you think? And even then, if it's not up your alley, you fall right asleep. And snore, too, actually. Speaking of, that should have been covered in our premarriage counseling: how to handle each other's snoring." He was practically yelling over the exhaust, and with the kitchen window open to the expanse of the shared backyard, where kids were playing and parents hovering nearby, Regina winced. She imagined the quick spread of gossip like peanut butter on toast that ended up all over the gosh-damn place—*Did you know that Regina Castro snores like a Mack truck?* That is, if the neighbors already weren't talking about their raised voices last night.

She could've clapped back that their pre-marriage counseling also didn't cover a husband who seemed incapable of acting like an adult. That somehow, his bachelor housekeeping skills had disappeared the moment they got married. Maybe that's why she couldn't stay awake. She was exhausted.

And yet, when he ditched the letter and cursed the pot of burnt noodles as he plated the dish, worry etched in the lines of his forehead, she refrained from saying a word.

He was joking. And neither of them was perfect.

She countered. "I dunno. It sounds interesting. I've never been invited to spouse stuff."

Being dual military sometimes put her in the between. She was sometimes accidentally excluded from spouse functions, because she herself was active duty. And the fact that she and Logan lived in the first community beyond Fort Fairfax's gates often kept her out of the loop of social functions. Though, interestingly, while she and Logan had wanted to be away from the pressure of living next to people they worked with and opted for Millersville, they soon learned that every single neighbor was also connected to the post.

"Should I go?" Regina asked.

"It's your call. Captain Chang is the new company XO. It would be a good way to get to know his wife before the unit deploys. He seems like a good guy, so she's probably nice enough."

Regina bit her lip, understanding the politics of it all. But she wasn't good with women. Men, yes. She could banter with her brothers, could shoot the shit with her cousins. But women? Maybe she was meeting the wrong kind of friends, but she had always been labeled rough, sarcastic, and competitive.

But it was important in any line of work to get to know the leaders, and Logan was right. Since the 701st Infantry Battalion would soon pack up and head out for their routine cycle in

Afghanistan in a little more than a month, it would behoove Regina to be plugged in. This was going to be their first deployment.

"*The Hunger Games* is a children's book," she said as a final objection.

"I've never even heard of it." He hiked his hands on his hips; his forehead was sheened with sweat. "But, um, babe?"

"Let me guess. We should order in. Or I cook."

He nodded guiltily.

Regina hefted herself to her feet and gestured toward the living room. "Out of my way, soldier."

She might not have been a big reader, but she could cook anything out of nothing.

CHAPTER SIX
Adelaide

August 2011

"This isn't your first rodeo. Buck up," Adelaide whispered into the antique gilded mirror she'd purchased from a *Flohmarkt* in Germany, she and Matt's last duty station. She'd haggled and gotten it for a steal at fifteen euro, though it could easily have cost her over three hundred dollars in the States, because despite its age, there wasn't a crack in the glass. And to her great amusement, it had fit into this tiny powder room in their new apartment.

Everything was minuscule in these Millersville Heights apartments. Small closets, tiny kitchen cupboards; arms out, Adelaide could've reached from one end of this bathroom to the other lengthwise. She wasn't sure how the movers had gotten her antique German *Schrank* through the narrow hallway. But housing on Fort Fairfax, which was larger, didn't allow certain dog breeds, and Scout, their seven-year-old bulldog, was like her son.

When Adelaide and her husband, Matt, moved in a month ago, it had seemed like a good idea to them to replace the standard-issue mirror with this one. It brought great light to the room. It also reflected off the framed prints of flowers hanging on the wall behind her, creating a chaos that caused her to shut her eyes as the sounds of laughter echoed through the door. The mirror showed every flaw on her face, from the dark hue of her evident exhaustion after unpacking feverishly the last month, to the blemishes that had erupted on her skin. It revealed the stress from the move, the upcoming deployment, and the nausea that had crept in the last two days.

She gripped the sides of the pedestal sink to settle her stomach. *Nausea is good,* she reminded herself. Nausea was perfect, because it might mean that she was pregnant. Her period— annotated in her bedside-table chart, along with her temperature and all the other tiny personal details—was two days late. She was cautiously ecstatic, though trying to appear her joyful, presentable self was another story. "You're fine. Everything's fine. You wanted this book club."

Books were Adelaide's escape. She read to experience. And she was tired of keeping her love of books incognito. During this time at Millersville, she'd made it her duty to get to know other readers. To boot, Matt was now in a leadership position, and she would be like Mama had been: a steadfast, optimistic military spouse that others could look up to.

She just hadn't anticipated that her planned night would coincide with what felt like hot flashes.

She patted her face with a damp paper towel and breathed in long sips of air. This was the first event in her home. At least twenty people had arrived, and she didn't know if she had enough food. She, for sure, didn't have enough chairs, and she could hear her mother, a triple threat in etiquette—Southern, career officer's wife, and former event planner—in her head. *Never run out of food, Adelaide, y'hear? That's the worst sin of hostessing.*

In her normal state, she'd have managed these issues with a passable imitation of her mother's grace, but currently? She didn't know if her own underwear was on inside out.

A knock on the door made her jump.

"Mrs. Wilson-Chang?" a woman said on the other side.

Adelaide's heart thumped an unsteady beat at the sound of the woman's formality. The whole *Mrs.* thing hadn't stuck yet, despite six years in the role. *Mrs.* referred to her mother, right? It was one thing when they were in the South, where the title was customary, but in this case, her title was due to the fact that her husband was a captain; Fort Fairfax was an operational unit, and folks tended to stand at attention until they were told to be at ease.

"Hello?" the voice said again, undeterred.

If Adelaide stayed still, if she didn't say a word, would the person go away?

"It's Sophie . . . and . . ." the woman started.

"Regina," a soprano voice added.

"It's Sophie and Regina. Are you okay?"

Golly. There were now two women outside her bathroom door, and Adelaide was causing a scene, and she didn't remember who they were. She was usually great with names, but after the first dozen introductions earlier that evening, Adelaide had lost track. She was living in a mush of timelines from their recent arrival and upcoming deployment, which had been hit with occasional bouts of confusion, all heaped up together into this one moment.

"Adelaide?"

The sound of her first name, now whispered softly, snapped her out of her runaway thoughts. "Um, yes, I'll be right there." She flattened down her flyaway red hair and then pressed her lips together to salvage whatever was left of her red lipstick. She noticed a smudge of mascara where a cat eye was supposed to be. *Dang it.*

She opened the door.

Two women looked at her with matching sets of concerned but friendly expressions. Then, slowly, after the rush of blood in her ears subsided, Adelaide pieced together who these two were from their introductions as well as from her "pre-event briefing" from Matt. *Know who your guests are before they arrive,* her mother had always said, and earlier that afternoon, Adelaide and Matt had discussed those attendees who belonged to the 701st.

The woman on the left, Sophie Walden, was partner of ten years to Jasper Clemens, a sergeant first class in Matt's unit, which made him one of the more experienced and seasoned noncommissioned officers around. She was Black, tall, and refined, classic in casual clothing, and a nurse. They'd arrived in the area about the same time, though Sophie didn't give any indication that she was at all stressed about it. Her demeanor was calm, professional, approachable.

Next to her was Regina Castro, Filipino, petite but with a personality twice her size from what Adelaide remembered from their brief introduction at the door. She was an active-duty quartermaster officer, married to Logan Hardin, who worked directly for Matt. Both were lieutenants. Today, out of uniform, she was in a red maxi dress and a leather jacket, hair loosely braided down the side. Adelaide recalled her making a beeline for a small group of attendees and chatting them up immediately.

"Are you okay?" Sophie asked.

"Yeah, of course. I was just . . ." *Getting my life together.* "Checking my makeup, is all."

"Okay," Sophie answered, though her smile

didn't reach her eyes. She saw right through Adelaide. "Thank you, by the way, for inviting all of us, and for picking such a great first book to read this month. I loved *The Hunger Games*. But I'm sure we'll chat more about it later."

Regina grinned. "I hope you don't mind, but we passed out drinks. The book clubbers were getting restless."

Adelaide's face heated. God, she was already failing. "Thanks."

Regina batted away her words. "No problem. It was easy, and people were more than willing to wait with a glass of wine. Great choices, by the way. Oh, I made an apple tart to share. It's made of puff pastry . . ."

Regina kept talking, about wine and hors d'oeuvres, and Adelaide shifted on her feet. It was all too much—the talking and the noise—and she broke out into a sweat. "I . . . I'm just going to sit," Adelaide said, and perched on the closed toilet seat. She cradled her head in her hands to block out the light and the embarrassment and the panic running through her. "I'm sorry. This is unlike me."

From above her, she heard Sophie whisper, the padding of footsteps, and the door closing. Then, the sound of rustling, and two thumps. She looked up to Sophie, who was on her knees, her face at eye level. "So, really, are you okay?"

Adelaide contemplated telling Sophie that

she might be pregnant. That for the second time this year, her period hadn't come when it was supposed to. But Adelaide had learned her lesson in the past. No one wanted to hear a sob story about miscarriage. Most people only wanted to see the good, the pretty. So, despite her desire to tell the world, her news would have to wait until she was in her second trimester. "I just need a second. I don't think I ate enough preparing for this."

"I can call Captain Chang, or send everyone away? Because I can; I can say you're ill."

Those two suggestions alone stirred up nausea. She hadn't even told her husband that she was late. "Oh my, no . . . no. Matt's out at a friend's house with my dog, Scout, and I just . . . I don't know . . . need to take a breath. Maybe a glass of water."

Sophie inspected her face. "I can definitely get you that. Anything else?"

"I . . . I don't think so."

"Okay, then, I'll grab you some water, and I'm sure Regina can keep everyone entertained. She knows half the people in there. In fact, she's already admitted to most everyone that she didn't finish the book." She cackled a laugh. "These young people, I swear."

With that, Adelaide smiled. It was a reminder that, by God, she could do this. This wasn't her first party, or her first duty station. She and Matt were rounding their sixth year; she had three duty stations and two deployments under her belt. Before that, almost twenty years following Daddy through ten different homes.

"I'll be back," Sophie said, standing. But as she turned to open the door, Adelaide called out her name.

"Yes?"

"Could we keep this . . ." Adelaide wasn't sure what to say that didn't sound fake or pretentious.

"On the DL? Sure."

She swallowed her relief. "Thank you, Sophie."

"Hey." She touched the toe of her flat shoe to Adelaide's boot. "What good are we if we can't handle a little SOS? We've each got to be someone's Katniss every once in a while."

CHAPTER SEVEN
Sophie

If Sophie heard Regina say "I volunteer as tribute" one more time, she was going to cry from laughter.

All the book clubbers were seated in different spots, plopped on couches, and on the floor around the coffee table. Of the twenty-one members who arrived, two were men. An hour in, most were tipsy, which meant that none of the book had really been discussed yet.

It was unlike any other book club she'd attended, where it had been serious, literary, and high-brow. Sophie hadn't been this relaxed since she and her family left their last duty station and home in Louisiana. It was exactly what she needed.

Everyone had gone around at the beginning of the night and introduced themselves and said what their spouses did for the Army. From there, it had been easy to deduce unit and possibly rank, and then age. All except Sophie were *spouses* to active-duty soldiers at Fort Fairfax.

Any person in this business with any kind of social awareness was careful to note where everyone else fell in the unit or on post, since at times the position of the service member transposed itself to the spouse. Sometimes, though not always, when the soldier rose in leadership, their spouse took on a greater role within the family-program structure. That spouse might be involved with unit social functions, with the dissemination of information. The bottom line, in this environment, was that no one wanted to insult someone with senior rank's spouse, unless, of course, they deserved it.

This meant Sophie always stayed on the right side of etiquette. She was still sipping the same glass of wine she had poured earlier that night. Despite letting her guard down a little, she wouldn't be caught doing something foolish when she didn't know these people at all. This wasn't Fight Club. Loose lips sank ships and reputations, even if this was a neighborly Army social function and not the Navy. Never, ever Navy.

"Okay, everyone," Adelaide said, tapping her drink glass with her fork. She was laughing now, seemingly one hundred times more relaxed than she'd been in her bathroom just an hour ago. She had repinned the sides of her hair into a loose victory roll. She was a really pretty woman and had great style. Earlier, Sophie couldn't stop looking at the trinkets behind the glass cases in her living room, the wall of hand-drawn sketches of the homes the Wilson-Changs had previously lived in. The pillows strewn across the sofa, the quilt folded and hung over an antique ladder— the decor was effortless.

It was like Adelaide was meant to be this Army wife, and there was no doubt that although she was new to Fort Fairfax, she had already been brought into the fold of the spouse social life. On the other hand, Sophie had to fight for her position as part of this community. Being a girlfriend didn't garner the same respect. Other spouses assumed the term *girlfriend* meant temporary, when in fact, she and Jasper had been together longer than many of their friends' marriages.

But so far, so good. She didn't feel judgment from this group, and she loosened up as the minutes passed.

"We should really talk about the book." Adelaide's voice took Sophie from her thoughts. "It's obvious that everyone seemed to connect with it. Which is great because I have a list of questions."

"Oh, I like this," Sophie said, settling into her seat. Themes, characters, plot—these were the things she wanted to discuss. Sophie read avidly and even reviewed books on a website called Goodreads, where anyone could spill their thoughts about a book. Since e-readers had come onto the scene, as flimsy as they sometimes felt in her hand, her library had grown rapidly.

To think she almost hadn't come.

Fort Fairfax was Sophie and Jasper's fifth duty station, a surprise—meaning, it wasn't *on* their request list. His aging parents lived in Orlando; they'd both wanted to be within a day's drive of them. In their almost ten-year relationship, they'd both agreed that they would always aim for southern locations, and so far had lived in South Carolina (Charleston was charming), Georgia (Savannah was delightful), Kentucky (those hats!), Alabama (not her fave), and most recently, close enough to New Orleans to properly celebrate Mardi Gras with her favorite guy.

Upstate New York wasn't on their radar, and yet, there she was. And though almost two months had passed, she still hadn't accepted that this was going to be home for the next two years. Her heart was still taped up in one of the boxes stacked floor to ceiling in their apartment.

She was tired of trying to find a spot for her old records, and what was she going to do with the curtains that once again didn't fit the dimensions of her current windows? And moving into these military towns just outside of post, versus on post, where new and bigger housing was being built, was more salt to the wound that she wasn't considered a legal spouse and, therefore, was not allowed to live on post.

Adelaide's face lit up. "Great! So this is my

". Would you have volunteered to save sister, knowing you would have to kill to vive?"

Sophie knew her answer, but she didn't jump in right away. She scanned the room, which seemed to have sobered as each person looked at one another for an answer.

Across from her, Regina tipped her wineglass away from her lips and set it down on the coffee table. "Oh my God, totally."

Sophie hummed an agreement.

Everyone eyes swung her direction. *Whoops.* Naturally, she felt compelled to answer. "I'm with Regina. I would have volunteered and thought about it later. Because we're talking about Prim here, my own flesh and blood."

Regina pointed at her in high praise. "Exactly."

"Oh, I don't know what I would do," Liana Folger said. She was originally from South Dakota, and she'd introduced her favorite hobby as knitting. She was, in fact, wearing a tricolor sweater she'd knit herself. "I'm not saying that I wouldn't have done it. I just don't know if I would have volunteered like that. It takes time for me to make decisions. To think things through, I guess. There're pros and cons to everything."

"That's just not me." Sophie felt the need to distinguish herself as loyal and steadfast. "I make a decision and a commitment for better or for worse."

"So you would commit to kill others to keep your family alive?" One of the men had raised his hand—Frank Montreal. He was married to a woman in the MP, or Military Police, unit. Cheeks pink from his drink, he wore rounded spectacles and was sitting cross-legged on the ground. "I mean, isn't that what the military does, in some cases?"

After a moment of silence, the room exploded in conversation. Wine be damned, the banter flew. The conversation meandered from the country's role in Syria, to its responsibility with refugees, and then to the portrayal of killing as part of life in *The Hunger Games*. After a bit, Sophie took a sip of her wine and found the glass empty and her mouth gloriously tired from talking and laughing.

By God, she might have found her people.

"So what does everyone think about doing this regularly?" Adelaide asked once the conversation lulled, setting the book down on the coffee table.

This time, Sophie didn't hesitate. "I'd love it. It will help pass the time, too, with the deployment." She was greeted with a collective nod from the group.

"How shall we choose books?" Colleen Lasseter, a woman who lived in Adelaide's building, asked.

"Let's do it the easy way," Adelaide answered. "Whoever wants to host can pick the book. Is everyone okay not voting for a lineup? This will make it flexible for people, since I'm sure some of us will pop in and out throughout the year, especially during the holidays."

Regina tentatively raised her hand. "Uh . . . is there, like, a mandatory 'you must read the book' rule?"

Sophie smiled and answered for her. "I don't think there should be, right? I used to be in a book club where there was a minimum-page read and it kept folks from coming. We should try to stay inclusive." She looked at Adelaide for confirmation. Already, Sophie felt a little protective over this young officer. This deployment had to be Regina's first as a spouse.

Adelaide gleamed. "I agree. Great!"

As the party died down, Sophie stood and made her way to the kitchen, straight to the sink, where cold water called to her. Above the squeak when she turned the faucet handle, she heard, "I wasn't sure what to expect from book club, but it wasn't this."

She turned and saw Regina. She was pouring herself another glass of wine.

"What did you expect?" Sophie asked her.

"I dunno. Academic? Stuffy?"

"Stuffy?"

"Yes. I guess it's what I first think of when someone says 'book club.' To be honest I was worried about how everyone was going to act.

I didn't want to lampoon myself since I'm not much of a reader. And working and playing in the same place where you live . . . it can get intimidating."

"I haven't had that experience." Sophie noticed a drop of wine on the kitchen counter, so she grabbed a napkin and wiped it up. The act gave her a moment to focus her words before discussing something that had been bothering her. "I quit my job a month before I moved here— I'm an RN and worked nights, and me and my coworkers . . . we bonded through our meals, in our break room." She smiled to herself, bringing back the memory of last Christmas, when the break room table was a buffet. "It improved our work because we became a team."

Regina's gaze dropped. "Yeah, it's not quite as friendly where I work. Not to say that I don't have good people working with me, because I do. But I'm not sure the Army's my forever career. I think I want to do something else. I guess I don't feel that . . . umph."

Sophie was intrigued. She leaned on her elbows. "What do you want to do?"

"If you're asking about my dreams? Something with food. I haven't really figured it out. But it doesn't matter. It's not what I want to do, really, but what I have to do and should do," Regina said. "I'm sorry that you had to quit your job. It sounds like you loved it."

"I did." Sophie shrugged. Because what else was she supposed to do? Complain? Every person in the book club had had to give up something to be there. So she changed the subject. "Anyway, you make a good book clubber."

"Thanks. I mean, I can definitely drink wine. And I promise that next time I will actually read the book all the way through."

"It thrills me that there will be a next time." Adelaide walked up, shaking the glass in her hand for a refill. "Just sweet tea, thanks."

As Regina poured tea from a pitcher, the sugar wafting into Sophie's nostrils, Adelaide continued.

"I wanted to catch y'all before you both had to go. I want to thank you for—" She gestured toward the direction of the guest bath.

"Oh my goodness, it's nothing," Sophie interrupted. "It's you who I have to thank. For inviting me."

"Well, of course, we're neighbors."

"But . . . because I'm not officially"—with her fingers she made air quotes—" 'a spouse.' "

Adelaide frowned and understanding flitted across her face.

Sophie continued, compelled to explain. "You don't have to defend the institution or tradition. I get why I'm left off a lot of the invites. And the ID card process. And medical and health care. We knew not tying the knot had its consequences.

But the hardest by far is just not being included in things like this."

"I'm sorry. It's a shame if you ask me."

"It's fine," she said, because that's just the way it was. "That's all to say, I appreciate this."

"This *was* something, wasn't it? Just like you both were something to me earlier, helpful without being judgy. It's admittedly always tough to find new . . . people to get to know. We should go for coffee. Something? Our husbands work together. We're steps away from one another. What do you think?"

"Sure," Sophie answered right away. In ten years, she learned there were a few things she never turned down: the flu shot, meals from neighbors or friends, and the first friend dates at new duty stations.

They both looked at Regina. Her eyes widened. "Me, too?"

"Yes, you!" both Sophie and Adelaide said. At the surround-sound answer, they laughed.

"Okay, then." Regina raised her cup. "May the odds be ever in our favor."

Sophie cracked up again and lifted her glass. "Indeed."

CHAPTER EIGHT
Regina

Regina was out of breath as she turned the corner to her apartment building. Her heels clacked against the sidewalk, and the sounds of the other book clubbers, all ducking into their own buildings, faded away. It was a little after midnight, and the moon was high, illuminating the empty street. Lush greenery swayed around the buildings, and she relished the feeling of the tepid wind against her skin. In her experience, this weather wouldn't last long. Upstate New York had two months of mild weather to ten months of chill and snow, and her time outside would soon constitute wearing cold-weather gear and her nose hairs freezing.

But right now, right now was perfect.

She couldn't stop smiling.

She passed Baby, parked perpendicular to the front sidewalk of the building and patted the hood. The car was her lieutenant mobile and had been a mess when she'd picked her up years ago, and most of her butter bar—or second lieutenant—salary had been spent fixing and maintaining her. That, and her growing collection of cooking gear—all of which Logan had beef with, but she digressed. Regina loved Baby because she was a diamond in the rough. She was a symbol of what could come with a little bit of work. She was also 100 percent Regina's, purchased by her outright, without a loan attached to her.

Regina took the apartment stairs up two by two. The sounds of voices and television filtered into the corridor from the other families. There were the Castillos in A, Sergeant Major Davis in B—he was geocaching it while his family stayed in Chicago—the Smiths in C, the Katz family with their four cats in D, and she and Logan in E, while F was empty for the time being. But when she approached her door, there wasn't a sound to be heard.

She turned the doorknob—locked. And after unlocking it and entering, she encountered a dark apartment.

Meow. Shadow greeted her at her door and immediately rolled to her back, an invitation to play. And, normally, Regina would have gone right down onto the ground to do so. Optimism ran through her veins, that their third year in Millersville would be better than the first. Perhaps this year, she would make real friends; she'd prove Logan wrong when he'd once told her that her *grumpiness*—that was the actual word he'd used, and she'd given him hell for it— was because she didn't know how to have a good time.

Instead she bypassed her cat and went straight to the bedroom, curious at the silence. No Logan. She searched the kitchen for a note—no dice. And then, she peeked out of the front windows, where sure enough, she discovered that his car was missing.

Which meant he wasn't in the neighborhood, wasn't holed up with his buddy Aaron, a single lieutenant who lived four buildings over.

She pulled out her BlackBerry, noticed no missed calls, and rang her husband, biting her cheek. Tingles ran up and down her arms—her nerves threatening to jump off along with her simmering temper. Two years they'd been married, and the man still ran his life as if he were single. Whatever happened to him leaving a note? Cell phones existed for a reason.

When the call went to voice mail, she hung up and dialed him again. This time, on the fourth ring, he answered.

"Hey." Logan's voice sounded like he was having a drink on the beach, all relaxed and unbothered. In the background, she heard the staccato of drumbeats and an electric guitar chord.

She controlled her voice. "Hey. Where are you?"

"Oh, I'm out."

"Where?"

"Just down the street. Listen, I can't hear you. Are you home?"

"Yes!" she yelled. Then, she girded her abdomen to keep her body from lurching with anger. "Where you should be."

He laughed—he was drunk. She knew then where he was. At the local Irish pub, aptly named Eyes Crossed Pub, with his buddies.

She dropped her head in resignation. *This* was another recurring fight they had. Their lives on the weekend rarely intersected except for the occasional movie together, a problem she attributed to their dating while Logan was at West Point. Because they hadn't dated in the way most college kids did—they hadn't had study nights and casual, last-minute adventures, but serious, planned occasions and intense school breaks—they didn't go out now. Yes, their sexual relationship thrived, their physical attraction oftentimes made up for their fights, but they didn't plan their lives like many couples mapped out their leave time together. Those things that she'd once bragged about—that she and her husband were individuals first, a team second; that they didn't feel the need to give each other permission—didn't feel so advantageous now.

Was it possible to go backward in a relationship? Because as each day passed, it was getting harder and harder to remember what brought them together in the first place.

"I'll be home soon, babe," he said now. A soft plea. "Another hour."

"Fine." Because what else could she say? "Take a cab home. You sound wasted."

"Yes, ma'am. Do you see me s . . . saluting you? I am." His voice muffled in her ear. "Don't get mad, baby. It's just me and the guys and beers. Thassit."

She rolled her eyes and took a deep breath. "Fine."

"Love ya!" he yelled, laughing. Logan knew that if he made it through this phone call and she went to bed, he wouldn't have to deal with her till morning. And since he would be leaving for Afghanistan soon, was a fight really worth it?

Logan was right. After he hung up, Regina moved on, changing into her pj's, playing with Shadow, and opening *The Hunger Games* to read the ending, which had been spoiled at book club—no big deal. She fell asleep with her thoughts jumping from the potential of new friends, to the book's ending (Oh. My. God), to Logan, who'd get an earful in the morning.

But when she awoke the next day, her husband wasn't by her side.

PART TWO

Everyone's got a different story.
—*Room* by Emma Donoghue

PART TWO

Everyone's got a different story.

—Room by Emma Donoghue

CHAPTER NINE
Adelaide

Present Day, Thursday

Despite the computer screen that separated them, Adelaide felt her husband's quiet judgment all the way from Wiesbaden, Germany, and it rivaled her mother's on a good day.

"Yes, yes, I know it wasn't okay," she said stubbornly. "I just thought . . . I just thought that if they got to see each other, in person and with me in the room as a buffer, that they would both be willing to work it out. They're my best friends, Matt. And it's time for this whole thing to be resolved. I had it all planned out."

"A plan?"

"Yes." Adelaide slumped in her seat and snatched her planner, turning it to a bookmarked page. A self-professed paper planner and journaler, she was met with an intricately doodled page after a night of insomnia. She heaved a breath, then lifted the page up to the monitor. "See."

He squinted as he read, tilting his head back— her poor husband needed reading glasses. " 'Write an SOS. Get them to stay.' Well, looks like step two got you stumped."

She closed the book and dropped her gaze to the desk in front of her. Her mama used to say, "Plan it and they will come," and that was what she'd done. Sheepishly, she said, "Well, I've got one here, at least."

"What's the rest of the list say?"

" 'Get them to bond.' And then 'get them to make up.' "

"Easy peasy, right?"

That gave her a chuckle. When she looked up, the screen was frozen, with Matt's mouth rounded into an *O*. Darn these old houses. She had a Wi-Fi extender plugged in for the upper floors, but somehow the connection was still glitchy.

The picture righted itself. Adelaide's heart melted a little at the sight of her hubby, who had broken out into a grin. It was adorable and mischievous, with a slight curl that made his dark eyes light up. Matthew Chang was wearing his brown T-shirt; he'd just gotten into his quarters from work, and while the lighting on his end was dim, Adelaide noticed the slight bit of shadow on his chin. It was his cozy look. She could almost feel herself nuzzled up against him, her nose at the crook of his neck. Usually, by the end of the day, he no longer smelled of after-shave but of a little bit of sun and a hint of bar soap.

God, did she miss him.

"You broke up there. What did you say?" she asked.

"I said, I'm thankful Sophie stayed, then."

"Honestly, the only reason Sophie's staying is for Genevieve. But she hasn't come out from the guest room."

"How *is* my little girl?"

"Good, still asleep." Adelaide eased at the change of subject, leaned to the left, and tilted the laptop screen so it centered the Pack 'n Play within its view. Genevieve had a glorious nursery that Adelaide had painstakingly decorated when they moved in, but her daughter preferred to nap near her.

Which was perfectly fine by Adelaide. Genevieve wouldn't be a baby much longer.

Their baby. She and Matt had waited a long time for her, an exorbitant feat interrupted by the Army's needs, but there they were. A pang shot up through her, at the bittersweetness of it all, that after the struggle to conceive, Matt had spent most of their daughter's life watching her grow through a computer screen.

"Man, I miss you guys," he said, cutting through the beginning of her emotional avalanche.

She smiled. "We miss you, too. One month, right?"

"I'm counting the days. The seconds." His gaze flickered downward. "I can't believe she's turning two next week."

I can't believe you're going to miss it was her first thought, though she bit back the words. She pried more gracious ones out of her mouth, peeled them from the enamel of her teeth. "I caught her the other day toddling right up to a Lab puppy being walked. Remember how she's normally so scared of anything on four legs?"

His face brightened. "Wow, that's great!"

"She kept patting it right on the top of its head." She smiled at the memory. "Pretty sure she's going to want her own puppy. I can tell."

He narrowed his eyes in jest. "Or maybe it's her mama who wants a puppy?"

"Maybe." She shrugged flirtatiously. It had been a couple of years since their last dog had passed, a geriatric bull dog they had adopted, the third foster in about a decade. And while she was ready for another fur baby, Matt wasn't keen on account of his allergies. But, like oil, the truth always rose to the surface. "A dog *would* keep me company."

"You know what would keep you company? Another baby."

"Um, no. Not when it's me who'll do all the work," she quipped, then bit her lip.

His grin fell into a frown.

"I'm sorry for that," she said. Matt had been feeling extra guilty and awful for not being able to come home for Genevieve's birthday or Adelaide's surgery, and she didn't need to lay the guilt trip on thick. Currently, he was on an eight-month unaccompanied tour in Germany, which would take him out of the next cycle of deployment. It had been the better of two options, though he still lived away from home. She worded her next sentence carefully. "It's because . . . I know we talked about two children, but with the pain I'm . . . I already feel awful having surgery when I know that Genevieve still wants to be carried and held—"

"No, you're right. You shouldn't have to do this surgery on your own. I'm sorry. I'm just excited to keep growing our family."

She nodded, though inside, a white flag waved. She didn't know when she would be ready. She had just started to feel more confident at being a mom when her gallbladder pain began, and the procedures, the journey of IVF . . . she couldn't fathom it right now.

She was raising Genevieve on her own. It was so easy for him to discuss children when it was she who had to live with the procedures, the prodding, and then the raising.

But she said none of this. Her complaint would surely just distract him, when he needed to show up to work with a clear head.

Their marriage—for that matter, her whole life—had been built around something bigger than the both of them. A false sense of security crept in when wars lasted too long, when the cause and the meaning sometimes faded with time and distance from threat. The current operational tempo was fast and quick. Military members were still dying, and while Matt wasn't in combat now, the risk existed. She, in the United States, despite being in pain and without the comfort of him around, had a nice mattress to sleep on, had meals with her family. She wasn't food insecure. She was privileged.

Adelaide offered him a smile. "No worries. Sophie's got you covered—*she's* taking care of me. Not that you won't have to make it up to me later on, because you will. Maybe with a trip to a local shelter when you're back."

He seemed to relax at her change in subject, slouching a smidgen into his chair. "Honestly, after all this, you can have an entire menagerie of pets. Except birds." He shivered. "But, babe. What are you going to do about Regina?"

She shrugged, her shoulders heavy from helplessness. "I've texted her, and called, but no response. She's been gone over an hour. She could be in Richmond by now. Yes, I know it was naive, but I had all these grandiose plans. That Regina'd start to cook, and Sophie'd take care of things around here, and soon we'd be one big happy family like we used to be. I figured I would explain my part of what happened back in Millersville, and we would move on. Then we could do all the local things around Old

Town. The Hop-On, Hop-Off bus in DC. A walk through Georgetown, maybe a visit to the Naval Academy. And then, of course, Genevieve's birthday—maybe a belated party."

"Besides the fact that Regina isn't there, that would have been a tall order. You have to recover from your procedure."

"Dr. Hakashi said that since it's going to be an outpatient procedure, I'll be on my feet soon." Something sour had developed in the back of her throat. Did she have to remind him of the many times she'd handled more in her schedule? The complicated moves, the last of which when Gen was two months old and Adelaide was still recovering from her C-section. Once, she moved on her own with a large truck through two states.

Hush. She knew better than to put it all on him. They both loved this life, down to its core.

She took a deep breath, noted that the pain in her side had returned. "I've got to go."

"What is it, did I say something wrong?"

"No," she sighed. From outside her door, she heard the doorbell ring. Her next instinct was to wince in expectation of a dog barking, then of the baby waking, but no—no dog. And Genevieve didn't make a peep. "Someone's at the door. Probably another solicitor. We really need to put up a sign."

His frown remained imprinted on his face, but

after a beat, he said, "Okay, babe. I'll call you later. Love you lots."

"Love you."

Adelaide pressed the hang-up button before she could think twice and exhaled the tension in her chest. She pushed their conversation down and away from her head. This irritation, too, wasn't new. Their split household sometimes resulted in their thoughts and wires being crossed. They couldn't snuggle and make up. So much was lost in translation when a wife couldn't touch her husband. Matt wasn't really trying to tell her what to do—he was just giving her his thoughts on the matter.

She passed the guest room door, which remained closed, though she heard Sophie's voice. She must be on the phone with Jasper. Then Adelaide padded down the stairs, slowing down just before she got to the bottom step, when through the front window sheers she saw the shadow of a coupe parked in front of the house.

A smile burst from her lips. She threw the door open to Regina, green suitcase by her side.

Regina's expression was nonplussed. "Look, I guess I'm staying but—"

Adelaide launched herself at her friend. "Thank you, thank you. You are the best in the whole wide world."

Regina mumbled an answer, but between the words was a laugh, and Adelaide would take it.

She'd take all of Regina's attitude knowing she'd decided to return. But when she stepped back, she noticed a stranger hovering outside her door.

A man . . . carrying two bags of groceries.

CHAPTER TEN
Sophie

Sophie heard the familiar rise and fall of two women's voices downstairs. Regina was back. *Damn.*

"Mother, are you listening?" a voice yelled through the phone in her ear.

"What?" Sophie shook off her thoughts and sat up in the four-poster bed of the guest room, cell phone pressed against her ear.

"I was just saying that I don't remember when you've ever left home. I think it's good that you're on a girls' trip," Olivia, the elder of her twin seventeen-year-old high school seniors, said.

"It's not really a girls' trip. You know that."

"Well, this is so very midlife crisis, and I approve."

"I don't," another voice said in the background.

Sophie shut her eyes. It was Carmela, the younger twin, but the more dominant of the two when it came to her opinions.

In Sophie's ear, the background noise amplified.

"You're on speaker now," Olivia said.

"Carmela," Sophie called out. "It's not a midlife crisis."

"It better not be." Carmela's voice was stern. "When are you coming home?"

Sophie lay back down, looked up at the ceiling, and sighed. "It all depends on how your Auntie Adelaide does."

"How *is* Auntie Adelaide?"

"Fine, so far. Surgery's tomorrow."

"And then, you'll be home right after?" Carmela asked. "Because I already miss you."

"Will you leave her alone?" Olivia piped up, sounding farther away. "Mama, you can be gone this weekend. We can handle the house and Daddy without you."

"Speak for yourself, Daddy will be a mess without her," Carmela said. "He was a mess today. He was moping around and eating all the junk food. It's bad, real bad."

Her girls continued to bicker, and Sophie shut her eyes in exasperation. Seven or seventeen, her girls hadn't changed. Their ideas were polar opposites, down to how they thought their mother—who was in her midforties and had earned her stripes, *thank you very much*—should handle her personal life. Then again, she had to be thankful that the girls even cared. Many of her friends had kids who simply took their money and ran off without even a thank-you text back.

"Hey, now. Liv. Carm."

When they fell silent, she continued, "I told

you I was keeping the return date open-ended. The clinic doesn't need me for a couple of weeks, so I'm going to play it by ear. Liv's right, Carm. Your daddy can take care of himself, and so can you."

"No, I can't. I need you," Carm said in her stubborn way.

Sophie imagined her face scrunched up, cheeks blown out in indignation. She laughed. "I need you, too . . . to understand. It's important I'm here."

"Fine," she whined. "But something doesn't feel right."

"Nothing's wrong." And yet, Sophie knew she was fibbing. Of the two girls, Carmela had a finger on the pulse of the family. She was like a sponge, an empath, and a lie detector. She knew that Sophie had basically run away from home.

As the girls jumped into describing what they'd done during school, Sophie examined the room she was in. It was like a Longaberger basket factory exploded in this twelve-foot-by-twelve-foot bedroom space. Square baskets lined a horizontal shelf mounted on a wall. Atop a pine armoire sat circular-shaped baskets tipped to their sides with faux greenery spilling from them. Two cylindrical baskets on the antique school desk in the corner were filled with pencils.

The baskets had been purchased at those multilevel-marketing home parties where the hostess plied everyone with drinks and food, and people threw down hundreds of dollars on baskets. Peer pressure and retail therapy in one afternoon—once upon a time, Sophie's life had been filled with those sorts of parties. It was another way for military spouses to bond.

Sort of like book club.

At the thought of book club, heartburn climbed Sophie's chest.

When her daughters began arguing on the other end of the line—one wanted LED lights hung around their room, and the other believed that it would interrupt their REM sleep—Sophie excused herself, burdened with her own warring thoughts and the voices of Adelaide and Regina downstairs.

"Girls, I've got to go. Call me, later?"

"Bye, Mommy," they said, almost in unison.

After Sophie hung up, she took a breath. A second later, her phone rang again. It could only be one other person. She lifted the phone to her face, pressing her lips together at her psychic ability. She clicked the answer button. "Jasper."

"When were you going to call to let me know you got there? I've been waiting."

Her first thought: *Damn it.*

Her second reaction: raised hackles. Really, Jasper's request wasn't strange, nor was it demanding, but this concern was extra. "It took forever to get out of Reagan, and I wanted to speak with the girls first," she said with more bite to her words than she'd planned.

"I'm sorry, I was just . . . worried." His tone switched to pensive. "You didn't exactly tell me your plans."

"I *did* tell you."

"No, you mentioned that Adelaide needed your help. But you didn't tell me the details until the day before you left!"

I mean, technically I did tell you.

"It's like you up and left me." A hint of anger sparked in his voice, and a sigh followed. "All I wanted was for you to call, and you didn't. So I'm sorry for sounding upset. I was in the dark, until Carmela buzzed me and said she was on the phone with you."

"That second daughter of mine," she quipped. Carmela, her intuitive young lady. "I'm sorry I didn't call you first."

A beat of silence passed, after which Jasper said, "I guess the girls have the whole weekend planned for me."

She drew on her patience. "Oh yeah?"

"Something about board games and making a music video on their phone."

"That's sweet." Sophie felt a tinge of jealousy. Not once had her girls asked her to be in a music video. Then again, as the person home every single day, she was old hat.

"I guess." He laughed. "They showed me a

move a little bit ago. I almost threw my back out practicing it."

Sophie cackled, softening. Jasper was the best father, despite having been absent half their girls' lives. She had to remember that she'd had twice the amount of time to parent their children. "Just . . . please, don't order takeout the whole time."

"Yes, ma'am," he said. "Though I hope we're not looking at too many days without you."

The mood plunged into awkwardness, reminiscent of the last few months. She didn't remember when their conversation turned into this weird walking on eggshells. When their nights in bed consisted of her pretending to sleep and wondering how he fell into slumber. What she did know was that things for her began to change when he retired from the Army after two decades, and the girls received their college acceptances. Suddenly, she truly gave no more fucks.

"Oh!" she said, snapping herself out of her thoughts. Speaking of giving no fucks. "Guess who's here?"

"Um . . ."

"Regina."

He gasped. "Regina? As in Castro?"

"The one and only."

"Wow," he said.

"I know."

"Babe . . . are you okay? That's it. I'm coming to get you."

Sophie's eyes brimmed with tears, and she patted her cheeks to keep them from flowing. Goodness, Jasper just had a way. His primary instinct was to think of people. To check in on her, despite the miles and the time apart that they'd logged during their twenty-year relationship. Knowing that Jasper had her back had been a consolation that superseded all notions of romantic love. Because in the end, wasn't that what successful relationships were built on? Friendship? Loyalty? Trust?

Despite her deep love for him, her feelings about their relationship were a dichotomy: live in comfort but in stagnation, or seek new adventures and the unknown. All she knew was that her time in Virginia would give her some space to think, despite her deep love for him.

Sophie forced herself back into the conversation, to the reason why she was hiding out in the bedroom. "No, I'm not okay."

"Then I'll come for you."

She shook her head. "No. I'm staying."

"Why should you subject yourself to something that you buried years ago?"

"I don't want to give her a single reason to think I'm running from her. I belong here."

"Soph—you've got nothing to prove."

"Still."

A phone rang on Jasper's end. "Damn it. I've . . . I've got to go, my other cell's ringing. And I've got to take it."

Of course he did. He was on the cusp of a new beginning and still worked with the same honorable fervor. Sophie knew her place in the mix. But this time, she was grateful that his attention had switched, because she didn't want to slip into the next line of their conversation, which was the crack in their common-law marriage.

"All right."

"But listen, from someone who was there, hear me out," he warned.

She shut her eyes. "Yeah."

"You are by nature a caring person. You've taken care of this family, and you tend to take care of everyone around you. But you've got to take care of yourself first."

"Okay. Thanks."

"Love you."

"Love you," she answered back, meaning it.

After hanging up, Sophie launched herself out of bed with one thought in her mind. That she was in Alexandria to not only take care of Adelaide but to also take care of herself, and she wasn't going to let Regina's presence ruin it.

CHAPTER ELEVEN
Regina

"I'll stay only under certain conditions," Regina said, drawing Adelaide's attention toward her. "And it's something that I'll need to say to both you and Sophie."

"Okayyy." Adelaide stretched out the word as she side-eyed the doorway. "But who is that fine specimen of a man?" She gestured with her head. "Out there."

Regina sighed; she wanted Adelaide focused on her. "You're just as bad as my mother." She turned to Henry and waved him in. Admittedly, if she'd passed him on the street, she would have been distracted, too. "This is the guy who you have to thank that I'm back. This is Henry Just, of Just Cakes."

"Just Cakes from down the street? My, my, aren't you a tall drink of hard lemonade."

Henry set down the bags and offered his hand. "It's very nice to meet you."

"The pleasure is surely all mine." As she shook his hand, she winked at Regina.

It took all of Regina's willpower not to roll her eyes. Instead, she said, "We've known each other for about a year now—"

"Ah, eighteen months actually," Henry said.

Adelaide touched Regina's arm. "Eighteen months. Get it right, woman."

"Anyway," Regina continued. She had to stir this soup before it got lumpy. She'd practiced her conversation points with Henry on their food-shopping trip, after she'd decided that the only right thing to do was return. "I stopped by his place when I left here—"

Adelaide's eyebrows rose.

"At the bakery," Henry confirmed.

"Right, and instead of heading all the way back to Georgia, which was my true intention, because I'm mad at you, Adelaide Wilson-Chang. So mad I could scream." She took a deep breath. "But . . . I realized, or he helped me realize, that I would have regretted it if I left without trying to stay under this roof, with *her*."

Adelaide nodded. The change in her expression was so drastic that a part of Regina wished she could have taken the serious stuff back, because Adelaide was fun, and damn, did Regina want to discuss Henry. She wanted to model-walk around like a queen because this man she'd known only through the internet was actually and truly real. Online friends didn't always translate to in-person friends. How many times had she attempted to meet people online, only to be catfished by their seemingly good looks and ability to write the perfect profile? Or the times when she'd been ghosted because there had always been something wrong with her.

Henry clapped his hands together. "Well, I think that's my cue. Regina, you've got my digits."

"Thank you."

"I'll text you later." He kissed Regina on the cheek casually, as if this was their usual farewell. The touch of his lips on her skin melted her insides like chocolate over heat.

When the door closed behind him, Regina lifted a hand toward Adelaide before she decided to say anything else. "We can talk about him later. Where's Sophie?"

"Sophie is right here." Sophie descended the staircase like a formidable ghost. She was a reminder to Regina that friendships and relationships could dissolve in a matter of days.

Stop it. That was the divorce talking. The breakup and the resultant breakdown of what had been her life had done a number on Regina's psyche. Hands down, her divorce from Sophie had been equally as devastating as her divorce from Logan, and even more difficult to reconcile.

Toe to toe, and no longer under shadows as they had been in Baby, Regina cataloged Sophie, ten years later. Could it be possible that she appeared stronger now? Because her posture was more confident, more poised than before. She was the kind of nurse all patients wanted around.

That was precisely why Regina had to return.

She couldn't allow Sophie to be indispensable. Regina was Adelaide's best friend, too. Regina had something to offer as well. Was it competition? Hell yes.

She stood straighter. "I'm staying, Sophie."

Sophie responded by raising an eyebrow.

"Do I like that you're here? No. But Adelaide called me, too. And as much as I don't want to admit it, you were right. This whole situation isn't about the two of us. It's about her, and it's about Genevieve, and we know that while you're a whiz in that hospital room, you'll need help with Gen. And frankly, out of the two of us, I'm the better cook."

Regina winced at her own words. She wasn't the only one who could cook out of the three of them, but being a credentialed chef was her only one-up.

Sophie crossed her arms. "You've always got something to say."

"That's right, just like you." Regina quipped back. "And I'm not done. I've got some house rules."

"Technically this isn't your—"

"It's okay, Soph," Adelaide said, then nodded for Regina to continue.

"The first rule is that I'm not sharing a room with you." She pointed at Sophie.

"That's fine." Adelaide answered quickly. "You can take Genevieve's room. A daybed's already set up. Genevieve is fine to stay with me, in her portable crib."

"Second is that I don't want to talk about the past. At all." She leveled a stare at the two of them. "Not even a whiff. I've moved on. It's been ten years."

Sophie crossed her arms. "Believe me, it's not on my docket to discuss."

Regina bristled at her answer, at the way Sophie had brushed off the event as if it were just a silly fight they had. It had taken months, years even, for Regina to even talk about what happened.

"Third—the kitchen is mine."

"Now, wait a minute." Sophie's face wrinkled into a frown. "You're being ridiculous."

"Hey. There can only be one in charge, you should know that. I'm a chef. This is my thing. I won't micromanage your care of Adelaide, you don't step into my kitchen, and we share Genevieve." At the expression that the two of them gave her, she added, "Years of therapy after a divorce, ladies. I'm asking for what I want. And I want boundaries."

"It's a yes from me, of course," Adelaide said.

They both looked at Sophie, whose face didn't betray what her upcoming decision would be. If she was being honest, Regina hadn't been worried about Adelaide agreeing to her terms. Adelaide knew how to apologize; Adelaide had actually gotten on the horn to weather her anger.

Sophie, on the other hand . . . she had sent weak emails and a passive-aggressive friend request on Facebook.

But finally, after enough mind-numbing seconds in which Regina was on the cusp of turning and walking out the door, Sophie nodded.

"Agreed."

CHAPTER TWELVE
Adelaide

September 2011

Adelaide wished for time to stop. With her hand ensconced in Matt's, protected and warmed from the chill that had started to invade their part of the country, she clutched on to the last minutes before her husband left for deployment.

"Babe?" Matt shook her hand. He was in full camouflage uniform, with a green duffel strapped to his back. His headgear, with its brim molded into a distinct downward curve, was tipped backward on his head, so she could see a tuft of his curly black hair—though he didn't keep much of it on his head at any one time—peeking from his forehead. His dark eyes gleamed, his cheekbones were high in a grin, and he gestured to a couple approaching them. Jasper and Sophie.

The lead-up to deployment had been hectic; the coffee that she had planned with Sophie and Regina never came to fruition. In the last three weeks, there had been meetings, and lots of them, with family members, where they'd discussed contingencies should emergencies happen downrange—the deployed arena—or on the home front. Adelaide had been a key player, since the company commander didn't have a spouse, and she had been more than happy to step up.

Now, seeing Sophie in front of her, her partner in crime through pre-deployment, she allowed herself to exhale.

Sophie leaned in for a hug. Adelaide squeezed her back with every bit of emotion she felt but couldn't show and received an equally strong embrace. Adelaide had been feeling like she'd been failing for a while, but she'd still ensured her face, her home, and her demeanor were perfect, with no one the wiser, her mother's good example pervasive in her thoughts.

"You good?" Sophie whispered.

"No? Yes? You?"

"Eh."

"Seen Regina?"

"She texted. She's running late. But she'll be here. I mean, of course." Sophie stepped back, a grin on her face.

That wry expression made Adelaide laugh out loud. How she'd come to rely on Sophie and that grin of hers. She had been the beacon of calm, Adelaide's rock when she'd begun to grow unsteady.

In the phase of pre-deployment, there was no time to get upset or to cry. It was straightforward: The spouse was to be unflappable. They had to keep it together. It was just good luck that her pregnancy nausea had abated a little, and she'd found the trick that a couple of crackers in the morning made all the difference.

Adelaide hugged Jasper, Sophie embraced Matt, then the two men sidled up to each other, a smile on each of their faces.

"Platoon Sergeant." Matt nodded to him.

"XO," Jasper said.

There was a bromance between the two men. They'd bonded over their love of the gym and football. Their relationship had given Adelaide some solace that Matt would deploy with someone he could consider a friend.

Sophie shook her head. "These two."

"Like peanut butter and jelly," Adelaide said.

"I'm the jelly, because I'm sweet," Jasper said. "Right, Soph?"

"Sure, if you say so."

"So what does it mean if I'm peanut butter?" Matt asked.

"Hm . . . that you're sticky?" Adelaide said.

"You're stuck with me!" Jasper added. The two men fell into laughter.

Sophie barked out a laugh. "Wow. That was a dad joke if I ever heard one."

"Speaking of, we've got about ten minutes before manifest, sir," Jasper said. His eyes jumped to Adelaide and then to Sophie. "Let's go find our girls?"

Sophie heaved a sigh. "Okay. Ad, I'll see you?"

"Yeah, of course." She feigned strength, though her voice cracked.

Three hours. They had been at this field for three hours, and it would all come down to these next ten minutes. In the distance, she could see the white buses that would take their soldiers to the airfield. And she hadn't been the only one to notice. The crowd around them quieted, and one by one, uniformed men and woman separated from their groups and headed toward the green space in front of them, where the final formation would be.

Pressure filled Adelaide's chest. She gripped her husband's hand tighter. She kept her eyes on him as he surveyed the goings-on, because she wanted to memorize every groove on his face. True, there was video chat. Yes, she would "see" him, but it wouldn't be like this.

Could she do this? Could she do this again? Nine months was a long time. Nine months felt unfathomable. How did her mama do this? How did Nana? How did they keep a straight face and wear their smiles and serve their meals and meet with people? In the media, in history, what was glorified were the military men and women who left, who fought wars, who put their lives on the line. Not often was it understood, was it shown, the mixed fear and pride of those who were left behind.

Finally, Matt looked down at her. He was a tough guy, always had been, always would be. Rough-and-tumble, rarely romantic. He'd choose outside activities over indoor ones any day of the week. He was also the first to laugh, and his booming personality filled their home.

Without him, the house would be empty.

"Hey, hey." He set down his duffel and rested both hands on her shoulders. He smoothed them down.

"It's just the worst possible time." The words slipped out of her mouth before she could stop them. They were whiny, accusatory, shaking from her desperate attempt to be the positive person her mother raised.

"I know. But I'll figure out a way to get back in time." His gaze dropped briefly to her belly, and a hint of a smile bloomed on the corner of his lips. "Until then, you're going to take care of you. The both of you."

She nodded and shut her eyes. "It's only been seven weeks. My first appointment isn't even until next week."

"Each day is another step closer. And we're going to celebrate every milestone."

She felt him tip her chin up.

"Open your eyes, babe."

She did and found his expression as loving as ever, even as the crowd began to clear around them. "How do you do that? Be so optimistic.

After everything you and I have gone through? This could all be nothing. And we could end up disappointed, again." More than disappointed. Heartbroken was more like it, but she couldn't put words to the loss.

"We could, but we might end up being the happiest parents on the planet."

Adelaide felt a surge of panic rush through her. "We need more time. Because if it doesn't happen, that's another nine months when—" Her fears spilled out. Six years they'd tried to have a baby, ever since they'd gotten married. And yet . . .

"Adelaide." He smiled thinly. Now she looked around and realized that they were truly the only ones still together. Off to the side, Jasper was waiting. Sophie had taken up a spot in the first row of the bleachers, an empty seat next to her for Adelaide.

"I love you. I love you. I love you." Adelaide wrapped her arms around his waist, feeling foolish at their wasted time, not just today but all the days they'd had since their last deployment.

He ran his fingers through her hair, then brushed her cheek with a thumb.

I'm not going to cry. I refuse to cry.

Matt kissed her on the lips, sweet and chaste. "I love you forever." Then he picked up his bag and walked away.

The rest of the morning was a blur. Adelaide

only remembered Sophie's warm hand in hers throughout the formation, and Regina, who she hadn't seen in days, sobbing on her other side. The march of soldiers to the buses, the trail of buses leaving the quad. Scout's cold nose against her elbow while she soaked in the tub later on that evening.

And starting to bleed that night.

CHAPTER THIRTEEN
Sophie

"It's time to get ready for bed. Unlock this door, right this second, you two." At 2101 Liberty Road, Apartment B, Sophie pounded on the bathroom door, her ear pressed against the wood. From the other side, she heard the giggles of little girls, the water running, and the clattering of something on the linoleum. *"Olivia Renee. Carmela Grace.* I swear to God above." She raised her eyes heavenward in a silent prayer and caught sight of the heating vent that was surely taking the sound of her voice and probably her very loud and frustrated thoughts up to her second-floor neighbor.

" 'Having kids is the greatest gift,' she said. 'Twins? Double the fun!' she said. You lied, Auntie May! Do you hear that, you two? Your great-aunt lied because she only had me to raise and had no idea that double the fun meant double the trouble!" She took a breath, then crossed herself for good measure, just so she wouldn't be proven wrong in her belief that ghosts didn't exist and superstition was a simple way to explain life's hard lessons. "Rest in peace, Auntie May. I appreciated all

111

the love you gave me. I didn't mean any dis-respect."

The door clicked open, halting Sophie's tirade, and she watched it widen to reveal two seven-year-old little girls, each with a face full of makeup.

"Oh . . . oh my!" Sophie rushed to the sink to turn off the faucet, which was on at full blast. She palmed her forehead, which was still damp with sweat. She'd accidentally taken a late-afternoon nap—her insomnia had been at full throttle since Jasper left a week ago—and mid-dream she was startled awake by what could've only been her sixth sense. Her mama sense, honed over the years of raising two very mischievous, like-hellions-when-they're-together little girls.

She took another deep breath to calm herself. Let it out slowly. This wasn't a big deal. Just because she'd spent a small fortune on her makeup didn't mean she needed to overreact. "Let's get you both cleaned—"

When Sophie turned around, she discovered the girls had taken off. But before she could formulate her next step, the cordless rang in her pants back pocket. She had a habit of carrying the cordless with her around the house, since her cell phone had horrible reception.

She pressed the on button. "Hello?"

"Hey, babe."

Sophie melted, right there on the lineoleum tile. Despite their decade-long relationship, she never got tired of this—his phone calls. There was something romantic about his voice in her ear, when she let her imagination wander to what Jasper was doing right at that second. Besides, it was easier to multitask on the phone; this moment was the perfect example.

"You have perfect timing." She tore a paper towel from the holder and dampened it with water to wipe down the smudges of lipstick and foundation in the sink. She hooked the phone to her shoulder, and tilted her head to secure it. "How are you?"

The girls cackled like hens in the background, and a second later, someone was screaming "Mama!" so she quit her attempt to clean up and padded to the kitchen, where Olivia had commandeered a boxful of fruit snacks. Olivia was two minutes and six seconds older than Carmela and was, as usual, attempting to assert her dominance.

"Okay. I just missed you, is all." Jasper's voice, a deep and sexy baritone, was smooth through the earpiece. When they'd first met, his voice was what drew her to him. Well, that, and all the sex appeal that came with him and the uniform he wore so proudly.

She shivered at the thought of him now, at the broad expanse of his chest, at how he could move into a space and take command of it without even raising his voice. Jasper had a presence; he garnered respect.

"It's only been a week. Don't tell me you're getting soft," she teased, wandering into the kitchen. She glanced at the calendar tacked up near the phone's base, where seven days were crossed out in pen. On the counter was a jar of jelly beans—one jelly bean per day of the deployment, per twin—that Olivia and Carmela dipped their hands into every morning.

"Actually that's why I called."

"What's up?" She frowned. The yelling between her girls escalated. To settle them, Sophie took the box from Olivia and divvied the bags of fruit snacks on the kitchen table, and then walked away, for space. She went to the living room windows, which looked out to Liberty Road. It was quiet, even for a weekday afternoon, with wet leaves scattering the asphalt from the bit of rain that had come down that afternoon. No one was out except for a couple of her neighbors walking their dogs.

"Have you been hanging with Regina?"

"Um . . . not the last few days. We had so much back-to-school stuff happening. And I sent out a couple of applications to clinics in town, so I was tied up with that."

"Oh, you sent out applications? I thought we discussed that you would wait a little?"

"Yeah." She paused, flashing back to that conversation. Since the girls were old enough to understand the dangers of deployment, she and Jasper'd both decided that Sophie would not work, to give the girls some normalcy by having a parent at home, if only temporarily. "Yeah, well . . . I miss working."

"Sure, but—"

As soon as Sophie heard the word *but,* she launched in. "Look, it's no big deal. If I get interviewed, I don't have to take the job." She couldn't bear to hear him utter the word *no*. This week, she'd begun to feel caged in, helpless. To think there were eight-plus more months of waiting. Waiting for phone calls and emails from Jasper, for him to come home.

To her relief, Jasper sensed her growing anxiety. "Yes . . . yeah, you're right. I was just surprised is all. Anyway . . . about Regina?"

Sophie jumped at this change of subject and dug her cell phone out of her purse and pulled up her last group text with Adelaide and Regina. "Right . . . I heard from her yesterday, actually. You know the Lasseters, right?"

"I do."

"Well, Colleen picked a book for October called *Room*, about a woman who was kidnapped and had a kid in isolation. Apparently, Regina's not in the mood to read it."

It sounds depressing was what the text read.

"Can you check on her?"

"Why, is something wrong?" Sophie stood and peeked into the kitchen at her girls—they were happily noshing on their fruit snacks—then made her way to the master bedroom. She pulled up her mini blinds, which she normally kept closed for privacy—the last thing she wanted was to be accidentally peeped on by kids playing in the communal playground behind their building—and she peered at the building across the yard, at the back windows of Regina's apartment on Bell Street. The lights were off despite the night sky.

"The lieutenant came in."

"Logan?"

"Yeah." He sighed. "I can't say what we talked about, and he didn't ask me to have you check up on her. But the conversation raised a flag for me. If you can swing it . . ."

Sophie heard the message underneath the words: morale check. "Of course. Yes, absolutely." With a tug, the blinds dropped closed. "I'll get on it."

Right then, she texted Adelaide to set a time for them to get together. Sophie had learned that Adelaide organized her life around appointments. And these days, Adelaide seemed to be busy, even sometimes too busy for a quick sidewalk conversation.

Adelaide
What's going on?

Gotta check in on our friend.
SOS

SOS?

I'll explain later.
Tomorrow afternoon?

Yes. 2pm?

Sounds good

"You're amazing, do you know that?" Jasper's flirtatious voice was back.

"I *do* know that." She smiled. "You're a lucky man."

"I know. And I was thinking."

"Yeah?" In perfect timing, her girls ran into their bedrooms across the hall. "Walk! Jesus, one of them is going to choke, and God knows I didn't stay home from work to do the Heimlich."

The voice in her ear laughed, deep-bellied.

"Oh, so you're enjoying this?" She hiked a hand on her hip.

"You know I am." He paused, bringing the moment down to serious. "I love it, hearing you."

"You're not so bad, either." Sophie perched on

117

the bed, and despite her attempt at deflection, her face warmed in the beginning of tears. In the four deployments they'd faced together, she'd cried twice, both during times like this, when she knew there was a novel in between his very few words.

She also knew what was coming up.

"Marry me when I get back," he said.

"Jasper."

"Look, I'm done with this rule you have about us not marrying while I'm still in. I've always said that you are first, our girls are first."

Sophie shook her head, eyes on the floor. At the peeling linoleum in the fifth kitchen she'd lived in since they'd been together. Five kitchens in ten years.

Sophie had been honest from the first day of their relationship. She wasn't convinced that marriage was necessary. Why did it take a ring and a piece of paper to declare commitment? And she was especially against marrying a man in the military for all the reasons why, despite her support of him, she was unnerved by deployment. There was simply too much upheaval, and she didn't trust the distance or the stress placed between them time and time again.

"Honey, we can't have this kind of conversation over the phone," she said.

"And when would we do it? I've tried in person.

Look, I've been doing some thinking. About us. And I think I'll be ready to get out soon."

Sophie's tongue tied into a pretzel, back going ramrod straight.

"You've given up your job and career, and here I am losing time with my girls. . . ."

Her heart beat hard and loud, in anticipation of the words she had been waiting for him to say for a decade though she had never demanded.

"Soph, as soon as I'm done with this deployment, I'm out. I'm out, and we can get married, and we will live in one place and have our happily-ever-after."

CHAPTER FOURTEEN
Regina

"Happily-ever-afters are lies. All lies." Regina threw a handful of popcorn at the television as the credits for *Notting Hill* scrolled up. Her voice cracked above the volume of the television, which she had set to the surround-sound speakers, and she leaned her head against the back of the couch. She wiped her cheeks with the palm of her hand.

From her periphery she saw the shadow of, well, Shadow. The cat sat just inches from her head and stared at her.

"Okay, yes, I'm crying because it was good. But that doesn't mean it's believable. Were they really compatible in the end? She was an actress, and he was a bookstore owner. How does that work, when the two of them are on obviously different tracks in life?"

Shadow responded by lying down; her tail whipped an objection.

"It's all about expectations. They have different expectations. It won't last."

Hearing herself saying these words, Regina threw herself off the couch. Her thoughts were meandering toward morose again. She approached the tower of DVDs and scanned the spines for another title. Except everything they owned was either a romantic comedy (her stash) or a war movie (Logan's), and the thought of watching anyone in a uniform in physical harm gave her nausea.

"Okay. How about *Fifty First Dates*? That's neutral, right?" She looked back at Shadow, who had taken her place on the couch cushion amid a fleece blanket and her favorite teddy bear, and was now writhing on her back. "No? *When Harry Met Sally*?"

Shadow had nothing to say, not even a purr. And it was just as well, because this darkness, the loneliness of movies and stale popcorn and her pajamas on the weekend, was now the essence of her life. Scratch that, the cat was probably sick of her, knowing that for the next nine months they would essentially remain in this state of limbo.

She pressed the eject button of the DVD player, and the disk slid out. As she put it away, the doorbell rang.

Regina frowned and straightened. She looked at the door, where shadows appeared in the sliver of light at the bottom. She'd received an email from Logan in the middle of the movie, so it wasn't an emergency.

"Regina?" A woman's voice.

"Yoo-hoo." A different woman's voice, now with knocking.

She glanced at Shadow and rolled her eyes. There were only two women she kept in touch with besides her mother.

She looked down at her disheveled pajamas. Touched the messy bun on her head.

Nope.

There was no way she was letting anyone in. She shuffled to the door and leaned closer to it. "She's not in."

Cackles ensued on the other side of the wood.

"For cryin' out loud, Regina! We heard Elvis Costello coming up the stairs. That last song in *Notting Hill* is iconic," Adelaide declared. "Open the dang door."

Regina growled. She even stomped her foot. Yes, she liked these women and she'd allowed them to get a little close, but that didn't mean they could just show up anytime. Then again, combined, Adelaide and Sophie could outlast the deployment itself; there would be no use fighting it. So, Regina opened the door wide and without looking at the women gestured them in.

Adelaide stepped in first, followed by Sophie. Both smelled good, which meant that Regina probably didn't. But she held on to her pride and crossed her arms. "What can I do for you?"

"It's dark in here." Sophie flipped on the lights.

"Hey!" Regina squinted against the brightness.

The curtains flew open. The windows creaked upward.

"Seriously, both of you? What is this? This is embarrassing." Her mind wandered to her dirty laundry. Had she put it away? Oh God, her sink was full of dishes. She rushed to the kitchen, to where Sophie had beaten her and was already clearing the counters of wrappers and containers from the last couple, or few, days.

Sophie shooed Regina away by putting a hand on her back. She led Regina to the round kitchen table and gestured for her to sit. "When was the last time you went outside?"

"Friday! I went to work."

"We mean, just to go outside. Go to the grocery store, the gym? When was the last time you cooked?"

She shrugged. "Are you guys stalking me?"

"Yes." Sophie took a seat across from her and mimicked her position: arms crossed, leaning back. "It's our job."

"As what?"

"As your girlfriends, what else?" Adelaide entered with a bag of groceries. "Look, we even got you fruit in case you're at risk for scurvy from hanging out in the dark, bless your heart."

"Ha ha, funny."

"Seriously." Sophie leaned forward and held Regina by her forearm. The act was comforting, grounding. "What's going on?"

"I . . ." A fresh round of tears bubbled under her eyelids. "I'm a mess."

Adelaide knelt down in front of her. "It's totally normal."

Regina shook her head. They weren't getting the full story. If they had known how she'd acted just days before Logan left, how she'd picked at the smallest things he did. That the morning he'd arrived after his all-night escapade, she'd actually packed up a suitcase and left it in the front foyer with an ultimatum that if he didn't shape up, she was shipping him out.

"You might feel better telling us. There's nothing that a good vent can't fix," Sophie said.

"You're going to think I'm the worst."

Adelaide took her other hand. "Honey, we've probably felt everything you're feeling. There's no judgment here, right, Sophie?"

"She's right. No judgment at all."

Now, tethered by both women, Regina forced out the emotions she'd kept inside for two weeks. "I have this feeling that I can't shake."

"What kind of feeling?"

"Feeling unsettled. Is this normal, during a deployment?"

"It happens," Sophie said. "But here's the thing. There's no normal deployment. It all depends on what unit he's with, what unit you're in, and where you are in your marriage. It is what it is, and I think putting expectations on it won't be fair to you or to him. I remember our first deployment together. Jasper and I were so green.

We only got ten minutes on the phone a week to work out our kinks as new parents. The phone would simply hang up when the ten minutes were up. Now that was rough." She half laughed. "So much was left unsaid."

Regina gathered her courage. If Sophie was sharing, she could, too. Besides, this feeling in her chest was overwhelming; if she didn't talk about it, she was going to scream. "If I . . . if I tell you both something, will you keep it to yourselves, for now?"

"Yeah, of course, anything," Adelaide said.

"It hasn't been right for a while, even before Logan left."

"Oh no, don't say that. You're newlyweds. You're getting to know each other," Adelaide said.

"But shouldn't we love each other more, then? Wouldn't our conversations feel more organic, and shouldn't we want to speak to each other the moment we're apart?" Her chest began to burn with sadness. "And shouldn't I be more sad that he's away?"

"So you're not sad because you miss him?"

"Yes, of course I am. I love him. I miss his company, and his presence. But I'm also relieved. It's like my whole body has exhaled this huge sigh. I told you. I'm a mess."

Adelaide shook her head. "Nope. You're not a mess. It's the deployment. It puts us in a situation where we're literally emotionally frozen until they walk out the door, and once they're gone and we finally recover enough to respond, they're not around to support us. But you're not alone. And you can't keep yourself in this house. You can't lock yourself in here."

"We won't let you," Sophie said. "In fact, I have a plan. It's something I like to do at every deployment. It's called the SOS."

"Ah, I get it now," Adelaide said.

Regina looked between the women. "Get what?"

"SOS. It's a simple text, three letters. If one of us types it, we come. No excuses." Sophie looked at her intently, then her gaze jumped to Adelaide. "But this only works if we want to be there for one another, and if we're open to being helped. We've got nine months together, and we can't do it alone." Sophie held out her hand, palm up.

"I'm in," Adelaide said, placing her hand on Regina's.

"You're serious?" Regina gripped the two women's hands, because she hoped against all hope that Sophie and Adelaide were serious. That she did, in fact, have friends; that she had these two people to lean on.

"As a heart attack," the two women answered.

The three burst into laughter.

"Okay. SOS. Got it." Regina sniffled.

"But you're not off the hook yet." Sophie eyed Adelaide.

"What is it?"

"Two things." Adelaide stood and dug through the grocery bag. "A box of waffle mix. Because what's better than waffles?"

"*Pfft.* Waffle mix, shmaffle mix. I can make waffles from scratch." It felt like a challenge. Regina's mind ran through the ingredients she had in her pantry, and for the first time in the last week, she actually felt like cooking. "In fact, I might have everything I need here."

"Even better. And here's the second thing." Adelaide lifted a book and presented it with a game-show-hostess flair.

Room, the next book club book.

Regina groaned. "I take it back. Turn down the lights. I want to be alone. Leave me to wallow and get scurvy. I'd rather be stuck in this room than actually read that depressing book."

"Nuh-uh. I think it's apropos, don't you think?" Sophie laughed. "You're stuck with us, lady. The two of us, and book club. Get used to it. And better start reading."

CHAPTER FIFTEEN
Sophie

October 2011

A few weeks later, and right on time, Sophie's waning optimism took a tumble in between helping others with their deployment blues and the next book club meeting—at an escape room, no less—that seemed to never end.

Nothing like a room one needed to escape to remind her she was enclosed in a time warp that would only end in eight months.

"This thing . . . it won't untangle!" Sophie's fingers fumbled with the knot in a rope that was tied to a key. Next to her, Regina and Frank Montreal struggled against their own knots for their own keys. The other end of their ropes were secured to a ground hook.

One of these keys would open the exit door.

"Almost . . . there," Regina squeaked. "Frank, how are you doing?"

Frank grunted next to her. The other three book clubbers behind them cheered. "I'm stressing! People out there are probably laughing at us. My fingers are on fire."

This was the first escape room in the area, and

the line for this challenge was long with other groups waiting their turn. They were also being videotaped.

"There's a nurse in the room just in case something happens, don't worry. C'mon, keep going!" said Sophie. The faster one of their keys unlocked the room, the faster she could go home and lie on her bed and simply read. "We've got five minutes left!"

Regina growled; Frank grunted.

"I'm almost there!" Regina yelled. "Oh my God, this is not what I signed up for. We're not even talking about the book."

"Shhh. Focus on the keys! You all are moving slower than molasses," Adelaide screamed.

"Someone, someone say something," Frank said. "I'm to the last knot. Distract me."

"Oh, okay, um, I really liked the book. It was devastating. I can't even imagine," said Colleen, shifting her weight from one foot to the other. She was a German woman married to an Army soldier. She was also a math whiz, which had been a help in the room. Without her, they would have still been stuck at the puzzles, which incorporated some geometry and algebra.

It was Colleen's idea to do an escape room challenge for October's book club. Which, at the time, seemed like a good idea, a great way to kick-start the neighborhood after deployment. Now Sophie couldn't blame those who had decided to bow out for the month. The sun was setting earlier, the air was getting chilly, and with Jasper not home, all she wanted to do was curl up and watch TV.

"Fear is what I felt," Frank said. Sweat bloomed on his forehead. "I know the story is told through Jack's eyes, but all I could think of was his mother. She tried so hard to make it the best life she could. A couple of times, I had to sit there and remind myself that it was fiction. This book wasn't a true story, but aren't each of us just trying to do the same thing—survive in our own bubble? In our own room?"

"That's deep, Frank." Sophie paused to appreciate that thought. Okay, maybe she needed book club for that aha moment. She *was* starting to hibernate. Lately all she wanted was to hide in her bedroom. "It was sad that Jack called each inanimate object by its name, as if they were human friends. It got me in my soft spot."

"Soft spot? You have a soft spot?" Regina grunted out.

"Hey, I'm a nurse, I have a soft everything."

"I beg to differ."

The team laughed.

"She's right, though, Soph," Adelaide said. "Don't be mad, you're just sometimes . . . well . . ."

"You're hard to read," Frank added, grunting. "And pardon my language, but you give no fucks. Which isn't a bad thing, mind you."

131

"Oh! I got another loop out! I'm almost there." Regina rested her arms at her side. "I need a couple of seconds."

The team cheered, and Sophie joined in, though the comments took her aback. Her fingers relaxed against her own knot. She'd known these people two months now, and their love language was teasing and sarcasm. All her life, Sophie had been able to dish as much as she could take. But in that moment, she felt raw. Her attempts at a clinic job had come up short; she hadn't even been asked for an interview.

Without Jasper around, she didn't have the daily pats on the back, the backup to remind her that she was amazing. Her twins wore her out daily, and this sometimes made her feel inadequate. The strength that she was supposed to feel, the steadiness of her experience, was starting to ebb. Everyone seemed to look to her, just as Jasper had asked her to check on Regina, because she was a caregiver.

But what if the caregiver needed caregiving? Caregivers were meant to hang in the background, to make up for the inadequacies of others without fanfare. They were just supposed to do the right thing when called upon. They were the worker bees, though often ignored.

It had never really bothered her, this idea of doing good just because, of sticking to the right road without the accolades. But sometimes . . .

Sophie felt a hand grip her wrist, bringing her back to the present. It was Regina, a key now in her hand. She looked at Sophie with concern, with care. "You're a badass, and we love you for it."

"We love that you don't give any f . . . flips at all," Adelaide chimed in, hugging Sophie and Regina.

"We love that you're always the voice of reason." Frank wrapped the three of them in his arms. Then Colleen joined Frank and Adelaide, and their quietest book clubber of all, Evelyn Oh, her arms barely reaching around, whispered, "No fucks."

The thirty-second warning bell rang, though none of them moved. And Sophie, for the moment, felt seen. Starting with Regina, these people, *her friends,* noticed.

She softened into this cocoon. For the moment, she didn't have to be the strong one.

PART THREE

The things of your life arrived in their own time, like a train you had to catch.

—*The Passage* by Justin Cronin

CHAPTER SIXTEEN
Sophie

Present Day, Friday

Sophie was back in her world: the sterile environment; among the smell of antiseptic; the big, bright windows; the curtains that squeaked as they swung closed for privacy; and the faraway beeping of someone's IV machine.

The hospital was Sophie's second home. This was where she spent most of her days, probably as much time as she'd spent mothering her children. Aside from pockets of time when she didn't work due to circumstance rather than choice—military-spouse jobs were few and far between, especially in small towns—at every chance she got, she donned her scrubs, and at every new hospital, she earned a quick reputation as an expert in IV insertion.

Hence her annoyance as she watched a young Air Force nurse attempt to insert an IV into Adelaide's arm for the third time. *Third.* In her experience, two times was all one got to successfully put in an IV, after which it was time to ask for help. Currently, Adelaide, wearing the faded hospital gown of Fort Patriot Community

Hospital, the DC metro's military hospital, was stiff, posture rigid with an arm out, sporting a tentative look.

Still, Sophie bit her cheek to prevent herself from jumping into the procedure herself. She schooled her expression. She'd hated it when other health-care workers micromanaged her, and her time was better spent calming a tense Adelaide.

"So if something happens to me," Adelaide was saying, "I have my power of attorney and will in the safe in my bedroom. It's in the purple folder. The safe's combination is my birthday." She sucked in a breath at the puncture of the needle, then continued. "And of course there's the Genevieve binder I left with Regina that has every bit of information needed to take care of Gen. But the rest of our paperwork, like my address book and passwords, are in the duck room."

Duck room? "Do you mean your office?"

"Yes, exactly. The room with the collection of ducks on the wall? All from when we were stationed in Alaska. *Waterfowl* is the more correct term, but Matt refuses to call the room by that name."

"Right. Waterfowl." Sophie tried to keep a straight face as she leaned against the wall and crossed her arms, instead of hovering over the nurse as she dug for the vein, willing the stick to be successful. To the nurse, she said, "Do you hear this woman? Will you let her know that she'll be home by this afternoon?"

The nurse visibly relaxed—success?—and flipped the toggle that allowed the fluid to shimmy down the tube from the bag hanging on the pole, and she pressed on the buttons of the IV machine. "She's right. I'm not sure if you should be telling her your safe's combination."

"Hey, don't expose that part." Sophie squeezed out a smile. "I want to be halfway to Florida with all of her Origami Owl necklaces before she wakes up."

Adelaide cracked up.

"What's Origami Owl?" the nurse asked.

"It's an MLM company for necklaces that twist open to hold charms. I think we all took a turn at being a hostess. And that lady right there—" She pointed at Adelaide.

"I like to support, what can I say?" Adelaide admitted.

"She bought a lot of necklaces and charms. And makeup. And baskets." Sophie rolled her eyes. "She's a sucker for home parties."

"*Collector* is the preferred term." Adelaide lay back onto the bed, cheeks pink at the banter, but finally, relaxed.

Sophie now understood why Adelaide had insisted that both she and Regina come. Neither, alone, would have been enough. Adelaide was uptight, worried about every little detail. She'd stayed up after midnight fretting about Genevieve's necessities. Anxiety had teemed off her like waves, and it took both Sophie and Regina to calm her. On the way to the hospital this morning, Sophie had held Adelaide's hand in the car like she'd clutched her girls' for any of their big moments.

The nurse noted something on her clipboard. "IV—check. Consent forms are done, so we're good to go there. In a little bit, your anesthesia provider will come by and chat with you, then we'll wheel you into the operating room. Ms. Walden, I can take you to the OR waiting room, where you can wait until Mrs. Wilson-Chang is out of surgery and in the recovery room."

Adelaide nodded, knotting her hands together.

"Can we get a couple of seconds alone?" Sophie addressed the nurse. Her friend needed a moment.

"Of course."

Once the door shut, Sophie perched on the bed and took Adelaide's hands in hers. They were slim, smooth, and cold, a contrast to hers, which were, frankly, rough. Sophie had nurses' hands, with layers of skin peeled off from the constant use of sanitizing foam and antibacterial soap, heavy from the persistent action of moving patients, pressing buttons, carrying, pushing, and pulling. "Tell me what you're thinking."

"That it's rare for us to worry about this, about our own contingencies. I keep asking myself if it's necessary for me to go under the knife. And then I reminded myself that two weeks ago I was in so much pain that I had to ask a neighbor I barely knew to watch Genevieve so I could drive myself to urgent care."

Sophie nodded, encouraging her to go on.

"How many times did we fill out that power of attorney for Matt and Jasper? We're always prepared for something to happen to them, for us to be left with the aftermath."

"We're definitely prepared."

"Maybe too prepared?" Adelaide said. "Because my mind immediately goes to the worst-case scenario."

"It's the way we've had to live. It's part of our survival. We can't be taken by surprise. We don't have that luxury."

"Right? My mama called me morbid because I thought about the probability of loss. All the time." Adelaide rolled her eyes and mimicked her mother's voice. *"Adelaide, dear, you're just invitin' trouble to your doorstep by asking it to dance."*

Sophie laughed, because she'd accused herself of the same thing. "We are a little morbid, but I think it's how we protect ourselves. We've known people who've been killed overseas, people who have died. We've comforted people who've sustained loss. We have lost people ourselves."

"Exactly, and right now, I wonder what if something happens to me—will Genevieve be okay? And I see what you're going to say next, Soph, and I don't want to hear it. I don't want to hear that nothing is going to happen to me, because things do happen. Things happen to service members, things happen to spouses. You're a nurse, and you know that things happen during surgery. God, the other day, I was driving by the oral surgery clinic and there was an ambulance wheeling someone out, probably from wisdom teeth removal. And yes, I have friends, but that mommy group I belong to? They are casual relationships. That's not all their fault, though; it's mine, because I am done opening myself to everyone and everything. It's exhausting to start and stop friendships. And then my family—I love them, but they're no longer young. They are, for a lack of a better word, *unreliable*."

Sophie didn't speak, not until she knew for sure that Adelaide was done. Because sometimes, her friend simply needed to vent. She had to express the worst-case scenario—its acknowledgment could strip away its power—before she composed herself once more. "Ad, I can't tell what's going to happen in surgery, or in recovery. No one can. But here's the thing I promise: I will do everything in my power to be here for you and for Genevieve. In all the ways. Even if it's just to grab you some ice chips or to feed you Jell-O or to hold up your throw-up bucket. And more, for the worst case. In the worst-case scenario, I will be here for Matt, for Genevieve, and I will make sure that Regina doesn't hog all of your baskets and necklaces because at least half have to go to me."

Adelaide cackled, face settling into a smile.

A knock sounded on the door, and the anesthesiologist walked into the room. Dr. Wong was spectacled and serious but had kind eyes. "Are you ready for me, Mrs. Wilson-Chang?"

"Yes, almost there." Adelaide squeezed Sophie's hand. "Please don't stay mad that Reggie's here."

Sophie hardened her poker face, gritted her teeth together in a Crest-white smile. "I admit, I wish you would have told me."

"One of you wouldn't have come if I had."

Would Sophie have refused the SOS if she'd known? Would she have missed this because of a decade-long unresolved situation between herself and Regina?

Sophie averted her eyes at her doubt. "Maybe. Maybe not."

"Well, thank you for staying, for not even thinking of leaving." She squeezed her hand. "I only have one last thing to ask. A huge favor. Massive."

"Anything, obviously."

"And I'm going to need help convincing Regina of the same thing."

"Okayyy."

"I think we should do book club again."

"Wh—I don't get it."

"I haven't been able to get a book club together here. And I figured, since you both have a week with me, that we could read a couple of books together."

"Noooo . . ." Sophie dropped her chin. She knew where this was going. "Adelaide, you and your plans. What is going on in that head of yours? This is ridiculous—book club won't fix Regina and me."

"Okay, so maybe not two books, but one. Something fun and quick."

"You're not hearing me. No, Ad."

"C'mon. You said you'd do anything. And this is easy. It's nothing really. I know you already have a Kindle full of books, and admit it, you probably have at least two paperbacks in your suitcase."

Sophie flattened her lips together. *Damn it.*

"So what's one more book? Pretty please with sugar on top." Adelaide's gaze strayed over Sophie's shoulder. She tugged on Sophie's hand. "Look, I've had to cancel Genevieve's party because of this surgery. And because I've been in pain, I haven't been out and about. Book club for the three of us—I want to look forward to that before we all go our separate directions once more."

"All right, Mrs. Wilson-Chang, we really must get going." The doctor approached her bedside.

"Say yes, Sophie," Adelaide said, as the room was rearranged, and the commotion began. "Say yes!"

And because her friend was about to go under anesthesia with all the uncertainty of surgery ahead of her, Sophie did what good nurses did. She gave her patient some peace. "Yes, fine. I'm in. I'll tell Regina. I love you."

"I love you, too!" Sophie said, waving like a pageant queen.

But as Sophie was escorted from the room, she wondered if this intervention Adelaide was planning, and which she had just agreed to, was a disaster waiting to happen.

CHAPTER SEVENTEEN
Regina

"Genevieve, your mama's seeing the doctor now." Regina looked up from Sophie's text update, which said that if there were no complications, the two would be home by dinnertime.

Regina texted back:

> She's okay?

Yes, but we need to talk.

> About what?

She wants us to do book club
while we're together.

Regina guffawed. Adelaide couldn't just leave well enough alone.

"Mama's with doctor?" Genevieve, next to Regina at the toddler-sized table and chairs, smashed a hand against the homemade Play-Doh, interrupting Regina's train of thought.

"Yep, and soon she's going to feel so much better." Regina tousled Genevieve's dark wispy hair.

"No more cry." Genevieve shook her head. "Mama no crying."

"No, no more crying." She stood, eager for some space. It broke her heart how much Adelaide had endured on her own, without family nearby. She knew what it felt like to struggle with something painful while alone.

The phone rang in Regina's hand, surprising her. *Henry.*

She stared at his name.

She'd been meaning to text him, but the last day had been consumed with getting settled and avoiding Sophie. And normally, unless it was Miko, she didn't take phone calls. Who had the time these days?

"The phone's ringing," Genevieve said pointedly. And she was actually pointing at the phone.

"Do you think I should take the call?"

Genevieve answered by grabbing the Play-Doh and squeezing it through her fingers.

"Okay, then." She pressed the green button. "Hello?"

"Hey, it's Henry."

Was it possible for his phone voice to be sexier than his DMs and his in-real-life good looks? According to her legs, which had turned to jelly, yes, it was. Regina swallowed her giddiness. "Hi. How are you?"

"Good. Great, actually. I was just thinking of you."

He was thinking of her. Of her! "Oh?"

"And I know you're busy right now."

Regina knew what was coming. He was going to ask her out. She hung on to the kitchen counter for support. "I am. Busy, that is."

"Oh, well . . . never mind, then."

She hit her forehead with a palm. "No, I'm sorry, I didn't let you finish. What did you want to say?"

"In one of our DMs, you mentioned how much you love cheese. And there's a restaurant in Old Town with your name on it. I thought . . . that when things settle down . . ."

Genevieve was staring at her with this goofy smile, and Regina realized the toddler was mimicking her own goofy smile. Then, Genevieve started to kiss the Play-Doh, which escalated to licking it, and then opening her mouth so wide Regina could see her back teeth . . .

With speed she hadn't deployed since she was in her twenties chasing around Miko, Regina leaped across the kitchen to snatch the Play-Doh from Genevieve's hand, and the little girl's mouth promptly clamped on her wrist with a vampire's sting.

"No!" she yelped.

"Oh . . . okay." Henry stammered. "No worries, I—"

"No!" she objected. "I wasn't talking to you, Henry. Sorry, I'm with Genevieve, my friend

149

Adelaide's daughter, and . . . anyway, cheese sounds wonderful. But can I get back to you with times? Adelaide's in surgery, now actually." She wiped the drool around her wrist against her jeans.

"Of course. Can I call you in the next couple of days?"

"Sure." She bit her bottom lip. "That sounds great."

"All right, then. I can't wait. I'll call you soon."

"All right. Bye."

When they hung up, Regina squealed. Then she jumped in place, then she did the running man.

Genevieve laughed. "You're funny."

"Why, thank you, thank you very much," she said, mimicking Elvis.

Genevieve's eyebrows plummeted, and she simply said, "I'm hungry."

Regina sighed and flipped the watch on her wrist. "Oh, it *is* lunchtime. Let's take a look at the manual, shall we?" Regina approached the one-inch binder with the spine labeled *All about Genevieve.* Parts were sectioned with tabs marked "About Me" and "My Schedule" and "Important People," and each topic was filled with typed instructions for Regina.

In the "About Me" section was a list of favorite foods, separated by types: entrées, fruits, vegetables, dessert, and with a separate section for pasta and rice. "You and me and carbs. Am I right?" She scrolled a finger down and stopped at something she was excellent at making. "Pancit? You eat pancit?"

"Uh-huh!" Genevieve piled a round piece of dough onto another one, and then smooshed it down with a palm.

"Let's see what we have for ingredients." Regina rummaged through the pantry. "Hmm. Instant mac and cheese? Sacrilegious. Oh, here's a package of vermicelli. Everything else, we can wing! Time me, baby girl. Twenty minutes."

But it took much longer than twenty minutes to make the pancit. Regina had forgotten how much toddlers got under one's feet. Every seemingly innocuous object was suddenly life-threatening: the under-the-counter microwave Genevieve stuck one of her metal toys in, the garbage can with the step handle that almost slapped her in the face before Regina edged her out of the way. By the time Regina got the bib on the little girl and settled her in the high chair, she was utterly humbled.

That explained the instant mac and cheese.

Still, watching Genevieve eat, a sadness came over Regina at how fast time had flown. Yes, she'd survived the toddler years with Miko— thank goodness—with the help of her mother, and Logan, who ended up being an excellent co-parent despite their divorce, but Miko was nine. Nine! Soon, he would be out of elementary school and then moving out somewhere possibly states away. Tears welled up in her eyes, and she punched at her phone. She and her son had texted several times that morning already, but she wanted to hear his voice.

"Hello," Miko said when he answered the phone.

Instantly, Regina felt better. "How are you? Did you eat this morning?"

"Yes, Lola made me my favorite breakfast. Pop-Tarts."

"Wow, yum." Of course her mother allowed Pop-Tarts. When Regina and her brothers were kids, her mother made eggs every single day. *Protein for muscle,* was what she would say without fail, convinced that cereal and pancakes and waffles were made of sugar.

Gloria hadn't been wrong. But it wasn't fun nor was it nearly as delicious.

Silence descended on his side of the world, and in the background Regina heard the faint, quintessential sound of lightsabers being wielded. "Anak, are you playing video games?"

"Uh-huh."

"Okay—" Their last conversation had been less than twelve hours ago—she'd let this go. "Give the phone to Lola."

"Okay. Lola!" A bedraggled scream pierced through the phone, and Regina distanced it from her ear. *Jeez.*

"Regina?"

"Hey, Ma, how are things?"

"Fine. Nothing's changed since last night, but Alexis is here. She wants to talk to you."

"Um, okay." It wasn't a surprise that Alexis was visiting the Castro residence, because Regina's mother was grandmother to everyone. When Alexis greeted her, Regina asked, "What's up?"

"I was in the neighborhood and thought I'd drop off invoices and receipts from the last event." Her voice dipped at the tail end of the sentence.

"Thank you."

"And I was hoping—do you have time to talk right now?"

"Yes, actually, I do." She and Alexis had skipped their monthly meeting in her haste to come to Virginia, and like a true soldier, her business manager was insistent on following up.

Regina hated talking about money. Besides facing the fact that she would soon have to make a decision about The Perfect Day Catering, money issues felt like a shameful secret no one should know about. It had been a prevalent pressure in her daily life as a child. Though not discussed around her mother's dinner table, Regina and her brothers had known there was little to go around, primarily as a result of their parents' divorce.

"We're crossing the three-year mark soon," Alexis said.

"Is it that time already?" Regina said airily, though a heaviness settled in her chest. It was slightly eased by Genevieve, who was eating the heck out of her pancit, loving every single strand of noodle, every morsel of green bean and carrot.

But Regina hadn't forgotten what she'd said to Alexis almost three years prior. She had been several years out after separating from the Army and Logan, with a child in tow, living back at home with her mother. With her savings from active-duty service—thank God she hadn't shared finances with Logan while married—she'd invested in her own business with one stipulation: that she'd give it her all, and if The Perfect Day Catering didn't feel profitable or promising after three years, she'd walk away. She'd estimated that in three years, she would feel the financial burden of debt, and sure enough, as the months passed with fewer clients than she'd anticipated, she was starting to be crushed by it. Her only solution was cash flow either in the form of clients or investment, and neither seemed to be on the horizon.

Right then, as Regina discussed numbers with Alexis, both agreed that the business was in a dire state. There were no optimistic words or encouragement as when they'd shared their first-year anniversary. Nor did Regina sound like a feisty business owner, fighting for her dream, as she had during their second-year anniversary.

This time, Regina expressed the inevitable. "I think it's time to start formulating an exit strategy."

"I'm sorry."

"It never has been your fault. In fact, you've helped me keep afloat. But unless a miracle happens in the next six months, we're looking at this same fate. It's me that's sorry. Can you give me time to get back to Georgia so I can think of next steps?"

"You sound like we're breaking up."

"I hope we're not," Regina said.

"I'm not going anywhere."

Silence descended, and despite the plate of pancit that had been calling her name, Regina's appetite disappeared.

"Well, how are things over there?" Alexis asked, finally breaking the moment.

"Fine." Regina heaved out a breath. "Just keeping Adelaide's kiddo happy while she's in surgery. I bought some ingredients with Henry yesterday to cook up some food, but I think I'm going to need a full-on shopping trip."

"Whoa, whoa, whoa there, little mama. Henry? You didn't text me anything about Henry." In a muffled voice, she added, "Yes, Lola, that's what she said; she met Henry!"

Her mother's voice came loud and firm through the phone. She must've grabbed it from Alexis. "So is he hot?"

"Mother!" Regina's cheeks burned. This was the reason why she hadn't told either of these women a thing about their meetup. They were on her like white on rice. "I'm not going to do this with you."

"Did you hold hands?"

In the background, she heard Alexis cackle.

"I'm going to hang up now!"

"Okay, iha. Remember, the red lipstick looks best on you. But make sure you dab a little powder on your lips, because when you kiss him . . ."

That was it, she couldn't do it. She hung up.

Seconds later, a text came in from her mother. It was a picture of her and Alexis pretending to kiss the book Henry sent her.

CHAPTER EIGHTEEN
Sophie

The sun had set by the time Sophie pulled up at Adelaide's townhome. The wind whipped her hair sideways as she assisted Adelaide out of the back seat, and they both took slow and sure steps up the sidewalk, the stairs, and through the door Regina was holding open.

"Hey, how did it go? How are you, Ad?" Regina asked, though she looked at Sophie for the answers. Their friend might have been awake and walking, but Adelaide was far from well. Her usual tidy hair had a knot in the back that Sophie wouldn't be able to untangle without a good brushing. Her skin had a dull sheen, a true sign of dehydration, and her hand hovered protectively over her belly.

"Surgery went well." Sophie grunted while guiding Adelaide to the love seat in the living room, then gently lowering her. "But recovery was a bit tough. She vomited and is still nauseous, though she's finally able to tolerate some fluids. Her pain level is pretty high."

"Oh."

"We're going to have to keep a close eye on her." She looked down at Adelaide. "Do you want to lie down here, or upstairs in your room? What do you think, mama?"

"Here, please," Adelaide said. They were the first words she'd uttered since she left the hospital. Her voice was hoarse and strangled. "Genevieve?" She began to lie down.

"She's sleeping now, honey," Regina said, though she turned halfway toward the kitchen. "I can bring her in, though, if you—"

"No, I don't want to wake her. Can you give me my phone? I promised Matt I would call as soon as I got home."

Sophie grabbed Adelaide's phone from her purse. "Let me guess what the code is . . ."

"Your birthday," Regina said at the same time as Sophie.

"Don't pick on me!" Adelaide raised a finger in a humorous warning before pressing on the screen. "Please, Regina, can I have an ice cream sundae and a root beer float?"

"I can whip that up. And how about a chocolate cake to go?" Regina countered, grinning.

"With buttercream frosting," she mumbled, her phone against her ear.

"Well, at least we know you're feeling less nauseous." Sophie made quick work of tucking Adelaide in with a quilt that had been rolled up in a basket next to the sofa. And as soon as Adelaide's head hit the decorative gingham pillow, her eyes shut.

"That is going to be a short conversation." Sophie raised her eyes to Regina, noticing that she was wearing one of Adelaide's vintage aprons. Her nose picked up the scent of something cooking in the kitchen. Then, her traitorous stomach growled.

Despite having eaten a hefty breakfast and a solid lunch at the hospital dining facility, her tummy was screaming for attention. It had been a while since Sophie'd nursed an adult. All of her patients were children, most often in the care of their parents. Earlier, she'd had to assist Adelaide to the bathroom, keeping her from hitting the floor, and her middle-aged bones felt every bit of effort.

"I did make food, for real. Not exactly cake, because I figured that would be cruel. But if you wanted a little snack . . ." Regina said, reading Sophie's mind. She sashayed toward the kitchen, in full understanding that Sophie was going to follow. Sophie loved food. She also remembered loving Regina's food.

When Sophie entered the kitchen, she encountered a room that had been turned upside down and inside out. Fresh vegetables decorated the countertop, and plates, cups, and utensils were out, buffet style. A large and a small pot piped tendrils of steam into the air, and the coffee maker dripped the playful song of java being brewed. "Wow."

"I took Genevieve out for a quick stroller ride—we both needed the break from being indoors—and the farmers market was today. Which, by the way, was interesting. Random moms with kids also in strollers stopped me because they recognized Gen but not me, and all of them expressed some kind of disappointment about her canceled party. There was one woman I recognized in the Genevieve binder. Her name's Missy, and she's a real estate agent. Did you know that Adelaide stages homes for fun? She's been working for free."

"She didn't say anything about that." Sophie shrugged. "But Adelaide mentioned the party. It made sense to cancel it."

"I know . . ." Regina's voice trailed off. "Except I feel bad about Gen not having a big to-do. You remember how grand her first birthday was. Adelaide set up a Pinterest board to public view just for it."

"Not our decision to make. She's the mama."

"Right." Regina sighed. "You're right. Anyway, I thought I would make a quick vegetable soup, and then decided, I might as well make a meat sauce for pasta tomorrow. The soup's ready, and I picked up a baguette and sourdough bread. Want some?"

The question wasn't whether Sophie would be able to eat, but if she would eat with Regina. While at the moment, Regina seemed amiable, they both were undeniably on shaky ground. But Sophie's tummy twisted with warning that she would soon be hangry, so she said, "Sure. All of it, please."

"That's what I like to hear." Regina busied herself getting a bowl together while Sophie slipped into a seat at the round antique kitchen table, surrounded by three different chairs.

Sophie examined them carefully. One was painted blue, one red, one white, with areas sanded down to the wood grain that made them look vintage and kitschy.

"Do you remember those chairs?"

"Hm?" Sophie looked up; Regina had her back to her. "They do look familiar."

"We picked them up on the side of the road that one day, on one of our flea market trips, er, the flea market trips we tagged along on. Remember?"

"Wait." Sophie frowned. "The free ones?"

"Yeah, I recognized the curve of the back in the chair you're sitting in. It looks like a heart."

Sophie turned in her seat and ran a hand over the wood. "They were gross, covered in soot."

"I know, right? Not anymore." Regina half laughed. "We could barely get them into that tiny car she had."

"I think I still have a bruise from one of the chair legs that dug into me during the hour ride home."

"It was a gorgeous day. I remember riding with the windows down. We had an argument about *Fifty Shades of Grey.*"

Sophie was taken back to the moment. Deployment had been underway, and loneliness and worry hovered in the background. The moments of laughter, of making plans about what to eat after their shopping trip, and then the book talk— her body softened at the recall. "I thought that there was something missing in *Fifty Shades*. People like what they like, and I'm not going to yuck their yum, but I was looking for more in terms of affection, you know?"

"I saw it differently. Grey showed affection in an unconventional way. Not every person shows love and commitment in the same manner. I mean, if anyone should know that, it's you."

Sophie frowned but didn't bite. This was a standard, straightforward answer from Regina. She guessed that caterers didn't get the same lessons on empathy as nurses did.

But, apparently, Regina wasn't done. As she served the bowl of soup, she stuttered. "Wh-what I meant was that you and Jasper obviously were able to circumvent traditions. Look at the both of you, being partners for almost two decades, totally outlasting most marriages. You barely showed any PDA, and yet, your love is stronger than any I know. Anyway, who am I to say? I'm divorced and have a crush on an internet friend."

"Internet friend?"

"It's nothing." Regina straightened. "Wait. Before you eat . . . can I take a picture?"

"Uh . . . okay?"

"It's for my catering company's page. Technically my manager's taking on social media while I'm away, but this soup ended up so pretty, especially on Adelaide's Fiestaware." Regina was already in the process of tilting the phone and snapping several photos in sequence. Sophie waited patiently—she would never admit it but she followed Regina, though not officially, on social media, and she loved her food photos.

"How's that going?" Sophie asked, testing the waters. "Your business?"

"Fine. Good." Regina's answer was curt, and as she thumbed the screen to post, she said, "All right. It's all yours."

"Aren't you eating, too?"

"Believe me, I *have* been eating all day, worried about Adelaide and trying to chase after Genevieve. I realized today that the only reason why I survived Miko's baby- and toddlerhood was because I didn't have a clue what was the right or the wrong thing to do. Today, I was with Gen for eight hours, and I'm paranoid that I've given her too much junk food or said something scathing."

The nervous chatter from Regina harkened back to the past, to the ease with which they'd bantered, even when sometimes their views clashed. Sophie thought it touching that Regina had appreciated her and Jasper's relationship despite her own divorce. It was a window of vulnerability that Sophie hadn't seen in a long, long time. She eased into her response. "That's what godmothers are for, right? What are we good for but to spoil? I tell the girls, as much as I can wait to be a grandmother, I also can't wait to be one, so I don't have to be in charge. I want to be able to be the good cop, for once."

"Yeah, you're right. I just didn't want Genevieve to worry. She called for Ad a couple of times, and my answer was always, 'Here, have something to eat!' "

Sophie laughed as she dipped the spoon in the soup, and as she brought it to her lips, her mouth began to water. Now that her kids were independent and always in some kind of activity away from home, she wasn't cooking nearly as much as she used to, and this was a treat.

When the savory broth hit her taste buds, she sighed with relief, with gratitude. What came with it was warmth, comfort. Maybe this time with Regina wouldn't be so bad. Maybe the rest of the next week would be like this, them on their best behavior. That would be good enough for her.

The doorbell rang.

"Are we expecting anyone?" Sophie asked,

though already standing. She didn't want for Adelaide to wake unnecessarily.

She saw a white van drive past the windows just as she arrived at the foyer. A package on the front step was addressed to both her and Regina. She lifted and shook the box.

"What is it?" Regina's voice filtered from the kitchen.

Sophie examined the next-day-delivery sticker with narrowed eyes.

"That's curious," Regina commented, once Sophie brought the package to the foyer table. She came at the tape with her car keys and popped the flaps open.

Two books. Both *Waiting to Exhale* by Terry McMillan.

Sophie side-eyed Adelaide, who was snoozing away. "She didn't waste any time."

In front of her, Regina groaned, face dropping into a hand. "Did you say yes to this crazy idea for a book club?"

"What else could I have said?"

Regina crossed her arms. "Don't you see what she's trying to do? She's trying to fix it. Fix us." Then, to Sophie's horror, Regina stomped over to the couch and nudged Adelaide.

"What the hell are you doing?" Sophie scream-whispered.

"If she can't follow the rules, then I won't, either."

CHAPTER NINETEEN
Adelaide

Adelaide gasped at Regina's angry face inches from hers as she crashed into a wave of consciousness.

"You keep pushing it, Adelaide," Regina said.

Pushing it? What in the heavens is she talking about?

"Leave her alone, Reggie. She's in pain, for God's sake." Sophie's voice filtered from farther away. Adelaide rubbed her eyes, focusing them. Sophie walked into the room.

"I don't care that she's in pain—well, I do care, but if she's insisting on forcing the issue, then let's discuss it." Regina propped both hands on her hips. "Are you lucid, Adelaide?"

"I think so." Adelaide blinked to clear the fuzz in her head, and the slow roll of her memory recounted the day's events. She had been in the hospital, then she'd come home. Everyone seemed fine when she walked in. The house had been quiet, but right now, it was like she'd turned on a reality show smack in the middle of a fight scene.

"There will absolutely be no book club. Sophie should never have agreed for the both of us.

And then you buying the books before you even asked? It's rude."

Oh . . . oh. Adelaide now understood. "I wanted . . ." She started but couldn't finish the sentence. Not when she couldn't sit upright. Not when she wasn't well enough to explain, fully, that what had happened between them wasn't as straightforward as the two of them assumed it was.

"Do you think this is a game?" Regina turned to Sophie.

"Don't look at me," Sophie said. "I walked into this place clueless, too."

Regina waved her away. "I appreciate what you're attempting to do here, Adelaide. I know that you've been trying to get Sophie and me to make up. But I don't want to make up, and do you know why?"

From where she was lying, Adelaide could see that Sophie had moved to the periphery of the room, near the window that looked out into the street. Her profile was illuminated from the streetlamp outside.

She looked sad.

So Adelaide sat up, and she felt every muscle as it contracted and relaxed. She'd known that at some point during this trip, they would have this conversation, that the truth would come out. She just didn't think it would be while she was getting over her anesthesia. But she would try to pay attention.

In the silence, Regina continued. "Because Jasper, your partner, Sophie, smeared my husband's reputation, which resulted in his reassignment to another duty station much earlier than expected, thereby leading to the end of my marriage. That's why."

From the window, Sophie snickered.

Adelaide's head began to pound as she tried to keep up with the conversation. What she needed was two seconds to jump in. "I . . ."

"You think this is funny?" Regina's voice echoed through the room.

"No, just inaccurate." Sophie turned back from the window. "Your marriage ended because your husband cheated on you and got caught, and *then* he was moved after you had Miko. *That* was what changed your life's course. I didn't cause it. *You* needed a scapegoat, and you picked me. You were so intent on blaming me, that you refused every apology I tried to make, even refused packages sent to you for Miko's birthday. As far as I'm concerned, as much as you want to, quote, 'have at it,' you might find that your take on history is revisionist."

Adelaide shut her eyes against the noise, against this fight. She just didn't have the physical energy. She could barely form the words to explain the reason why she had called the both of them here.

Exhaustion had taken up every cell in her body. What pulled at her was sleep.

One nap. One nap was all she needed and she would tell them straightaway.

So Adelaide did what she'd done so well the last decade. She shut her eyes and told herself that she was fine, that everything was fine.

CHAPTER TWENTY
Regina

Day Before Thanksgiving, 2011

Regina knew her body, and something wasn't right. The last couple of days, she'd felt alternately full, then nauseous, then starving. When she got out of bed that morning, her belly grumbled and her legs felt like they were tied down with bricks. And now at her daily 6:00 a.m. unit physical training, bleary-eyed and in her matching Army gray sweats, beanie, and black gloves, she hoped this sickness would simply pass. It was the day before Thanksgiving, and there was going to be some major eating at their combined book club and Thanksgiving dinner to discuss *The Passage,* and she intended to enjoy it.

"So what do you think? Should I go out with him?" Next to her, First Lieutenant Cynthia Kelkirk jogged in time. The formation had been broken up into running groups, and she and Cynthia had naturally partnered up because of their similar mile pace and because they shared an office cubby.

Regina woke from her hazy trance. "Oh, who?"

"You're not listening! And we're not even going fast. Porter and Gaines got ahead of us half a mile back."

Porter and Gaines were the slowest soldiers in Charlie Company, but at the moment, Regina didn't even have the energy to care. "Sorry."

"Pshhh, you're not sorry," Cynthia said in jest, then did a double take. "Are you sick? You're looking pretty ragged."

"Gee, thanks." Regina grinned, or tried to, anyway. "I don't know. Maybe I'm coming down with something."

Cyn snorted and exaggeratingly placed an extra foot between them. "Well, don't give it to me. I've no time to be sick. T minus sixty-eight days before I'm out of the Army, thirty-eight days if I decide to use up my leave. I've got appointments up the yang to prep me for my transition out."

"You're making me sad. There'll be no one to complain to about the weather."

"Yeah, I'm not going to miss Upstate New York."

"What's the plan, then? For after?" Regina licked her lips, and then cursed herself because her lips felt even colder.

"Anything. Everything." Cyn smiled. "But seriously, I'm meeting with a headhunter after work on Tuesday—he's got leads for a couple of government contractor positions."

Grunting a greeting, they passed a walker, a

soldier with an injury. The pause allowed Regina to take a deeper breath. She wasn't lying to Cyn when she said she was sad. She was just getting used to the deployment routine, and one of her comforts was having Cyn, at work, to chat with.

"Don't worry, you'll get there, too," Cyn said. "What did you and your husband decide on? I know the two of you were discussing what's next."

"We'd like to PCS out of here at the same time to the next duty station—that's, like, the priority. So far, so good. We're supposed to move this summer. Assignments branch is working on the logistics now. There might be jobs at Fort Benning for the both of us, and I have my mom, who lives right down the road in Columbus, and his parents are in Savannah." Regina coughed against a tickle in her throat, to keep herself from delving into the fact that these decisions had not been easy to come to. She and Logan had fought through most of it, tooth and nail. Regina wanted to head to duty stations where she'd never been to, whereas Logan wanted familiarity. But she also knew that the dual active-duty life required negotiation. "Do you ever feel guilty?"

"About what?"

"I don't know. For wanting to leave the Army?"

"No, not at all. We're serving now, Castro. Here's my thought on the matter: it's better to run *to* something than run *from* something. So I say, have a plan, and if that plan sounds better than what you're doing now, then go for it." Cyn spared Regina a glance as they turned the corner. "You know that you can't own and operate a food business while on active duty, right?"

"Shhhhh. I said that when I was drunk." She looked around for prying ears, and remembered she'd revealed the same thing to Adelaide and Sophie the first night they met.

"Why is it a secret?"

"Because that's not what I went to college for!" A wave of emotion rose in her chest. She didn't graduate from a great college and then join the Army so she could eventually grill burgers whenever her husband burned dinner. Nor would she give up the security of being able to support herself to chase a pipe dream of being a chef. Not only would she have to go back to school (um, no), but her projected income would be pennies for a long time as she established herself.

She had always been a responsible person. She had great credit, and she helped out by sending cash to her brothers, who were still in college.

At the thought of burgers, her tummy growled, and she laid a palm against it. "Ugh."

"Oh God, you don't sound so good."

"I did stop by my friend Sophie's place the other day. She had a houseful of kids. We were making Christmas cookies to send downrange. Maybe I got sick from them?"

At the mention of cookies, she detected a butter aftertaste in the back of her throat, and her nose conjured up the smell of cookie dough. A quiet burp escaped her, which gave her a moment's relief, but what followed was a bubble of disgusting, sickening air. Cyn was still chatting away as the bubble rose up higher and higher, until Regina felt it in her nose.

Regina halted a quarter mile away from the run's end point, and in between the winter-hardy holly bushes that lined the trail of the running path, she bent over at the waist, both hands resting on her knees as she heaved, though nothing came out. Tears leaked from her eyes at the effort, and her chest burned, body lurching in between the gasps.

"Oh my God. Are you okay?" Cyn ran toward her.

Regina shook her head, eyes wet. Then, another bubble rose from the pit of her stomach, and this time, she gave into it. Sure enough, last night's dinner, along with half her intestines, came up and out.

The effort put her in a daze, so much that she didn't know how she made it back to her car and then home. But with Cyn to help her, she somehow climbed up to the third-floor apartment without upchucking in the stairwell. She hobbled into the apartment, beelining straight to the bathroom, passing by her bedroom, where she caught sight of her hanging calendar over her desk.

She knelt in front of the toilet. Cyn rubbed her back as she emptied her tummy again.

It had been years since Regina had hugged the porcelain goddess, and even then, she could count on one hand how many times she'd drunk enough to feel sick. Throughout the years that were supposed to be the wildest in her life, she'd kept the fine balance of working hard and playing hard. There was too much pressure on her to succeed. Excuses were not tolerated in the Castro family, especially from her, the eldest and a girl.

Her heart dropped.

She was a girl. A girl who could become a mother.

"No, no, no, no, no." She shook her head. Thoughts on the calendar she'd seen a moment ago, her mind counted down the days since Logan left. About eight weeks. Had she had a period in between?

"What is it?" Cynthia said, coming from the kitchen, a glass of water in her hand.

Reality crashed down. "Oh God."

Regina and Logan had decided to wait to get pregnant. If she was indeed pregnant, Logan would miss the entire pregnancy. They would somehow have to work together, harder—they couldn't be dysfunctional. They could not continue on the same contentious road they had traveled the last two years.

Regina shut her eyes and leaned back against the porcelain tub. Breathed in deeply, exhaled slowly. She imagined herself physically pushing the nausea back down her esophagus.

She had to calm down. She had to think.

CHAPTER TWENTY-ONE
Sophie

"I don't think this is a good idea, Mommy," Olivia warned Sophie from the back seat of her SUV.

"Mommy, they're fighting!" added Carmela, who was looking out her window.

In front of them was a blooming confrontation. At the parking lot of the post office, next to the only grocery store open in town, the night before Thanksgiving, Sophie watched as a woman exited her vehicle to yell at a man who'd crashed his shopping cart into her front fender.

'Tis the holiday season.

"We'll walk the other way. Mommy has an important thing to drop off at the post office that can't wait."

"Is this for your new school?"

"Maybe, sweetie, maybe." Sophie swallowed her giddiness.

The last couple of months had been tough. Harder than it had been in the past, perhaps because now, her schedule oscillated between stark loneliness when the girls were at school to chaos when the girls arrived home each day. Sophie, proud of her profession, of managing a challenging work schedule, had found herself with little to do that was for herself. Since the deployment, she'd decluttered everything in her home twice over, caught up on all the shows she'd been recording on the DVR, and even meal planned through December.

Then, the other week, Sophie'd read an article about being able to earn a master's degree online. She'd undertaken a deep dive into the different schools and what kind of degree she could get, the requirements and cost, and if she'd needed to take the GRE. She discovered that with some nursing master's programs, it wasn't necessary, though she would need to coordinate her clinical rotations with a local hospital.

It was doable. At the very least, something to look forward to. The prospect of work, even if it was school, settled her anxiety about the future; just doing something about the situation made her feel better.

But the application process was frustrating. Her computer was slow; it was fussy. The internet kept cutting out with the snow. So she completed the forms the old-school way: she'd downloaded them and filled them out by hand. With the deadline at the end of November, it had to go into the mail that day.

"Ready, girls?"

"No," Carmela said intently. "It's cold."

"I'm tired," Olivia added.

"How about this?" She caught her daughters' eyes in the rearview mirror. "After the post office, we can swing by the grocery store for a little treat. Maybe doughnuts?"

As she'd expected, their eyes lit up. They both jumped out of the minivan with glee, and after a short wait at the post office, skipped alongside Sophie to the grocery store, where she filled up a small box with a half dozen doughnuts.

On the way to the register, Sophie remembered that she needed tampons, so she and the girls detoured to the feminine hygiene aisle, where only one person lingered. The woman's high ponytail was distinct. The way she stood was striking and familiar, with one hand on her hip, the other holding a box, as if she were in an argument with it.

"Reggie?"

Regina jumped. "Oh my God, you scared me!"

"You mean like Babcock?"

Sophie was met with a blank expression.

Sophie eyed the woman. "Really? It's from *The Passage*, the book that we're supposed to have read by tomorrow. Babcock was one of those vampire-ish monsters who . . ."

Recognition flashed. "Oh, yeah . . . right. I only got a little more than halfway."

"That's more than four hundred pages, so I commend you," Sophie said slowly, catching sight of what was in Regina's hand.

181

A pregnancy test.

Regina's lips began to tremble ever so imperceptibly. "There are so many choices, you know? Three-minute tests, one minute, plus sign indicators or without? Generic or brand name?" She gestured to the shelves below them, to the condoms and contraceptives and lube. "It's ironic that they stock these together."

"Reggie, do you think you're pregnant?" Sophie eyed her girls; they'd wandered across the aisle to the baby toys, where they squeezed stuffed animals hanging on hooks. Normally she wouldn't allow them to play in the store, but her priority at the moment was Regina.

"Y-yes." Her hands wandered to the right of the tests, to the ovulation strips. "When didn't my birth control work? When was it all decided that I would be part of the point-three percent of birth control failures?" She covered her mouth. "Oh God, I'm going to be like my parents, who didn't plan for me. Am I even ready? Is Logan?"

Sophie wrapped her arms around Regina. Hugging was not something she did for everyone, but right then, Regina had triggered the mother, not the nurse, in Sophie.

"You're not your mother. Logan is not your father."

"What if I suck at even doing this? At hugging?" Regina said, through tears. "I've never been really touchy-feely; I don't know how to talk to kids. I mean, do your twins even like me?"

"What?" Sophie half laughed and pulled back. "No, you're not going to suck at hugging, or at talking to kids. I promise you. And watch this." She looked over her shoulder. "Girls, do you know this lady?"

Olivia frowned. "Yeah. That's Ms. Regina. Duh!"

"And do you like Ms. Regina?"

Both girls grinned widely. "Yes!" Carmela said. "She gives us candy."

"See?" Sophie said, then took her voice down. "Now tell me. Why do you think you're pregnant?"

"I'm late, and I was sick today."

"The only definitive way to find out is if you get a blood test. But in terms of over-the-counter tests, any one of these will do." She touched the row of boxes, read their specs, settled for the eeny-meeny-miny-mo method, and plucked the winner. She carefully worded her next question. "Would this be good news or . . ."

"I think so?" Regina's face was blank. "I'm not sure. Logan and I are . . . complicated. I thought we would have more time. . . . Look at me making excuses."

"It's okay." Sophie put a hand on her arm and took her phone out of her pocket. She flipped it open and dialed, and the sound of the buttons echoed through the silent store.

"Who are you call—"

Adelaide answered after the first ring. "Speak now or forever hold your peace!"

She was always so extra. "Hey, Ad. SOS. Meet me and Reggie at my house in about a half hour?"

"I'm there! Wait, I lie. I have a pie in the oven. Cripes."

"Really, you don't have to—" Regina tugged Sophie's arm.

Sophie gently pushed Regina away. "Ad, how about we come to you?"

"Sounds good. Shall I open a bottle of rosé?"

"Uh . . ." Sophie looked at Regina. "Maybe? But we'll grab more sustenance."

When she hung up, she linked her arm around Regina's. "You can't do this on your own. This is an SOS situation."

"But . . ."

"No buts. Let us take care of you. Grab some snacks, like Twinkies and Bugles or something. And maybe your favorite soda."

Sophie trailed after Regina as she grabbed exactly the things she loved the most: Fanta. And vanilla ice cream. Little Debbie pies and Funyuns. They upgraded from a basket to a cart, which hadn't looked so sinful since high school.

That night, she and Adelaide and Regina snacked and watched Regina's favorite movie, *Titanic*, which Adelaide happened to have on DVD, and after getting Sophie's kids to bed in

Adelaide's extra bedroom, they stayed up past midnight to watch Adelaide's favorite thing: infomercials.

At two in the morning, when Regina finally summoned the courage, she tore the pregnancy test's wrapper and walked into the bathroom. Sophie sat, her back against the closed door, with Adelaide. Three minutes later, the door behind them opened, and Sophie looked up to Regina, holding up a test stick with a positive sign in the little window.

CHAPTER TWENTY-TWO
Adelaide

Thanksgiving Day, 2011

Adelaide took a sip of her beer and suffered through the brain freeze, willing the numbness to spread throughout her body. She was huddled around Frank Montreal's coffee table for November's book club, with a portable heater set up behind her. And yet, she felt cold all over, stiff and unfeeling.

Regina was pregnant. Pregnant, and not even on purpose.

The next second she was hit with a wall of guilt—she should've been happy for her friend. A million things had to go right to ovulate, to inseminate, to survive. Apparently, it just happened for lots of people, including Sophie, now Regina, and pretty much everyone who came to book club, but not her.

"Thank you everyone for making this a potluck. Otherwise, we'd all just be eating chicken wings and Doritos chips." Frank entered their circle, carrying a hefty hardback in his hand. "Are you ready to talk *The Passage*? I personally think that it's all perfectly timed. The people in the book are doing everything that we're simply trying to do during deployment and the holidays: survive."

A round of *hell yeses* and nods and *um-hmms* responded back. Adelaide took another swig of beer, because she might as well. Neither being healthy, nor responsible, nor eating only organic, nor sleeping for eight hours had yielded her a baby, so what was the point? She couldn't seem to get pregnant, and when she was pregnant, she couldn't bring a baby to term.

And yet Regina, who wasn't planning to have a baby, got pregnant while on birth control.

Adelaide had been doing fine. After her miscarriage earlier in the deployment, she'd visited her doctor twice to follow up. She'd chosen to keep the incident to herself—only Matt and her mother knew, and telling them was traumatic as it was. As the days passed, the cloud lifted just a little.

That is, until last night, when Regina appeared from the bathroom holding up a positive pregnancy test. Adelaide's emotions had swept her up like a tornado.

There was a crash in the bedroom area, taking Adelaide out of her thoughts. It was followed by the chorus of children saying, "We're okay!"

Now that their spouses were gone, it was an unspoken rule that sometimes book club would include babies and children, and that meant interruptions. As the parents around her laughed, Adelaide joined in, because that's what she did. *Smile, dear. No one likes a grumpy goose,* was what her mama always said. Patricia Wilson, despite her shy nature, was 100 percent hospitable and gracious 100 percent of the time, never once succumbing to TMI.

"You picked a winner, Frank," Adelaide said now, pulling the book from her tote bag and willing the meeting forward. "It was meaty but fun, and exactly what I needed to get away from the real world."

"And thanks for giving us till the end of the month to read this," said Wendy Proctor, a first-timer. She was a teacher at the elementary school. "Everything was due from the kids the last couple of weeks, and I needed the extra time—especially for a book that's eight hundred pages."

"I needed that week, too, to get myself together," Frank said. "The deployment hit me hard this time. The kids are so confused. The last time Mel deployed, the kids were toddlers and now—well, sometimes they're angry that she's not around."

Frank did have a dark hue under his eyes, and his hair, usually cut short, was shaggy around the ears. Admittedly, Adelaide didn't think of the guys having a hard time transitioning. And since the unit had deployed, she hadn't checked in with Frank.

She vowed to do better.

"And are you? Getting yourself together?" Sophie asked, joining the circle, with a plate of dessert in her hand.

"No. Not even." Frank gestured at his outfit. "I'm really not sure if this shirt made it to the laundry this week. Tuesday, I lost my car keys. Then I thought I would call Mel so I could pick up our spare from her at the office, and then I realized—nope. She's not here." Frank rolled his eyes. "I had to call a locksmith, and it was a total scam. Anyway"—he drew out the word, and pressed his palms against his cheeks—"I'll stop now. We're all in the same boat."

"But it doesn't mean we can't feel what we need to feel," Sophie said, reaching across and squeezing his hand.

"Oh my God, she *does* give fucks," Colleen said, now settling into an empty seat, a plate in each hand. To the book clubbers who'd missed the escape room, whose glances bounced among the circle, she said, "See what happens when you miss book club?"

"On that note"—Frank shook his head, laughing—"I have questions about the book." He stood and passed a piece of paper to every book clubber, then stopped at an empty chair. "Regina!"

"I'll be there in a sec!"

Adelaide turned to see Regina coming out of the bathroom. Her face seemed withdrawn, and

Adelaide quickly looked away, pain striking her heart. She had probably just thrown up.

Adelaide, too, had been sick during all of her short-lived pregnancies. Her longest pregnancy was thirteen weeks, but before she lost that baby, she felt the full pain of hyperemesis. She'd welcomed it, though. Welcomed the surge of hormones because that meant her baby had been growing. Until the baby no longer did.

"Get your dessert and sit down before the children decide to become the Twelve," Frank said.

"Don't even say that. That freaks me the hell out," Kerry DeGuzman, one of the newbies said. "Have any of you ever startled awake in the middle of the night to see a child just looking at you?" She shivered.

Most in the circle nodded. One started to commiserate about the strange sleeping habits of her child, and the whole conversation simply became too much for Adelaide. She stood abruptly, unintentionally interrupting. "Oh, excuse me. I forgot to grab dessert."

As she walked to the kitchen table, Frank said, "Oh, by the way! Regina mentioned last month that she liked to cook and bake, so I asked her to make a special dessert today. Red velvet cake. Is that too much with the vampire theme?"

The crowd answered with a resounding no.

"Cake is cake." Adelaide took Regina's side—

191

her plate was empty. Her friend had a hesitant look. After surveying the table, Adelaide placed a dinner roll on Regina's plate, whispering. "Bread is pretty safe to try. But you've got to eat when you can."

"Thank you." Regina nodded.

"How did you even make the dessert?"

"I sucked it up. I didn't want to disappoint him or the rest of the group."

Adelaide admonished herself and her selfishness. Here was Regina, who made a cake for others while feeling unwell, and Adelaide had thought of no one but herself. She filled a glass with ice and lemon water and handed it to Regina. "Go sit, rest."

As Adelaide contemplated having two pieces of red velvet cake to drown her sorrows, the group's topic of conversation switched to food. She piled her plate and returned to the living room.

"I'm not a cook," Adelaide admitted.

"You can cook," Sophie said, with an overfull mouth, the bottom of her lip smudged with frosting.

"Yeah, but only simple stuff and appetizers, and easy dessert. But not meals—Matt is the cook. He grills. He has all of his family recipes. I've got mac and cheese, and I still get that wrong, though don't tell my mama, else I'll have to cash in my woman card. During our last deployment, I think I lost ten pounds because after a while, Burger

192

King and Subway just turned my stomach." She flattened her lips into a line. Around her, the clubbers reflected back pity. "I just wish deployments weren't even a thing, y'all. I don't know how you've done it all this time, Soph. Four times in ten years! This is our third in six, and I'm tired already."

"Is it horrible to say that I'm happy they're gone?" Nadine Sox interjected. She was older, with teenagers. "The last couple of weeks before they leave is always chaos. This last time, the tension was so high, none of the kids slept, which meant I couldn't sleep because to sleep with teenagers roaming the house is just asking for trouble. I hate to sound like a brat, but I needed to breathe, and the only way that was going to happen was when he left. Though it's just as hard now that they're gone. My only consolation, seriously, was this book." She lifted *The Passage* from her lap. "I kept thinking about Amy and her journey. How in the beginning she was caught up in the unknown but had no choice but to trust in whatever that force was. But in the end she was given all the extra powers to do good."

"You mean she was injected," Wendy quipped, raising an eyebrow.

"Sure, injected. Sort of like us." Kerry laughed. "When they raised their right hand, it was like we did, too."

Adelaide was mollified. Everyone was in the

same boat, but there she was, complaining to herself, and she didn't even have any kids. She didn't have other humans to take care of, or any extra responsibility that fell onto her lap. It was just her, her beautiful apartment, and her dog.

Some XO's wife she was. She had everything she ever needed but couldn't seem to focus on it. Instead, she was jealous.

It was shameful.

Adelaide straightened her posture. *I can do this. I've done it before, and I can do it again.*

"I'm sorry. I acted pathetic earlier," she said. "It doesn't help for me to be so negative."

"It's all right. The first couple of months are always the hardest," Sophie said.

Adelaide nodded at Sophie's calming words. In the last two months, Adelaide had begun to see Sophie and Regina as bookends. While Regina was young and idealistic, Sophie brought sage advice and logic.

Still, despite her respect for these women, Adelaide had not told them about her lost pregnancies because that was too intimate, made her too vulnerable.

So she put on a smile despite feeling raw, while the eyes of the group were on her. She didn't want to be judged or pitied. Nor did she want the group's mood to plummet with her personal issues. "I know. I'm just glad you're all here with me. I don't know what I would have done without you. I definitely don't know if I would have read this eight-hundred-page book."

The comment brought on a collective exhale, and they launched into their discussion and talked about life until most of the food was gone and half the kids were asleep on parents' laps. And while Adelaide was glad the conversation had moved on, it became clearer to her that no one could understand her situation. Every person there was a parent or was going to be one. And even at a welcoming Thanksgiving meal of unlikely friends coming together, Adelaide couldn't shake the loneliness that surrounded her.

CHAPTER TWENTY-THREE
Regina

Day After Thanksgiving, 2011

Regina accepted the video chat with a tinge of fear in her heart, and Logan's face materialized on the screen. He had the camera angled so his normally square jaw was rounded and his left cheek was twice the size of his right. His side of the world looked as if it were filtered with green, probably from the dim light in his trailer. But one thing was clear: he looked exhausted.

Her heart squeezed, and she admonished herself for her initial reaction. She'd spent the last day obsessing over the moment when she'd tell him about the pregnancy, and she'd forgotten that he was clearly a man who had volunteered his life to serve others. He was good. And she had nothing to worry about.

Hope filled her that her announcement would put a smile on his face.

The truth of the moment sank in a little deeper. They were having a baby.

A baby!

Regina knew that she was lucky. Her college best friend had had an accident as a teen and couldn't have a baby. There were new studies about this thing called PCOS that caused pain and often infertility.

This baby would come from her. This baby would be her bond to the world. And she knew she would be a good mother. Regina would be protective and doting and present.

This baby could be the thing that would finally make her and Logan's relationship feel real and on solid ground.

"Hey, sweetie," Regina said, heart heavy with all of her self-talk. Her hand covered the ziplock bag containing the positive test, as if Logan was in the same room and could have peeped into the contents. "You must have gotten my vibe, because I was planning on Skyping you just now."

He yawned. "I'm headed to bed. I barely made it to my CHU. What's up? How was today? Feeling better?"

"Yes. Er, and I found out what was making me sick."

"Yeah?" His eyes wandered above her face, distracted. "Hey, I see lights behind you."

Regina turned around, to her artificial tree. "I put it up right after Thanksgiving dinner, as usual. I'm hoping to add more ornaments this year."

"Wanna see my tree?" He turned the camera so it tilted to his bedside table next to the twin bed. His bedsheets were crumpled in the middle, but

Regina ignored that big pet peeve of hers. "I just got it today. Along with all the treats and cards you and the neighborhood sent. Tell them thanks. The company loved it. The cards from the kids made some of the soldiers tear up."

Her face flushed at the natural segue in the conversation. *Oh my God, he is going to freak out.* "I'm so glad they got there. And um . . . well . . . speaking of kids." She swallowed a breath, wishing that there was a way she could've said all of this in person, because it would have been easier. Right now, his attention seemed scattered. On his side of the world, his small TV projected background chatter.

"Yeah?" he asked absentmindedly.

Regina heaved a breath and spit out the words. "I'm pregnant."

His eyes snapped to hers. "What?"

"I'm . . . we're . . . pregnant." Except this time, she said it with gusto and a bigger smile, with an enthusiasm that she was sure would transfer across the screen.

He sat up and leaned in toward the screen. "Pregnant, like with a baby?" His face looked bewildered. "You?"

"Me." Worry rushed up her spine. "I mean, I still have to get a blood test, but I've got this." She showed him the baggie, held it close so the plus sign was right up to the camera's view.

"I . . . oh . . ."

She waited for more. She chewed the inside of her cheek, and counted the seconds that passed. *One . . . two . . . three . . .*

"I . . . I thought we were waiting to . . . and your birth control."

A niggle of annoyance zinged through her. She intuited the beginning of a fight. "I took my birth control on time. But it isn't a hundred percent. We *were* waiting, but we're not anymore, obviously."

His mouth fell open, though nothing came out of it.

"Do you have anything else to say?" she said, after several painstaking seconds.

"What did you expect me to say?"

She felt a mix of confusion, then some empathy because she had been speechless herself a couple of days ago. And then came shame, as if this was only her doing. As if she'd engineered this pregnancy to raise the stakes in their marriage.

"I . . . I don't know, except it wasn't this." Her voice shook. Having a baby, making a baby, was not a one-person endeavor.

Regina's fear from the grocery store returned. It rose like a tide in her psyche, coming from deep inside her. Up to this point, she'd done everything she could so she would have choices in her life. What if she and Logan were going to be like her parents had been, forced into staying together for the sake of a child?

You're not your mother. These were Sophie's

words to her. Her friend had spoken with sureness, and just as that statement had convinced her then, Regina, in recalling it, believed it now.

She gathered her courage. "Logan, if you're not ready for this . . . because I am, and I intend to be the best mother this child could have."

"Whoa," Logan said. "Regina. Don't get this wrong. At all. Babe, I'm just in shock." His eyes rounded in fright. His Adam's apple bobbed, his sign of insecurity. "I'm . . . scared, too. But it doesn't mean that I'm not with you on this." And as if reading her mind, he said, "I know what you're thinking right now."

Logan indeed knew exactly what she was thinking, so she gave words to it, intending on making it clear. "My father left us, Logan. He left us for an entirely different family, and I don't want that to happen here. I want us to be honest with each other."

After seconds of silence, her husband spoke. "This is our baby. Yours and mine. I will love this baby as much as I love you."

Regina felt tears well behind her eyelids. She nodded, her anger subsiding. She had to remember that she'd had over forty-eight hours to process this news. That in the beginning she was shocked herself. "I love you."

His eyes softened, and a soft smile graced his face. "I'm going to be a dad. You're going to be a mom."

"Yes, yes. We're going to be parents." Regina's face warmed, and her body sagged with relief. *This* was the Logan she fell in love with.

"We have a lot to discuss. About our plans, together. How can we raise a child if we're both on active duty? But how can we do it without the both of us working? Babies are expensive."

She nodded. "I was thinking the same thing. But we have time to talk about it."

"You're right. Yes, we do." He held up a hand and pressed his palm up against the screen, and she did the same, not quite lining up with his. She shut her eyes, hoping to feel his comfort through the image.

They were in for a long road

PART FOUR

Whatever the problem, be part of the solution. Don't just sit around raising questions and pointing out obstacles.

—*Bossypants* by Tina Fey

CHAPTER TWENTY-FOUR
Sophie

Present Day, Sunday

Two mornings later, Sophie leaned back against the leather chair and pulled on the wooden handle. Her legs jerked upward, and she sighed at the instant relief. It had been a long night; she had forgotten what it was like to have a toddler in the house. Babies had their sixth senses, too, and no bribe could get Genevieve to settle the last couple of nights, not in the playpen next to her mother, and especially not in the crib. Regina, who had been sleeping in Genevieve's room, had not been able to sleep, either, and soon, Sophie and Regina ended up sharing the poster bed, with Genevieve somewhat asleep between them.

The arrangement wasn't ideal, especially since their blowup the other day had erected a tougher barrier between them. But they did what they had to do for sleep and sanity.

Sophie's phone buzzed in the chair's cupholder, startling her. Jasper's name appeared on the screen.

Haven't heard from you. Check in?

She debated on how to respond and if she even should. Jasper would simply insist that she return home now that Adelaide was on the mend, in her second day of recovery. That Sophie mustn't subject herself to her and Regina's former drama.

As if her partner had read her mind, another text flew in:

Hope Regina's on her best behavior.

Instead of answering the text, Sophie opened her new-to-her copy of *Waiting to Exhale.* She intended to stay in Alexandria as long as she needed to, and he would have to accept it. So she focused her attention on the previously loved book, pages yellowed and dog-eared, with pencil markings in some corners.

It was ridiculous for her to be reading a classic when she had an entire Kindle app full of books, many of which had been published in the last year. Heck, she had her current book club book—she'd found and joined a neighborhood book club in the subdivision they had moved into—yet to read. *Dominicana* by Angie Cruz promised to be a page-turner.

And yet, here she was. Surely, *Waiting to Exhale* no longer held the same kind of meaning and emotion almost three decades after it was written. But she would read the book in the name of friendship—with Adelaide, of course.

Not with Regina. Sophie prided herself on not going back on her word, and she wouldn't start now. At the end of the week, whenever Adelaide wanted "book club" to occur, Sophie would be ready.

From upstairs, she heard a thump from Adelaide's room. She had checked in on her earlier that morning, and her friend was wide awake and reporting more pain on board. Admittedly, Sophie didn't like the way Adelaide had looked—her walk and demeanor were those of a patient fresh from surgery. By now, she should have been up and about, albeit moving slowly.

When no other noise followed, Sophie settled into the seat.

Before she knew it, Sophie had read thirty pages of the book and her body felt the telltale signs of relaxation: legs crossed at the ankles in front of her, her shoulders no longer at the level of her ears. And she was properly put in her place—the book *still* did have relevance. So much time had passed since she'd read *Waiting to Exhale* years ago that it felt like she was meeting these women for the first time. The characters' personalities jumped off the page, and Sophie was already invested in their lives. Sadly, the movie version also played in her head. The catch-22 of book-to-movie adaptations: the scenes were created for the reader.

"Ahem," a voice said, and Sophie peeked above her book. Regina was leaning on the doorjamb, holding a fork. "I've got breakfast ready. Pancakes, bacon, and eggs."

Sophie pressed her lips together. Regina had beaten her to the kitchen that morning and shooed her away, a cup of coffee pushed into her hand. If Sophie had not been exhausted, she might have been insulted at not being asked to at least help.

"Thank you."

"I see you're reading the book."

"I am. We said we'd do it."

"Correction. You said you would, and you agreed for the both of us. Which was wrong."

Sophie laid the book on her lap and leveled Regina with a glare. Apparently, their fight the other day wasn't enough for her. "So you're saying you're not going to read it."

Her face crumpled slightly. "No. I'm just saying I didn't get to agree myself." She sighed. "How far in are you?"

Sophie paused at this unexpected reaction. Was that acceptance? "Three chapters. You?"

"Um . . . same."

Sure.

But before Sophie could challenge Regina, a thump upstairs brought their gazes to the ceiling. "I'll go check on her," Sophie said.

"I'll come with you," Regina said. "I just need to grab Gen."

"No worries, I've got it." Sophie stood up to make the point. Truly, too many cooks spoiled the broth, didn't Regina know that?

Sophie continued her imaginary argument until she reached the second-floor landing, where she heard sniffling.

Adelaide. She rushed to the door and gave a cursory knock, though not even a half second later, she pushed through. On the bed perched Adelaide, pressing a pillow against her belly. Tears streamed down her face.

"Ad, are you okay?" Sophie glanced at her handwritten notes on the bedside table, and sure enough, it wasn't time for Adelaide's next dose of pain medicine. In fact, her pain meds were maxed out.

Her voice croaked. "It hurts. I woke up and everything hurts. And I just got sick in the bathroom."

"You threw up?"

"Yeah."

"That doesn't sound good. I think I should call your doctor."

She groaned. "No. I don't want to be away from Genevieve."

"Right. I know you don't." Sophie took a second to soften her voice. "Ad, sweetie . . . it's obvious that your pain meds aren't sufficing. Let me take a look at your incisions."

"Okay." She lifted her nightgown, and Sophie

spied the incision sites. There were two, and they looked clean, though slightly red. But Adelaide's belly was distended, and it radiated heat. At a slight touch, Adelaide sucked in a breath.

Oh dear. Sophie's mind ran down the possibilities of what could be causing these symptoms, and it immediately jumped to the worst-case scenario, as it always did.

Infection.

Sepsis.

Sophie grabbed the thermometer from the bedside table, and seconds after she stuck it in Adelaide's ear, it beeped: 101.3. "You have a fever."

"So what does that mean?"

"That means I'm calling your doctor right this second."

Footsteps sounded. "Hey, is there anything I can do?"

Sophie turned, and Regina was at the doorway, with Genevieve just behind her, hair matted and messy, and with a finger in her mouth. Her chin was wet with drool.

"Mama okay?" Genevieve said around her finger.

"Oh, baby," Adelaide said. "I'm okay, baby. I'm okay." She turned to Sophie. "I don't want her to . . . to see me like this."

"Reggie, grab that bag over there and fill it with underwear, pants, and a shirt maybe. Toiletries,"

she said slowly, thumbing her phone screen at the same time. Her first thought: *Text Jasper*. He always knew what to do.

> Can you get a hold of Matt for me?
> SOS but unofficial?

Then she punched Fort Patriot Community Hospital's phone number, written on the discharge form, also at the bedside. In the background, Genevieve, sensing the emergency, melted into a puddle of tears. Regina held the little girl tightly in her arms.

Thank goodness Regina was here to manage Genevieve, because Sophie's priority was to get Adelaide to the emergency room as quickly as possible.

CHAPTER TWENTY-FIVE
Regina

Regina lunged for her phone when it rang three hours after Sophie took Adelaide to the ER. "Hello?"

"It was a bile duct leakage," Sophie said without pretense.

"Wait, what?" Regina asked.

Genevieve, lying on her belly on the living room couch next to her, looked up from a video on the iPad. Her eyes were droopy, and her hair was disheveled—just about how Regina felt. Standing, Regina went to the foyer to pace out of earshot. Toddlers knew and absorbed more than adults gave them credit for.

"It was a bile duct—"

"No, I heard that part. Was that what caused the infection?"

"Yes, but they won't know how bad it is until they go in."

"*Go in* meaning s—" She lowered her voice. "Surgery again?"

"Yes."

"Did you get a hold of Matt?"

"Jasper did. I spoke to him briefly, too."

"Damn." Besides her relief that Adelaide was

exactly where she needed to be, Regina was impressed with Sophie's clear head. "Thank you for telling me. I was so worried."

"How are you guys doing?"

Regina half laughed, looking around the house and then at her copy of *Waiting to Exhale* cracked open and turned pages down on the couch. In the hours since Sophie and Adelaide had left, ironically, she could only read. Somehow, she felt a little closer to Adelaide by doing so. "Yeah, I'm totally fine. Genevieve is calm, the house is standing, and there's food in the fridge. And I'm at the part where Gloria's ex-husband came out as gay to her and she's in denial." She stopped, cringing at her earlier lie. "So I guess I can admit that I'm not at a hundred pages."

"It's all right, I knew."

"Busted." She looked at the floor. "Sorry."

"That's okay, I was plotting on getting up early tomorrow so I could beat you to the kitchen."

"God, we are petty." Regina shook her head, though at that moment, she was grateful. Grateful that, at least, at this moment, they were able to put things aside.

"As can be. Or in denial."

"Like Gloria."

"Now that was a book club statement. Who *are* you?" Sophie laughed.

Regina remembered their first book club together, their first threesome conversation when

Sophie assured her that she belonged in book club. The decade had flown, though the days had been protracted. But those almost nine months together at Millersville had been filled with great memories.

"Soph, I'm worried."

"Me, too, Reggie." After a pause and a sniff, she said, "The doctor said that this would be an overnight stay, maybe two."

"Okay, well . . . do you want to switch off, if that happens?"

"That sounds good. Let's play it by ear?"

Regina sighed. "Okay. I'll probably take Gen out on a stroller walk after we get off the phone, maybe to the park. I think she and I could use some air."

"Okay. I'll keep you posted."

"And hey, Soph?"

"Yeah?"

"You were amazing. I don't want you to get a big head about it, but I'm glad you're here."

"I'm glad you're there for Gen. Maybe Adelaide had a sixth sense about this all. We needed all hands this morning."

"Even Jasper."

Another pause. "Yeah, I guess that guy, too."

Regina couldn't discern Sophie's tone, if it was loving or sarcastic. But as she opened her mouth to ask, the doorbell rang. "Someone's at the door."

"I've got to run, anyway. I'll keep you posted."

With a supervisory glance at Genevieve, Regina padded toward the front room. "Just let me know if you need food. I can bring you some from home."

"Thank you. Bye."

Regina stuck the phone in her back pocket and opened the door, belatedly thinking that she was no longer in small-town Georgia and perhaps she should have checked the peephole.

But she was rewarded by a sight for sore eyes.

She felt her body give. "Henry." Under an arm he carried a box, and with the other hand, a reusable bag, with the blooms of flowers overflowing out of its top. On his face was a tentative, shy smile.

"I know I should have probably called, but your last text was—"

She rushed to him, and wrapped her arms around his torso. What was it about him? Her usual defenses were nowhere to be found. Though logic would insist that she make sure he hadn't misrepresented himself these eighteen months, her instincts eased her worry. The fact that he was at the front door after her last text, a simple *I feel so helpless,* meant that he listened to her.

Then, she realized how much she was squeezing him, and stepped back. "Sorry, I—"

"No, no need to apologize. I . . . I kind of liked

it." His cheeks pinkened. "Anyway, I'm not here to impose. I just wanted to drop this off." He shook the box. "Pastries from the shop, and I remember you eyeing the flowers at the market the other day. I figured . . . well, my sister, Carolina, loves fresh flowers. So anyway." He held both packages out.

God, he was so . . . thoughtful. "Do you want to come in?"

"Oh, nah . . . I mean, not unless you want me to."

"I do. Want you to." This felt like first loves, teenage angst, and her heart thrilled at it. With Logan it had never felt that way.

Quit comparing the two.

Still, when he entered the town house, she cataloged the way he moved, lithe instead of bulky and hulking. She watched him greet Genevieve like she existed—while Logan treated Miko, until he was much older, like a plaything rather than a person. And when he plated the pastries and then promptly cleaned up after himself, it sealed the deal.

Henry was different.

They were sitting as a party of three with Genevieve at her toddler table, with a plate of pastry each in front of them, when Henry asked, "Do you want to talk about it?"

Regina Velcroed Genevieve's bib. "About what?"

"Feeling helpless."

She split the croissant on her plate, and it flaked on her fingertips. She marveled at its perfection, made better when it melted in her mouth. It allowed her a moment to wonder how much she should reveal.

Henry waited patiently. Again, unlike Logan.

"Usually, if there's a problem, I'm fixing it. If Baby's broken, I fix her. If someone's hungry, I cook. If someone needs help, I . . . do. And right now, I feel like I'm not doing enough."

"I bet your friends don't feel that way."

"Yeah, well . . . Sophie's really doing the heavy lifting."

Henry took a bite out of his croissant. "I don't think it's a competition."

She shrugged. "I dunno. For a decade now, Adelaide has been closely in touch with each of us, with Sophie and me not being in touch with each other. It's been weird, to say the least, to still have the ghost of her around."

"What you're doing here is equally important." He reached the short distance across the table and touched her forearm, grounding her. His thumb feathered across her skin and drew her arm closer. "And I bet Sophie has missed you, too."

The idea startled her. "Miss? I didn't miss her."

His expression turned thoughtful. "No?"

Regina opened her mouth to rebut. Because no. She hadn't missed Sophie. She was angry, and rightly so. But she was interrupted by the sweep of Genevieve's arm and the accidental swipe of her sippy cup onto the floor.

"Uh-oh! Sorry!" Genevieve yelped.

It broke the moment, and it was probably a good thing. This was why Regina, six years postdivorce, never did get past that first date. There was too much at stake. And it wasn't just because she was a mom or that she was always busy or that she was living in her mother's home.

There were too many feelings involved. She couldn't look a man in the eyes fully. She double-checked all friendships, only letting a few in. She preferred to pass once it got serious. It had been safer that way.

Henry was at the sink before Regina recovered from her thoughts; he ran water over a sponge. "Don't worry about the milk—I can wipe it up."

"Oh, okay."

He bent down and picked up the cup and assessed the floor for droplets of milk. "I bet that sippy cup claims to be spill-proof. And yet."

She giggled at his intensity. "Are you in the market for sippy cups?"

"No, but . . ." He straightened, and he swooped his hair back with a hand. "Maybe one day. Carolina's a single mom, so I'm around young kids pretty often. I love kids."

He said it so seriously that Regina stilled.

He stood swiftly and rinsed the sponge at the

sink and washed his hands. Correction, he was scrubbing them raw, as if in deep thought, suds blooming on his hands. He opened his mouth to speak, then shut it.

Regina willed the moment forward, because in between the words he spoke was a message, though she wasn't willing to investigate it. Not yet. So she changed the subject, swiftly. She said the next thing that came to mind— something that had been simmering in her quest to feel more helpful while at Adelaide's. "You know, Genevieve's turning two next week. I was thinking—why not have a little celebration here at home?" Then, as the words left her mouth, the more inspired she became. "This is probably last-minute, but do you have time for a cake order for next Saturday? Nothing too elaborate."

Startled, he said, "Yeah, sure. I can check. Our schedules are back at the bakery, but I can call you to confirm. For how many folks?"

"Um . . . ten? Fifteen? Or can I confirm in a couple of days?" Regina's to-do list materialized in her head. She would need to figure out what people to invite, food to plan, and decor to buy.

"That might be something I can fit in. But listen, Regina—"

"Great! Well!" She bent down and wiped Genevieve's face with a napkin. And because she wasn't yet ready for whatever he wanted to discuss, added, "I think you're done with your snack, little girl. Do you want to get ready to head to the playground?"

With the word *playground,* Genevieve bolted out of her seat.

"Oh, okay, well, I really should get going. You'll call me about the cake?"

"Yes, I will." She swept crumbs into her palm and took a breath to recover. "Thank you for coming by. It was so thoughtful."

Somehow, she negotiated Henry out of the town house with a kiss on the cheek, and hoped that it showed her gratitude, despite how she'd blundered the end of their visit.

When she was sure Henry was far enough away, Regina schlepped the stroller out of the hallway closet.

She was the one who needed the walk to the park.

CHAPTER TWENTY-SIX
Adelaide

Adelaide awoke to the sounds of beeping, her vision hazy. She was discombobulated, unsure where she was, with a white dotted tile ceiling above her. It was the complete opposite of how she had fallen asleep the night before, ensconced in the warm blue of her walls and the textured curtains she had painstakingly researched before deciding on the perfect pattern. The bed she was lying on surely wasn't her Tempur-Pedic, nor was she covered by her luxurious organic cotton sheets.

Then the memories trickled back: the surprise of extreme postoperative pain, her gasping for her breath from it. The drive to the ER at Alexandria General instead of Fort Patriot Community Hospital because they were at capacity. The worried expression of the ER doc on call, who had quickly discerned that surgery was necessary.

She lifted her arms off the bed, where two IV lines ran bags of fluids. A peek downward showed the thick tube of a urinary catheter running from under her blanket to somewhere over the side of her bed. She'd remembered having one when she had Genevieve, for her C-section.

Genevieve.

Her spine straightened at the thought of her daughter. Genevieve had cried out for Adelaide as she was being helped out the door this morning. Her sweet little one was probably worried and all alone.

No, not alone, with Regina.

Adelaide breathed a sigh of relief.

A quiet knock sounded at the door, and then it opened to Sophie, who was carrying a to-go cup. Her face lit. "You're awake."

"Yeah." Adelaide's voice croaked; she cleared her throat. "Just now."

"Don't try to sit up." Sophie set down her cup on the bedside table, then pulled a chair closer to Regina. She sat. "You need to take it easy for now. And really, you should take advantage of it, because they're going to walk you soon enough."

"I feel like I lost a week of my life. "

"Your body went through the wringer trying to right itself. But I just spoke to the nurse, and she said that surgery went well, and your doctor should be here in a bit to let you know more. But let me tell you, your husband and mother are blowing up my phone. They're both so worried. I do think, young lady, that you should call your mother."

"What did she say?" She wiggled in discomfort and flushed with an unknown feeling. Her mama was boss and priest and parent all at once.

Sophie was already pulling out her phone. "That I should have you call as soon as you woke up."

Their conversation was interrupted by another knock at the door, and a man in a lab coat walked in. "Hello, Adelaide. Do you remember me? I'm Dr. Popov. I did your surgery."

She sat up in bed. "Yes. Thank you, for everything."

His smile was gracious. "Just doing my job, though it's really our ER doctor who made the right call to admit you. It was especially wise of your friend to bring you in this morning. It could have been so much worse. May I sit?" He gestured to the chair.

"Sure," Adelaide said.

"Your surgery went well, and so did your initial recovery. I wanted to chat with you about upcoming follow-up care. You'll be checked regularly by nurses on the ward, though I'm hopeful the rest of your recovery will be smooth. There will be quite a bit of teaching, especially with diet for the short term. But I'll be back to check in on you tomorrow, and your discharge should be on Tuesday, with your first follow-up about three days after discharge. As usual, if there's anything you need at all, please let one of the nurses know and they can always give me a call." With a nod, he left the room, leaving the space thick with emotion.

Sophie smiled. "That sounds promising. Home in a couple of days."

"So fast," Adelaide whispered. Everything had happened so fast. And now that she was up and lucid, the full consequences dawned in slow motion. "You're supposed to leave on Tuesday."

Sophie shook her head. "I'm not leaving on Tuesday."

"But your work?"

"Work will be fine without me, and before you even say his name, so will Jasper. He knows me better than to think I'd leave Regina to take care of it all."

"I feel bad," Adelaide said, though she didn't mean just about Regina or Sophie. It was about everything. She was taking so much of everyone's time. The worry she caused. She felt bad that her body turned against itself and put everyone through an emergency. She could have died with all these unresolved feelings about her family. She could have died before even verbalizing what she wanted in her life, caught up in what was supposed to be her plan.

"Don't say that."

"But I do." Adelaide scooted up in bed. "Soph, I don't think I want to have another baby."

"Whoa. Where's that coming from?"

"I don't know." Adelaide took a deep breath to make way for the avalanche of emotions that had been released by surgery. "While I was in pain at home, I was so scared and so confused. And with everything this morning. All I know . . . is that I want to do things different from now on." Adelaide leaned back onto the pillow. "I'm allowed to change my mind, right?"

"I . . . yes, absolutely. I don't want you to think my shock is about that. It's just that I thought . . ."

"I thought, too, for a long time. Even in the haze of Gen's babyhood, my eye was on the prize of a second baby. I was an only child, and I wished I had a sibling, especially when we upped and moved around. I wanted a playmate. Now that my parents are old, I wish I had someone to commiserate with, someone to help me take care of them. But I don't know if those reasons are good enough, because somewhere deep inside, I'm no longer feeling it." She shook her head. "I don't know why. Two babies makes so much sense. It's the perfect number. You have two babies. One each for you and Jasper. One each for me and Matt. It's what I always pictured. A white colonial with a wraparound porch, a long driveway, and a picket fence. Two babies and a dog." She looked up to Sophie's wry expression.

"Ah, Ad, it never does quite turn out that way." Sophie laughed. "Goodness, I can't even remember what my dreams were when I was in my twenties. Life pushes us in different directions. Sometimes it's hard enough to just keep one foot in front of the other."

227

"And we've made choices to accommodate for the surprises or to try something new, right? Like living in a town house instead of picking a colonial."

"True," Sophie nodded. "Like going to grad school in the middle of a deployment."

"Soph." Adelaide dug deep into what she'd wanted to ask, to the bottom of it. If there was someone to ask, it was Sophie, who had been on this Army life road longer than her, who had survived it. "What if I want different? It's okay, right?"

"Of course it is." Sophie's answer was swift and quick. Then, she took a moment, looked down into her coffee. "We're not saddled with permanence, you know? Sort of like the books we read, the characters. We get to have an arc, too. We get to change, even if it's unexpected. But I do think we've got to let someone know when things change. Like the characters in books, they've got to talk to one another." She wiggled her phone in the air.

"Maybe you're right," Adelaide said.

Their conversation trailed when a nurse came in to take vital signs, and in the break, Adelaide thought of Matt and her mother, the other characters in her life's book. It was one thing to think about and want change, and it was another to actually admit it.

CHAPTER TWENTY-SEVEN
Adelaide

December 2011

Before Adelaide knew it, the snow came in full force, and it was Christmastime.

Three months down, and six to go in this deployment.

Deployments passed much more quickly when Adelaide had things planned, when she had things to do. Distraction, after all, was the best solution to malaise. And while she'd allowed herself to grieve the loss of another pregnancy, to dither about what her life could have been if she had been the one pregnant was useless. So she'd decided to try to just "get over it."

Still, Adelaide regressed, at times. When their spouses came home in six months, Sophie would have thriving twins to meet Jasper, and Regina would have a baby—a baby! And what was Adelaide going to have to show for it?

Adelaide dipped the paintbrush into the can with a little more force than she'd intended and got her thumb and index finger painted along with the brush, ruining her manicure. Alone, on her knees in Regina's spare bedroom, soon to be nursery, she took a deep breath.

She was doing a lot of that these days, this deep breathing.

She glided the brush against the baseboards, turning them from natural brown to white. Regina had wanted a white nursery. White on white, with pops of yellow. And Adelaide had agreed to help. She was more than willing to fill her days, even if it was just to volunteer to decorate.

"I wish I could help you," Regina said from the kitchen, where she was chopping veggies.

Regina was only twelve weeks pregnant—she finally had her first appointment a couple of weeks ago, which Adelaide had attended—and while Regina wasn't showing yet, Adelaide could already tell a difference in her. Regina was a little fuller in the face; she glowed. "No way. Even if this paint is supposed to be fume-free, why risk it?"

"I just feel really useless."

"You're not useless. You put up your Christmas decorations. You're getting ready for your mom's visit. You go to work every day. You're growing a baby."

"I guess I am, right?" She lay a palm against her belly. "My mom's going to freak when she sees me. Honestly, sometimes I forget I'm pregnant. Since my morning sickness went away, all I feel is a little bloated, though I've been perpetually hungry. I've been cooking up a storm."

I would never forget. Adelaide's brush went off course with the thought.

"I hope you don't mind some vegetable fried rice for lunch. I'm trying this new recipe out."

Adelaide was thankful for the change in subject. "I'm more than happy to taste test every one of your dishes through whatever cravings you may have."

"Have I said how great you are? Sophie, too. Especially on the day I found out I was pregnant. I was in shock, and if it wasn't for the both of you—"

Eyes on her work, Adelaide steadied her hand. "That's understandable. We're on our own, not exactly ideal for finding out such life-changing news."

"And thanks, too, for keeping it secret for now. I'm not ready to tell the rest of the world, not until I'm further along."

That halted Adelaide, and she sat back on her heels. A pain started in her chest, and Adelaide bit her lip to temper her jealousy. She should've been happy for Regina, end of sentence. "I totally get it. Your secret is safe with us."

"You're amazing at this, Adelaide."

Adelaide looked up to Regina, who was watching her from the kitchen. Her cheeks warmed at the compliment. "Do you mean volunteering myself to make your bedroom into one of my design experiments?"

"Yes, exactly that. First, for coming over today when you could be planning your trip to your parents', and second, the painting. It's so overwhelming to figure out what to buy and where, and honestly I wasn't expecting to have a nursery. We're due to move right after the baby's born."

"Nonsense. Can you imagine the kind of empty boxes we'd live in if we didn't actually settle into our homes? You've got to make it like we belong here, or we never will. Besides, what we're doing isn't hard to rehab whenever it's time to go."

"Still! You got right down to the core of what I wanted for the nursery. I feel like you were made for this."

Adelaide shrugged. "That part's easy for me. Kind of the one thing I'm good at." She dipped the brush into the paint can once more, continuing her work. "With everything else, I'm a Jill-of-all-trades and a mistress of none. My path has been a pretzel. I have a business degree but never used it. We moved all the time and I've been"—she counted it out on her hand—"a substitute teacher, a post day-care worker, a Gap seasonal cashier, and a part-time administrative assistant. All good jobs, but none that spoke to me as a career."

Saying it all aloud made her chest flutter in

mild panic. Like she was lost and couldn't find her way out of the woods.

How was it possible to feel lost despite being around friends and without any real worry?

It was possible.

Because she'd thought she'd be pregnant by now. She'd thought she'd have a family. She hadn't insisted on solidifying a career because children were supposed to be on the horizon.

And yet.

And yet.

Regina spoke over the oil sizzling in the pan, and the fragrant scent of garlic wafted through the room. "That basically tells me you're good at everything. You're great at coordination. I think there's a career in that. And I mean, you did start the best book club in the whole world."

Regina's words knocked Adelaide out of her spiraling thoughts, thank goodness. "Speaking of book club, how's *your* planning?"

Regina had volunteered to host the next meeting. "I was giving it some thought. Since we're skipping December and this is the first book of the New Year, it should be something good."

Adelaide's ears perked. Regina, doing research? About book club? She stood and went to the kitchen, and leaned on the doorframe. "Yeah?"

Regina pan-fried the veggies and added cooked rice. "I've been hearing about this great nonfiction."

Adelaide leveled her with a look. "Regina Castro—nonfiction. Really?"

"Yes?" An eyebrow scrunched down.

"I . . ." Obviously everything was surprising her these days, "Never mind. Okay, I'm listening. This nonfiction."

"*Bossypants*. Have you heard of it? It's Tina Fey's memoir."

This was getting more and more interesting. "Of course I have."

"It felt, I dunno, perfect for what we are now: Bosses. And since Colleen *did* start the precedence with the escape room."

Adelaide read the woman's mind. "Are you planning a road trip?"

"Yes! I found a travel agency that plans overnight trips to New York City. While being on an actual tour, we get to hit the highlights, maybe opt to tour NBC Studios. This could be a good way to get out of here without any of us truly taking the responsibility of driving there. There are tours in February, and that will give time for everyone to read the book during the holidays."

"I love that idea." Adelaide nodded.

"It makes me want to read the book, too." Regina sprinkled salt and pepper, and added soy sauce to the fried rice, causing Adelaide to drool. "Though I have to admit, I'm being selfish. I'm not sure how hard travel is going to be with a baby. I'm considering this one of my last hurrahs.

Soon I'll be inundated with diapers and strollers and baby gear. Which I have to find room for." She gestured at the growing mound of still-boxed baby gear in the living room situated around a lit but sparse Christmas tree.

"I'll help you get organized once the room is painted," Adelaide reassured. Admittedly Regina's place still had the vibe of a college dorm. Adelaide could do a number with a modest budget. "Your kitchen, though. Your kitchen is always so clean and neat. You know where every pot and pan and Tupperware cover's at. And you have every cool kitchen tool."

"Only because Logan isn't here to mess this place up. But kitchen stuff is fun because everything I make in here goes into my belly." Regina created a well in the rice dish and cracked an egg into it. As it cooked, Regina walked past her and to the bedroom. "Wow. What a difference a day makes. I didn't realize how much natural light was in here."

"It's going to be more beautiful when you have the bedding and the decor up, but that's for another day."

Noise from the open window summoned them to it, and looking down, there was Sophie with other adults supervising a gaggle of kids attempting to make a snowman.

"Playdate," Adelaide said. "It's why she couldn't come over for lunch."

At that moment, Sophie broke away from the crowd and went to her backpack. She burrowed, head bent into it, then rushed to a crying child.

"Uh-oh, someone's hurt," Regina said. "But, of course, Sophie's ready." She sighed. "One day I hope I can be as good a mom as her. She has it all together." Regina sauntered back into the kitchen.

Adelaide was left staring at the group, at the adults in parental solidarity. And then at this room.

At least she had this room that she fixed up all on her own.

At least she had book club to tout.

These were things she could show six months from now.

At least.

CHAPTER TWENTY-EIGHT
Sophie

Sophie heard the mail truck before she saw it come up the crest of Bell Street, and she excused herself from her building playdate for a quick getaway. She high-kneed it through the snow, and by the time she got to the building mailbox to meet the truck, beads of sweat had covered the back of her neck.

"Good morning, Jimmy."

"Morning." Jimmy was their usual neighborhood postal worker, known for his colorful and decorative scarves. Today's was holiday themed, with gold bells. It probably wasn't regulation, but no one was going to tell on him; this man brought them letters from their family members downrange. As far as Sophie was concerned, he was Santa Claus incarnate.

He flipped through the stack of mail in his hand. "Here's yours. And tell your girls I say thanks for the cookies. They were . . . well . . ."

"You don't have to say a thing. They insisted on making them themselves."

He beamed. "Then tell them they were the best I ever had."

"You're a sweet man. But don't be surprised if you get more." Sophie laughed.

"I look forward to it."

Sophie walked away and looked down at the first letter. It was from The School. It was a legal-sized envelope, and thin, surely containing only one piece of paper.

Her heart dropped into her belly; she pressed her lips together to keep from crying. It had to be a rejection. Of course she didn't get in, why did she even hope? She was never the model student—they must have seen that in her application.

She flipped through the other letters to catalog them, and by the time she made it to the backyard, she had gathered enough courage to open the envelope. Better to face the music. Patients did this all the time—they faced diagnoses despite their fear. This was not life and death.

Amber Hayes, one of her building neighbors, was at her side. Amber had become another good friend. She had a daughter a year older than Olivia and Carmela, which made for great playdates, and she was born in Freeport, Bahamas. With her paternal side of the family from Nassau, Sophie had locked onto this common thread.

Amber brushed at her scarf, which was caked with snow from playing with the kids. "What's up?"

"I applied to grad school."

"Wow!"

She lifted the envelope. "But I don't think I got in."

Amber frowned. "But you haven't opened it."

"They only send little envelopes if you don't get in."

Amber's gaze bounced to the envelope, then to Sophie, and back. "If you don't open it, I will." She shook Sophie's elbow. "C'mon."

"Okay, okay." After heaving a breath, Sophie slipped a finger under the flap. She bit against her cheek as she pulled out the letter.

"Read it out loud," Amber prodded.

She unfolded the thin paper with dread. " 'Dear Ms. Walden, I'd like to take this opportunity to welcome you—' " She paused, looking up. "Holy shit . . . 'into the Department of Nursing Masters of Education program!' Oh my God!"

Amber screamed and clapped. She scooped snow and threw it up in the air. Soon, all the little girls milled around them and were also screaming.

"Do you mind watching the girls?" Sophie asked Amber. "I want to head over to Regina's."

"Absolutely! I'll be right here."

Sophie ran—er, she stomped, quickly—across the backyard snow, to the next building, then around the corner to the gate. She pressed the doorbell.

"Who is it?" Regina's voice was airy.

"It's me! I've got news."

The door buzzed open, and Sophie clomped up to the second floor, and then to the third. She'd done this climb more than a dozen times the last couple of weeks. The neighborhood had been a ghost town since Thanksgiving, and they'd spent a good bit of time taking turns having dinner at each other's places.

The door was already open when she got to the top step. As per usual, she kicked off her shoes, and for good measure she shrugged herself out of her coat and snow pants. Down to her yoga pants and sweatshirt, she entered, and Regina greeted her with a bowl of rice.

"Hey! That was fast!" Regina laughed.

"What's going on?" Adelaide stepped out of the bedroom with paint-stained clothing. She wiped her hands on her jeans.

"Sit down." Sophie gestured to the couch, which the two women took.

"This is good, right?" Adelaide asked.

"Yes . . . Let me think of how to say this." She started to pace. Because what she was about to say was intimate. This was about goals, and dreams, and the future. Which she never talked about with anyone because . . . because these were things she kept close to her heart.

"Sophie, I swear," Regina warned.

"Okay. I applied to school. To a master's program."

"You did? When?" Adelaide asked.

"Around Thanksgiving."

"You didn't tell us?" Adelaide shook her head. "Go on, I'm sorry to interrupt."

"It wasn't something I told anyone, really, just Jasper. I was feeling a little low, you remember. I felt like I had hit a dead end . . . anyway, I thought I would give it a chance and apply." She waved the letter around. "I got in."

Regina and Adelaide leaped to their feet and cheered; they hugged her in tandem.

"We need to celebrate," Adelaide said.

"Later, yes! The girls are outside with Amber, so I can't stay long."

"Then let's at least break into dessert. I made cookie dough the other night. I've been on a cooking spree. You can take some to the kids." Regina popped into the kitchen and pressed the buttons of her oven, then dug into her refrigerator and took out the cookie dough.

"Okay, I can stay a few minutes." Sophie migrated and sat at the kitchen table, with Adelaide next to her, remembering three months ago when they'd consoled Regina. "I feel like time is moving so quickly. It's Christmas in a couple of weeks, and then soon—"

"Ahhh!" Regina said shaking her head. "I don't even want to think about it. It's so overwhelming. I was just telling Adelaide that I want to be like you when I grow up. You always seem to have it together." She made quick work at dropping spoonfuls of dough onto the pan.

Sophie snorted. "Believe me, I don't have it together."

"You remind me a lot of my mama, actually," Adelaide chimed in. "You always have a wise word. I don't think I've ever seen you do wrong. You must have been an easy child to raise."

"I was far from an easy child." She leaned back into the wrought iron chair and watched Regina put the pan in the oven. "It's why I wasn't sure I'd get into grad school, because up until my . . ." Her voice choked.

"What's wrong, Soph?" Adelaide asked.

"It's just that I don't really talk about it all the time." Actually, Sophie didn't talk about it at all. It was better, sometimes, to forget, to move on, rather than linger in the past. It had become a skill for her, in fact, as a nurse, to leave one patient behind and enter another patient's room with a renewed attitude. But right now, with her friends, she felt safe enough to say. "I was a tough child. Headstrong."

"Nuh-uh," Regina said, in jest.

"Believe me. I ran with the wrong crowd through high school. My parents—I can only imagine the headaches and the worry. Fast-forward to when I was a freshman in college. And I was out, partying as usual on a Friday night. Got drunk, all that. And got in at dawn to find my RA at my door. My mother had passed away."

Sophie looked up, and sure enough, her friends were both staring at her. A part of her warned that she'd said too much, that they would judge her and her terrible decision, but she didn't see any of that in their expressions. Instead, she saw love in their eyes. She saw care.

"So, that was the end of my bad ways."

"Oh, Soph, you weren't bad," Regina said.

"I know." She shrugged. "But since then, and the way things work in the Army, with our close quarters, I always mind my p's and q's. So, yes, I do try to do things right. I'm always trying to move forward. But it doesn't mean I'm calm about it. I'm like a duck, all calm on top and paddling under the water."

"Well, you don't have to paddle too hard around us," Adelaide said.

"Anyway. Sorry, that was deep. This was supposed to be a short announcement. Hopefully my kids are still okay out there."

"You know what?" Regina said, a grin growing on her face. "Let's invite everyone up here. I don't have a lot of chairs, but I have enough cookies."

"Really?" Sophie said, standing.

"Yes! Like you said, it's a celebration. Adelaide, wanna yell for them?"

"That's . . . that's a lot of mess we'll be bringing into the house," Sophie objected, while following Adelaide to the open window.

"Nonsense. Reggie's right. Families celebrate. And we are Framily."

"Framily?"

"Friends who are family. Chosen family." And without another word, Adelaide yelled out the window. "Hey, y'all! Get yourselves up here. Apartment E! We got cookies!"

Sophie's face warmed. She had framily.

CHAPTER TWENTY-NINE
Adelaide

February 2012

"Happy Valentine's to us. We're here. We're really here." Adelaide stepped down the three steps from the double-decker tour bus to the pedestrian-filled sidewalk. Times Square was up ahead, with billboards and flashing signs trailing up to the blue sky. She tightened the thick woven scarf around her neck, ignoring the twenty-degree chill because hello! She was in the Big Apple. It was going to be perfect if she could help it.

Regina was a genius for suggesting this adventure.

Adelaide walked a few steps from the bus and turned around to watch the book clubbers spill from the narrow door. All fifteen were accounted for among the other patrons of this Hop-On, Hop-Off trip that would comprise about six hours of their day, before they headed back to the pickup spot, where a charter bus would take them all back upstate.

She spotted her friends. Sophie was chatting away, and Regina was standing in the rear of the group. She had been late to the charter bus pickup and almost missed loading entirely, and when Adelaide had passed her while going to the bus restroom, she was sound asleep. Adelaide had been eager to chat, to update her on the itinerary. Since Regina had been too busy with work, and the second trimester had left her exhausted, Adelaide had been more than happy to step up to lead the day-of details.

"Do you feel Tina Fey here?" she asked Regina now.

"What I really feel is hungry." Regina's answered was curt. She sniffed the air, expression softening a bit. "I smell french fries, or fried something. Before we do anything can we eat?"

"Of course! Our NBC tour is in an hour, so we definitely have time to pick up a quick snack. I looked up a sandwich place that's just straight ahead." Actually, Adelaide had researched everything, from the restaurants they would frequent and the sights they would see, with their pregnant host, their most high-maintenance participant, in mind.

Adelaide led the group down Seventh Avenue. The book clubbers trailed her like little ducklings.

Except their group split, distracted by another restaurant with wide-open doors and a doorman beckoning inside.

"Wait a minute. You guys? That might be a sit-down place," Adelaide said.

"Oh dear, I think you're losing them." Sophie

passed her, as with the rest of the group. A slew of other tourists mixed in between their bodies. "If you have another place in mind, you might want to yell it out now."

She found her itinerary. Multipage, stapled, and printed from her brand-new inkjet. She waved the papers up in the air. "People, come back!"

At first, no one else turned around, so Adelaide yelled, "Millersville Book Club! Hello!"

Finally, the group meandered Adelaide's way. She breathed a sigh of relief, though pedestrian traffic ballooned where they stalled. Someone shoulder-checked her from behind. She gathered her bearings and said, "We're going *that* way."

"Oh, why didn't you say so?" a voice said. "No big deal."

But as the day progressed, everything became a big deal. It started with the group's complaints at the NBC Studios tour, which couldn't fit their entire book club without having to split up into three groups. There were rumblings at how it was too cold to be using public transportation. One of the ladies forgot her purse on a bench at Rockefeller Center, and they had to backtrack for that. It was Adelaide's responsibility to know where the restrooms were at all times, apparently. And she was informed that there hadn't been enough time allotted for the World Trade Center site, and that they all should demand a refund.

The day that was supposed to be perfect had

been reduced to a string of complaints and misguided suggestions.

Dinner was the last of their activities before they boarded the bus for their late-night travel back to Millersville. Adelaide had chosen a pub that, while on paper sounded ideal, was the worst restaurant she could have picked. Three of the book clubbers had one too many drinks and were properly tipsy and cantankerous well before their food came. Add the clank of dishes and the roar of the crowd, and Adelaide's nerves were on overload.

And yet, she kept the smile on her face; she was going to fake it till she made it.

"Hey, are you okay?" Sophie said.

It made Adelaide jump. Her friend was sitting across from her. "Oh, ah, yeah, I'm good."

"Okay, it's just that you had this look."

What look? Adelaide forced her smile wider apart; she realized book club loyalist Frank next to her had stopped his conversation to watch them. She scrambled for an answer. "No, I was just thinking, you know. About *Bossypants*."

Sophie pasted on a frown. "I wasn't a fan. I don't know why, but I look for struggle in my nonfiction because I want to learn. I didn't have much to learn from her."

Kerry, from three seats down in their long table, nodded. "She mentioned her scar, though. I kind of wish she went into that."

Colleen unrolled her napkin and put it on her lap. "Her thoughts on improv as it applies to life were good. I liked the one where she encouraged the concept of saying 'yes, and . . .' I took it as encouragement to take an active role in change and society."

Everyone at the table nodded, including Adelaide. But the message hit her in the space in the middle of her breastbone. It brought back everything she had thought of when decorating Regina's room. What had she contributed lately, except for a field trip half the book clubbers hated? What exactly was her purpose?

At the other end of the table, Regina cackled. "I love how she describes her father, that she grew up with a healthy sense of fear of him. I totally related to that. Even if my mother's barely five feet and I'm this age, I have never once talked back to her." She placed a hand on her five-month bump. "And I wonder, too, how am I going to parent?"

"Being a parent is a job where you never know where you stand," said Weston, who'd moved into their neighborhood a month ago with his wife. They were in the Air Force, and parents to one college-aged daughter. "One day you think you're doing okay, and the next you feel like you suck at it."

Sophie cackled. "That is ten thousand times the truth."

Across the long side of the table, Abby, a new book clubber yelled, "I can't hear you guys down here!"

"What are you even talking about?" Next to her, another newbie, Carla, placed a hand behind her ear in emphasis.

The table then recounted the discussion, and the level of noise ratcheted up to what Adelaide could only describe as five million decibels. Then, someone complained that their food was taking too long.

Everyone was obviously tired and hungry. To help distract the clubbers, Adelaide flipped through the itinerary only to realize she'd forgotten to bring questions.

"Adelaide," Sophie said.

She startled out of her thoughts. "Yeah?"

"I'm going to the bathroom, wanna come with me?"

"Sure." She stood, eager for peace, and with what she hoped was some kind of an excuse, followed the back of Sophie's colorful shirt.

Finally, she made it to the bathroom. It was quaint but clean. There was a woman wiping down the sink, who first nodded at the both of them and then sat on her stool and looked back down at her book.

"Here, Ad." Sophie pushed a damp brown paper towel into her hand. It was cool to the touch, and Adelaide pressed it against her eyes, first the right, and then the left, as her breathing escalated to a chaotic pattern. "What's going on?"

Adelaide kept her eyes shut. She felt the cold bathroom tile against her back, a slight reprieve from her churning thoughts. "I'm just so mad."

"About what?"

"It's hard to explain."

The door flew open, and Regina appeared. She had a hand on her belly. "What's going on?"

"God, it's nothing." Adelaide half laughed.

"Obviously, it *is* something." Sophie voice was calm and nonjudgmental.

"Ad." Regina placed a hand on her shoulder. "What is it?"

Adelaide heaved a breath. She knew it would feel better to let it out, but it felt so heavy, like a mountain to move. She leaned into it, if but a little. "I . . . couldn't stand it anymore."

"Stand what?" Regina said.

"All of it." Adelaide dug into her heels. "The talk about kids. It's getting to be too much. Not because I don't like kids, but because I love them. I want them. I—" She looked up at her friends, and exhaled the truth. "I lost a baby at the beginning of the deployment. I have lost babies before."

"Oh, Adelaide. Sweetie." Sophie's expression softened.

Regina's eyes began to water. "I'm sorry."

"Not to say I'm not happy for you." Adelaide

251

scrambled to explain, realizing that she'd put Regina on the spot. "Because I'm *so* happy for you. I am, so much. I just wish sometimes that it was me."

Adelaide tore her eyes away from her friend's face. There was no time for pity, there was no room for sadness in her life. She had all she had ever truly needed, and had no reason for complaint. She infused a lightness into her voice. "But I'm fine. Really I am. I just needed a break from all those people out there. I was just having a moment."

She pushed herself off the wall. Her tears threatened to bubble over, but her stubbornness, thank goodness, pulled her through. She made it to the sink, turned on the faucet, wet her hands, and patted her cheeks. It was only then that she took a good look at herself under the gloomy light casting a foreboding glow on her face. The bags under her eyes cast a purple hue. In her eyes were exhaustion, and something more. Something she was perfectly happy ignoring.

So she took a deep breath, imagined oxygen flowing through her lungs. She tried her lips to see if they could still smile. They did. She spun around. "All right, I'm ready to go."

"Adelaide." Sophie's tone was a warning. "You don't need to do that."

"Do what?"

"Pretend," Regina said.

She shrugged. "It happens to one in four women. It's just par for the course."

"Jasper and I lost a baby," Sophie said. "And I was sad, for a long time. It's okay to be sad. Though I'm not going to assume how you feel, or assume you'd want to tell me, pretending these feelings don't exist won't make them go away."

Adelaide crossed her arms and hugged herself. "I'm sorry, Soph."

"Me, too, but this is not about me. This is about you."

"And this is about us," Regina added. "Because telling me about what happened won't lessen my joy. I care about you. I want to be there for you, too. Like how you showed up at my apartment that first week, and when you were there for me when I took my pregnancy test? I'm here for you."

Adelaide lowered her head. "I was not raised to be a sob story, to have a sob story, or to tell it."

Sophie laughed. "You are far from a sob story. Are you kidding me? Look how you brought us together, how you help people every day." She lowered her voice. "But even if you did become a sob story, I'm not going anywhere."

"I'm here, too, Ad. To support you every step of the way, even if you become really, really pathetic." Regina pressed her lips into a grin.

"The way you two turn a conversation. You don't give me a chance to stay sad. You guys are the epitome of *Bossypants*."

"Har har." Sophie smiled. "The book was *eh*. Funny, yes. Insightful? The jury's out on that. Although"—she looked up at the ceiling—"she talked about what makes a good boss, and she said it was about hiring people and getting out of the way. That's what we do for one another. We look out for one another and see in what way we can or can't help, and where. So, when you see me and Regina, know that we can help. And then get out of your own way so we can work our magic."

Regina took Adelaide's hand, and Sophie's with the other. "Exactly. Remember. The SOS applies to you, too."

PART FIVE

*But going forward required a
singular leap of faith—and he was
a man of little faith, particularly
when it came to himself.*

—*His at Night* by Sherry Thomas

CHAPTER THIRTY
Sophie

Present Day, Monday

By Monday morning, Sophie waved the white flag that she needed a hospital shift change. Her back hurt from the visitor pullout chair, and her lungs craved fresh air. After Adelaide's admission that she no longer wanted another child, Sophie had begun to feel claustrophobic. Because while she had agreed with Adelaide that a person should be able to change their mind at any time, it was also an entirely different issue to actually move forward with it. Change was harder when it involved other people. Change required knowing exactly what outcome one wanted, didn't it?

Sophie had scheduled the Genevieve handoff at 9:00 a.m. so mother and daughter could share a few moments together, and Regina, fresh and energetic, would take the hospital shift until the next morning. But when the two arrived, Adelaide was asleep, so they migrated to the hospital cafeteria instead.

Sophie's phone beeped a notification while in the hallway, a reminder of her flight back home. It was scheduled for the next day.

She couldn't leave, could she? Neither she nor Adelaide had planned for this extra surgery, and while Regina was staying the rest of the week, Regina wasn't tuned in to Adelaide's needs. Their roles had divvied up naturally, and Sophie would daresay it was working, though things were still slightly awkward between them.

But Sophie's biggest obstacle was not Regina.

While at the elevators, Sophie went to her messages app and clicked on Jasper's last text.

> **Hey, I'm not coming home tomorrow. Adelaide still needs me.**

Little dots showed that he was responding.

> **Seriously?**

> **Seriously.**
> **I'm changing my flight to Sunday.**

"Everything okay?" Regina asked minutes later while buckling Genevieve into a child's seat. "You look upset."

"It's nothing."

Regina's eyes gazed downward at Sophie's phone, which flashed with text notifications. "Sure?"

"Yeah. You know Jasper . . . he doesn't know how to insert a line in his texts. He literally

258

sends every sentence as a separate text, and my phone blows up unnecessarily." She smiled with effort. While every part of her wanted to divulge her issues with Jasper and what Adelaide had revealed—because she knew it would release some of this pressure from her chest—she reminded herself that she and Regina were not on solid footing.

Regina shrugged. "Okay. But look, I have something to tell you." She sat down, and from her backpack she pulled two brown bags: one for Genevieve and another for Sophie.

"For me?" Sophie was gobsmacked at the gesture. "Thank you."

Regina waved it away. "It's nothing. Just some cinnamon rolls. But anyway, listen up. I ordered a *c-a-k-e*."

"A *c-a-k-e* for what?" Sophie dug into the bag.

"For who else?" She covered Genevieve's ears. The little girl stared up at her and smiled a toothy grin, all the while clutching her sippy cup with one hand and crackers with another. "For her party," she whispered.

"What party?"

"The party I'm planning. For her birthday." She lowered her hands. "This weekend. First of all, are you going to be here? I'm planning it for Saturday, since I leave on Monday. Get this, I even elicited Missy to help."

"Who's Missy?" Sophie unwrapped the warm

cinnamon roll from the plastic wrap. "Wow, this looks amazing."

"Remember? One of Adelaide's contacts in her binder? Anyway, she said she would handle the invites on her end and can almost guarantee that mommies in their circle could be flexible with the timeline. I was thinking that maybe we should have everyone come over while Adelaide's out for her follow-up appointment. We'll soon find out what time that will be, right?"

"Yes, we should actually know before we leave the hospital tomorrow." Sophie took a bite of the roll, and its taste distracted her for a moment.

"Good?" Regina asked.

"It's perfect." Sophie licked her lips. Then she shook her head as the conversation caught up to her. "I've still got to update Jasper with everything and change my flight. But hold the phone. You've scheduled a *p-a-r-t-y* for the child of a mother who just had surgery, a mother who should be recovering the rest of the week, and then made it a surprise not only for the child but for the mother?"

"You make it sound so horrible." She shrugged. "Birthdays are such a special time. And you *know* that Adelaide hates the fact that she's not throwing one for her own baby. The woman loves parties. So yes, the party is for her, too."

"I don't know, Regina. Why would you think that she wouldn't want to plan this, at a later time? On her own?"

"Because! Like you said, she'll be in recovery. By the time she's up and about, it may be weeks. Adelaide loves birthdays as much as I do."

Sophie's taste buds were having a party in her mouth after another bite of the roll, but she frowned at Regina's implication. "And I don't?"

"I'm just saying that you're not one for parties."

"We like our birthdays low-key."

"But that's not our friend, is it?" Regina heaved a breath. "And honestly, this will give me something to do, to give back. I feel helpless. I want to show her how much I care about her. I want to make Ad happy."

Sophie paused for a beat. "I think that us being here alone shows how much *we both* love her, and I've no doubt she's happy that we're here. And I also think that this party will stress her out."

Regina tipped her head back as if in exasperation. "Sure, maybe a little at first. But in the end you know she'll love that we got a cake and some decor and sang the 'Happy Birthday' song. Depending on how Missy can swing it, maybe we can fill up Adelaide's house like how it used to be when we got together. Adelaide thrives having folks around. She's an extrovert."

"Only when planned," Sophie emphasized.

"Small detail. And this is a special circumstance."

Adelaide *was* an extrovert, this was true. While

Sophie wasn't social like the two of them were, she could respect it. A memory rushed back, and Sophie smiled. "I remember the time when she wanted a karaoke night, and you brought your karaoke machine to her house. And the apartment HOA came and asked us to turn it down."

"The nineties tunes were what brought us to the dark side. Those ballads. They were like battle cries of freedom."

Sophie could hear it now: the loud feedback from the karaoke machine in Adelaide's house, the television speaker all the way up to high. Neighbors filtering in to check on the commotion. Everyone singing along in their different pitches.

Sophie giggled, and it felt good. To let go of what was in her chest. Her worry for her friend, her worry for her and Jasper's relationship.

"So you'll help me?" Regina prodded. "We've got less than a week, and I've got a list to go through."

Sophie pressed her lips together. "I swear, you and Adelaide and your plans."

"Is that a yes, then? Adelaide will be so much better by the weekend, and what better time to celebrate than with both godmothers present?"

"I guess . . ." Sophie hedged. All said, it was a good idea. It was thoughtful. And a part of her liked this teamwork, at being addressed as "both godmothers," as if their friendship had turned around. And yet, she also wanted to play hard to get—it was so complicated, this push and pull. "I'll help, willingly and without argument, if you actually finish our book club book."

"Ugh. I was hoping you wouldn't say that. I was perfectly happy putting the book away before something bad happened to the characters."

"What can I say? I like to be consistent. But if we're talking about supporting Adelaide— then having our little book club would make her happy. And she might be a little less pissed off when she sees you've invited people without telling her."

Regina grunted.

"I'll fill goody bags and can blow up balloons and make a big fuss even when I don't think we should," Sophie said, sweetening the pot.

Regina bit her lower lip. "Fine. Let's do it."

"Great." Sophie turned to Genevieve. "Ready to see your mama, Genevieve? She's going to love a hug from you." She stood and plucked her out of the chair. "And I can't wait to go home and go to bed. It's been a day. And by the way, Reggie?"

"Yeah?"

"You're not helpless. Look at how happy this kid is." As Sophie gestured toward Genevieve, the little girl smiled with all of her teeth. "And that cinnamon roll really hit the spot. It might have been the best thing I've eaten that you've made."

"Thanks." A second later, Regina's eyes narrowed. "Is this a prank?"

Sophie threw her head back and laughed. "No. No, it's not."

CHAPTER THIRTY-ONE
Regina

Present Day, Tuesday

Sitting contorted in the pullout hospital guest bed and tangled in a stiff blanket, Regina startled from her Candy Crush game by the synthesized beat of a phone ringing. As she sat up, her book, which she had failed at reading, crashed to the ground. Kicking the blanket off her, she leaped to her feet so she could turn off Adelaide's phone before it woke her.

But the phone stopped ringing, and the room plunged into pitch darkness.

Regina sighed, thanking the heavens above. As she lay back down, the phone rang again. She lunged toward the noise, bone-weary from the uncomfortable cushions, skin dry from the recycled air, to Adelaide's beside table.

She turned the phone over—it was Matt.

This was probably Matt's fifth attempt that she'd witnessed—the last one at 11:00 p.m., when Adelaide was watching *Property Brothers*—and not once had her friend taken the call. There had always been a reason: exhaustion, headache, and at the moment, sleep.

It was understandable. All night, beeping machines, the footsteps of nurses, and the quiet whisperings of caregivers had kept both she and Regina awake. Hospitals were not meant for sleep.

But Matt must've been out of his mind with worry.

She swiped the phone to answer it. "Hello?"

Matt's voice was faraway. "Ad?"

"No, it's Regina. Hold on, okay?" She bent down and placed a hand on Adelaide's shoulder and nudged her gently. "Adelaide, it's Matt."

Adelaide grumbled. Another nudge—and her eyes fluttered open. "Hm?"

"Matt. He's on the phone."

"I'll call him later." She shut her eyes.

Regina gripped the phone in midair. She looked around the room for an Adelaide stunt double who would actually take the time to talk to her husband. This was strange. Admittedly, Adelaide had not been talkative overnight, but Regina'd chalked it up to pain.

Okay, then. She bit her lip as she put the phone against her ear. "Matt?"

A pause, then Matt spoke. "She doesn't want to talk to me?" he said, resigned.

"No, not that, she's sleeping. Perhaps try to call later? Rounds will be in about an hour, and she'll be up from then on."

"Yeah, okay. Thank you."

"You're welcome."

"Regina . . . she's doing okay, though, right?"

"She is, yes." Regina smiled, hoping he'd feel it somehow.

"Okay, goodbye."

After hanging up, Regina couldn't go back to bed. Anger bubbled from deep inside, at secrets people kept from others they claimed to love when physical distance kept them apart. It wasn't fair to Matt, just as it hadn't been fair to Regina, ten years ago.

The interaction she'd witnessed was too complicated to think about without some real caffeine in her system. After writing a quick note to Adelaide that she'd be back in a couple of hours, she decided on a walk down from the hospital to Burg Street, about a half mile away, where the city was just starting to wake. She loved the vibe and nostalgia of the early mornings, the dimly lit sky and the stillness of the world. It reminded her of the long runs she used to take, the early formations with her Army unit. On a scheduled catering day, Regina also used the early mornings to do her prep. Knowing she'd accomplished so much before the rest of the world had awakened—that by the time she'd drunk her second cup of coffee, half her checklist had been checked off—was satisfying.

Inspired, she took a picture of the sky for her Instagram. She hadn't kept up with the feed—

despite being in a bustling town, Regina felt out of touch with reality, especially without having her family to ground her. She equally was out of words for the morning, with so much on her mind, so she left it without a caption.

Her phone buzzed, first with a notification that Just Cakes left a comment on her photo, and then second with a text from Henry.

You're up?

> I am. Looking for coffee near Alex General.

Old Town Coffee & Tea is on Burg, two blocks down from the bakery. It's small. Look out for the green awning or you might miss it.

She bit her lip and decided, what the hell.

> Are you free? Want to join me?

Absolutely.

> Great. I'm on my way.

Sure enough, Regina almost missed the entrance of Old Town Coffee & Tea since its building facade was narrow and smooshed in between an art gallery and a museum, but two women in workout gear passed her with bags of pastries. Her taste buds and attention woke at the scent of butter and java, and she entered the shop, hanging by the door to wait for Henry, heart pounding in anticipation of his arrival. To distract herself, she scanned the cozy coffeehouse, immediately landing on the chalkboard menu behind the counter.

Genevieve's party could have a chalkboard theme! She tapped into her phone as the flood of ideas came. Chalkboard menu on the tables, then maybe colored chalk for the kids to play with in the backyard. Non-helium balloons on the ground for the kids to kick around.

She took a photo of the scene, of the long line and the chalkboard menu, to save for inspiration, only to be asked by someone if she was in line. Her heart squeezed in envy. To be a business, any business, that bustled like this was the dream. And in her gut, she knew it was possible. The Perfect Day Catering could thrive in a historic town like this.

Would she really be able to shutter the doors in six months? Would she be able to tell Alexis that she would have to move on? Could she let go of her employees? Could she afford not to? Every bit of saved money, except for a small amount earmarked for emergencies, had gone toward her venture. Yet, what had she gained?

Headaches, yes, but joy, too, and pride. That she'd created something from scratch, made from her own sweat and tears. This was something no one could take away.

She shook her runaway brain into focus and started on the food list. *Cake from Just Cakes. Tea sandwiches, 3 types (cucumber, cheese, ham).*

Someone cleared their throat.

Baby pink tablecloths.

"Excuse me, are you in line?" A low voice said behind her.

Tent flags draped in the living room.

"Uh-huh," she said.

"The line moved."

Goodness, Northern Virginians were impatient. She sighed, thumbed a final word on the phone, and looked behind her, eyes ready to roll.

Only to meet Henry Just's level gaze.

"Hey." She felt her entire body relax and warm. "I mean, I'm glad you could come."

"I'm glad you asked me." He drew her into his arms. He smelled good, like sugar and vanilla. "How was your night?"

"Okay." She nodded and pulled back. The line had in fact moved, so she scooted forward. "Adelaide's doing really well. She's going to be discharged today sometime."

"That's great. You don't sound so . . ."

"Oh, I just have a lot on my mind." Her fingers found their way to her forehead, because yes, her brain had an overflow of unresolved issues that she didn't quite know what to do with. "Plus, not enough coffee to function."

"I get it. I mean, good, because I thought it was me. Since the last time we saw each other . . ."

She was now in front of the counter and the barista looked at her expectantly. Out of haste she ordered her usual, a latte, though a second later she wished that she had something sweet to go with it. She was a mess, trying to manage this crush-filled moment, and a little sugar always made her feel better. Henry handed his credit card over her shoulder and ordered for himself with his easy demeanor and casual familiarity.

As they waited for their drinks, Regina said, "You didn't have to do that."

They were shoulder to shoulder, and his hands were stuffed in his front pockets. He was half looking at her, half at the baristas making their drinks. Next to the bar counter came the loud roar of the milk steamer. "Regina, I don't mind getting you coffee. I like you."

The words seeped in slowly.

How was he so open, just saying what he felt? And why couldn't she be like that, too?

She looked up at him, at his seemingly shy demeanor. His cheeks were slightly red, vulnerability in his eyes. "You like me?"

"Yes, I do. So meeting you for coffee, even grabbing you coffee. Sending you a book, hanging out with your goddaughter. I'm down for it. I hope I'm not too forward, but your time here is short. . . . And at the same time, I don't want to be a creep, to be around when you might not want me, because I'm not sure if you really want me to be here, or if I'm just forcing something." The red in his cheeks bloomed to the rest of his face.

"No, I . . . I like you, too." The words popped out before she could stop them. "I'm . . . I don't do this a lot, and I'm out of practice. I don't know how these things progress." She laughed at how this all seemed so backward. "I mean, you know that. But I really like that you're around, and that you're here."

"Likewise. And great." His smile reached from ear to ear.

It was good the barista called his name, and he stepped away to retrieve the cups of coffee, because Regina had to control her own heated cheeks.

He handed one cup to her. "Do you have time to sit?"

She looked at her phone. "I've got to get back to the hospital soon. But maybe you could walk me there? We can talk about the cake."

His expression slackened. "Right, the cake. Speaking of, I have some time later on today and you can pick out what you'd like, on the cake."

"And maybe"—she dared to step out of her

comfort zone—"maybe we can talk about where you can take me. After we talk about the cake, I mean."

"Oh—I'd like that." His smile swooped all the way up to his eyes. The sides of his mouth wrinkled, which filled Regina with innocent giddiness.

He wanted to go out with *her*. She didn't have to beg him for time, nor did she have to guess how he felt.

He was doing everything right. But as she pushed the glass door open and the chime overhead rang, Regina wondered if, in exploring her affection for him, she was adding to her growing list of unresolved issues.

CHAPTER THIRTY-TWO
Adelaide

Adelaide had just endured another visit from a resident, baring her abdomen yet again, when her phone rang. Matt's name appeared on the screen, along with a photo of him holding Genevieve when she was born, wrapped in a faded, striped hospital blanket. Her daughter was a pink, screaming bundle. Matt's glasses were slightly askew, a perfect representation of those three days of chaos, from Adelaide's water breaking in the middle of dinner in a fancy restaurant, being induced, to an eventual C-section, and a second surgery from a nicked bladder from the C-section.

Soon after giving birth, Adelaide had forgotten all about the trauma, which was superseded by the priorities of motherhood. She'd forgotten it, anyway, until now, when she was again in a hospital, with a second surgery after a first failed one. Now, when she felt all the consequences of single motherhood, of what was like a single marriage. Yes, she had all the trappings of marriage: support, love, financial backing, and yet, she didn't have the most important part—her husband.

Adelaide wanted more. But to say it aloud would make her sound selfish. She'd grown up with a mother who'd endured this life with ease, and Adelaide saw this role as its own brand of heroism. By admitting she found it lacking sometimes—it would make her less of the Army wife she aspired to be.

Now, all she could do was look at the phone in deliberation. Should she answer it? The last time she'd spoken to her husband, she was still a little out of it on pain meds before emergency surgery, but she was thinking clearly now. A lot had happened in the last three days, and it wasn't just her physical recovery. It was the realization that came afterward, and what she would need to tell him.

In a brief interlude of bravado, she snatched the phone off the nightstand and clicked on the green button. "Hello."

Matt's voice was haggard. "Adelaide. Damn it. Gah, I'm sorry. I'm just . . . I am literally about to go out of my mind. Why won't you speak to me?"

Adelaide felt his panic; she could see his face as he spoke, and a wave of guilt crashed upon her. "I'm sorry, babe."

"Don't *I'm sorry* me, because now I'm wondering what's going on. And don't tell me it's medical, because I know that's not it. Whatever it is, just say it instead of letting me sit here in

276

another country to try to sort out where I went wrong."

Matt's stress level had always come first. And she didn't think this was some sort of martyrdom—it was the truth. Not only was he the breadwinner, but in the entire scheme of their world, as dramatic as that sounded, her stress paled in comparison to his. Her entire mission up to this point was to grow and keep a family. She wasn't sure how to explain that she had reached her limit when she had lived such a privileged life.

"Baby?" Matt prodded, taking her from her thoughts.

"I . . . want to revisit *us*."

She heard him gasp and then realized that might have been the wrong way to start the conversation.

"What I mean is, Matt . . . I don't know if we want the same things, for the future." Then, she winced, because that was worse. "Oh my goodness. This isn't coming out right."

"Adelaide." Matt's voice was serious now. Somber. "Please. Please just come out with it."

Adelaide shut her eyes and took a deep breath. She counted to three. "I don't think that I want to have another baby."

His answer came quickly. "Well, of course not. You've got to recover. I would never force it. Babe, we have time. There's no reason to rush."

"What I mean is—I don't want to have *any* more babies." She took another breath. "I know this isn't something you want to hear. But I've been thinking about it for a while."

"A while . . . ?" His voice trailed off.

"I wasn't completely sure until . . . until all this . . . mess here. I had been getting hints but not truly understanding what I needed. And now I do."

"I thought that us waiting to have a baby had everything to do with me"—his voice croaked into a sob—"being away. That's it, right? You don't want more kids with me because I'm always gone?"

"That's part, though not all of it. There's something more, deeper."

"And what's that?"

"I . . . I don't know. I'm still processing it myself. Are you mad, Matt?"

"No." His answer was definite and clear. "No, I'm not mad. I'm not here to pressure you, Adelaide, but I guess I have to be honest and say that I'm a little sad to think about our family being complete. And I'm confused because I feel a little sideswiped. But no, not mad."

"Okay."

"But it doesn't change how I feel about you, or our family, or Genevieve. And it sure as hell doesn't mean we can't talk to each other. The worst of all this, for me, was not hearing from you. I was falling apart over here. I was worried—"

"I don't want you to worry."

"I . . . of course I worry about you. Because I miss you, and I love you. You're my best friend. Even if you're sitting on some beach somewhere having a margarita, I'll still worry." He inhaled. "What can I do, from here?"

"I don't know. We can just keep talking, I guess."

A knock sounded at the door, and a nurse hovered by the entrance. The day shift had commenced, and this new nurse's demeanor was fresh and awake. "Just checking in, Mrs. Wilson-Chang."

Adelaide nodded. "Matt, I have someone—"

"I know." His voice was tender. "Just give me a call later, okay? We need to keep talking. Love you, babe." Matt hung up without listening for her answer. Inside, Adelaide felt a mix of pain and relief. But she slapped an imaginary Band-Aid on it, pressed her hair in place, and once again smiled. She nodded for the nurse to come in.

The nurse glanced at her clipboard. "I have an order here for discharge."

"What time?" She couldn't wait to go home. She missed her bed and Genevieve. She wanted to see where these new feelings took her, and she was eager to recover her time with her friends.

"Looks like if your afternoon vital signs and pain level are in control, you have the green light." She looked around the room. "Do you have someone who can take you home?"

"Yes, I do."

"Great! Let's schedule it for me to come in an hour to do a full assessment and some discharge teaching, and aim to get you out of here at around three p.m.? Is that good?"

"Sure. It sounds good." Adelaide emptied her lungs of air. Her mind wandered to the nest of emotions that were tangled together, but with the light of hope behind it.

Yes. She was definitely good.

CHAPTER THIRTY-THREE
Sophie

March 2012

The first day of spring brought the sun and a blessedly quiet afternoon.

The day's snowfall was different. It wasn't a thick blanket of ice that blocked the vision outside one's windows. Instead it fluttered downward to the ground as if Sophie's little neighborhood were ensconced in a snow globe, like the world was at the tail end of hibernation. The temperature had climbed into the thirties most days, with the general mood of the neighborhood rising with it.

On this day, in a miracle, Sophie's girls had been content playing in their rooms and were now taking a late-afternoon nap. The free time allowed Sophie to read. As of yet, no one had volunteered for the next book club meeting nor had a book been designated, so she dug into *Breaking Dawn*, the fourth installation of the Twilight series by Stephenie Meyer. Sophie had become hooked on the series, though she hadn't admitted to anyone else how deep her obsession was. At book four, she was still #TeamJacob all the way.

Six months into deployment, Sophie had gotten into a groove. Her family routine was working. She and Jasper were solid. Her friendships were thriving. Grad school would begin in June and she looked forward to it. There was no drama. Aside from a couple of check-ins with Adelaide and supporting Regina as her belly grew, things were calm on her side of the door.

So when Sophie's phone buzzed on the couch cushion—a call from her cousin Mario—she sent the call to voice mail.

It was an unkind gesture, and Sophie felt a pit of guilt in her belly. Family was a subject she didn't really discuss but that remained an ever-present shadow in her periphery. Over the years, she'd simply disassociated herself from her father and extended family; she'd let go of all the distraction and emotions that used to invade her heart for days after communicating with them. But what came with that understanding was the knowledge and sometimes the guilt that it was her choice to break away from them. A good choice, but a shameful choice to make nonetheless.

Mario only called to update her on her father. The two men lived together in Nassau, where her paternal family came from. Her father had returned to his childhood home after Sophie's mother had died, abandoning her to her mother's sister—may she rest in peace with the angels—who comforted and cared for Sophie in every way. In her mind, she was orphaned the day her mother passed.

And she wasn't in the mood, not today.

The last time Mario called, he'd asked for money, insisting that her father didn't have enough to buy his medications. Drama had ensued in her refusal to send money when he had never lifted a finger for her, when at the time, she didn't have enough money herself—young soldiers were paid in pennies, and at the time Jasper was a Specialist and she was pregnant with twins and on bed rest. In her empathy, in the past, she'd often taken her family's issues to heart. Sometimes she'd even try to solve issues not in her control, and these days she couldn't take responsibility. She had her own little ducks to keep safe.

Unless someone was part of the military community, they—her own family included—did not understand what it meant for a family to have a deployed soldier. They seemed to forget that it was *she* who was alone, that it was she who needed support.

The phone beeped with a voice mail message. But instead of listening to it, she drew a bath.

She turned off the ringer of her landline, set her cell to vibrate, and left the door ajar so she could hear her daughters while water filled the tub. She inhaled the scent of the rose bath oil she poured into the water—smelling the roses—for the first time in forever.

She sank into the water. She wiggled her toes against the warmth and relaxed in it. She turned on the iPod and stuck an earbud in her ear, and marveled at how this tiny square could hold her most favorite songs, and then shut her eyes.

Why didn't she do this more often? Why didn't she take care of herself first? A bath every couple of weeks, a shopping trip for herself. Maybe a movie on her own. She thought of the upcoming months and promised herself time and space . . .

The next second, she awoke to her girls rumbling around the house. She blinked, eyelids heavy, skin pruned. She scanned the bathroom for her cell—she must have forgotten it in the bedroom. But the water was tepid at best, so it had to have been at least an hour.

Time to face reality—Sophie supposed that she had to resume her motherly duties. She unplugged the tub stopper and turned on the faucet to warm, drew the shower curtain, and rinsed off, taking her time, while commotion ensued in her apartment. Her girls yelled for her. Which, on some days, was par for the course, but along with the humidity of the bathroom, a heavy feeling descended around her.

Her sixth sense started tingling. Shrugging into her bathrobe, she popped out of the bathroom. "Girls?"

The girls were giggling, and when she discerned that there was nothing else beyond that, she sighed with relief. She followed their voices into the living room, where Olivia and Carmela were piled up on her office chair. Olivia pressed on the mouse button with a forefinger, and the other typed on the keyboard.

"Hey, you two. What did I say about playing on the computer?" She laughed to release some of the tension that had built up in her chest, but Carmela was pointing at the screen. "We want to call Daddy."

Sophie clicked on the mouse and onto Skype, and sure enough her girls had tried to call him. She clicked to try the video chat again, but it went unanswered. "He's probably not in yet. I'm sure he'll call soon. It's his nighttime."

She scanned the living room, but nothing was amiss, so she squashed down her hypervigilance, padded back to the bedroom, and threw on sweats. She picked up her cell phone, still facedown on her bed.

She'd missed nine calls and nine voice mails.

Then the doorbell rang.

A memory flashed: of Sophie at nineteen, stumbling home after a perfect party night, exiting her dorm building elevator, a smile plastered onto her face, sleep calling for her, none the wiser until she turned down her hallway.

Today has been too perfect.

Sophie's knees buckled. She steadied herself on the bed, slightly hunched down. The girls erupted with their announcement that someone was at the door. Numbly, she made her way to the front of their apartment, clutching her phone in her hand. The path to the front door was not far at all, three hundred meters at most. But she took forever to get there, her legs weighed down like sandbags.

They'd talked about this moment, at pre-deployment briefings. The technicalities of what must happen at the Notification. The war had been going on for a decade now, but people were still dying. Many were getting injured. She'd witnessed some of the aftermath of a tragedy. The funeral, the ceremonies. The grieving fellow soldiers and family members left behind. The memorial runs where they'd write the names of the fallen on their running bibs.

The risk still existed. Sometimes, Sophie's denial made her forget how much danger Jasper and their unit was in. She'd needed to get out of bed every day to take care of her kids, to take care of herself. Everyday life had to occur, and Sophie had to keep her head clear.

Holding her breath, she watched herself reach out to open the door, and it swung open to her friends on the other end. Regina and Adelaide. Her eyes darted behind them; there was no one else. No soldier in a uniform. No chaplain.

"Oh my God. Is it Jasper?"

As if reading her mind, Adelaide said, "No, no. It's just us. No one else. Oh, Sophie." Her friend rushed at her. "It's not Jasper. But I'm so sorry, Sophie—"

"Not Jasper," she heard herself say, still stuck in the moment of fear, and yet it transformed to confusion. Because Adelaide was still hugging her, and Regina's face was crestfallen, her eyes glistening with the beginning of tears.

"Jasper called us. He's been frantic, because your cousin emailed him. Because he couldn't seem to get a hold of you."

"I was . . . I was taking a bath. With earbuds. And I napped for a bit," Sophie babbled. She was being led by the hand, she realized. She sat on her couch. "What is it?"

"It's your father, Sophie. I'm so sorry, but he passed."

The world twisted on its axis. "My father?"

It was the last thing she said before the world went dark.

CHAPTER THIRTY-FOUR
Regina

Regina couldn't get the sight of Sophie fainting out of her mind. A full twenty-four hours after she and Adelaide had showed up at Sophie's front door, Regina was still shaken up. Sophie was an edifice of strength, and Regina'd wrongly assumed that Sophie's family was similarly unflappable.

When asked when she would leave for the funeral, Sophie had said the cost would be prohibitive. Flying to Nassau with two children—who didn't know her family—would be too challenging.

And that was why Regina was on the phone now, speaking to the one person *she'd* felt orphaned by. She had sympathized with Sophie; through her, Regina had realized that there would come a time that one couldn't keep denying their past. And if there was a time to bring herself to face rejection, the time was now, when something beneficial could come from it.

"Regina?" Emilio Castro's gruff voice brought a pang to her heart, and an equally bitter taste in her mouth. It was familiar and strange all at once, and took her back to when she was a little girl, nuzzled up against him, the whiskers of his five-o'clock shadow rough against her forehead.

"Dad."

"Iha, it's been a long time. Is everything okay?"

She winced at his insinuation that she'd only call if she needed something. Then, she reminded herself that yes, she was there for a favor. She couldn't be ashamed now, not after what he'd done to their family. She had the upper hand.

"With me, yes. I'm fine." She held back from mentioning the pregnancy. She was already exposing herself with this call. She hadn't spoken to him since she was commissioned an officer almost three years ago, because no matter how hard he'd tried over the years to mend their torn relationship, she wasn't yet willing to stretch her comfort.

So she plowed right into her prepared speech. "But I have a friend here in New York who isn't okay. Her father died. The funeral is in Nassau. Her husband is deployed, as is mine, and she's alone with two twin girls. I thought that maybe, with your pilot and airline benefits, you could . . ."

"Oh." The dip in his voice was evident, and a sure sign of his disappointment that this was not a social call. Beats of silence passed.

Regina hung on like she was climbing a rope in training. All arms and legs even if her heart screamed, *Just forget it! Why are you doing this to yourself?*

Because this was the man who had disappointed her, time and again, despite a piece of her that would always wish for the quintessential father-daughter relationship. That she could get back the good times and purge all the bad.

Sometimes, hope hurt the most.

After a long pause, he said, "When does she need to fly out? Three tickets or for just her?"

She croaked an answer, taken aback. "Um . . . as soon as possible, and for three, if you can swing it."

He mumbled something indistinguishable, which indicated he was working out a few things in his head. She imagined him sorting through a pile of paperwork, perhaps looking at his calendar on when he needed to fly next.

Her father had been an adventurer. Add the pilot's license, and he had lived his best life, amassing pictures on film he'd develop when he returned, showing her mother all he'd seen while she stayed at home to take care of Reggie and her brothers. None of those pictures depicted him with the other woman he ended up settling with, or other women prior to that, whom he had brief affairs with. Of him exploring this hidden other life he thought he was missing out on.

"Iha, give me the day to work this out." He cleared his throat. "I'll call around to see the best way to get this done and how many tickets I can get. Since she's under a tight time frame, and it's the peak season for travel, I can't make any promises."

"Okay. Great," Regina said, gratefulness rushing out, though hindered somewhat by pride. "I didn't expect this."

"I'm sorry that you thought that. Because all I ever wanted was to be your dad. Your mom and I didn't work out, but you can always come to me—you and your brothers. I want to take care of you."

"And yet—" she began, and then stopped. She shut her eyes. Now was not the time to rehash years of anger, because it was never about money. It was about him stepping up, about him running away.

She couldn't mess this up for her friend. She tried her words again. "Thank you. Will you call me back and let me know, soon?"

"Yes, of course. But, Regina—"

"Bye, Dad," she said quickly, and hung up. She pressed her hand against her belly, against the baby that was growing in it. She apologized to its spirit for her rush of emotions, for the anger and the disappointment.

She also promised it that she would do everything in her power to keep it from heartbreak.

CHAPTER THIRTY-FIVE
Adelaide

"Promise me you won't worry about the girls. Reggie and I have them," Adelaide said to Sophie, while standing at the restricted boarding area of Syracuse Hancock International Airport. The airport was bright, airy, and modern, but among them was the feeling of urgency. She handed Sophie a lunch bag. "From Reggie. A sandwich and brownies."

Sophie's face crumpled. "You guys are just so good to me."

She smiled lightheartedly. The last thirty-six hours had been a whirlwind for all of them. With the help of Regina's father, Sophie was registered as his guest and could fly at a discounted fare. To their surprise, Sophie chose not to take her kids with her, since the experience could potentially be more traumatic than helpful.

Since Jasper's parents were on a cruise, Adelaide had jumped at the opportunity to care for the girls, and Regina followed suit. Despite their short friendship, Adelaide considered Sophie every bit her family.

But leaving the girls with Adelaide and Regina required paperwork, a medical authorization for care in case of emergency, arranging for both ladies to stay at Sophie's apartment so the girls could be as comfortable as possible.

"We're good to you because you're good to us, and because I think you, too, forget to activate the SOS. It's what friends are for." Adelaide pushed a book against her chest. "And to start, here's part of your SOS plan."

"You and your plans." She scanned the cover and raised both eyebrows. "*His at Night*. Historical romance?"

"Yes. It's amazing, and perfect for this trip. It's about faking it till you make it. It's the third book in the series, and the author, Sherry Thomas? She's a talent."

"The almost kiss on the cover's telling me that this will be a good distraction."

"More than, Soph. There's love. And well, sometimes it's all you need. I promise it will make you smile. That's what happily-ever-afters will do for you."

"Is there sex?"

"More than we've all had the last few months, that's for sure."

Sophie threw her head back in a laugh; Adelaide softened at the sound. They'd had such little laughter the last three days. Longer than that, really, from the lingering tension after New York City, mostly coming from herself. Adelaide had had to take a hard look at her expectations of herself and of her body, and at what she'd assumed people expected of her. Thank goodness for the new therapist she started seeing last week—she'd found another outlet where she didn't feel like she was burdening anyone. Speaking to a stranger had its own comfort; she didn't feel judged.

Sophie took a deep breath, her smile tight. "I can do this, right? I'm flying into a mess. I didn't want the girls to have to face a funeral of a grandfather they didn't know, but I don't even know how *I'm* supposed to deal with this."

"You can, and you will, because of who you are. You're truly one of the strongest women I know."

"I don't feel that way right now."

"Oh, c'mon, are you kidding? You're raising twins. You are calm all the time. You are a leader without having to raise your voice. And you know how to read people, how to help them through tough situations. You will do what you need to do in Nassau. But if you don't go, then you'll always wonder."

Sophie nodded.

The squeal of little girls took their attention, and Olivia and Carmela ran up to their mother, each with a chocolate bar in their hands. Trailing behind them was Regina, who dragged a back-pack and a tepid smile. The girls' faces were smeared with chocolate.

"We got sucked in by the magnets and couldn't get out without bribery." Reggie was out of breath, hand on her belly. "Man, having two is a handful."

Sophie lowered her voice. "I'm asking too much, aren't I? I should stay."

Adelaide couldn't let Sophie worry. She touched her on the elbow. "But there are two of us."

"Sophie, listen," Regina said, "if for some reason, the two of us can't handle a few days, we have a bunch of parents at book club who will help us figure it out. It's a seven-hour flight to the Bahamas, and you'll be gone four days. Easy-peasy."

Sophie heaved a breath. "You're both right. Okay, I should go before I lose my nerve. She wrapped Regina in a tight hug. "Reggie, I don't know what I would have done without you and your dad."

"Um . . . it's okay. You'll just owe me one." She grinned.

Sophie stepped back and got down on one knee. She scooped up her children into her arms and kissed each one on the cheek. She whispered *I love yous* into their ears, then finally stood. "All right, ladies. Here I go."

"Godspeed." Adelaide kissed Sophie on the cheek and, after one more round of extended goodbyes, watched Sophie's back as it disappeared down the long hallway, toward the security area.

The crying began as soon as Sophie was no longer within sight, starting with a sniffle from Carmela, which turned into a full-blown sob from Olivia. It took both adults to coax the children from the terminal and into the frigid parking lot, then into Adelaide's car.

"It's going to be a long four days," Regina said to her now, and peeked over her shoulder.

Adelaide bit her lip. "I know, I'm worried about bedtime. We might have to get creative, maybe make a slumber party out of it?" She stuck the key in the ignition, and her cell phone rang in her purse. "Let me get that. It's Matt's day off today, so I don't want to miss his call."

Sure enough, the BlackBerry flashed his name. She answered the call, then turned on the car anyway to get the heat going. "Hi!" She mouthed the word *Matt* to Regina. Regina turned around and put a finger against her lips.

"It's Mr. Matt," she whispered.

And like good military children, they took their voices down to a low roar.

"Hey," Matt's voice was rough-edged, and Adelaide pictured him lying in bed, comfy under his fleece blanket. A feeling of yearning shot through her. "What are you doing right now?"

I wish it was you. Adelaide heated as the thought materialized in her head. Six months was a long time to be celibate. "We just dropped Sophie off at the airport. We're in the car now."

"Who are you with?"

"Me and Reggie and the twins. What's up?"

"I can tell you, but you've got to keep it on the DL for now."

She looked askance at Regina, who was playing a game on her phone. "Got it."

"I've got some news. The advance party is coming home in April."

The advance party was the first wave of soldiers who redeployed back to post to help set the stage for the entire unit to return.

She felt a smile push through her lips. "You?"

"No, not me."

"Dang it, I was hoping . . ." Then, when Regina turned slightly in her direction, she smiled brightly despite her disappointment. She should know by now that she couldn't rely on hope when it came to Army plans. Nothing was real until they actually got on that bus, or plane.

"Sorry, babe. Also, you'll most likely hear some grumblings about someone specifically who's coming home. There are other things going on—rumors."

It was vague, this information, and she would need to find some alone time the next few days to follow up with more questions. The mere fact that Matt didn't come right out with the rumor told her that it was highly sensitive and important.

"All right. Well, I love you and I'll talk to you soon!"

"Love you, babe."

As she backed away from the space, Regina asked, "Everything good with the guys?"

"Oh, yeah, everything's fine. Just fine!"

But as usual, and now against everything she was learning in therapy, she was faking it, because everything was not fine.

CHAPTER THIRTY-SIX
Sophie

Adelaide had been right; Sophie had been saved by *His at Night*. As it was Sophie's first romance novel, she hadn't been sure how to approach it. She usually lifted her books to eye level when she read, but on her flight to Nassau, she'd kept the suggestive cover out of sight of the other passengers, especially while cramped in the middle seat.

But when she cracked the spine and read the first chapter, she was thrown right into its historical world despite her skepticism.

And damn, did that book take her out of her funk. It eased her worry as the miles between her and her daughters increased. She loved that she was able to hold the book with one hand and flip its pages with a thumb while she ate her peanuts.

She finished the book the first night she arrived in her father's home, just in time to deal with her cousin and the death of a man she'd been estranged from. She felt entrenched in two worlds: Victorian England, where Lord Vere and Ellisande Edgerton of *His at Night* found their way to each other, and sunny, breezy Nassau, where she had to face strangers who were also family.

But just as Vere and Edgerton had to fake it to make it, Sophie did, too. For four days, she girded herself against the puzzled looks, the judgment, and the impending grief that would take her years to process, because it wasn't going to happen in Nassau, where she couldn't let her guard and emotions down. For four tortured days, only made better by her phone calls back to Millersville and a reread of the book, it became undeniable that family was born not of DNA but of connection and loyal love.

At her layover stop in Orlando, Sophie hit pay dirt after scouring through three different airport bookstores—she found one that had a shelf of romances. She didn't read any of the back covers, but simply took a copy of each and stuffed them in every crevice of her carry-on. The tail end of deployment was still up ahead; the maddening wait was like senioritis in high school and college, but magnified to the nth degree. She would need all the love to pad her heart.

Her first night back, Sophie's girls tutted and crawled all over her; they even checked in on her while she was in the shower. Travel exhaustion had settled in by the time her girls finally succumbed to slumber. It was glorious then, the silence. She hadn't had any for at least a week. To sit there and do nothing—hear nothing but the hum of the light bulbs in her kitchen—was a sublime kind of luxury.

Until she couldn't stand it anymore.

Sophie never could just sit.

So she cleaned her kitchen, though it was already immaculate—Adelaide and Regina had done everything perfectly and correctly. Still, the act of tidying calmed her nerves, so she wiped down her kitchen counters and cleaned out the fridge. She swept the linoleum and spot-cleaned her cabinets. And since it was almost the end of the month, she went to the computer to pull up her Excel spreadsheet of the bills that needed to be paid.

Her email was already opened, the in-box holding one new message. From Jasper.

Their emails had continued while she was in Nassau, and there, she'd clutched on to them like a life preserver in rough waters. Jasper understood the whole story; he had seen her attempt to deal with her family, from the guilt of being out of touch with them to the freedom resulting from the separation. And Jasper came through the best way he could. He'd encouraged her, emboldened her, become a true, real-life conscience as she muddled through her trip.

Sophie's love for him had grown a hundredfold in four days.

And yet.

Her tummy turned with a tinge of sadness.

Because now that the waters were still, she wished that the life preserver had been a rescue boat. She wished he had been there for her, physically by her side, throughout the entire ordeal.

It was no fault of his own—she knew this. Their love had been tested and proven like a diamond out of the rough—she knew this, too.

And yet.

Sophie clicked on the email to a four-line note.

Soph-
Lots of drama over here. Coming home with the advance party to take care of it. More later.
Glad you're home. Love you.
—J

She sat up in her chair. Jasper was coming home, and early! Sophie looked left and right, around her living room, the redeployment list materializing in her head. She'd need to hit the grocery store for his favorite food, the Walmart for decorations, and . . . "Shit. I need a pedicure."

But the rest of the email sank in.

Drama?

The mere mention of drama meant that there was an overwhelming amount of it.

And invariably, it had to involve someone they both knew.

Sophie shot off a quick email back and pushed down all her mixed feelings. There was a new timeline at hand, a new end date, and that took precedence.

Her baby was coming home.

CHAPTER THIRTY-SEVEN
Regina

"Who knew that redeployment would be so high-maintenance?" Regina said while on her back on a salon reclining chair at Total Spa Care at the Millersville mall. Above her was Janis Northrop, also a book clubber, though at the moment she was in full work mode as an esthetician.

"At least you get your man home early." Janis applied warm wax to the undersides of Regina's eyebrows. "And you got a quick salon appointment. In a couple of weeks, you wouldn't have been as lucky to get an appointment anywhere near Fort Fairfax."

She hummed an agreement, then closed her eyes for the tedious process of removing most of the unsightly hair from her face. To her left, she heard the sound of Adelaide's happy squeak; she must have been thrilled with her manicure.

"How are you feeling these days?" Janis asked.

Instinctively, Regina's hand made its way to her belly, and she chose her words carefully despite the temptation to let loose a joyful scream. She was aware that Janis's husband wouldn't be part of the advance party, so she was careful not to rub it in. "I feel pretty good! Baby's doing well, too. I'm grateful Logan'll be here for the birth—it was a miracle that the request was approved. I know I'm lucky."

"Okay, breathe." Janis had applied paper under one eyebrow. With quick movements, Janis pressed the paper against her skin and tore the hair out. "You okay?"

Regina patted the sides of her eyes; waxing always made her tear up. "Yes. Man, the stuff we have to do. Wax, dye, have babies. We should get hazard pay, too!"

"You're telling me." Janis handed her a mirror, and Regina inspected her face. Nope, not a strand of dark scraggly hair.

"Thank you for taking care of me the last couple of hours." In the mirror, Regina took in her reflection. Her hair was now highlighted with ash brown—her OB had given her approval for the third trimester—and layered for more volume. "I wish I could duplicate this blowout. Can I just have you with me on reunion day?"

"He's going to be so happy to see you—no matter what," Sophie said, from the waiting room area.

The patrons in the room nodded in solidarity. Still, Regina couldn't help but be a little worried.

Her husband had left a woman who was trim and fit. And now here she was almost seven months later, with a belly big enough to take up half their queen-sized bed, quite literally. She was now eating kimchee over rice every day, because cravings. The movies that she'd loved now made her cry—she refused to watch *Titanic*, her favorite of all time, because she couldn't think about all that death right now.

Adelaide stood from the manicurist's chair and tugged Regina out of hers. "C'mon, we need to celebrate with some ice cream before we all lose touch."

Regina gasped at the implication. "Lose touch? We won't lose touch."

"There will be a little bit of losing touch, and that's okay." Adelaide smiled pensively. "It's natural for the attention to shift."

Regina and Adelaide paid and met Sophie outside. Sophie's appointment was scheduled for the next day but she had joined the two and shopped when they were in the salon. She was holding two bags from Dillard's.

"Someone was busy! What do you have in there?" Adelaide asked, using a finger to peek inside.

Sophie widened the opening. "A little somethin' somethin'." She winked. "Lingerie."

"Getting serious," Regina teased. "But I only say that because I'm jealous. My lingerie wouldn't fit over my thighs at this point. I did, however, fill the freezer with Logan's favorite ice cream. That should count for something."

"Don't worry about that belly," Sophie said.

"Be proud of it. That and the stretch marks after. I have an added bonus of a C-section scar."

"I didn't know you had a C-section!"

"The girls came early, at around seven and a half months. I had high blood pressure, but we were all well taken care of. They stayed in the NICU to feed and grow. So, see? Imperfect bodies are strong bodies."

Next to her, Adelaide heaved a sigh, heavy and mournful, and the expression on her face was the absolute opposite of her cheerful, glittering nails.

Guilt overcame Regina, and she flashed Sophie a look. As if understanding, Sophie slinked her arm around hers. "Let's go have some ice cream."

"I changed my mind. I don't want ice cream. I want my husband back," Adelaide said quietly, shoulders dropping. She stuck out her bottom lip. "I want him back so we can resume our life. I miss him."

"C'mon. I have to talk to both of you about something anyway." Regina tugged Adelaide by the elbow.

"Fine," Adelaide relented.

"Where do you want to go?" Sophie asked.

"Let's go back toward home. I think the ice cream shack opened up."

Regina had learned that ice cream was sacred in their part of the world. These mom-and-pop ice cream shops were set up like tiny homes along the sides of the highways, each complete with a walk-up counter and a couple of picnic tables. Full fat and full flavor.

For what Regina wanted to propose, they deserved the best dessert.

Fifteen minutes later, all three women had ice cream cones and were sitting in Sophie's minivan, still running with the heat on. Regina, in the second row behind Sophie in the driver's seat, made good progress on getting her rocky road ice cream down to a manageable size before saying, "So, I'm not sure how to do this, but I was wondering . . . you two have been everything to me the last seven months. You really took me under your wings, you know? And while my mother is going to kill me because she fully expects me to ask my cousin who I haven't seen in ten years and who's, like, sixteen years old . . . will you be my baby's godmothers? Being a ninang is a big deal. It's not just about presents, but being there for them, when I need a stand-in."

At first, Regina was met with silence. Then, tears. Both of her friends started bawling over their ice cream.

And then suddenly she was crying. *Damn these pregnancy hormones.* She pressed her napkin against her eyes. "Is that a yes?"

"That you're stuck with us? That I get to send noisy presents forever and ever? Of course, yes!" Sophie said.

Adelaide's tears turned into a waterfall of sobs.

"Oh my goodness, Adelaide." Sophie turned toward the passenger seat. She reached across the first row and clasped her hand.

"It's just." To Sophie she said, "I'm fine. Everything's fine."

But Adelaide's sobs continued. This was a woman who never had a hair out of place. Her emotions were never too extreme.

"Adelaide?" Regina asked.

Adelaide hiccuped. "It's just that . . . I hear my mama in my head all the time, during the good times, but especially when things aren't going well. I had a plan, still have a plan, about a family, and the last few months I realized that maybe, God, that I may not get it. But spending time with you both, and with Olivia and Carmela, and now I'm going to be a godmother. I just realized that it's . . . it's still heartbreaking, but it's also okay, and also joyful. You two have helped me accept. Being with you both, with your kids, Sophie, and you growing yours, Regina, has helped me heal a little."

Regina had all but forgotten about her ice cream, and she felt the first trickle of melted chocolate on her hand. "I don't know what to say, Adelaide."

"You don't have to say a thing. This is a good cry. This is me accepting, a little of myself, and your offer. Of course I will be this child's godmother. I will be there, one hundred percent. Even if we lose touch, this child will always have me."

Regina scooted up in her seat and wrapped her arms around the passenger seat and somewhat around Adelaide. It was awkward and made them both laugh. "Less than a year ago, I didn't have any friends, and now, I have you both. How lucky am I? How lucky is my baby?"

Regina heard a beep, and both sides of the automatic minivan doors slid open. Then her friends climbed out of the driver and passenger seats, and stepped into the van's second row and hugged her from each side. She felt herself relax into their embrace. She allowed the joy of the moment into her heart and cherished that momentary feeling of perfection, that she had these friends, soon she'd have her husband home, and shortly after would be able to hold her baby.

Regina pocketed that feeling when they returned to their apartments, and as she made her welcome-home meal menu. The next day would be a grocery day, to pack her cupboards with Pop-Tarts and salt-and-vinegar chips and Coke Zero.

But her smile extinguished the moment she saw her husband's crestfallen face on Skype later on that evening. "What's wrong?"

"I have to tell you something."

Her heart plummeted. *Of course, of course.*

Didn't she know by now? Nothing was easy; along with the good, the bad always lurked nearby. But she kept her smile, because she was jumping the gun, right? She and Logan had spoken almost every night during deployment—their relationship had reached another level. Regina's admiration for Logan had grown; their friendship had been rejuvenated.

He rested a hand behind his head. "There are rumors, Regina. I'm sorry. It's a whole big mess, and I swear. I swear to you, they're all untrue."

His plea was like a crowbar to her heart, threatening to unhinge it from her chest. "What rumors? What are you talking about?"

"They're saying—"

"Who's saying?"

"The commander . . . said that there are rumors being circulated, about me and another soldier."

"What?" she whispered, watching his lips move, not fully understanding what he was saying. She brought her hand to her heart, then lower, to her belly.

"But none of it is true." He started to cry then. There were tears on this man who never showed pain, never complained. He was coming unglued. "There's nothing wrong with making friends, is there? I mean, just because we had meals together. If I spent the same amount of time with Torres or Hayworth, no one would've given it a second look. C'mon, it's Chandler. She's just a friend."

Regina took in all of it. She had no choice but to listen, because Logan didn't stop speaking. He explained all the times when he and this Chandler spent time together. And all Regina could think was: *Why hasn't he mentioned any of these moments?*

And her prevalent thought . . .

"Who is she?" she asked. "What's her first name?"

"Becka."

"Becka as in Rebecca?" He was calling her by her nickname? "But, but if you're just friends, why haven't you mentioned her?"

In the back of her mind, within the deep folds of her intuition, whispers of warning trickled in. She recalled her mother and father fighting. Her father begging, always asking for forgiveness, and her mother predictably listening and accepting. There was so much shame in a marriage breaking up. It wasn't supposed to happen in Filipino families, and her mother pretended for so long that their relationship could be fixed.

"I . . . I don't know. Because it's no big deal."

"Obviously someone thought it was a big deal. Do you know who spread the rumors?"

"I've got suspicions. But I don't want to talk about that." He had calmed down; he scraped his hand down his face. Her husband looked so tired. He'd lost weight, his wedding ring no longer resting at the bottom of his finger but sliding toward the knuckle. "The worst part of it was that no one gave me a chance to explain myself. The commander and XO literally got me into the office and then told me that I was going home."

"Captain Chang?"

"No, not even him. The big boss. The battalion commander and XO. It skipped Captain Chang altogether. Otherwise, I might have—I mean, I know he would've listened. But I tried. I told them that it wasn't true, that I shouldn't be punished for something that's hearsay."

Regina was knocked back into her seat, and the confusion cleared into fear. Adultery was a crime punishable under UCMJ, under military law. "You can get in serious trouble for this."

"That's the thing. They've got nothing on me." His face neared. "I would never. Not to you and especially not to our baby. I know that we fight, I know we don't get along sometimes, but we've been golden since I left, haven't we? We've worked it out. I never have, and I never will cheat on you. And now that I'm being watched, I need you, babe. You've got to believe me."

She looked at her intertwined hands. At her wedding band, embedded in her swollen finger. She remembered the promise she made with this ring, and how, when her father didn't keep his own promise, she had suffered as a child. And now she was going to be a parent.

She couldn't act irrationally. She looked into

the screen, into his hope-filled eyes. And she saw the man she fell in love with, the father of her unborn child. She had to believe him—she needed to trust him. "I believe you."

But now, a shadow had been cast over her perfect day. Someone had gone above and beyond to threaten her livelihood and marriage, someone who didn't give either one of them the benefit of the doubt.

Regina made it her priority to find out who this person was.

PART SIX

*Some things you got to release. . . . The
more you hold them in, the worse you get.*

—*The Immortal Life of Henrietta Lacks*
by Rebecca Skloot

CHAPTER THIRTY-EIGHT
Regina

Present Day, Tuesday

Regina zipped up her windbreaker and pulled on her hood to protect herself from the hostile wind, but she exhaled a sigh of relief as she stepped out of the town house for Just Cakes. Getting Genevieve down for bed had been tough. The honeymoon period was over between her and the toddler, apparently. Earlier, at the playground, after Regina had switched shifts with Sophie for Adelaide's discharge, Genevieve had refused to leave with Regina, despite coercion attempts, and she had a meltdown. At dinnertime, Gen launched her pasta bowl to the floor. And when her mother arrived from the hospital, groggy and exhausted and unable to play, Genevieve threw a tantrum that Regina could only describe as like a hurricane.

Then again, if I were her, I would be throwing a tantrum, too.

Perhaps Genevieve felt the stress of her mother's pain. Children were infinitely wiser than grown-ups assumed they were. Miko had been only three when Logan finally moved out—

though they'd been sleeping in separate rooms for over a year—and she remembered his bout of insomnia and separation anxiety.

Her Apple Watch beeped with a call.

Speaking of Miko . . .

She slipped her wireless earbuds into her ears, then accepted the call. She looked both ways and crossed the street. "Hey, sweetheart."

"Mommy, Lola says I have to eat all my vegetables."

She found a bench across the street from Just Cakes to sit on, slinging one leg across the other and stuffing her hands in her pockets. "I hope you ate them."

"I didn't. I told her that you don't make me eat my veggies so I shouldn't have to do it while you're away."

"You said I don't make you eat veggies?"

"Yes." He harrumphed.

She dipped her chin to her chest. She was going to get it from her mother, for sure. He wasn't lying—she didn't *make* him, but that was because sometimes it was easier just to sneak them into his food. She didn't want to spend their precious time together fighting. Especially since he preferred hanging with Logan more and more these days.

"Well, you know that when Lola's in charge, you have to do what she says. It's her rules."

"But whyyyyyy?" he whined.

"Miko."

"All right," he said finally. "I'll eat them."

"Anything else?"

"Dad called me. He told me to tell you hello."

"That's nice. What are you guys planning this week?" Logan had taken leave for the rest of the week to take Miko.

"We're going camping."

"Great. That sounds great." With these words she smiled. Actually, physically smiled in hopes that it made it to her voice.

Regina was grateful that Logan was attentive, that he was a good dad. That he paid attention to when Miko's school and social events were, and attended them when he wasn't out in the field. Miko was the only reason Logan continued to try to get stationed in Georgia, since, after she'd left active duty, it was the easiest place for her to settle. He understood that their son needed stability and found pockets of years when he worked within at least a few hours' drive away.

Still, sometimes she was jealous of their small bonding moments. If she and Logan had worked out, it would've made everything so much easier, for all of them. Right now, with how much Miko clamored to spend time with him, she wished she was a part of that fun, too.

She pulled herself out of her meandering thoughts. "Speaking of, sweetie. Ask Lola to help you pack, okay? Since you're going camping, I don't want you to forget anything. You can't just pack T-shirts and your LEGO sets and one flip-flop like last time."

He laughed, and she imagined his bright, wide grin. "Okay, Mom."

"Okay." Regina caught a whiff of sugar, a reminder of her appointment, and she turned, facing the storefront of Just Cakes, across the street. An outline of a figure passed through the front windows. Her insides fluttered.

"Mom?"

And then her flutter crashed into the door of her conscience. Miko was part of her package, and she'd soon have to address it if this crush with Henry grew. Which meant she couldn't let that flutter get out of control.

No one could be above Miko.

"Yes, babe."

"Are you having fun?"

"Me? Yeah, sure, but I'm not here for fun. I'm here to help your Ninang Adelaide out."

"Can't you do both?"

"I can, I suppose."

"Do you know what Daddy said?"

Her next words came out wryly. "What did your father say?"

"He said that you two had so much fun once."

The statement stunned her. Logan had said those same words to her long ago, during a fight.

She'd accused him of being irresponsible, and he answered back that she'd lost the ability to have fun.

"Is that what he said?" She clicked on the messages app on her phone, to Logan's last text, which was a short thread about their camping logistics. She shot him a text:

You told our son that we had fun once?

I mean, did we not?

Not cool to disrespect me in front of our child.

How was that disrespect?

Logan.

Reg.

She took back her previous wish that she and Logan had worked out. A good father did not equate to a good partner.

She mustered a sweet tone for Miko. "Well, honey, you just remind your daddy about all the fun you and I have on Friday movie nights."

"I will. We do have so much fun."

"Yes, we do." She stood then, catching sight of Henry at the doorway. He was leaning on the doorjamb, staring right at her, hands in his pockets. All at once, her heart jumped in her chest. "I've got to go, okay, hon? I'll call you later."

"Bye, Mom."

She took off her earbuds and tucked her devices in her pocket. Henry straightened and walked curbside as she crossed the street. Oh, to have a man greet her like this every day.

Henry's smile was genuine, he wore that apron so confidently, and he smelled so sweet—from the sugar he worked with, undoubtedly—that she suddenly craved *him*. She wanted to touch him.

So she did, leaning up for a hug. "Hey."

After a moment's hesitance, his arm linked around her waist, and the strength of his hold, lifting her lightly, took her breath away. "Hi. I'm glad you made it."

After he set her back down, she swooned ever so slightly. "Me, too. Is your event over?"

"It is. You have perfect timing. You ready for some sugar?"

Why the idea of baked goods turned her on, she didn't know, but her face heated with pleasure. "I am." She followed him into the bakery, where she was greeted by a dimmed room with candles lit at every round tasting table. Twinkle lights were draped across the ceiling, casting a romantic glow. Soft jazz music piped through the surround-sound speakers. "Oh, wow."

The kitchen door swung open, and a woman stepped out, untying her apron. "So I'm heading out. Henry, don't forget to . . ." She startled. "Oh, hello, there."

Regina stunned, said, "Wow, hi. I'm Regina Castro."

"Carolina Just." Carolina took her hand, a smile on her face. She was the female version of Henry, though an inch shorter. She had the same orange-red hair, the same pink cheeks, and the same warm demeanor.

"I . . . I know." Regina covered her mouth with a hand. "I'm sorry, I'm a little starstruck. You once made a six-layer Doctor Who cake with all the doctors included."

"Thank you. It was a feat, so I'll take the compliment. I'm pleased to meet you, too, Regina. So you're the reason why my brother insisted on taking over our IG account."

"Okay, sis, don't you have to go?" Henry said.

She laughed. "Yes, yes. I, too, have a rendezvous." She took off her apron with a flourish and hung it on a hook.

Regina's cheeks burned. Was this a *rendezvous?*

"And with whom?" Henry asked.

"None of your beeswax." She winked at Regina as she passed. "But I hope to see you again soon,

Regina. Glad to meet you, finally." She opened the door with a hand up for a final wave.

Regina was still rooted to her spot. "That. That was Carolina Just."

"Carolina Just, who has a date with someone I don't know about. Interesting." He walked to the window and watched her stride around the corner. Then he looked at the ceiling. "If I hear any thumps or moans up there, we may have to do an intervention."

She followed his gaze. "Wait. You live up there?"

"Yeah. We own the entire building. It's very convenient, for when I have to babysit. And spy on my sister—though obviously I haven't been on my game." He shook his head, as if to focus. "Anyway, yes, the music and lights. We had another fundraiser. We find that the more romantic a setting is, the easier it is for folks to empty their wallets." He pulled out a chair. "Sit, and I'll be back with samples."

"Actually, I think I already know what I want—chocolate. It's both Genevieve and Adelaide's favorite." She fiddled with the napkin at her table setting, her nerves catching up to her. "I suppose I could have just called with the order."

"And say no to free samples?" Henry reappeared with a plate of tiny slices of cake. "Listen. You might think you want chocolate, but why not try another flavor? It might even become a new favorite." He slipped the plate under her nose.

Her eyes grew wide with anticipation at what she knew were the three specialty flavors of Just Cakes: chocolate, red velvet, and carrot. That carrot cake recipe was how she'd begun Instagram-stalking the bakery. Regina had been looking for a recipe for her mother's birthday and went down the rabbit hole through Pinterest, then landed on Just Cakes' Instagram page, on a video of Henry icing a cake with precision and competence.

She probably watched the video a dozen times.

Henry appeared with a glass of champagne. "And of course, no cake tasting would be complete without a little bubbly."

He took the seat in front of her and linked his fingers together. She avoided his intense gaze, hoping he wouldn't see right through her, to the extra effort she'd made with her hair, the red lipstick she braved. She focused on cutting into the carrot cake with her fork.

The fork glided in; the cake didn't crumble, a sure sign of its perfection.

"All right, then. Don't keep me hanging. Taste it already!"

A burst of flavor greeted her with her first bite. The cake was spiced, the cream cheese frosting just mildly sweet. It melted in her mouth. "Wow."

"Is it good?"

"Mm-hmm. It's really good."

He let out a breath. "That makes me feel better."

"Really?"

"Yes. You're a chef. Whenever I bake, I always hope that I don't sacrifice taste for decor. Your praise means a lot." His voice was low, almost seductive, and her upper chest warmed.

"Tell me more," she said, to cool the moment. She was here to taste cake, not to ogle him. "About the shop. What are you raising money for?"

He seemed to recalibrate, and the expression on his face changed. He reached behind him, to the shop countertop, and snagged a brochure, setting it in front of her. "We're starting a nonprofit, in conjunction other Old Town businesses. There's still quite a bit left to do when it comes to equity within education. Most schools in our district require the use of tablets and computers, and many loan them out to kids, but oftentimes they're not in great condition. We're trying to get tablets to each child in our local schools."

"What a great idea."

"We hope it will be. Carolina and I didn't have much growing up. Anyway, we're just at the beginning, so we haven't yet announced it on our socials. Though it's made for some late nights while we fundraise."

This was the first Henry had brought up his childhood; Regina realized then that the expression on his face? It was pride. The same kind of pride she held for The Perfect Day Catering. "Wow."

His smile dimmed. "Then why the frown?"

Was she frowning? "I . . . It's nothing."

"Eh, I don't think it's nothing." He reached across the table. "What's up?"

She shook her head. "This was your moment. I don't want to make it about me—"

"It's our moment. After all, this is a conversation. I want to hear what you're thinking."

She waited for a sarcastic remark, reminiscent of her "conversations" with Logan way back then, when they either fought or she'd backed off to avoid silence. But none of that came. "I've told you about my three-year limit to my business."

He nodded. "A self-imposed limit."

"Yes. It lines up with the renewal of my commercial-kitchen lease contract. I'm about six months away from it."

His eyebrows rose. "And how do you feel coming up to the date?"

"To be honest, not good. Do I love the work? Absolutely. Do I see myself doing this forever? Yes. But our books tell me the opposite. And deep inside, I think the business is not a perfect fit for the location."

"It sounds like you know what to do." His gaze

331

dropped. "Though I get it's not an easy decision."

"No, it's not. And not just for my employees. What scares me more, to be honest, is what comes next. Do I go back to a desk job? Do I try to start something new or revamp my current business somehow to fit what my community needs?"

"Or do you change your community?"

Her gaze snapped to his face. "Move? But my Mom lives in Columbus, and Logan's stationed there, too."

"But Logan isn't always stationed at Fort Benning."

"I mean . . ." She looked back at the last eight years, and true enough, Logan hadn't lived in Georgia for half that time. "No, but still."

"Consider this: You love The Perfect Day Catering. You've already taken a risk. Maybe explore other options on the table, even one that's far-fetched and bonkers? Not that I have any say."

"No, thank you." She smiled, though her mind was in her commercial kitchen, with the entire family and employees milling about. "It feels good for me to talk this through. Sometimes I feel like I'm . . . alone in this."

"You are most definitely not. You have your friends here. You have me." He clapped down on the table gently. "But go ahead, taste the rest of the cakes." He watched her as she took a bite of each sample. It took all of Regina's effort not to let her eyes roll back in pleasure.

"Is that a moan I hear?" The right side of his mouth quirked up into a grin.

"Maybe?" She covered her mouth with a hand while her face burned up like a furnace.

"Well? What's the verdict? Still chocolate?"

"As delicious as the carrot and the red velvet are—"

He peered at her playfully. "It was worth a try, though I thought I could tempt you."

"Listen, if I could have a cake with a layer of each . . ."

"I seem to remember a certain Instagram story when you and your son flipped a coin over who would pick that evening's pizza. And whoa."

She laughed. "You didn't like my anchovies and olives with pineapples?"

He splayed his hand against his chest and coughed. "The thought alone gives me heartburn."

"What can I say? I have an advanced palate." She beamed.

She stuck her fork in the cake and took another bite as she listened to him describe his adventure making sourdough pizza crust. His lovely voice filled her with earthy and sunny goodness. She had to shut her eyes to savor it, using all her senses, enjoying the hint of his cologne that wafted from across the table. She imagined what it would feel like to wake up next to him, under the crook of his arm, her nose nuzzled into him.

Her eyes flew open at how quickly her mind spiraled downward.

He grinned, leaning back, crossing his arms, appraising her.

She sipped the champagne to reset her palate and to get her mind straight. "So, yes. Chocolate."

"All right." He scribbled her order on his notes. "And design?"

"Simple, waved sides, ombré white to pink, a big number two, maybe some gold sprinkles. Enough for twenty servings? That should be safe. But really, I leave the design up to you. I trust you. But can we move my order to Friday? That's the day Adelaide's follow-up appointment will be."

"Friday is definitely enough time."

"Thank you for doing this."

"Of course." He stood, and he stuck a hand out to help her off the stool. "Are you doing anything right now?"

"This was my big plan for the evening."

"Would you like to head down to La Cremerie? That's the cheese shop I told you about."

Regina looked at her watch. Surely they wouldn't need her the rest of the night. Soon enough, she would be back to reality, not just at the town house, but in her home in Georgia, where her nights consisted of helping Miko with homework and sorting out bills, not twinkle lights and cake and nighttime strolls. "You know what? Yes."

"Great. Just one minute." He untied his apron and draped it over the countertop. He blew out all the candles and, leaving the lights on, led her out the door. After he locked up, he offered her his elbow.

This time, Regina didn't feel the wind. Nor did she feel the time fly. Though, an hour later, under the dark, star-dotted sky, she absolutely felt his lips on hers for their first honest-to-goodness kiss.

CHAPTER THIRTY-NINE
Sophie

Present Day, Wednesday

The next morning, Sophie woke up in an empty bed. She sat up, bleary-eyed, and grabbed her phone from the nightstand. It was 8:00 a.m.

"Damn it." Jumping off the bed, she threw on a robe over her pajamas. Exhaustion clung to her bones, but she ignored it, irritated that she hadn't woken up to her alarm for Adelaide's 6:00 a.m. temperature check. Both she and Regina had pulled long shifts the night before—Regina for Genevieve and Sophie for Adelaide—and Sophie must have crashed hard after Adelaide's 3:00 a.m. medication.

Sophie padded to Adelaide's room and peeked in. The morning sun filtered through the sheer curtains. The outline of Adelaide's body under the covers rose and fell in a calm pattern. Sophie pushed the door—it opened with a creak—and picked up the thermometer on the bedside table. With a gentle tap, she said, "Just taking your temp, Ad."

Adelaide mumbled an okay, and Sophie stuck

the thermometer in her ear. After a short wait, the device beeped a verdict, and Adelaide let out a breath. Her temperature was normal. *Thank God.* After a brief glance at the medication record she drew up for Adelaide's pain meds and antibiotics and noting her next dose, Sophie left the room, shutting the door.

Her phone buzzed with a notification: another text from Jasper. Since she changed her flight, he had been nonstop with questions. Despite her attempts to calm him with logical reasoning, he was unsatisfied with any of her answers.

Sophie stuffed the phone back in her robe pocket and squashed the ire rising in her chest. She wasn't going to get into it with him first thing in the morning, without a cup of coffee in her system. He would have to wait.

Sophie smelled the food as she descended to the first floor. Bacon. And as she neared the kitchen door, she heard music.

She peeked into the kitchen. Regina was belting out a song by Taylor Swift while she stirred a pot before moving on to chop something into smithereens. Then she halted to send a text. Genevieve was on the floor surrounded by Tupperware and its covers emptied from one of the bottom cupboards. She lifted a blue cover in a wave.

Sophie put a finger up to her lips in a sign of *shh,* and Genevieve imitated her, lips pursed.

Regina broke out into a small dance.

This was so . . . cute. Sophie tried to contain her smile and instead crossed her arms and waited patiently for Regina to turn, which she did after a strike-a-pose move with a hair flip.

Regina started, and brought her hand to her chest. "Good God. How long have you been standing there?"

"Enough to see that *someone's* happy." Sophie approached the kitchen counter, lifted Genevieve into her arms, and kissed her cheeks until she giggled before setting her down. Then she poured herself some coffee and sat at the wooden table. Her phone buzzed in her pocket, but she ignored it, focused on this singular conversation with Regina.

Up to that point, their interactions had been transactions, save for a couple of friendly comments. Mostly, their communication revolved around the Genevieve pass-off, the Adelaide care plan. The chores they'd split up, and yes, the party on Friday. They'd even shared a bed, but they hadn't spoken despite the close quarters. As soon as their heads had hit their pillows, slumber overcame them. But the past hung over them like a chandelier too big for a room, and Sophie craved a simple conversation.

In Sophie's opinion, the loss of a friend was just as devastating as a romantic breakup. In the decade Sophie had missed, she never got to support Regina through her divorce. She had never sent Regina's son those noisy presents she'd promised in her minivan on that ice cream trip, though not for lack of trying.

"It was just a song," Regina declared.

"Mm-hmm. Right, as if I don't know you. You have that look."

She stopped stirring. "What look?"

"Giddiness."

"I mean, maybe I am a little giddy. . . ." She stirred again.

Giddiness usually meant romance, but maybe Sophie was wrong. "You're going to leave me hanging? Is this about last night, with your date?"

"It wasn't a date. It was about the cake. Which reminds me. This evening, I'm going to have to sneak out again. I need to buy decor."

"With?" Sophie waited a beat for an answer, then added, "Adelaide told me that this was an internet friend."

"Maybe you and Adelaide shouldn't be talking about me." She gave Sophie the side-eye.

Ouch.

Genevieve threw one of the plastic containers into the pile, as if in anger.

"Oh, Genevieve, no throwing," Regina said.

"Yes!" Genevieve said.

Sophie's phone buzzed again. She took it out of her pocket.

Carmela
Mama, why aren't you home yet?
Why are you being such a cactus to
daddy? All prickly.

I love you.
I'll be home soon.
I need to stay for Adelaide.

You're using her as an excuse to stay
away.

The phone rang in her hand. She clicked the red button to send it straight to voice mail.

"Mine! Mine!"

When Sophie looked up, Regina was kneeling next to Genevieve. "Be nice to the bowls, okay? Or else I'm going to put them away."

"It's like we need to take our own advice," Sophie said.

"Uh-huh," Regina said. "Some of us more than others."

Sophie put the phone screen side down and frowned.

"Look, you're hiding something, too." Regina stood and shut off the stove and leaned back against the countertop. "Maybe you should share first. What's the deal with ignoring Jasper's texts the other day, and then now, sending Carmela to voice mail?" At her silence, Regina added, "C'mon! I saw that contact photo—it was her." She crossed her arms. "That sixth sense you always talked about? I have it now, too."

"How funny that you remembered me using that phrase."

"I was twenty-five and pregnant, and you were the best mom I knew. I watched you so closely I was practically taking dictation. It's why it just pissed me off so much when . . . when . . ." She pressed her lips together.

When everything happened.

"You thought I was the best mom?" Sophie asked instead, stunned.

"Yes. But you're changing the subject." Regina's tone changed. It hardened into bricks. "It's not just you. Adelaide was ignoring Matt, too, at the hospital. The bottom line is that there can be reasons why we keep things to ourselves."

Sophie snorted. Speaking to this woman was like picking up a needle with points on both ends. There was no way she was going to come out of it unscathed. "Damn. I was just curious why you were acting so weird."

"There you go, judging."

"I don't judge!" Sophie huffed. And now, she had no idea where the conversation had meandered to. "I swear, talking to you is like talking to one of my children."

Regina laughed. "There you go again. You're

such a good mama and nurse, but sometimes you're such a"—she opened her mouth, then, as if thinking twice, eyes darting quickly to Genevieve, who was slack-jawed and watching them, reconsidered—"pill."

Sophie didn't know whether she should clutch her pearls or kick this woman's butt. "That's rude."

Regina lifted her hands up, as if in surrender. "It wouldn't hurt you to lower your standards for normal people like me. We can't possibly accomplish everything you have and still be gorgeous and have a social life. The perfect Army wife. Oh wait!" She laughed. "Except, you aren't."

It was a low blow, even if Sophie knew that it was true. No, she wasn't technically an Army wife, but she had lived long enough as one to count.

Sophie stood, giving up. "It's obvious we're having two different conversations—I have no idea what the hell you're talking about. I won't stand for this kind of tone from anyone, not from my children, not from strangers, and certainly not from you."

"And I'm surely not going to sit here and *share* and pretend that what happened so long ago is water under the bridge. Because it isn't. Sure, ten years have gone by, but I have neither forgiven nor forgotten."

"None of what happened back then was my fault."

"Are you serious right now? Yes, it was."

Sophie hung her head, though inside she was shaking. "You need to direct your anger to the right person. Besides, how many times do I have to apologize for any of my and Jasper's involvement? I tried over the years, Regina. I've sent emails, presents to Miko. What more can I do?"

"Keep Miko out of this."

"How can I? It wasn't just us who split up, it was our families, too." Saying this all aloud brought back the chaos of their last days together in Millersville, and the hurt that ensued.

"There are such things as consequences," Regina said, bending down to pick up the scattered plastic bowls, a dismissal. "We've got to live with them."

CHAPTER FORTY
Adelaide

Adelaide couldn't go back to sleep after Sophie took her temperature, and after looking up at the ceiling for minutes on end and hearing the muffled noises of the world moving on below her, she decided it was time to get up.

Slowly, gingerly, she sat up in bed. Determining that her medication hadn't rendered her dizzy, she stood, then made her way to her dresser and pulled out a nightgown, a comfortable, soft flannel number that she'd used postpartum. Then, she went to the bathroom, where she confronted herself in the mirror.

Heavens, she looked rough. Her skin was dull; her hair was matted and stood up in places. Forget bags, she had steamer trunks under her eyelids, and her lips were not their usual shade of pink. "But at least you're standing," she said aloud.

Adelaide lifted her nightgown over her head inches at a time; she spied the dressings over her sutures and peeled the tape from her skin. To her relief, the incision sites were dry and clean, and the skin around them wasn't red or swollen.

On the struggle bus, she continued attempting, and failing, to fully raise her arms over her head.

She sweated bullets as she tugged the clean nightgown over her body. Every muscle, some seemingly new ones, protested all the movement. But this was no time to give up. She'd awakened with two goals in mind.

To be with her daughter, and to get her friends to bond over *Waiting to Exhale*, if they hadn't done so yet. So far, much of her comfort came from knowing her friends had found a way to work together, but she'd hoped the book would bridge the remainder of the gap between them.

Adelaide shuffled to the top of the stairs, holding on to the banister with a vise grip. Older homes like hers had tall, narrow stairways, and with every creaky step downward she felt her soul lighten. It was a one-foot-at-a-time operation, and she grunted with effort. When she reached the bottom step, both Regina and Sophie were looking up at her. Regina was giving Genevieve a piggyback ride.

She'd heard Genevieve in the middle of the night, crying for a bottle and a snuggle. It hadn't been but a few minutes before the hallway light turned on, a sliver spilling under her doorway. Next came the sounds of footsteps going to her daughter's room. Adelaide couldn't tell which godmother was dealing with the baby, but it didn't matter. Genevieve would always be able to look to either of them for help, at any time in her life.

Sophie crossed her arms. "I cannot believe you just did that. One of us could have helped you."

"I'm fine," she uttered, though she had to catch her breath first, her eyes solely on her daughter. "Hey, baby girl."

Regina brought Genevieve closer.

Genevieve stuck her arms out and leaned out of Regina's grasp. "Carry me, Mama."

"Whoa there, not yet," Regina said softly.

"Oh, I so wish, sweetheart." A primal mothering urge rose within Adelaide. She wanted to take Genevieve into her arms, stick her in a pocket like a joey to keep her safe.

"Just another day or so, okay?" Sophie said, more to Adelaide than to Genevieve.

Adelaide looked around at her house. Her daughter's toys were not in the normal places, and little tokens of her friends' things were littered all over the living room. Their purses and jackets hung at the foyer umbrella stand. On her pedestal table were books and receipts.

Almost an entire week had passed, and life had gone on. Her house still stood. Her daughter was taken care of.

It was both a shock and a relief to Adelaide's system that the world continued to spin without her. Yes, she had full confidence her friends could handle the task, but to see it . . .

She had placed so much pressure on herself to keep the home fires burning, to be absolutely indispensable, but she *was* dispensable. Things were all right without her.

Tears clouded Adelaide's vision.

Sophie looked around, as if she were checking for a fire. "What's wrong? What did we do?"

"Nothing." Adelaide couldn't put into words that she was both relieved and disappointed that everything was better than okay.

"I know what it is." Regina made her way to the kitchen. "You're hungry. You need calories to heal. Well, don't you worry. I read up on the dietary restrictions of someone who's had your surgery, and most of what I made this morning is bland and soft and without any kind of substantial deliciousness, but exactly what you need."

"How about you head to the back deck?" Sophie added. "Getting some cool fresh air might be good for you. I can bring one of your blankets out."

"Agreed. I'll bring the food out." Regina set Genevieve down and disappeared around the corner.

"That sounds great." Adelaide began her shuffle to the back of the house, passing her L-shaped couch with *Waiting to Exhale* cracked open upside down. It looked like Sophie was halfway through the book.

A grin threatened to burst from her lips. The plan was working. She'd caught Regina reading the book at the hospital when she spent the night, and now Sophie. And—she realized—she herself had better catch up.

Genevieve got ahead of her and started to tug at the door. "Hold on, baby," she said, looking down, noticing that the top of Genevieve's head was as tall as the windowsill. Had she grown overnight?

And then she remembered. Genevieve was turning two this weekend.

Two.

When Adelaide had canceled Genevieve's party a couple of weeks ago in preparation for her surgery, she'd been filled with regret. She'd waited to become a mother for a long time and was committed to celebrating every milestone.

But even she knew she had her limits.

Adelaide opened the door and gently sat down on a cushioned chair, while Genevieve pushed her trucks across the slats of wood on the deck. Regina came out first with a tray and set it down on the table in front of Adelaide. On the tray was a book, her copy of *Waiting to Exhale*. She recognized the first edition with its well-cracked spine.

"Oatmeal and *Waiting to Exhale*. And I think I'm ahead of you in the reading," she said.

Adelaide raised her eyebrows. "That was your book on the couch?"

"Yes. A certain somebody kept nagging me to read. As if we weren't in the same book club."

"But, if I remember correctly, Sophie and I took to finishing a book in a few days, and you liked to stretch it out for weeks."

"I liked to take advantage of the full deadline. And also." Regina handed Adelaide her phone. "You left this downstairs before you went to bed last night, so I charged it for you. And I noticed you have a ton of phone calls to return. I swear you and Sophie are the queens of avoidance. What's been going on?"

That got her attention. "What do you mean, me and Sophie?"

"Am I the only one who notices things around here?" Regina snorted a laugh. "You need to call your mother."

Adelaide knew her mother had been trying to reach her, but she hadn't had the nerve to call back.

"What's going on?"

She picked up her spoon. "I can't put it into words. I've been feeling conflicted about life in general for a while, and with surgery and emergency surgery, things have, I don't know, shifted. I told Matt that I don't want another baby."

Regina leaned back in the chair. "Wow. What did he say?"

"He was sad, and I don't blame him. I figured that he would be shocked and would need some time to process, and we'd talk about it some more. Matt and I—we talk about everything.

My mother on the other hand . . ." She stirred her oatmeal. Steam rose above the bowl. But Adelaide was far from hungry. On the contrary, she felt full. Full of confusion, of thoughts, of new ideas and possibilities. "I don't want this whole situation, the way I feel, to become like one of those informercials we used to watch."

"I don't get it."

"Like the more I watch one, the more I soften to the idea, and then soon I'm buying the two-for-one special with added subscription." She sniffed a laugh, remembering the Orange Glo and the Snuggie and countless other things that she'd bought over the years. "I don't want to accept my feelings as status quo and ignore them."

"Look, Ad. I lost my marriage. Not my fault, I know. I wasn't the one who couldn't keep it in my pants. But I learned from it, too. I learned that if you don't hit the topic straight on, there's so much room to avoid, and so much room to lie."

Adelaide stuck a scalding spoonful in her mouth. *If only you knew how right you are.*

Regina continued. "You know what to do. It's the same thing that helped way back when. Keep speaking to Matt, to your mom, to me or Sophie. In fact, do it now. I'll try to keep the old lady away." She gestured at the glass door with Sophie's outline at the kitchen table.

"You did not just call her an old lady."

Regina shrugged. "We're all older now. Just

calling it like it is." And before she stood, she handed the phone to Adelaide. "Call your mother."

Adelaide found her mother's number in her recent-call list, pressed the call-back button, and put the phone against her ear.

"Adelaide." Patricia Wilson's enunciation of her name was its own tune. From it, Adelaide knew that while her mother was happy to hear from her, she was in a little bit of trouble.

"Hello, Mama."

"I was worried. I left a lot of messages with you and with the hospital and—"

"I know, Mama, and I am sorry. It's been a rough few days."

Patricia sighed. It was breathy, the kind that said that she was frustrated. "But you're okay now?"

"Yes, ma'am."

It was her standard answer to her mother: *Yes, ma'am. Of course. I agree.* All versions of agreements, of yeses, of her being all right. But as soon as Adelaide said it, she knew she was lying.

"Actually, I'm not fine, Mama."

"Tell me, baby."

"I wanna know how you did it. How you just grinned and bore the Army life. And how you made gravy out of grease."

She was answered with silence, followed by a full-on cackle. Adelaide took the phone from her ear and looked at the screen. Yep, she was definitely talking to her mother.

It had been a while since she'd heard her mother's laughter. "Are you . . . okay?"

"Oh, baby, if you feel like that's what I did, I sure pulled the wool over your eyes. I did *not* always grin and bear it. And most days were greasy and just plain messy."

"Really? It always felt . . . perfect. Like you had it together."

"Looking isn't always the same as being."

"I know that." Adelaide worried her lip. She and her mother had discussed the Army life often, and she'd heard everything, every story, every warning. Patricia had passed down all the rules, the etiquette.

"What's going on, sweetheart?" As usual, her mother heard right through her questions.

"I just find myself not wanting the things I used to want. And I don't know how to deal with it."

"These things you now want, are they productive? Are they good?"

"That's the problem—I'm not sure what those things are yet, except that I want different. But what if they're not what Matt wants? You know the Army, so many things are laid out in front of us, and its needs, my husband's needs, come first."

There was silence on the other end of the line, then her mother's voice piped in, loud and angry.

"Do you know the term I hate the most? The word *dependent*. It's what they call us, the spouses, the children. We are associated with the *sponsor,* and all your life, you were linked to your father's social security number as a dependent, and now to your husband's. It really does give a skewed impression of where we rank, doesn't it?"

Adelaide hummed an agreement.

"Of course we love your father and Matt and our lives. We also understand the mission. It's not a question of love or appreciation, so I hear you, Adelaide. Sometimes we get lost in the sauce. Who we are, where we stand, whose career takes precedence. People assume that since we knew what we married, that we should simply accept. And sadly and wrongly, we believe what these people say at times.

"Well, it's okay to wonder. It's okay to try to figure it out. And you might be surprised at how well Matt might come along. Here's what I like to think. We're called dependents because the service member depends on us. Without us, how do they have that support, that extra bit of love? Without us, what is there to defend or fight for?"

Adelaide pressed her hands against her face, now wet with tears. "I miss you, Mama."

"I know. I miss you, too. I regret not being there—"

Adelaide shook her head. "Daddy—"

"Your father, if able, would tell me he wished

we were both there, too. That's how much we care about you, and how proud we are. We're proud of you and all of the choices you've made, and the choices you will make. Don't you forget it." In the background, the doorbell rang. "Sweetie, I have the visiting nurse here. I've got to go. But call me soon? Don't wait so long next time."

"Yes, Mama. I love you. And thank you."

"Love you, baby girl. And tell my Genevieve I love her."

Adelaide glanced up as Genevieve toddled to the sandbox. She stuck her fingers in the sand, scooped them up, and watched the grains cascade out of her fingers.

"I will."

She hung up and turned to the French doors, where her friends lingered in the kitchen, and then down to her oatmeal, which was now undoubtedly cold. Her tummy rumbled with renewed vigor. It was time to get better, and to be better.

CHAPTER FORTY-ONE
Regina

"I just couldn't believe Sophie's audacity," Regina said to Henry later that night, voice croaking. Her fingers and forearms strained with the weight of the bags of decorations she was carrying. "To assume that I could just forget." She stopped, then set the bags down. "Can we rest for a sec?"

"Sure." Henry rotated slowly, tipping sideways to balance the mesh cornhole game tucked under one arm and the toddler bowling set under the other. "Let me get this straight. Because of what Sophie did, you and your ex were transferred to Georgia."

She'd been explaining the complicated story of her and Sophie's friendship and the blowup that basically ended it, the details she'd skipped in their DMs. "That's the short of it."

"But you were already hoping to move there."

"Yes, because both our parents lived in the state, but Logan was rushed out, essentially right after I gave birth to Miko, which was complete chaos."

"And you had proof that it was Sophie who put the nail in the coffin."

She lifted the bags again and grunted. "Not technically, but yes."

"But not technically."

She speared him a look.

"Look, we have scales in the kitchen for a specific reason. Cups of flour end up drastically different depending on who's measuring them. And now that I've changed the subject I have an idea," he said. "How about we drop this off at the shop to keep it out of sight? I don't think everything will fit in the trunk of your car."

"You sure?" Regina sighed, then picked her bags back up. They resumed their slow trudge toward Burg Street. "I really should have planned this better. I should have told you to stop me when I went above and beyond my list. Party stores are my catnip."

"When are you planning to put these up if Adelaide's home?" he said over his shoulder.

"My plan is to put Genevieve down for a nap as soon as Sophie and Adelaide leave for her appointment. It's at Alexandria General, and they should take at least an hour if you include check-in time. I've got Missy—Adelaide's friend—at the ready. She'll bring her army of friends over after Adelaide's gone to help me set up."

"I can try to be available, pending, of course, the schedule. And I've got storage at the shop. Not to worry."

"Have I said thank you already?"

"You have." He grinned. "But I don't mind hearing it again."

"You are absolutely the best."

"Oh, yes. More."

"I owe you not just one, but two or three favors for how awesome you've been."

"I love it, keep them coming." He laughed.

"Don't push your luck, buddy." She rolled her eyes just for effect, though her body felt light despite the bags weighing her down. Henry knew how to speak to her, to inject levity and humor, and even some flirtation, in between the tough conversations. It helped to keep everything in perspective, including the kiss they shared the other night.

"Still trucking back there? I can see the shop's light!"

"I'm coming, I'm coming."

After the next block, they crossed the street, and with the awning of Just Cakes within view, they passed another shop that displayed a wedding dress with its skirt stretched to the width of the window. Regina slowed, eyeing the charm of it all. "I love that everything is right here on this street. Just Cakes"—she looked up at the wedding shop's name—"Rings and Roses. La Cremerie. Old Town Flowers. Have I mentioned I wanted to live in this area? I wanted to get stationed here."

"You're here now, sort of stationed. What do you all call it?"

"TDY," she said. "Temporary duty."

"TDY. So it worked out." They'd made it to Just Cakes, and he set down the boxes to unlock the door.

"It did." But in the back of her mind, a thought arose. Was it too late, or too hasty, to do one more thing she wanted? "Do you know what they used to say?"

"What did they used to say?" The bell rang with a chime as he stepped in.

Regina followed him in, grunting. "What happens on TDY stays on TDY."

"Really now?" He set the boxes down, and he turned and eyed her. The look, and the fact that they were alone in a darkened space, caused her to shift her feet. She sucked in a breath to settle herself.

He approached her, stopping less than a foot away. She stilled, the air around her warming. "Here, let me grab that from you," he said. "I'll make room behind the counter."

"Okay." She swallowed the moment, orienting herself as he relieved her of the bags. She shook out her limbs as she watched him stack the decor.

"Would you like a tour? Of the kitchen?" he said after a few moments.

And once again, the vibe changed. Curiosity took hold. This was the kitchen she'd seen in part through Just Cakes' photo feed and stories. "Um, yes!"

She followed him through the swinging door, to the impressive, sparkling-clean stainless steel commercial kitchen, with a center counter and three industrial mixers next to a floor mixer. "It's so pretty in here."

"It's a small space for six people, but it's laid out nicely." He waved her toward the back. "But if you want to see small, let me show you the office."

She stepped into the doorway. The office was as large as the guest bathroom in her mother's home. "Whoa. This is tiny, but you've used the space well." She scanned the shelving that went up to the ceiling, which held baskets and binders.

"My sister is type A, as you can see." Henry came around her. He snatched a pink Post-it stuck on the computer.

"What was that?"

"Nothing." He brushed past her, sighing, and as if relenting, showed her the Post-it. "A note from my sister."

Don't be a slowpoke.

"What does that mean?"

He ran a hand through his hair. "It's her way of giving me a hard time."

"Oh?"

"Encouragement. To not be so nice, or I'll be slotted into the friend zone."

"With whom?"

"Who else? With you."

He gestured for her to take the lead, to exit. Regina mulled his words as they walked back through the kitchen. She thought of his honesty, of his ability to tell things like they were but without pressure or expectation. Laying a hand against the swinging kitchen door, she paused, compelled to return the sentiment. She looked up at him. " 'Nice' matters to me. I like nice. And being nice has nothing to do with being slotted into the friend zone. And being friends doesn't mean being slotted into the friend zone. And for the record, what others might consider a slowpoke, I consider very much right on time."

"Really?"

"Yes, because—" Bravado rose within her. In all the talk of change, here was something she had control over. She might not have had control over her marriage, the rate and speed her son was growing, or this situation with Sophie, which was a whirlwind on its own. But this, with Henry, she could manage. "Because you're letting me find my footing. So I can do this, on my own time."

His Adam's apple bobbed. "This?"

"Yes, this." She placed both hands on his chest, letting them slowly slide up his shoulders. She felt his heat on her palms; she heard each breath he took. "This okay?" she whispered as she lifted to her tiptoes.

"Just . . . perfect." He met her in between, his lips finding hers. His hands came to rest solidly on her hips.

But unlike the comforting hug of their first meeting, the casual kiss on the cheek afterward, their friendly lunch at Genevieve's mini table, and their good-night kiss the other night, this was hot. It escalated to the tangling of limbs, of clothes being tugged out of place, of locking up the store. Together, they took the building steps two at a time to his third-floor apartment. There, in his bedroom, they tumbled and kissed, then gave in and made love in the same way they talked and messaged: with an equal give-and-take.

The night was, indeed, perfect.

CHAPTER FORTY-TWO
Sophie

"Perfect. Just perfect." Sophie licked her lips as she set the glass of Moscato on the side table. She kicked her legs up on the ottoman and sighed. She'd earned this moment of relaxation, and she intended to savor it.

"You don't have to rub it in." Adelaide, reclined in the La-Z-Boy, peeked above her book.

"You'll have some soon enough. Alcohol and narcotics do not mix." Sophie cracked open her copy of *Waiting to Exhale*. Now on page 201, she was well into the book and enjoying every page. And the wine, of course.

"I haven't had a narcotic since this morning. Only ibuprofen," Adelaide whined.

"Still. Not tonight." Sophie lifted the book to her face, ready to immerse herself in the book's world.

To Sophie, books always carried secret messages tailored specifically to her. They were like horoscopes, giving her exactly what she needed at the moment. Right now, she pretended that she was with her three friends in Sun City trying to figure out what in fact had happened in her life, though she hadn't quite decided if she was Bernadine, Savannah, Gloria, or Robin. These four women were drastically different, and all were dealing with troubled love lives, and reinventing part of themselves in the process. Sophie saw a little bit of herself in each of them.

It had flown by, this real life of hers. Looking back at raising her children, at all she'd accomplished, Sophie had to admit that she hadn't done a bad job. But while her friends throughout the years had taken girls' trips to glamorous destinations to practice self-care, or cruises and adult vacations with their spouses, Sophie had not.

It hadn't been about the opportunity, or even about the ability. In raising her kids, her focus had been on being there for them, always. She'd wanted them to have a parent to come home to. She hadn't wanted her children to have to miss her in addition to Jasper, nor did she want to miss a moment of their lives. Had she been a helicopter parent? Proudly so. She had no regrets.

And now her girls were independent.

Being here in Alexandria, away from her responsibilities, Sophie realized that she had missed out. She had been so focused on being good, on doing good. Soon, her babies would be off to college. Adventure was calling.

A knock sounded from the front door. Sophie met Adelaide's eyes. Regina was out but had a key, and it was eight o'clock, well past time for solicitors to come around.

Sophie stood. "Are you expecting anyone?"

Adelaide shook her head.

The knock sounded again. Sophie looked down at her outfit to make sure she was decent. Then she opened the door. A delivery person stood on the threshold, dressed in a purple collared shirt and a purple hat branded with *Flowers-R-Us*.

"Ms. Sophie Walden?"

"Yes?"

He held out a package. "Delivery."

Delivery? "For me?"

"Yes, ma'am."

She frowned, taking the box hesitantly. "Okay."

He tipped his head forward. "Have a great day."

Sophie weighed the box in her hand, then read the label printed with a message.

Sophie,

Remember me. Remember us.

Come home.

Jasper

Her heart softened, and then she rolled her eyes. If there was anyone who should have known she didn't like flowers, it was Jasper. Sophie considered flowers a waste of money because they died no matter how often she changed the water. Besides, she had more important things to worry about than changing out the water of plants, like taking care of humans.

But, typically, Jasper didn't listen to her. When it came to logistical information—that, he was good at. On the days she'd worked, he knew how to manage the children's schedules. Jasper was not helpless, nor did she ever need to thank him for babysitting his own kids. But it stopped there. Because anything above and beyond, he'd forget. He'd sent flowers anyway on every occasion, until she'd given up trying to correct him and instead learned to say thank you.

After locking the door once more, she turned. Adelaide had sat up in the recliner. "From Jasper?"

"Mmm," she answered, not really willing to explain more.

"Looks like flowers . . ." Adelaide added, as Sophie brought the box to the living room. "Is this bad? Usually flowers make people smile, and you're not smiling. Are you two all right?"

"Yes. No."

"No?" Adelaide gasped. "But you guys are . . . perfect."

"There's no such thing as perfect, Ad. There's only work, and then suddenly an absolute silence."

Sophie started to tear at the tape at the top of the box.

"Silence? What does that mean? Did you guys just stop talking?"

The top flaps popped open. "One day the girls got older, and Jasper and I had little to say to each other. And I realized. Twenty years, Adelaide. Twenty years that man and I worked to keep our family together. Did we have fun? He just retired, and he slid right into a government job. I'm in a new job, too. So what does that mean? Another twenty years there? It feels . . . so mundane."

"Are you saying that you . . ."

There was packing material inside, which Sophie pulled out. *Really, Jasper, what is the point of this?*

"Sophie Walden! It just dawned on me that you ran away from home! I'm so disappointed. I'm going to tell that man that I did not mean to harbor a criminal."

"I hold your pain meds, lady. Watch it." Sophie looked up. "I just don't understand him some-times. I've been gone for a week. Surely he could survive it without having to send me a care package."

"It's probably because he thinks you're never coming home!" Adelaide put her hand on her forehead.

Sophie stuck her hand in the box and felt a sting at the end of her middle finger. She retracted her hand. "Ow!"

"Thorns!" Adelaide said. "Must be roses."

"Can't be. They're too short to be roses." Sophie tore at the corners, peeling back the box, and finding the offending plant. A cactus. "Wow."

Adelaide threw her head back in laughter. "Oh my God, it hurts to laugh. Ouch!" She held the pillow against her stomach. "That is classic."

Sophie fumed and held up the ugly thing. It was round with tiny, spiky thorns. "Carmela called me a cactus the other day. She must have picked up the term from Jasper. What the hell is this supposed to mean?"

The door opened, and Regina walked into the foyer. "Hey! I'm back."

Sophie tried to put the cactus out of eyesight. The last thing she needed was more teasing from Regina. But little could be done before she walked into the living room.

"What's going on?" Regina unwound her scarf.

"Sophie got a cactus. From Jasper," Adelaide said.

Regina turned to hang her jacket on the hallway tree. "Ha! Because you are prickly as hell."

Adelaide clutched her pillow against her tummy and cough-laughed again.

"Thanks, you guys. Thanks a lot," Sophie said.

"I guess that means you have to actually speak to him now." Regina looked at her pointedly.

Sophie was left without a comeback. "We'll see."

CHAPTER FORTY-THREE
Sophie

May 2012

It was reunion day, the day Sophie and her girls had been painstakingly awaiting the last eight months. The vibe around her was electric. People milled with chaotic energy. Sophie felt anxiety in every part of her body. And, per usual, the buses' arrival time had been delayed.

While others simply looked off into space, in the hopes of catching sight of those buses sooner rather than later, Sophie pulled out *The Immortal Life of Henrietta Lacks* for book club next week, hosted by Kerry. Her bag was never without a book, and these days, usually two, with at least one romance novel. But the priority was *Henrietta Lacks*.

Except, Sophie hadn't gotten past the prologue in the last six weeks since Kerry had announced this title. The prologue set a serious tone, and while Henrietta's story was clearly important, Sophie wasn't sure she had the emotional fortitude to read this story of injustice, not with their family reunion on the horizon. Not when another huge feat would have to be completed: Jasper's reintegration home.

She gripped the sides of the book with the same fervor she gripped her children whenever they crossed a busy street, in hopes that her nerves would remain still and steady for the next few minutes.

"The buses are about ten minutes out," the announcer on the loudspeaker said, snapping Sophie out of her thoughts.

She called out to her girls, who had been playing with other kids, and they ran toward her. They were in matching red, white, and blue dresses. Sophie hadn't told them that Jasper was coming home until that morning. From her experience, it was best to hold off for as long as possible. It was tough enough for adults to comprehend if a flight was suddenly canceled or delayed, but the children? These children were placed under enough pressure.

Not to say she didn't prepare. She'd filled up the fridge with Jasper's drinks of choice—chocolate milk and Mountain Dew—and the cupboards with pork rinds and dark-chocolate-covered pretzels. She'd purchased the girls' dresses and her own outfit this week, then gotten her hair and nails done. She had also shaved her legs, braving the forest that had grown all winter.

All the while, she felt the pressure of transition. Soon, she would not have the bed to herself. She would have to consult with Jasper on parental decisions. All completely understandable, but still, it was a change.

Once the girls were seated, Sophie turned and searched the crowd for Regina, for whom she'd saved a seat. Above the heads of seated families, her friend was nowhere to be found. Adelaide was with the battalion commander's spouse, doing her duty and making the rounds to greet families.

"Regina's not here yet," Annie Rodriguez, an occasional book club member, whose husband was arriving early as well, said. "You don't think she went into labor, do you?"

"She better not have! She's only eight months along. But I should text her." Sophie took out her phone: no texts from Regina, but one from Kerry. "Hey, I just got a text from Kerry. One of her kids has hand, foot, and mouth. So no book club at her place. She asked me to pass on the message."

Annie made a face. "Oh man, we had that a couple of years ago, and I am not envious. But maybe it's a good thing. I haven't even cracked the book open. You?"

"Honestly?" Sophie said. "No. I can barely keep my mind straight."

To the side, the unit military band had begun their set with an uplifting patriotic instrumental, signaling the arrival of the buses. Smiles appeared in the crowd, the anticipation rising.

Sophie's heart thumped in time with the music, and she tapped her heel-clad food onto the ground. Her girls began to dance next to her.

The rush of emotions was like the rising of the tide, looming above surfers, enormous. That tide represented the length of separation, the struggles of the last eight months, the triumph of survival.

When Sophie saw the flash of the white buses, knowing that in one of them was Jasper, the wave crashed down. Her emotions jumbled in the foam, with no way of knowing up from down in all that rushing water. She wanted to cry, to laugh, to clap, all the while finally experiencing the belated worry that she could have lost Jasper during the last eight months, when most days she'd been able to ignore this fact altogether.

Forgetting her intention to text Regina, Sophie reveled in the anticipation of seeing her partner: How he would look, surely different from on the screen. How he would feel in her arms. A smile bloomed on her face, so big, so bright she imagined he could see her smile, too.

The white buses parked quite a ways from them, just as they had at deployment. Except this time, when the doors opened, bodies in camouflage tumbled out. Family members began yelling names; children were crying. Sophie began to tear up. It wasn't just for her soldier, but also for the others, some mothers and fathers, all sons and daughters, friends and neighbors. These soldiers stumbled out, with wide smiles and bright eyes, radiating joy. Their faces said that they were home. Finally.

And yet, formality must be observed. The formation's march to the front of the stands. The stillness of their proud bodies. And while they stood there, at parade rest, Sophie did what everyone was doing; she searched the sea of faces for her loved one.

"Where's Daddy?" Olivia asked.

"I'm looking for him, baby," Sophie answered, then hooked an arm around each one of her daughters' shoulders, shocked at how tall they'd gotten. They bowed their heads at the chaplain's prayer and then waited patiently through the general's brief speech.

"I see Mr. Logan," Carmela said, pointing up ahead.

"Oh, you do?" Sophie's curiosity was again piqued after the reminder that Regina was not there. Or maybe just not next to her. The crowd behind them had grown, and Regina could have been in the back somewhere.

Then her eyes darted to the left of the formation as if directed by her sixth sense, and there he was. Fourth row from the front, second from the right.

Her Jasper.

She squeezed her daughter's shoulders. "I see him, girls. I see him."

And finally, at the commander's command of "Fall out," the people rushed out of the stands. Holding her girls' hands, Sophie ran toward the love of her life.

CHAPTER FORTY-FOUR
Regina

Regina had been there all along and watched the people in the stands spill onto the field. From her vantage point, she had seen the empty space next to Sophie, too. Her friend was probably worried; her nurse's mind had likely gone all the way to premature labor. But Regina had needed space; she wanted privacy. She wanted to see her husband's face from far away, to assess it without seeing the judgment of others or being influenced by the rising excitement of the crowd.

And she'd found him, singular and still among the rushing parents and children, spouses, and significant others. He looked like she felt, a little lost and alone. This should've been a happy reunion. The commander had cited her pregnancy as the reason why Logan was coming home early, and Logan had vehemently dispelled the rumors that would surely spread now that the first of the unit was home. But she couldn't shake this unsettling feeling brewing in her belly, like yeast fermenting.

Then, he spotted her in the stands. His eyes locked in on hers. His gaze was unreadable, but for the sake of the moment, she plastered a smile on her face. She was relieved that he was home, that he'd made it home, that he was safe no matter the circumstances of his return. Even if people believed ill of him, of them as a couple, those people would not see them struggling.

She finally walked up to him, careful in her wedge espadrilles. The field was a mess of rocks and uneven ground. She squinted, facing the sun, and when she got close enough, saw tears in his eyes. He looked down at her belly; he touched it with a palm.

"Hi, Logan."

"Oh my God, hi." His voice choked out a reply that rattled Regina's soul. He kissed her on the lips, and on the cheek, then on the neck, as if breathing her in, and he got down on one knee, a hand on her eight-months-pregnant belly. "I made it, baby."

Regina's tears came hard and fast, and they were from relief. She'd survived the pregnancy without him; she'd made it through their first deployment as a couple. She'd endured those first torturous and lonely weeks, and come out almost nine months later, thriving.

A camera started to circle them—local press. The internet was hungry for reunion stories. She knew because she hadn't been able to get enough of watching the taped encounters on Facebook while wishing for her own. But she didn't want anyone to see her face, to detect the mixed emotions in her heart.

She pressed her hand against the top of his shoulder, a sign for him, and he stood. "I need to grab my duffel. They've unloaded them against the side of the building," he said.

"Let's go," she said, and allowed him to take her hand. It was rough, just as she remembered, a sign of his hard work. He hated lotion, didn't think that skin care was something infantrymen practiced, but at times she'd rub lotion into his hands anyway. Touch kept them together. They could calm each other with it. Their worst fights were neutralized by a kiss.

This time, holding hands would have to do, because they said nothing as they traversed the busy field to the quiet side of the building, where a group of soldiers watched over neatly arranged gear. Logan spotted his name painted on one green duffel among the others and slung it over his shoulder.

She led him to Baby.

But once he stuffed his bag into the trunk and climbed into the passenger seat, the mood plummeted.

Regina wanted to speak to him; she wanted to hear his testimony before she went any further. So she silently drove the car to an empty parking lot a few buildings down, where there were fewer vehicles around. Home would've provided zero privacy. As soon as neighbors knew Logan was home, the doorbell would ring and guests would arrive, and a barbecue would begin, and all of her questions would've had to wait.

She turned in her seat as soon as she stopped the car. Logan's head was already in his hands, and he fully understood that this conversation was going to happen right there and then.

"I haven't been able to sleep, or think, Logan."

"Me, either. The stares, the judgment. I see it everywhere." He rubbed the heels of his hands into his eyes. "You don't understand what I've been through."

"I don't understand? I think I do." She made nail marks with her thumb on the foam of the steering wheel, because, of course, he was only thinking of himself. "I haven't been able to talk to my own friends about it, either. Because surely they know, too, right? But that's not remotely as important as what's happening between us. Or what's going to happen, with you."

"I don't know what's next, babe. Everything is on hold right now. I'm just . . . supposed to wait."

"For?"

He shrugged.

"And this other"—she wanted to say *woman* but couldn't—"person."

"She's back, too."

Regina straightened in her seat. "She is?" She

had been out there in the crowd, in the same formation?

"Yes. Command thought that it would be better to get rid of the so-called problem, which was us, I guess."

Regina's insides trembled slightly, like a fault on the verge of cracking wide open. Her husband referring to himself and someone else as "us" was a slap in the face. But she shook the sense back into herself.

She believed him—there was nothing going on—and her anger was misplaced. "Will you tell me who accused you of having an affair?"

"I . . . I don't know for sure, but I've been told by others that it might be . . ." He looked out the window.

"Who, Logan?"

"It's someone we know. Personally."

No. *No.* It couldn't be. No one they knew would do this. And if so, why wouldn't they have told her first?

"But that's not what's important," he warned. "Everything is on the line. I . . . we . . . have to hold out. We're supposed to move, remember? Who cares about all of these rumors when we'll be out of here soon enough? I wanna keep lying low. Promise me that you'll do the same. Let me handle this."

Regina nodded, but did not promise, because she intended to get to the bottom of this.

CHAPTER FORTY-FIVE
Adelaide

"I feel like I'm missing an arm." With Regina on her mind, Adelaide peeked over the top of the food truck's counter to watch the mini doughnuts cook. She was riveted as she tracked the dough being piped into the hot oil, forming into a circle, and then moving on down the conveyer belt. The entire process took about a minute and fifty-six seconds—she had timed it while the customers in front of her ordered theirs—and Adelaide knew that her pregnant friend would have appreciated this little but mighty machine. "Regina would get a kick out of watching these doughnuts being made."

Sophie unwrapped her turkey leg from its foil. "It was inevitable. She and Logan are having a baby, and they have a lot to catch up on this week. Though she did say that they were coming. I bet they're around here somewhere." She spun around and peered out into the crowd. "Do you know where Jasper and the girls went?"

Adelaide took a requisite look. "Nope, I don't see them. But maybe Jasper found them already? Maybe I should order extra doughnuts."

They were at the Millersville May Festival and

what seemed like the entire community had congregated in the town square. The sun was just about to set, and the festival signage and rides lit up the sky. The sounds of carnival games and roller coasters were like white noise, punctuated by the occasional screams of riders. With the sudden shift in weather to hint that summer was around the corner, it was a perfect night, and Adelaide was relishing it.

It also helped that Matt's return date had been solidified. The last of the unit was coming home in a week. Just one more week and she would see her husband, finally. She was counting the days until her best friend would be home, her lover would be back in her bed, and they would hopefully start their family.

Thank God.

"I'll have a dozen, please," Adelaide ordered, then turned to Sophie. "Have you been hearing . . ." Adelaide hedged on the question that she knew she shouldn't ask. Matt had been terribly secretive, but sure enough, there had been some grumblings among the returned. She took another stab at the topic. "The other day, at a spouse luncheon, I overheard a group of ladies talking."

"Oh?" Sophie's face was unreadable.

The spouse's club on post held a luncheon every month that was an opportunity to socialize while learning about a local business or charity.

"They alluded to the fact that Logan was in the advance party because he couldn't keep his nose clean downrange."

"Mmm." Sophie noshed on her turkey leg, which she was obviously using as a distraction.

Adelaide, feeling closer to the answer, decided to tackle the question from a third angle. "Did Jasper say how they chose who would come home on the advance party?"

Sophie side-eyed Adelaide, glancing a moment at their surroundings. Her voice plummeted to a whisper. "You know we can't be talking about this."

"Why not? It's just you and me." It sounded like the truth was at the tip of her friend's tongue. "Regina's been curt on text."

"When is she ever not curt?"

"You know what I mean. She's been unreachable. I understand she needs space. But after all the time we spent together, and add in the rumors . . ."

Her doughnuts made it to the end of the line, and they fell into a strainer. The food truck worker picked them up with tongs, dredged them with powdered sugar, and threw them into a paper sack. Adelaide began to drool when the sack was handed to her, warm to the touch.

"So you're saying you've heard the rumors?" Sophie asked.

"Haven't you?" Adelaide pried, feeling like she was pawing her way to the truth.

"You know as well as I do that rumors are bad news and many times aren't even true."

Adelaide peered at Sophie, master of the poker face. "You're being so vague."

"Because the situation is vague. For what it's worth, I've probably heard the same things you have. But none of us really know what's happened. The fact that Regina hasn't come to us directly means that all the rumors are just that—rumors," Sophie said. "Let's go find our people."

"Fine."

They followed the path around the game tents, and Adelaide waved at every baby in a stroller. With Matt almost home, the excitement of trying for a baby threatened to bubble over. To be part of a family like Sophie, to have a child to love, was all Adelaide could think about. "Thank you for including me in your people, and for asking me to come out with your people."

"Of course." Sophie tugged on her elbow. "Hey, you okay?"

"I'm fine. No, let me take that back." Adelaide was learning a little more about herself every day, and telling the truth about her emotions was something she had to work on. "I'm feeling out of sorts, I guess. It's another transition, with you and Regina actually having other lives than our threesome. It's great, of course, and I'll get my reunion, too. But it's a sign that things change, whether or not we're ready."

"I'm always here, though," Sophie said.

"How are you and Jasper? I haven't even asked."

They took a few steps without Sophie answering. They stopped at the low metal barrier of the Octopus, a ride with tentacle-like arms that spun cars of passengers. "Do you think Jasper and the girls are in there? He loves this ride."

The roller coaster's music began, and the cars began to move and spin.

"Soph?" Adelaide didn't like this attempt at distraction.

Sophie sighed. "We are fine in every sense of the word. It's been intense, is all. You know how it is. Even the joy is a lot. It still feels fragile."

"Oh, uh-huh," Adelaide answered casually, though she saw through Sophie's flippant answer. There was more on her friend's mind. But she didn't push it; marriage and relationships like theirs had too many layers for other people to judge outright, especially a marriage that had just endured separation. She smiled to lighten the moment. "I understand. Intimately. We're so excited for them to be back—"

"And then, the toilet paper roll doesn't get replaced, and then I start crying for no reason. I go from feeling so grateful, to wondering why his socks are all over the floor."

Adelaide threw her head back and laughed. "It's such a mess."

"Right? Oh! There they are!" Sophie reached high in air and waved.

Adelaide followed her gaze, to the Ferris wheel, a ride over from the Octopus. Jasper was in between his girls, an arm wrapped around each, as their carriage was carried upward, slowly. Their faces were lit up by the carriage lights, and the twins' expressions were either of terror or sheer delight.

Adelaide wondered what Matt would be like as a dad of twins. When she became a mom . . .

If she became a mom . . .

She shook away the thought. She shouldn't do that to herself.

"Hey, where'd you go right there?" Sophie asked softly.

Adelaide bit her cheek and debated on how much to say, then tried for another stab at vulnerability. "I'm afraid. I'm afraid I won't ever be a mom. All I've ever wanted was two kids and a dog and a picket fence. What if I don't get the thing I want the most?"

Sophie slung an arm around her shoulder. "It's normal to be afraid. And though I can't predict the future, I'll be here for you, and Regina will, too. For anything. And I guess Matt will be there for you, too, right?"

Adelaide laughed. "I guess I do need him."

Sophie scrunched a cheek. "Well, technically, you don't necessarily need him."

"True. But I want him." Adelaide grinned. Feeling better, she popped a doughnut in her mouth, savoring it as it melted on her tongue. Her mind whipped back to their biggest dessert aficionado. "I think we should have a baby shower."

"I'm down," Sophie said. "It's about that time."

"Yes, and before it gets too busy. Once the rest of the unit returns, we might get less of a turnout." Adelaide gave her the side-eye. "And in case things get . . . complicated?"

Sophie's eyebrow rose. "Are we still talking about this?"

"Regina deserves a shower despite . . . what we might be hearing. I want her to know that we support her, no matter what. Maybe at our next book club?"

"It's my month. We can make it a surprise. I was thinking of another YA book."

"You're really liking YA."

"YA and romance. You really corrupted me." She side-bumped her. "Actually, the right word is *enlightened*."

"You're welcome!" Adelaide yelled. The people in front of them turned around, confused.

Sophie laughed, sinking her teeth into the hunk of meat.

"By the way, you are the first person I've ever known to buy a turkey leg."

"It's damn good." Sophie took another a bite,

chewed, and swallowed. She looked over her shoulder. "Look, Ad. Ultimately, whatever's going on with them is their issue. Not our monkeys."

"But we have such a small unit. And we're friends. We should be there for one another in spite of it all."

"The line is thin and very fuzzy."

In front of them, Jasper and the girls appeared. The twins were chatting nonstop about their Ferris wheel ride. Jasper was out of breath, laughing.

"It's your turn, Mommy," Carmela said. "Daddy wants to take you on there." She pointed to a kid's train roller coaster that turned corners at lightning speed so that adults disembarked nauseated.

Sophie eyed Jasper. "That ride isn't meant for anyone who's had a baby."

"C'mon, don't be a fraidy-cat," Jasper challenged.

"Come with us, Adelaide."

Adelaide laughed. "Heck no! I haven't had a baby, and it makes *me* want to wet my pants. You guys go. I'll watch the girls."

With that, Jasper pulled Sophie away, faux kicking and screaming, and got in line with the next group. With the twins, Adelaide watched the two get seated.

From behind, the music tent played a seventies disco song. The roller coaster began, and the screeching noise of the wheels was drowned out by the music, and soon, the crowd around them began to sing. The twins, who'd climbed up on the metal barrier, belted along, and Adelaide found herself humming to the music.

And for the first time in a long time, she was at peace.

She didn't know what brought it on. Perhaps it was the knowledge that everything was all right at this moment. That Matt would be home soon. That she was watching a friend scream her head off on a roller coaster, that she was eating fair food, and was tapping her foot along to disco.

Perhaps this was enough, this peace. That even if she never became a mother, her life could be just as fulfilled and content as this moment, with a family that cared for her, with a body that was healthy enough to be out enjoying this night, with these little girls she loved like her own, and, yes, with the book club that she'd given life to.

She pocketed this feeling and promised herself to hold on to it as long as she could. Because her instincts also told her that trouble was brewing.

CHAPTER FORTY-SIX
Sophie

Sophie ended up needing to go to the bathroom after the kiddie roller coaster, and she left her girls with Adelaide and Jasper at the game tent. Walking swiftly, she crossed the park to the fair's only set of restrooms. The sun had set, and the music was in full swing. The dinner crowd had arrived, and she was starving.

There was a line for the ladies' room that snaked outside the little building. She followed it to the last person, an older woman who shifted from one foot to the other. "Damn."

"You're telling me," the woman said.

Sophie crossed her arms and looked up at the sky. She counted the stars, then sang along with the NSYNC song being blasted over the loudspeakers, all in the name of distraction. She should have known better than to have waited too long—it was a lesson she'd tried to impart to her girls. The moment one was desperate enough was exactly the time there would be a long line.

She heard a couple arguing. She turned to see a man and a woman behind a tent, mostly shrouded in darkness.

"We can't do this here," he said. "My wife's

literally in the bathroom, and she'll be out any second."

"You can't just walk away. What about me?" The woman's voice was shrill.

"You knew this was temporary. . . ."

Sophie couldn't hear the rest of the man's words, though he continued to speak. His profile and build were familiar, though she couldn't place where. He was holding the woman—shorter by a head, with a ponytail—by both shoulders. His tone was pleading.

Curious in the same way she frantically paged through the black moment in books, Sophie wandered to the space, her conversation with Adelaide earlier replaying itself in her head. What she was witnessing was none of Sophie's business, but she was drawn to it.

And with every step, the man's profile became clearer.

The man was Logan.

Please, God, no.

Sophie had put on a poker face for Adelaide earlier, but yes, Sophie had heard the rumors, too. That Logan was back early because he and another soldier had been inappropriate; adultery was suspected, though nothing could be proved. Even Jasper couldn't confirm it despite her inquiry. And she knew better than to push.

Sometimes, it was better not to know.

Because right now, seeing Logan with this

woman, touching her, looking into her eyes, Sophie realized that the rumors were true. If the two had just been friends, wouldn't they be conversing out in the open like everyone else? Would they be in a heated argument?

Sophie stepped on a soda can, and the noise drew the two people apart.

Shit.

There was no way out of this but through. Sophie pressed her lips together in what she hoped was a smile. "Hi. Logan?"

"Yeah?" he frowned.

She approached them, leaving the bright spotlight of the tents. "I'm Sophie Walden. From the neighborhood. My husband is Jasper Clemens."

The woman backed away. "I've gotta go." She turned without another word.

Logan's face broke into a smile, though it didn't quite make it to his eyes. "Oh, hey, it's nice to see you again."

"Yeah, welcome home." She crossed her arms. Her curiosity had flipped to protectiveness.

"Thanks." He mimicked her stance. "Regina should be back soon. And that was . . . someone I worked with."

She assessed him, though red flags waved in front of her eyes. Bullshit—that woman wasn't just a coworker. And Sophie was going to tell him that she knew. That she'd seen enough! And how could he be such a lying jerk?

But Sophie also envisioned Regina's expression at finding out that Sophie had not gone to her first, and thought twice.

She would have to speak to Regina first, and alone.

"Oh, hey, babe!" Logan raised his eyes to the space over Sophie's shoulder.

Sophie shut her eyes. She took a breath. She schooled her expression as she would with a vulnerable patient.

She turned. "Hey, Reggie!" Her voice sounded fake, but she went with it. "I was just in line for the bathroom and I saw Logan, and he was . . ." Her brain stuttered a step. "Waiting for you. I thought I would say hi."

Regina's expression was flat. "What were you guys talking about? It looked serious."

"Nothing, just asking how he was settling in." Sophie turned to Logan. "Right?"

"Yeah. And I was wondering where Sergeant Clemens was."

"And I was saying that he's . . . actually with the twins and Adelaide just on the other side. You guys should join us if you haven't eaten. We grabbed a picnic bench and everything." Sophie felt sweat beading on the back of her neck from the suspicion in Regina's eyes.

"We've already eaten," Regina said.

Sophie was desperate to lift the mood, to buy herself some time, to look less conspicuous.

"Did you end up reading this month's book club selection? The one that Kerry had to cancel?"

"Uh, no." Regina's face relaxed. "With redeployment and the third trimester, whenever I sit down, I end up falling asleep. I heard it was heartbreaking."

"It is. It's a nonfiction about the HeLa cells, which were taken from a Black woman and then grown for research, and yet, her descendants haven't received a dime. At the heart of it, the book's really about doing what's right and calling out the wrong things when it's necessary." She wasn't sure why that came out of her mouth, except that she felt a rush of protectiveness toward her friend.

Regina raised an eyebrow.

"Anyway, next book club is at my house. I'm sending out an email soon. But I've got to run. Seriously, my bladder." She leaned in to hug Regina, an overkill, but necessary. "Come join us at the picnic tables, by the game tent, if you can."

"Uh, sure."

Sophie rushed to the bathroom line, which miraculously had shrunk, and she heaved a sigh. She really could have messed things up back there. This was not about her; this was about her friend. Her pregnant friend.

She had to protect her, though she didn't know how to.

PART SEVEN

You can tell your story any way you damn well please. It's your solo.

—*The Sky Is Everywhere* by Jandy Nelson

CHAPTER FORTY-SEVEN
Adelaide

Present Day, Friday

What a difference forty-eight hours had made. On Friday morning, Adelaide was up at 9:00 a.m., feeling a million times better. Her energy had increased with more of Regina's home cooking, and her spirits lightened with Sophie's company. Though she still needed her pain meds, she'd worked up the energy to follow Genevieve around to make up for the days she'd been unwell, taking breaks as needed. This morning, she even put on some makeup and a little bit of lip gloss, and she looked forward to leaving the house, even if it was for her follow-up doctor's appointment.

Most importantly, she couldn't wait to celebrate her daughter's birthday, even if it would be an intimate affair.

Adelaide entered her walk-in closet. She reached up to the topmost shelf, croaking from the anticipation of pain, and grabbed a hatbox. She opened it to a teddy bear smooshed to fit. The fibers of its fur were the softest she'd ever felt, and she'd known that her baby girl would love it. She pressed on the paw of the bear, and it spoke—with Matt's voice.

When she finally arrived downstairs, close to 11:00 a.m., with the bear in the hatbox, she detected a frantic energy in the air, though nothing was amiss. Sophie was on the phone in the backyard, Genevieve playing just beyond her reach, and Regina was in the kitchen.

"Hey, look at all the food!" Adelaide looked over Regina's shoulder.

"Hey, mama. Since today's a special day and you're up and around, I thought I'd make a little extra. We can always freeze leftovers for later."

"You are the best! I have Genevieve's present all ready. She can open it when I get back."

"Oh, that's right. You have your appointment," Regina stated, not looking at her.

"Yep, at noon." She went to the sliding glass door and knocked on the glass.

Sophie turned and made a sign that she would bring Genevieve inside.

"I feel really good today," Adelaide said to Regina.

"That's great. Why not extend your field trip today? Take a walk after your appointment?"

"Yeah, maybe." Adelaide was getting a strange vibe from Regina but pushed it away. Whenever the woman cooked, she was in her own world. "I'll wait for Sophie in the living room. Might as well check emails."

She sat down in the small office area in the

living room and opened her laptop. It had been almost a week since she'd been online; she could just imagine the notifications on social media and unread emails.

She logged into her email first. One was from Missy Stanfield, one of her mommy friends. She was a real estate agent and Adelaide had staged a few homes for her, just for fun.

Subject: What do you think?

Hi Adelaide!

I know you're tied up with your surgery, and I sure hope I'm not bothering you while in the midst of recovering. Because if I am, then by all means you have to get off this email now, young lady. But if and when you are up to it, I'd love to follow up about what we discussed earlier, about you maybe working for me part-time? You were the first person I thought of. Give me a buzz whenever? I promise to only take a few minutes of your time! I still do want to stop by to bring over a present for Genevieve like I mentioned last week. I know you've got your best friends there, but I bet they can't make my cream puffs. I'm just saying!
xo,
Missy

Adelaide laughed. Missy always had a way about her. She didn't hide her ambition, and with her, Adelaide felt creative and energized. Unfortunately, Adelaide was also going to have to disappoint her. It didn't make sense for Adelaide to accept a job knowing she would eventually have to let it go. They were due to move after Matt returned from Germany, and preparing for a PCS was a full-time job.

At the thought, Adelaide's chest ached with what felt like heartburn. Her next thought was to shut down her negativity. Moving was an inevitability in the Army. But dang, did she love it here in Old Town. It was a nice change from all the small posts they'd lived in. She felt at home in the DC metro area, more than other places. In Old Town, she felt like she could blossom.

Was it normal to feel so young in your midthirties? She was just starting to feel good in her skin. Having to start somewhere new always put her on the outskirts, and with that came insecurity, over proving herself to others and sometimes to herself. And unless she knew someone from another duty station, making friends, even for an extrovert such as herself, was hard. It wasn't the superficial meet-and-greet moments that she worried about, but the tearing down of her walls, and the exposure of herself that rendered her vulnerable.

Would she allow herself to get close to people

this next time around? How much investment would she put into this community before having to pick up and start over elsewhere? It was a fuzzy line to toe.

She just wished sometimes . . .

She cut out the thought before it came to fruition. And instead, she pressed reply:

> Hi Missy,
> I'm doing well, thank you. But one of these days I'm going to have to tell you the entire surgical ordeal. I would love to see you, soon, and while I cannot have your cream puffs (much too rich for my blood, and not in a metaphorical way—my lack of a gallbladder means my belly just won't be able to tolerate all the delicious cream for a little while), I do want you to come over soon! As for the job offer . . . I'd like to chat about it in person.
> Best,
> Adelaide

Her reply came quickly:

> I bet we'll chat later. ;) Talk to you soon!
> M.

Adelaide pondered Missy's odd response.

The sound of fast-moving footsteps took her attention, and at the sight of her beautiful daughter entering the room, the rest of the world shrank in importance. Adelaide opened her arms to greet Genevieve, and her baby girl rushed into her arms. Genevieve felt bigger, heavier, and it sparked a sad nostalgia of time passing much too quickly for her taste. "Hello. Do you know what today is?"

Genevieve giggled, a little bit of drool pooling on the sides of her lips. "My birthday!"

"Yes, it is! Mommy just needs to go somewhere with Auntie Sophie, then I'll be back and we can have cake."

"Cake! Mr. Henry!"

"What?" She half laughed and looked up to her friends, who hovered by the living room doorway.

"Is that his name?" Sophie turned to Regina.

"Okay, okay, so I kind of showed her their Instagram feed." Regina tapped on her watch. "But more on that later. You all should go."

"Yep. You're right. Thank you." Adelaide heaved herself off the couch.

The doorbell rang.

"Lemme get that!" Regina jumped and spun away.

Once alone, Adelaide said quietly, "What the heck's up her butt? She's being really weird."

Sophie cackled.

That, too, was weird.

From the door came the sound of a man's deep voice, then the shuffle of feet. A figure appeared at the doorway, a person so familiar, though Adelaide could not place him. He was Black, in his forties. Fit. Clean-shaven and bald. He was wearing jeans and a gray long-sleeved Henley. He carried a small gift bag with one hand, and held a small plant in the other. A cactus.

Next to Adelaide, Sophie breathed out his name. "Jasper."

CHAPTER FORTY-EIGHT
Sophie

"What are you doing here, Jasper?" Sophie asked after she kissed him on the cheek. He'd handed her the cactus, and she gripped the side of the pot with force.

Was she dreaming?

"Now, if that isn't a welcome, I don't know what is," he said, face crestfallen. He turned to his left. "Adelaide."

Adelaide hugged Jasper. "Oh my God, I didn't recognize you right off the bat. Talk about a blast from the past. Matt's going to be so jealous when I tell him. Anyway"—she bent down and directed her daughter by the shoulders—"we're going to leave you two for a few minutes to catch up."

"Wait a sec." He stopped at seeing Genevieve. "Is this the little one?"

Sophie made introductions. "Yes, this is Genevieve. This is Mr. Jasper, my . . ."

She tripped up at how she should describe him. Husband, according to civil laws. Still simply a boyfriend according to the Army. To adults she introduced him as her partner, but to a two-year-old?

"I'm her baby daddy," he jumped in.

"Jasper!" She nudged him playfully with an elbow.

"It's true, isn't it? Well, this is for you, Miss Genevieve. Happy birthday." He bent down and handed her the gift bag.

"That's so sweet of you Jasper," Adelaide said. "Isn't it, Sophie?"

Sophie, still in shock, caught up after a beat. Jasper really *was* here. "Yes. So sweet."

"You're talking to a father of two girls who expected gifts whenever I came home from out of town. I knew not to arrive empty-handed."

"You've got ten minutes," Regina said stiffly. "Before Adelaide's appointment. Remember?"

Sophie nodded and watched the three go.

Jasper dipped his chin. "You don't look happy to see me."

His expression sent a twinge of regret through Sophie's heart, and she shook her head. "I'm sorry, I'm just surprised. Shocked." Belatedly, her body sprang awake, and she leaned in to hug him again. She felt his body soften toward hers.

"I was shocked, too, to receive your note," he said. "But I got here as soon as I could."

"Which note?"

"The one where you asked me to come."

She pulled away from him. "I did what?"

He frowned. "You sent me a letter, for me to come. Then Carmela insisted that I bring you a plant. She told me you had fallen in love with cacti so I picked one up at the garden center right off of I-95."

Carmela.

She threw her head back in laughter. "Did you send me a cactus in the mail?"

"No. Why would I do that?" Jasper read her expression. "Did she . . . Were we just tricked?"

"I think we were." She sighed and gestured to the couch and sat next to him. She was surprised to find her heart trilling like a hummingbird. She was nervous. "That daughter of ours."

"I think she's worried about us. And I don't blame her. I'm worried about us." He shook his head, his fingers linked tightly together. "The sporadic texts. The avoidance. Even that kiss. It didn't feel . . . I don't know . . ."

A flash of what their real kisses had been like popped into Sophie's head. They'd started with a yearning in her gut that would spill out into an insatiable need. She couldn't get enough of him. But in the last few months, she hadn't been able to put her finger on this sadness she felt—nor could she remember the last time she'd kissed him with the same fervor.

"Sophie, I remember a time when we used to greet each other at the door. Something was there, between us. An excitement."

She sniffed a rebuttal, then said, "It wasn't always so easy for me to greet you at the door, because you left more often, and for longer chunks of time. I'm not saying you didn't make your own sacrifices, but being the one left behind was tough."

"It wasn't fair, I know."

"It wasn't about being fair—you're getting it wrong." She took a breath. "To be honest, I kind of enjoyed when you were gone. Not because I didn't miss you, but because I was able to become who I wanted to be. It was only me, and my schedule, and the girls. When you were gone, I took my dreams and my goals and ran with them. Even after we left Millersville and you stayed on active duty, I was fine with it. But now, with retirement, it just feels different. I loved our life, but now I wonder how much more there is out there."

"Oh, Sophie." Tears sprang to his eyes.

"I love you, Jasper. With all my heart. We never needed a ring or a piece of paper. I love you, and I know you love me. But I feel restless, and with you getting the job you always wanted . . . God, I am so proud of you—"

"But it all doesn't mean a thing without you."

She offered her hand then, and he took it. She padded her finger across his knuckles, and her heart was speared with pain. This man was crying, and the only other time he had ever cried was when their twins were born. He had bawled the moment they were brought to the warmers and intermittently until they were discharged from the hospital.

The truth dawned on Sophie. She'd worried him. She'd hurt him while she was in her own head. "This crossroads took me by surprise. I didn't know what to do with all this stuff in my head and in my chest, and when this opportunity came up, to help with Adelaide, the only thing I wanted to do was to get some space, to think."

"And now that you have? Thought, I mean. What do you want to do?" he asked.

"I . . . don't know. But I have loved being away. This week, and looking back at our life, your career especially, I realized I loved learning about new places. I really liked to travel. Now that the girls are months from college, and you're also done with the Army, the load on my shoulders has lifted. We were so good, Jasper. Good all the way through. On the narrow road of parenting. We hovered over those girls. We gave them the best example. And now I want to be bad. I want to be spontaneous, run away sometimes. I just didn't realize it until I got here."

"Sophie, if you want me to quit this job, I will."

She shook her head. "We've always done what we wanted in our hearts. This isn't even an ultimatum."

Jasper tugged her hand. "Just as you have done for me, I go where you go, Soph. Bad or good, temporary or permanent. Overseas or here. We will work it out. If you still want me."

"I have never not wanted you," she said. "This was never about not loving you or wanting you or needing you. I'm sorry, Jasper."

He looked down for a beat. "I admit, I was really mad you left for this trip. Then, the more I thought about it, I remembered that there were nights when I lived like a bachelor, without having to make sure that our girls were okay. My trips and my deployments put you in a situation where you had to do it all. You've had to face a lot of decisions on your own. The least I could do was to give you space to think, even if it was killing me."

"Thank you for saying that."

He nodded. "But, Soph, do you remember what I told Carmela that one time she ran away from her classroom when she was five?"

Sophie thought back, pre-Millersville, to her kindergarten girls, who had been separated into two different classes. Carmela had been upset by the arrangement. One day, she simply walked out of the classroom when her teacher's back was turned, marched to Olivia's classroom, and demanded to be let in. "You said she could go anywhere she wanted. She just needed to tell someone." She eyed Jasper. "But I did tell you."

He considered her a moment. "Sophie, we only made a couple of promises to each other. We said that we would always talk to each other, and that we would tell each other what we needed. We can't go back on those promises."

"I know. I'm sorry." Humbled, it was her turn for tears—he was right. Their vow was simply based on a promise of communication. Nothing more, nothing less. And despite her own transition, there he was, supporting her need to figure out who she was in this second half of her life. He'd understood that her leaving was never about running from her responsibilities. "I love you."

"I love you, too." He tilted her chin up, gazed intently into her eyes. "Always, Sophie. Before children, after children, young, middle, and old age. Through all the changes." He leaned forward and kissed her gently on the lips, and the need that Sophie had thought had disappeared rose from inside her. It surged through her body, and she felt every bit of his love to the tips of her fingers and toes.

She felt a small hand tapping her on the back. Then, Jasper's lips stiffened. Sophie opened her eyes.

"You're kissing," a sweet voice said.

Sophie turned to Genevieve, who was smiling. Then, her eyes trailed to the kitchen door, where Adelaide and Regina stood, with sheepish expressions.

CHAPTER FORTY-NINE
Regina

Regina spied out the front windows as Adelaide, Sophie, and Jasper climbed into Adelaide's car.

Holy hell.

"What you lookin' at?" Genevieve said behind her.

"Your mommy, Aunt Sophie, and a blast from the past." She did a double take. Genevieve had a Tupperware bowl on her head.

"Mommy's out the window?"

"Mm-hmm. What a strange and unnerving day."

When she'd opened the door to Jasper, Regina felt as if she were teleported back in time à la *Back to the Future*. For a moment, she'd lost herself in the space-time continuum, and they were in Millersville. And in her shock, she had forgotten that she had a grudge against Jasper and welcomed him into the home without hesitation.

It wasn't until she closed the door behind them that reality hit.

How many times over the years had Regina envisioned a moment when she could give Jasper a piece of her mind? More than she cared to share. And she'd had the opportunity, only to let it pass her by. Her guard was lowered because

she'd accepted Sophie's presence and importance in Adelaide's life. Because despite their
squabbles this week, she and Sophie had worked
well together.

Regina walked to the staircase and sat on the
first step. She needed a breath, a moment.

Genevieve sat on the step next to her. "You
sleepy?"

"No."

"You need a hug?" But Genevieve didn't wait
for an answer. She leaned against Regina and
stuck her pudgy arms out only to reach halfway
across Regina's body, grunting in effort.

It was exactly the hug Regina needed. She
leaned down and pressed a kiss against Genevieve's forehead. "Thank you, sweet girl."

"Y'welcome."

But Regina also needed strength, someone to
bolster her, to remind her to keep vigilant and
angry. So she took out her phone and dialed the
only other person who was directly associated
with The Fight.

Logan answered on the first ring. "Hey. This is
a surprise. Is Miko's phone off? I'm grilling, and
Miko's in the tent. Miko—" he yelled.

"Actually, I wanted to talk to you."

"Oh." In the short silence, she heard a wood-
pecker. "What'd I do?"

"Nothing, this time anyway." She half laughed.
"I've something to tell you."

"What's up."

"When I arrived here about a week ago, I found out that there was someone else who was invited."

"Uh . . . did you want me to guess?" Logan chuckled.

"Yes, goodness. Anyway, it's Sophie."

"Whoa."

"And guess who's here now."

"Um . . ."

"Jasper."

Something sizzled in the background, and it filled the silence.

"Hello?" she asked.

"I'm . . ."

"I know, right?"

"He seemed okay?"

She frowned. She hadn't expected for that to come out of his mouth. "Y-yeah. He's fine. He's retired now. But anyway. You don't sound pissed."

"Are *you* pissed?"

"I . . ." Next to her, Genevieve stood with a flourish and toddled toward the living room. Regina followed a step behind, and with the brief distraction, thought twice. "I don't know how I feel, except weird."

"It kind of brings it all back, doesn't it?"

"It does." Still more silence.

"Adelaide had some guts."

Regina laughed. "I know. I was so mad, I even walked out until . . ." She paused just before she rolled right into her story about meeting Henry for the first time. "It's been a week."

"So what do you need from me?"

The question snapped her back from her previously comfortable state. A reminder that Logan did not comfort. For him, it was about who or what someone needed, a transaction.

As if sensing her change in mood, Genevieve got tired of the living room and went to the kitchen, to her standing easel. "I guess I wanted to discuss it, with someone who was there."

"But there's nothing to discuss. We're divorced already. What more is there?"

"God, Logan."

"I'm just saying. We're years past this," Logan said. "I've said sorry, and I'm doing my part to make it okay with my son. I'm not sure what you want to discuss."

"Never mind. You're right. There's nothing to discuss." It was easier for Regina to quit the conversation. They were exes, not friends. "Miko doing okay?"

"Yes. He caught a fish earlier today."

"That's great."

"Yeah, it made it easier for me to tell him that I'm PCS'ing this summer."

"What?" Regina's voice echoed in the kitchen, so loud that Genevieve peeped from behind the easel to look at her. Logan moving was out of the blue. "You've only been in Georgia for a year."

"It's to the Pentagon."

"Here?"

"Yeah. Funny, right? Actually, not funny, because I wish I didn't have to be away from Miko. But the job's a good one to have right before I retire, and there's a civilian job I have my eye on that I can probably slide into after. After all, I can't stop working—we've got a long way before our boy's through college."

And this was why, despite her annoyance with Logan, Regina had done all she could to keep father and son together. Logan took this responsibility seriously. "If this is a good move for you, for our son, then congrats. I just know that he's going to miss you. . . ."

"Would you consider . . ." He heaved a breath.

Coming? Regina finished the sentence in her head. But Logan had gone silent, and so had she, and her brain was now running down a path that had suddenly unrolled in front of her. There was nothing defined about its destination, but she felt herself taking steps.

Her brain mulled the facts: She was already closing down the shop in six months. Logan was moving to the DC area. She'd always wanted to be stationed here. She loved the area now. And there was Henry.

Henry.

She was interrupted by Genevieve's singing.

"It's a berfday! My berfday!"

The Tupperware bowl, still on Genevieve's head, was visible over the top of the easel and it rocked while she wiggled her hips. Like she was having a one-person party.

Except there was an actual party today.

Which Regina was supposed to be preparing for.

"Oh my God. I was so caught up. I have got to go."

"Okay?"

"We'll talk later. Tell Miko I love him." She hung up. Then she texted all those who were involved with the party: Henry, Missy, and Sophie. Coast is clear! Come on over!

Finally, she sent a final text to her business manager, Alexis: Would it be bonkers for me to move the business?

CHAPTER FIFTY
Adelaide

Adelaide's anticipated hour at her doctor's for her follow-up had taken only fifteen minutes. She'd received a good bill of health, and she was ready to celebrate Genevieve's birthday, now with an extra person, Jasper, in attendance. But Sophie had insisted that they go for a short walk to show Jasper a little bit of Old Town. At first, Adelaide resisted, but as soon as she stepped onto the cobblestone sidewalk, her spirits lifted.

While Adelaide still had a winter coat on, the sun was warm against her face. She felt the vitamin D seep into her skin. She stopped to admire the newest shop window dressings on Burg Street. She took in the sounds of the neighborhood as it relaxed into its Friday afternoon vibe.

She was sitting at one of the Burg Street benches, waiting for Jasper and Sophie, who had decided to grab an ice cream cone, when she heard her name. Turning, she saw Missy coming down the street, with an elegantly wrapped gift. She was dressed in yoga pants and a quarter zip, with soft fuzzy boots on her feet. She was glowing, cheeks pink, blond hair coming out of its ponytail. "Hey!"

"You look great!" Missy's eyes scanned Adelaide from top to bottom. "How was your appointment?"

"It went well. You off to a party?"

"Uh, yes." Her smile tightened, and she took a seat. "I was just thinking of you. Are you able to chat now?"

"Um, sure . . . I'm waiting on my friend Sophie." Yet, with how Missy crossed one leg over the other, as if to settle in, Adelaide didn't have much of a choice.

"So, it's been years of planning and saving, but I'm veering from my original role as a Realtor to flipping homes."

"I . . . I know." This wasn't news to her, but Missy plowed on and explained her life story and her newest business venture. Adelaide said nothing because it would be rude, and quite frankly, it was nice enough to be outside and chatting.

But as the minutes wore on, Adelaide glanced at her phone, at the time. Sophie and Jasper were taking forever.

"So," Missy continued, "I need someone with an eye for both style and the bottom line to design these homes, and I want it to be you. It's only one house to flip for now, and we would be learning together. I would pay you fairly for your time. But here's the new news: I know that I had said that you could take your time, but I'd actually need the answer in the next couple of weeks."

Adelaide straightened, gingerly. "You need an answer that quickly? I . . ." Her first instinct was to scream *Yes yes yes!* The mental image of her putting design and colors and textures together to create beauty sent a feeling of joy through her. "Genevieve *is* starting part-time preschool in the fall."

But could she do it?

A body rushed up to them. "Hey, ladies!"

"Janie!" Adelaide waved. Janie Woo had her son, Malcolm, by the hand. She pushed her plate-sized sunglasses up to her head. The woman leaned in to give both Adelaide and Missy a kiss on the cheek. "What are you up to?"

"I was just headed into the toy store and . . ." Her eyes widened.

"You're headed to a party, too?" Something didn't sit right in Adelaide's gut. Two of her mommy-group friends buying presents the same day, for a party that Genevieve wasn't invited to?

"Um, no?" Janie said.

Adelaide shook her head, confused. "Did I miss an invitation while I was down for the count?"

"Oh, no!" Missy squeezed her forearm. "She and I, totally separate gift reasons. Right?"

"Right! Anyway, I have to run. Oh my God, I need to use the bathroom all of a sudden. You know how it is—mom bladder! Love you both.

You look fabulous, Adelaide. I can't wait to have you back to full swing." As if given a boost of adrenaline, Janie kissed the both of them goodbye and hustled into the store.

"That was odd," Adelaide said, more to herself.

"You know Janie. She's everywhere." Missy coughed. "So, about my proposal. I know we're not in a boardroom or anything. But I think we'd be great together."

"You do know I'll be leaving, probably in a year."

"I understand."

"And I wanted to be a stay-at-home mom to Gen. All of the work I've done for you thus far has generally been when I can get literally the only sitter I trust . . ." Then, realizing that this part wasn't Missy's job to figure out but hers, she said, "But I'll get you an answer soon."

Two weeks. In two weeks Adelaide would have to find a more reliable sitter. And she'd need to be at 100 percent. And she'd have to talk to Matt about it.

"Awesome. Well, I've got to go, and so do you," Missy said.

They both stood from the bench. Adelaide raised an eyebrow. "What do you mean I need to go?"

"Uh . . . because you . . . need to lie down." She leaned in for a hug and patted Adelaide on the back. "I'll see you. Okay?"

"Okay."

But as she watched Missy hike up the road, she caught sight of Henry, with a tall box in his hands, darting down the street. Both going in the direction of her home.

She texted Sophie: Where are you guys? I'm ready to head back.

Something was definitely up.

CHAPTER FIFTY-ONE
Regina

June 2012

Regina arrived at the clinic for her thirty-six-week appointment and clutched her yoga-ball belly after her short day's work. Her uniform was feeling tight, her pants' elastic band cutting off her circulation. She was officially over the pregnancy—gone was the third-trimester euphoria. Her once almost manic energy that compelled her to scrub the baseboards was replaced by an all-time record exhaustion.

She was sweating just thinking of it.

Regina was given a clipboard of forms to complete, and she sat on a plastic chair in the crowded waiting room. She placed her bag on the empty chair next to her, for Logan, who was on his way, and she worked on the forms methodically.

But Regina's mind wasn't on the page. She was thinking of her friends who she hadn't seen in about a week, since the festival. During previous appointments, Sophie and Adelaide had been by her side, even at her first ultrasounds, filling exam rooms with banter and laughter. Her current surroundings were the complete opposite.

Adelaide had been right about priorities shifting, but Regina hadn't realized that with it would come melancholy. Grief.

A tightening began on the underside of her belly, and Regina shifted in her seat. Braxton-Hicks, she was sure of it—she'd been having the false contractions for a couple of weeks but without any real pain. She was probably dehydrated, not to mention sleepy from insomnia that had kicked in full force.

The stomp of boots down the hallway snapped Regina out of her thoughts, and she looked up, a smile ready on her face for Logan. But instead of her husband, it was Lieutenant Gabby Cole, her current work-cubby mate, also in uniform.

"Hey!" she said. "Appointment, I see?"

"Yep, an ultrasound. How about you?"

She held up a green file folder in her hand. "Ophthalmologist. Yours is way more exciting than mine. You alone?"

"No, my husband will be here soon."

"Ah, you sure?" An eyebrow raised.

Regina laughed at this. What an odd question to ask her. "Yeah."

"Oh, I thought I saw him heading off post. Blue pickup truck, right?" She hiked a thumb above her shoulder, then her gaze dropped. "Or maybe it wasn't him? Anyway, I'm actually late. See you at work. I hope things . . . work out well. In there. The ultrasound, I mean."

She frowned at the other woman's skittishness. "Thanks. I'll see you when I get out of here."

Regina stared back at her phone, faceup on the chair next to her. Not a single notification from her husband, despite her having reminded him of her appointment before he walked out the door that morning.

She sent another text: **Hey, did you forget my appointment? In five minutes.**

She bit her lip, unable to shake the odd vibe pricking her senses. She wished that with all the technology of these phones, there was a way to log into Logan's phone to see exactly what he was doing.

She shook her head at her silliness. Doubts and suspicions were unlike her, though they were rearing their ugly heads. The other day, she glanced over at his phone when it buzzed in the middle of the night, and it ended up being his mother, which was not unusual. And then Regina had been on him about his schedule lately. She often wondered who exactly he was going out with.

She was being ridiculous, because Logan had also shown he was trying to change. He'd come home early from work when in the past he'd worked overtime. He'd checked in on her throughout her day, just to say hi. The other night, he'd scrubbed the house from top to bottom, and then run out to get groceries, and had insisted she sit when she was perfectly capable of taking out the garbage.

This was a new side to him, a softer side, a more thoughtful side. Was he overcompensating to make up for the drama? Yes, of course—she wasn't a fool. But she believed *him,* though she was still bothered by whoever had turned against him. Was it someone in the neighborhood? Was it someone in the unit? She'd discounted Adelaide and Sophie. Sophie, who'd acted weird at the festival but who texted her often to ask about her pregnancy. And Adelaide, who texted her about great baby toys and organizational strategies. Regina, at least, knew that with them, she was safe.

The other two hadn't brought up the rumors but Regina didn't mind because she didn't want to discuss them, either—it was humiliating, with everyone connected somehow. Her and Logan's problems needed to remain theirs, solely.

But no matter what, these women were her sisters through it all.

The door squeaked opened across the way, and Ms. Samson, her midwife, walked out, wearing scrubs. Behind her was a couple: the pregnant woman was in uniform, the man in civilian clothes. She had a strip of ultrasound pictures in her hand, and her face was flushed with a definite glee. The mood was contagious and put a smile on Regina's face.

"I'm ready for you in the other room, Lieutenant Castro. Is there anyone with you today?"

"Yes, my husband, but I think he's just running late."

"No problem. When he checks in at the front desk, they can bring him to this room. I'll have the nurse hook you up to the monitors so we can check your baby's heartbeat and check for contractions, and I'll return and check you out."

She texted this information to Logan, and while she removed her uniform top and draped it on the chair and sat down on the reclining examination table, she patiently waited for her husband to answer back. A nurse entered and took her vital signs, then motioned for her to lie down so she could get hooked up to the stress test machine.

Regina gripped her phone in her hand and took a deep breath as a puddle of warmth spilled on top of her belly. She shut her eyes for a brief moment and calmed herself. She had read that babies felt all the feelings of their mother, and Regina refused to pass on her suspicions to her child.

The nurse guided the transducer over her belly in search of the baby's heartbeat.

"Is everything okay?" Regina asked.

"Absolutely." She moved the transducer to the right side of Regina's belly, and smiled. "Your baby's active." Then suddenly the heartbeat thudded on the monitor. "There he or she is. Did you find out the sex?"

"No, we want it to be a surprise."

The nurse applied a second transducer toward the top of her bump to detect contractions. "All right. I'll be back in about fifteen minutes."

Regina stared up at the ceiling, at the square tiles and the tiny holes. Where was her husband? She checked her phone again, as if she hadn't been clutching it all this time, and then tested the volume. Anger zinged through her, then concern, and then suspicion.

She pushed it out of her head. *There's nothing to be suspicious about, Regina.* Still, she sent another text to Logan: **Where are you?**

And then, as if her friends knew that she was in a state of confusion and frustration, a text flew in.

Sophie
I hope your appointment goes well today.

Thank you!

Adelaide
OMG, I almost forgot! Matt's flight is landing tomorrow, and it's all I can think about. Good luck today.

Sophie
So excited for you, Ad.

YAY for redeployment!

Adelaide
I took bets. Everyone says it's a girl.
Only one person said it's going to be
a boy.

Sophie
That one person is me. C'mon, I'm
right about these things. I've got the
touch.

<3

Regina's eyes watered—goodness, her emotions were everywhere. She was grateful for these women, that they had intuited to text. She took a deep breath to calm herself.

Sophie
What does Logan think? Boy or girl?

Oh God, Regina actually didn't know.

We just pray that the baby
is going to be healthy.

Sophie
Aw, I like that. Priorities.

Adelaide
I still think she's a girl.

Regina heard footsteps and the sound of voices, but none were Logan's. Her mood crashed.

> Gotta go. Not supposed to be using my cell phone.

The door jiggled and Ms. Samson came in and looked at the monitor. "Baby looks great on the monitor, but it seems like your body is trying to gear up for labor."

"Really?" She turned her head toward the machine, where Ms. Samson lengthened the narrow strip of paper.

"Contractions are coming every three minutes. You're not feeling it?"

"I am. They feel like tiny cramps." She put her hands on her belly, keeping clear of the equipment, and, yep, it was tightening. "That is a trip."

"We might need to admit you if we see cervical changes."

"Okay." She watched Ms. Samson type information into the computer, and her heart sped up. Was her bag packed? Did she need to do anything at work? Oh God, she hadn't shaved her legs in days. She had been planning the hair-removal ordeal this weekend complete with pedicure so she wouldn't frighten everyone in the delivery room.

Then, she felt a gush of warmth between her legs. "Um."

"If you're in the latent stage of labor, we could also send you home, where you'll be much more comfortable—"

"Ms. Samson?"

"Yes?"

"I . . ." *God, Logan, where are you?* Her belly tensed, much harder than in the past, and—"I feel something, down there."

Ms. Samson's eyes widened. "Well, let's see." She lifted the blanket. "Ah, it looks like you're definitely staying. We'll have to swab to make sure, but I think your water broke." She patted Regina's knee. "Did you get a hold of your husband?"

"No, but . . ." She felt like a fool having to explain. Because she didn't have an explanation. What would she say? That her husband simply forgot, and apparently didn't know how to answer his texts or phone calls? She stuttered an excuse. "H-he'll be here soon."

"Great." Ms. Samson continued the barrage of mundane questions, which Regina was thankful for, because focusing on her answers kept her from crying. This was supposed to be the happiest time in her life, but she felt lonelier than ever.

CHAPTER FIFTY-TWO
Adelaide

T minus twenty-four hours until Matt's arrival, and Adelaide was in her apartment enjoying a glass of rosé. The house was clean, the menu planned for the rest of the week. She and Matt's block leave plans were all set—they were taking a trip to Sedona, his way: camping. While her choice had been a Greek vacation with the best their money could buy, at this point, any time with her husband would suffice.

In the last two weeks, Adelaide's life had gone from bustling to quiet. With two of her best friends' spouses returning, her daily social calendar was as stark as Texas on a blistering summer day.

Not to say that events weren't happening. All around her, the majority of the neighborhood had awakened. With troops slowly returning, though not exactly back at work because of block leave, the neighborhood streets teemed with people. Families were catching up, taking walks, having informal barbecues in backyards, gathering under porches and at the playground. Through the evening, the sounds of laughter permeated the air. It was like summer vacation for adults.

Adelaide was happy for these families. She loved to hear them celebrate; she relished in the happy smiles, and watched nostalgically as couples held hands.

She just wished it was her turn.

And tomorrow, it would be. There were only a few spouses left who were expecting their loved ones, which meant a small formation, an informal drop-off. A bummer for her husband, who liked a little bit of fanfare. Who didn't, when they hadn't seen their family in months?

She had finally cracked open *The Sky Is Everywhere* for book club at Sophie's next week. At the moment, snuggled into her couch with a blanket over her legs, with Scout lying over the covers at her feet, she'd rounded out the first twenty pages. The book's content was heavy; it was about death, and offered a sharp contrast to what she was feeling. But she was connecting with the seventeen-year-old main character, Lennie, who lost her sister. She empathized that changing tides always brought a little bit of grief.

This was why she loved book club—it required her to read books she wouldn't have picked herself. This year, she and her friends had read seven books together, exceeding her expectations. She might not have a child but she had book club. That was her baby. Her offspring, and she would forever hold that as her legacy.

The doorbell rang, and she frowned as she put

down her book. In the front foyer, where she had a mirror hanging, she checked her hair and her lipstick, puckering and then wiping the lipstick from under her lip. She opened the door and stuck her head out. Through the grate was Sophie.

"Hey!" Adelaide pressed the buzzer.

Sophie was free of children.

"Where are my babies? Are they okay?"

"With their father." She grinned.

Adelaide pressed her palm to her forehead. "I keep forgetting!"

"Isn't it weird? Honestly, I almost took them with me and then remembered that I can rely on someone else."

"Well, don't just stand there." She opened the door, wide. "What's up?"

"You're coming with me."

"Where are we going?"

"The hospital." Sophie's face fell. "You haven't seen the text traffic?"

"What?" Adelaide rushed to where her phone was plugged in and realized that she'd left it on silent. Her fingers couldn't seem to work fast enough on the buttons. "Damn wine."

"Forget the phone. Regina's water broke. C'mon."

"Oh my God!" Adelaide rushed to her boots next to her hallway tree. "Are we allowed in? Did she say?"

"She texted that she can't find Logan. So it's going to have to be us until he gets there."

Once both her feet were snuggly in her shoes, she looked at Sophie, and for a moment they both didn't speak. Understanding passed between them. Matt had continued to be tight-lipped despite Adelaide's curiosity, but it was becoming more evident there was some truth to her suspicions.

In the car, finally, Sophie spoke up, though her voice shook. Her face was wrinkled into a disturbed expression. "I've got something to admit. I don't know who to talk to. And everyone I trust is involved somehow," she began.

"This doesn't sound good."

Sophie shook her head.

"Christ on a cracker." Adelaide leaned back in her seat. Maybe she should have had more wine.

"I witnessed something. Something that could be innocent, or . . . not. Something that I might have had suspicions of but did not believe until I saw it with my very own eyes. I don't want to name names, Adelaide."

"Okay. But what did you see?" Adelaide asked. "But before you start, put on your seat belt." She was stalling, because whatever Sophie had to say was ultimately in confidence. Then again, there were ethics involved. Friendship ethics, Army ethics, and the fact that secrets never remained so.

Sophie put on her seat belt, then started the car. She backed out of the space. "I saw one of our friends' spouses in an intimate conversation with another woman."

"Oh God."

"I saw it." Sophie clutched the steering wheel. "At the festival, while waiting in line for the bathroom. The husband was there, with another woman. They were arguing, about ending things. About not wanting to end things. I wanted to tell him that what he did was wrong, because his wife was already . . . in a *state*. I went up to the couple, and they were jumpy. The guy was shaking like a leaf. He knew I saw. Then, the wife arrived."

"Oh my God."

"But by then the other woman was gone."

Finally, all the pieces came together for Adelaide in an undeniable fit. Why Logan was home early, and why Matt refused to talk about the situation. The swirl of rumors that followed Logan at redeployment. How Regina had pulled away, just ever so slightly.

"Here's my question," Sophie continued. "Do I tell this woman, my friend, first? Do I tell her and be the person to ruin their marriage? Would I want her to find out from someone else? Because this thing, this indiscretion, is all made worse by the fact that . . ."

Adelaide read her mind. "It's not over between them."

"No, I don't think so," Sophie said.

Adelaide's foot tapped of its own accord as anger built inside her. How could Logan? How could he do this to his pregnant wife? Did he know how lucky they were to be starting a family? "Well, we can't just sit by and . . ."

"But how am I supposed to tell her? And should I even? Is this my business? And this woman . . . she's going to kill the messenger."

Adelaide now looked ahead at the busy street, packed nose to tail waiting for entrance through Fort Fairfax's gate. "We're stuck," Adelaide declared. "In more ways than one."

CHAPTER FIFTY-THREE
Sophie

When Sophie and Adelaide arrived at the labor and delivery ward, the secretary stationed in front of the locked double doors directed them to the waiting room. "We have increased security here. Labor coach or significant other only, with identity bands."

"She just called us," Sophie said, taking the lead since the hospital was her arena. "She's alone—could you double-check, please?"

Without fanfare, the woman picked up the phone. And while Adelaide wrung her fingers together, Sophie made sure that she kept the smile on her face. The ward secretary was the key to the L & D world; that person held the power to open the locked unit.

The secretary turned in her chair, presumably to speak without being spied upon. After a few moments, she spun back around and hung up the phone. "I'm sorry. They want privacy at this time."

"What does that mean? Does that mean she's in labor?" Sophie asked.

"And wait a minute, did you say 'they'? She's not alone?" Adelaide interjected.

"I'm not at a liberty to say otherwise. Perhaps one of you can call her."

"We did call her. She's not answering." Adelaide raised her voice. "Can we get her room number, at least? Don't you have a board back there with their names?" She got on her tiptoes.

"Ma'am!" The secretary stood.

Sophie grabbed Adelaide by the elbow. The last thing they needed was for the secretary to call the MPs. "C'mon, tiger, let's go."

Thank goodness, her friend followed, and they reconvened near the elevators.

"So I guess she's okay?" Adelaide asked, taking out her phone. "It doesn't look like she texted, though."

Sophie had an idea. "Here, turn on your camera." Adelaide had a new iPhone 4 with a camera that was unbelievably sharp compared to her BlackBerry. "Let's take a picture together." They snapped a selfie. "Go ahead and send it."

"Okay. I texted her and told her we're here," Adelaide said.

"Let's wait a second to see what she says."

They commandeered seats in the packed waiting room, where the tension was thick with worried family members. Still, after thirty minutes, there was no return text.

"What do we do?" Adelaide asked.

"We should just go home."

The ride back to the apartments was long despite

being only a short five miles, the car filled with silence. All the while, Sophie worried for Regina. Even single active-duty soldiers who were in labor had company, either by their choice, or assigned by the unit—a woman should have support in every step of the baby birthing process.

It physically pained her that she couldn't be there, at this moment. Alongside that pain was anger, at Logan.

When she dropped off Adelaide at her apartment, Sophie asked, "What do we do? About the conundrum I'm in . . . with that couple?"

"I don't know."

"What would you do?"

Adelaide shrugged. "I'm stumped, too. Let's think about it. We can't be rash."

"Okay."

After they said goodbye, Sophie headed home. She entered her apartment and went straight to make herself a cup of chamomile tea, in the hopes it would give her the clarity she needed to unload this guilt. At the counter she felt arms around her waist, and she girded herself to keep from jumping. It was Jasper, of course, and it was silly to be startled, but she'd gotten used to not being touched so intimately. Sure, she was always ready for the kid tackle, but she was still reacclimatizing to having her man at home.

But the next second, she melted into his arms,

especially as he kissed her on the back of the neck, all the while being heckled by their girls from their bedroom.

"Aren't you all supposed to be sleeping?" Sophie said as she turned to face Jasper. She wrapped her arms around his neck. She needed this hug, to help lift the weight she was carrying.

"I didn't want to go to bed without you."

They were still in the honeymoon phase of reunion, and she was intent on enjoying it to its fullest. Soon she would be tired of the laundry on the floor, and him forgetting that the dishes were his to load, too. There was more to catch up on, like the nitty-gritty of his deployment not covered in their emails or phone calls, things said in the dark that couldn't be repeated.

"You okay?" he asked. "How's Regina?"

"Okay, I hope?"

He frowned. "What does that mean?"

Sophie realized her faux pas. "I'm sorry. I'm sure she's fine. No need to call the cavalry."

"Infantry, babe."

"That's what I meant." She grinned. "We couldn't get in to see her, which means she's either in labor or just had her baby. I'm sure she'll call soon."

"All right. Well, I'm glad you're home because"—he glanced over his shoulder—"can we talk?"

Sophie's sixth sense rang a bell so loud that she

448

blinked repeatedly at him, to steady herself. His language the last few days had been of feelings and emotions. They'd talked about their future, their children's lives. His hopes for them, and of building a life together. There had been no real talk of work. "Aren't we talking now?"

"It's about our plans."

She took a step back. It was a purposeful move, to remind herself that she could stand on her own two feet. Because she could sense that what he was going to say was going to rock her world.

"I had a physical today."

"Jasper?"

"It's . . . nothing."

"If it were nothing, then you would have already said it."

"Okay, okay." He leaned back against the counter. "The doc found something. A lump. In my testicle."

Sophie watched as his Adam's apple bobbed. "Cancer?"

"I don't know yet. I have an MRI next week."

She threw her arms around his waist. "Oh God."

"Soph." He pushed her away, gently. He was asking her to be strong with his eyes. "But if I do. Have it, I mean. I can't do what I promised. I can't get out. I won't. The health care, the life insurance. The girls and you."

"I don't care about that. I only care about you,"

Sophie said, definitively, scooping up all the strength in her being. She changed out her partner-hat for her nurse-hat. To her surprise, her voice emerged without any trace of fear. "If this is cancer, we stay in and we will get you well."

CHAPTER FIFTY-FOUR
Regina

The next morning in the hospital room Regina was awakened by the sound of knocking. "Come in," she said reflexively, while pressing her hand against her cheek. Her eyes darted about her surroundings. She was, momentarily, discombobulated. She was lying in a quiet and dark room, free of monitors and machines, and at her bedside table was her copy of *The Sky Is Everywhere*, a tray of food, and a bottle of sparkling apple cider. Then she looked down to her belly, which was decidedly no longer taut and round.

With this recalibration, her joy was renewed. She was a mommy! Last night had been painful and confusing, full of tears and a crying baby.

Closely trailing was the realization that her body ached, everywhere.

She sat up gingerly, to see Sophie come in with a basket and balloons. "Hey."

"Hey, mama." Sophie set down the basket and leaned down and hugged the top part of Regina's body. Sophie's giddiness could be heard in the shake of her voice. "Congratulations. How are you feeling?" She stood and looked around the room. "Is the baby in the nursery?"

Regina nodded, parched still. "Just to be checked out."

Sophie perched by her legs. "Look at you. You're beautiful."

"I don't feel beautiful." She pushed her hair back, though she knew her ponytail was trashed. "Thank you, though."

"What did you name him?"

"Logan Michael. We're giving him the nickname Miko."

"Miko. I love it." Sophie peeked at Regina's bedside chart, which happened to be hanging on the footboard.

"Are you checking out my paperwork?"

"Maybe." Sophie grinned. "I want to make sure you're set up well. Also, Adelaide—"

"I know she's busy with reunion. She texted, actually, to let me know, too. I think the buses should be there right now." Regina flushed. She had a lot to explain about yesterday. "I'm sorry I didn't let you all come visit yesterday."

"You don't have to mention it. You were in labor."

Regina winced. "Right, but when you got here, I wasn't in major labor yet. It's just . . . it's just that Logan and I had to work something out. To be honest, we got into a fight."

"Are you guys okay?" Sophie's face sported a frown.

Regina jumped in with her answer. "Oh, much

better. I think I was just anxious and I felt a little out of control. . . . Anyway . . ." Her voice trailed off at this partial truth. The rest of the story was that she hadn't wanted her friends to see her so angry at Logan.

"Well, I'm here now, and can stay to help out for as long as you need. Like if Logan needs a night to himself, I don't mind taking a shift."

Regina exhaled a breath. The last twenty-four hours had been stressful, mostly occupied with her labor, enjoying Miko, and attempting to figure out how to diaper and swaddle a wiggly baby, but also partly managing how to handle her lingering questions regarding Logan's whereabouts the day before. He had made it to the hospital two hours after Regina was admitted, and by then, she had been on the verge of exploding in anger, not to mention completely dilated and ready to push. He'd claimed he'd misplaced his phone—and what could she say about that? "I would love for you to stay. I need your steadiness. I need help feeding Miko. Breastfeeding is so hard, and the nurses are great, but they have other patients, too."

Sophie smiled back. "Then I'll be here. When's Logan getting back?"

"I'm already here," said a low voice at the door. Regina's husband sauntered in with flowers and a teddy bear, then gestured at Sophie. "What are you doing here?"

Regina didn't like Logan's tone, especially because he was just recently in the doghouse. "She's here to meet Miko and possibly stay overnight. I thought that since you said you were so tired—"

"I didn't say that." He set the items on the windowsill. "And I don't like the idea of her staying."

Regina bristled at the implication that she'd misheard and didn't have a choice, and embarrassment filled her that she was being disrespected so fresh postpartum. "Um, I think that I can make that decision."

His gaze swung to her. "I'm your husband, and the father of this child."

"But I am my own person, and Miko is my son, too."

"It's okay, Regina. I . . . I'll go," Sophie said quietly, gathering her coat off the bed.

This was wrong, so wrong. Regina sat up in bed. "Sophie, no. Please stay."

"I absolutely forbid her to be here," Logan said.

"But why?" Sophie whispered softly.

"You should ask your partner," Logan said.

"My partner?"

Regina's eyes darted between Sophie and Logan as bits of information from the last two weeks collided. Logan had mentioned that the cheating allegation was brought to the commander from

454

someone they knew. "It was Jasper?" she asked the both of them.

"Jasper what?" Sophie stood straighter. "What are you saying, Logan?"

"He's the one who went to the commander and told them that Becka and I . . . you know. He probably told everyone. It's his fault that I have a target on my back."

Sophie seemed to rise onto her toes. "Don't bring Jasper into something you did. He hasn't even said a word to *me* about it. He had the respect to keep it from even *me*. The reason you have a target on your back is because you painted it there yourself."

"Excuse me?" Regina scrambled to try to catch up with what Sophie had said. Did she just accuse Logan of having an affair?

"I said what I said," Sophie whispered. "I saw it myself, at the festival. He was talking to a woman. They were fighting."

"You what?"

"Get out. Take your lies and get out of here, Sophie," Logan growled.

Regina shook her head, unable to sort the truth from the lies, who she should believe, her husband or her friend. No, not just her friend, but Sophie, who was more like a big sister.

Sophie looked back at Regina. "I'm sorry, Regina. I'm telling the truth. I wanted to tell you but didn't know how."

Regina understood, then. She felt in her soul that her suspicions were true. Sophie didn't lie.

She touched her belly, a habit.

But she didn't say a word. Stunned, she simply watched as her husband ushered Sophie out.

When the door clicked shut, it cracked Regina's heart a sliver.

"You can't believe her," Logan said. "C'mon, babe. I've been home—you know nothing's going on. Yes, I was talking to a woman at the festival. You remember that night—so many of our friends were there."

The man was so smooth, so unflinching. Regina searched her mind's cupboards for how he'd acted since he'd returned. Where else had he been spending his free time?

"I don't want any more lies, Logan."

The smile died on his lips. With it, the crack broke Regina's heart clear through.

PART EIGHT

*I realize that just because I want to settle
down doesn't mean I have to settle.*

—*Waiting to Exhale* by Terry McMillan

CHAPTER FIFTY-FIVE
Regina

Present Day, Friday

Regina checked her watch; she had thirty minutes left until go time. The guests would arrive soon, and Henry was on his last trip back, with the cake. She'd successfully put Genevieve down for a nap, and in the last hour, Regina had gotten started with the decorations.

She twisted the pink tulle through the banister, her mind already on the next task: covering the tables with white tablecloths.

Her phone beeped a text, the fourth beep in probably ten minutes. Then again, her phone had been beeping nonstop since yesterday between Missy and Henry, preparing the final touches for the party. If she stopped each time someone texted her, she wouldn't get anything done. What she did know was that Sophie and Jasper were stalling Adelaide in Old Town until she got the signal from Regina. So she ignored the texts for now, and focused on tying the last bit of tulle at the top of the banister so that it looked like a bow.

The front door opened, spilling light into the foyer. Henry came through, this time followed by Carolina.

"Regina, cake's here," he said, with a whisper.

"Yay!" she whisper-yelled from up top. "The cake table is that circular one right there. Thank you."

"Have a great party," Carolina called up.

"You're not staying?"

"No, I've got another cake to deliver. See you soon?"

"I hope so." And she meant it, smiling. *And maybe more often.*

When the door closed, Henry looked up at her, mischief in his eyes.

She felt tingles running through her. "Henry . . . we're alone again."

He stopped fiddling with the boxes and ran a hand through his hair. "Yes, yes, we are." He strode toward the bottom of the stairs.

Ever since their night together, they hadn't been able to stop kissing, to keep from touching. At any private opportunity, she put her lips on him. This day alone, with the three trips he'd made back and forth from the cake shop, their work was interrupted by their hormones.

"What should we do?"

"I was thinking. Something"—he took two steps up—"naughty."

Her breath left her, replaced by need. She took

the next four steps down, meeting him. "I like naughty."

A growl escaped his lips, and it revved her engine. She felt mischievous. She took his hand; their fingers entwined. A step above him, she was even with his height, his lips an easy reach. They kissed hotly; his hands roamed her body; hers entangled in his soft hair. Her imagination ran ahead by a mile.

But his hands settled on her hips, and with gentle pressure, he pushed her away an inch. His face was regretful.

"I know. I know. Guests are coming in like ten minutes," she whined.

"Rain check," he said, not asked.

"Definitely."

"Okay, I'm going to let go now, even though it's going to kill me."

She bit her lip at how sweet he was. "Back to work, Mr. Just," she whispered.

He nodded and turned.

She slapped him on the butt. He laughed, spinning around. Regina ran up the stairs and he chased her; her heart in her throat, this time with joy, until he caught her and turned her around. His kissed her fiercely then, and she submitted to him. Her spirit fell into his. "We're going to wake the baby."

She'd said it with such innocence, but it changed the mood.

"I don't want this to stop," Henry said. "I know you have to leave in a couple of days, but I don't was *us* to end."

Regina's mind went blank, and the right answer evaded her. She wanted to agree with him, but her soldier instincts prevailed. *Nothing's set until the orders are cut,* or, make no promises until the logistics are planned.

In the pause, Henry's expression fell. His grip around her loosened.

"Henry—"

"No, it's okay. I'm sorry. That was too forward."

"No, that's not it. It wasn't too forward, I—"

"Hello?" A woman's voice echoed from downstairs. "The advance party's here. Put me to work! Anyone here?"

She shut her eyes. "It's Missy. But our conversation isn't over," Regina said, her focus divided. She wrapped her arms around his neck and planted a kiss on his lips. "Okay?"

"Yeah, okay."

From the bedroom came the cry of Genevieve waking.

"Gosh, um . . ." Regina started.

"I'll take care of her, and you can deal with Missy," Henry said.

"Do you know how to . . ."

"Grab a child from a crib? I think I can handle that. Go do what you need to do."

"You're the best." She let go and ran down the

stairs and encountered the woman she'd met just briefly but had bonded with. "Hey!"

Missy gave Regina a hug. "Did you get my text? I just saw Adelaide."

"What? Where?"

"By the toy store, about twenty minutes ago. I tried to stall." She turned toward Henry, who was coming down the stairs, holding Genevieve's hand as she stepped down. "Well, well, well." She winked at Regina.

Luckily, Henry was cordial as ever. He shook Missy's hand and somehow glossed over the entire awkward moment as Regina excused herself to the bathroom. Describing the meticulous methods of frosting, he fixed the two-tier cake upon a whimsical pedestal. He was a consummate professional.

Meanwhile, when Regina looked in the mirror, she saw a woman in the deep throes of longing. She would have to figure this situation out with Henry but until then: *focus*. Genevieve's party.

Missy's words caught up to her. Regina stepped out of the bathroom. "Which toy shop?"

Missy was setting the table like a good mommy-friend (Regina was impressed). "Four blocks away, on Burg."

Crap. "Do you think she knows?"

"Not sure. Another friend came by but I think we deflected the situation."

The doorbell rang. As Henry grabbed the door,

Regina retrieved her phone from the charger. There were messages from Sophie, updating her every couple of minutes, noting their location. And the last text, sent two minutes ago: *I can't stop her. She's literally walking home.*

Mothers and toddlers spilled in. Missy corralled the mothers and assigned them duties. Kids sprinted through rooms.

Regina went to call Sophie, and turned just in time to see Adelaide come through the door. "What on God's green earth is going on?"

Regina hung up.

Behind Adelaide, at the doorway, Sophie appeared. She had an exasperated look on her face.

The room silenced. Regina moved in front of the crowd. "Um . . . surprise?"

CHAPTER FIFTY-SIX
Adelaide

Her home was full of people. People were in rooms she wasn't finished decorating. There were children in every nook and cranny. One toddler was climbing up the stairs. Someone was coming out of the powder room.

"Surprise!" Voices chimed in, though not in unison.

Behind Regina, someone clapped. It was Genevieve. "It's my party!"

Adelaide was confused, but also joyful, and shocked.

Despite her warring emotions, Adelaide understood that she had to remain calm because there were too many people for her to lose her cool. This event was evidently for her daughter, but thrown in Adelaide's honor, whether or not she'd consented to it. So she plastered a smile on her face and grabbed Sophie's hand behind her. "We need to talk." Together they walked to the center of the foyer. Adelaide scooped up Regina's hand and dragged both her friends up the stairs, smiling, hoping people didn't notice her anger.

Finally behind her closed bedroom door,

Adelaide shut her eyes. "Who is responsible for this?"

"Me," said Regina.

Adelaide turned. "Why?"

"Because, I thought . . . you love birthdays and parties, and you said you were sad that you weren't throwing Genevieve a party." She took a step forward. "Look, I know I didn't ask permission."

"No, you didn't. And you know . . . *you know* that my home is so special to me, that it's important for me to prepare it myself. I feel like sh—doo-doo. Did you even think about that? And to reach out to these people? You can't just snoop or jump into people's lives."

Regina's chin dropped into her chest.

"It wasn't just her. It was me, too. I helped," Sophie said.

Regina threw her head back and laughed. "Oh my God, you can't be a martyr here, too. I can't even take the blame on my own."

"What are you talking about?" Sophie asked.

"Please. You did nothing for this party. And you couldn't even do the one thing I asked you, which was to keep her away until I gave you the okay."

Sophie hiked her hands on her hips. "Wait a minute. I can't help it if the patient went rogue. Who was the one who didn't keep an eye on their texts? I tried to help."

"Here we go again," Regina said, crossing her arms. "I hate to bring the past back up, but you 'helping' is something I can live without."

"Whoa," Adelaide said. The conversation was spiraling out of control.

Regina threaded her fingers in her hair. "I feel like I'm in an alternate universe. You, Ms. Picture-Perfect Adelaide, are yelling at me for doing something nice, when it's not my fault you arrived too early. All this after you fooled me into coming to Old Town in the first place to deal with this lady"—she gestured at Sophie—"when you knew what I went through after Miko was born."

"What do you mean by that?" Sophie asked.

"I ended up having postpartum depression." Regina frowned. "It didn't help that my birth experience was the worst. Not only was Miko a vacuum-assisted delivery, but he was blue coming out. I was already furious at Logan, and then there was . . ."

"The Fight," Sophie added.

"And then we found out that Command put Logan on orders months before we expected."

"No." Adelaide had had enough. "Stop it. The both of you. I'm sick of the both of you fighting. Because you shouldn't be fighting each other. Because this is all my fault." She let her gaze rest on each of them briefly, breath heaving. "Can you guys take a seat, please?"

"What—" Sophie started.

"Just do something once in your life without questioning me, please?"

Sophie took a seat on the wingback chair, and Regina perched on the bed.

"Regina, I know that you and Sophie had a fight after Miko was born. But it wasn't her fault that Logan got reassigned so quickly, truly." Now, it was Adelaide who had to sit. She took the chair next to the door, precariously. She swallowed the nervous bubble rising in her throat. "It was me."

Regina frowned. "What do you mean?"

"I mean that Sophie and I met up quickly after her visit with you. Matt had just come home, so I really didn't have time to socialize."

"I remember that," Sophie said. "You met me outside your building."

"You were crying," Adelaide continued, her heart hammering in her chest. "It made me upset for you. To be honest, I hated Logan for all of us. He had a baby coming, and he was lying to everyone—you, Command, Sophie, even Rebecca Chandler. By the time I walked back into the apartment, I was so upset, shaking even, and I had to tell someone, else I was going to explode. So I told Matt."

"Matt?" Regina asked.

Sophie laughed. "Matt told the commander."

Adelaide nodded. "He had to, at that point. While Sophie's impression was nothing concrete,

468

it was enough to expedite Logan's move. For the morale of the unit."

"So the unit's morale was improved by my husband leaving his postpartum wife and infant?" Regina said. "And you didn't say a thing. You let me blame Sophie."

"I'm sorry," Adelaide said, voice croaking. "I'm so, so sorry. But I didn't want to upset you more. You were alone. You needed someone."

Regina was shaking her head. "All this time." She fixed her eyes on Sophie. "I'm sorry, Soph. I'm sorry I let it all fall on your shoulders. I was a bitch. A bitch over a marriage that wasn't going to last, not really." She half laughed. "What's funny about all this is that I was thankful for the transfer in the end. It really made me who I was meant to be. I left the Army when my obligation was finished. I realized, truly, that my marriage was over. I went back to school. I started my own business. And I raised Miko."

Adelaide's tears began to flow. Now that the truth was out, she realized that by admitting it, she could lose her best friends. "I . . . don't have any excuses. It was a choice I made, which I regret."

"And knowing that I took the blame? That she blamed me?" Sophie stood. "Adelaide. All these years, I beat myself up over this. Sometimes I doubted myself as to whether I did the right thing. When I'd see Regina post on your Facebook feed,

I'd feel so sad and so left out. I often wondered what I could have done better. I . . . I can't be here right now. We've got a houseful whether we like it or not. I'm going downstairs, where we've got a little girl to celebrate."

Adelaide stood and reached out to Sophie, but her friend sidestepped her. "No, Adelaide."

Regina followed. "I'm going downstairs, too. If anything, my goddaughter deserves a great day."

Adelaide watched as both women went down the stairs. After several minutes, she did what she did best. She put a smile on her face and walked out the door.

Instead of being full of a loud crowd, the foyer was silent. A dark-haired man stood at the open front door. He was dressed in jeans and a polo, with a duffel slung on his back. His head was partly shaved, skin sun-kissed, and he had a distinct dimple on his chin. The same Genevieve had on hers.

"Oh my God, Matt." Adelaide held on to the banister, sheer determination keeping her upright.

Then she allowed herself to cry, in front of the entire crowd.

CHAPTER FIFTY-SEVEN
Sophie

The party went off without a hitch, in large part because of all the tiny details Regina planned, from the food to the outdoor games set up in the backyard. Not one bit of love was spared. But the party was also saved by their significant others.

Sophie had been in a daze when she'd descended the stairs, even when she'd witnessed Matt walk in the door. Her smile had been fake, her brain solidly still in Adelaide's bedroom, processing what her friend had admitted. Luckily, Jasper stepped into conversations with his charm. Henry chased after used paper plates and napkins. And Matt headed up the games—he was a child whisperer. The three men filled the room with their booming laughter and nonstop chatter.

Sophie was cleaning up as the last of the guests trickled out, when she felt hands on her shoulders. They were solid and heavy and comforting, squeezing gently. Jasper stood flush against her side. She turned to him, wrapped her arms around his waist, and rested her forehead on his chest as she'd done more times than she could have counted. "You survived it," he said.

"*We* survived the party. But the rest of it? It's not over yet."

"What are you going to do?"

"I don't have to do anything. In this case, it's me who has the upper hand. I'm wildly hurt that the truth didn't come out years ago. What do you think I should do?" She leaned back and looked up at him.

He rested a hand on the back of her neck. "I don't know. But I understand the thin line we used to walk between professional and personal. We lived in the shades of gray."

From her periphery, Sophie noted movement and turned. Regina, standing next to Henry, slung a scarf over her neck. At her feet was her green rolling suitcase.

"Hold on a sec, Jasper." She let go of him. "Reggie." When she approached, Henry stepped aside, into the living room. Regina continued knotting her scarf.

"Where are you going?" Sophie asked.

"I'm staying at a hotel."

"I know that this is a hard ask, but please don't go."

Her gaze shot up. "That *is* a hard ask."

"You said so yourself. Didn't everything turn out the way it was supposed to?"

"She lied to me. I love that woman, and she . . . I hate when people lie." There were tears in

472

her eyes. "She also knew about the bad blood between you and me. Years of me stewing. I'm surprised you're not packing up your things. She lied to you, too."

"I know." Sophie touched her forehead. "I can't seem to wrap my mind around the whole thing. But what I know for sure is that I can't leave. Because then I would lose her, and if you leave, you'll lose each other, too. You and I have already lost years together, and that has been painful enough."

"What are you saying?"

"I'm saying don't be rash about it. One bad thing shouldn't negate all the good between us. What if you hadn't come back a week ago? What if I had headed home mad? We wouldn't be here today. We wouldn't have tried to keep it together. And as much as we had our moments this week, we had some okay ones, too, didn't we?" Sophie sighed. "I don't know. But Jasper's here, after months of me pulling away, and Henry's here by your side, helping you as an equal. I have to think that means something."

"I can't even think." Regina brushed past her.

"Where are you going to stay?"

"I don't know, an Airbnb or a hotel somewhere? There's surely something open." She wheeled her suitcase out of the room and walked down the steps. "I need to figure out the rest of the logistics tomorrow. I'll text to let you know where I am, and to let her know, too, because I know she's going to worry."

"Okay," Sophie said, and with a nod to Henry, made way for him to catch up.

"I'm sorry for saddling you with the cleanup," Regina said.

Sophie smiled at both the thoughtfulness and the silliness of it all. "You threw the best party, in the shortest amount of time, with the least amount of help. You made that little one's year, and even if Adelaide didn't say it, I know she's grateful. So I think the least we can do is clean up."

Regina nodded, took two steps, then looked back. "I'm sorry for everything, Soph."

"I'm sorry, too."

CHAPTER FIFTY-EIGHT
Regina

Regina stuffed the suitcase into her trunk, and when she finally sank into Baby's driver's seat, the gravity of her conversation with Sophie caught up with her. She'd been so engrossed with the party and making sure people enjoyed themselves that she'd had very little time to think about what came next.

She leaned to the passenger-side door and opened it to Henry, who had been standing on the sidewalk, patiently.

He held up two hands. "I'm sorry to sneak up on you. I just wanted to make sure that—"

She gestured with her head. "C'mon in."

The car rocked as Henry got into the passenger seat and closed the door. The car tipped like it was on water.

"I neglected to give introductions the first day I arrived, but Henry, meet Baby. Baby, meet Henry. Baby was my first car and still is my only car. I bought her with my own money. She was a scrap heap when I got her, and now . . . now she is magnificent, though slightly temperamental."

"She's pretty."

"She is. But do you know why I love her so

much and why she matters to me?" She turned her face to the right. "Because she's mine alone. My name's the only one on the registration. When I first took her home, my family thought she wouldn't last. But all she needed was a little love and someone to trust." She paused, feeling her heart crack open again, a decade later. "Isn't that all anyone needs? People who love them? Who are willing to see them through the bad times?"

She rested her hands on the steering wheel, bent her head to lean her forehead against it. She shut her eyes. "Can you believe she said, 'Don't be rash'? What a total Sophie thing to say. But then I think: Am I rash? Did I not think in there? Was I part of the problem a decade ago, when I didn't listen to Sophie? And what am I supposed to do with all of this information? Am I just supposed to forgive someone who's lied to me for the last ten years?"

She turned her head to the side. Henry stared back at her intently.

"What are your thoughts?"

"I . . . I don't know. But it's obvious that those two care about you. A lot. I don't know what it is. Maybe it's because you were together at an impressionable time in your lives, or at your most vulnerable maybe? But a deep undercurrent runs through the three of you. For the three of you to have been in the middle of a fight, and with no one else at the party noticing it—that says something. Anyway, I can't even imagine what you're going through, but I can't let you stay at a hotel when I have a perfectly good place." He held up his hands. "Not for anything but a place to sleep tonight, if you wish. I promise."

"I know. I trust you." The words came out of her mouth before she thought twice. And she realized she meant it. She'd trusted him all along. "Listen, I know that we need to have our own conversation, about us."

He turned in his seat. "You and I have spoken or messaged almost every day the last eighteen months, Regina. You and I are good. Right now is not about us. This is about you and your friends."

"How are you like this?"

An eyebrow rose. "Like what?"

"So good, and understanding. And nice."

"Is that good? Should I be an asshole?"

She laughed. "No. But you make it so easy, which makes it all so hard, too." Her mind was ping-ponging from Sophie and Adelaide to Henry, and to her business, and . . .

"Argh." She laid her forehead on the steering wheel once more.

"Hey, it's okay." He placed a hand on her back.

"Is it?" She looked up ahead, to the bumper of the car in front of her, as if to find her answers there.

By the time she'd left Millersville, her friendship with Sophie had been in ashes. She'd remained friends with Adelaide, and to this day she swore it was Adelaide who'd helped her survive her first postpartum week, until her mother had been able to take over. In the years following, it was Adelaide she had turned to. "I don't want to lose Adelaide. Sophie, too."

He offered his hand; she set hers on top of his and held it firmly, as if it was a lifeline. "Deep friendships are complicated," he said.

She looked up at him, at his beautiful face and sincere expression. "Do we have a deep friendship, too?"

"You're changing the subject, Ms. Castro."

"Is it working?"

"Yes." He leaned toward her and kissed her sweetly on the lips. "Look, everything feels daunting, but you have choices. You have the choice to stay or go, to forgive or not. And no one says you need to make that decision right now, either. It's like cooking: you measure as best you can, you time according to the recipe, but the rest is just your gut."

He planted another soft kiss on her cheek. And as Regina felt the tingles travel through her body, she knew he was right. She just had to take a moment to actually hear what her gut had to say.

CHAPTER FIFTY-NINE
Adelaide

"I can't believe you're home," Adelaide said to her husband in a hushed tone. They were lying side by side, facing each other, under their covers. Their hands were intertwined in between them. Next to the bed, Genevieve snored in the Pack 'n Play.

He shook his head, face dimly lit by the moon through the window. "I was stupid to not ask for the time off. I don't know what was going on in my head, except that I took you for granted. I just always assumed that you'd handle everything, as you have all this time. But that second surgery woke me up. My commander didn't think twice about letting me go on leave."

She nodded. "Can I be honest?"

"Yes."

"I was really mad at you. And I was starting to resent you, and your work. I am done being second."

"You're not second."

"I'm not?" She laughed softly, though she tried to ease the sting with a smile. "I am, and why this has worked for so long is because I accepted it. And now, I'm at a point . . . I want there to be more than this. I need more." Adelaide swallowed her nerves. "I don't know what that means yet, totally. But I've been offered a job. Something that I could be damn good at, Matt. I want to see where it goes."

He took a breath. "Okay. Of course I support that, but . . . I still have the rest of my career. My pension. We need it."

"Oh God. I'm not asking you to quit the Army, babe. I know you love the Army. I love it, too. But I'm asking you to make this work. To be my partner as I have been yours, through everything. That means accommodating my plans in the process, even if we don't know how it'll work out."

She could see that he was biting his cheek. He did that when he was in deep thought. That and the furrow on his forehead. She spied the little gray hairs that had popped out since he left for Germany, evidence of their time apart. "I think I can swing some jobs in the area, maybe even until retirement. And with the daily stuff—to be here more often."

"You don't mind trying to stay here? At least for just a little while?"

"No . . . God, no. Adelaide, you are my life. And you are first. I don't want to you feel second ever again."

"Are you upset? About not trying for another baby?"

He shut his eyes and shook his head. "No, I'm not upset."

"Are you sure? You can tell me."

"Adelaide, children have never been a given for us. You and I have been trained to know this, for lack of a better word. I'm thankful for a healthy you, for Genevieve here with us. I want to be the best person for the both of you. Even if you still wanted kids, it's more important for the two of us to get it right, first."

"I love you."

"I love you, too."

Adelaide kissed her husband, wrapping her arms around his neck. She relished the comfort his lips brought, how he cradled her face with his strong hands, and the sweet familiar smell of his aftershave. A need grew within her, and their kissing intensified, but she pushed him away gently. "We have to be good, for now. I'm still in a little bit of pain."

"When you're ready, I'll be ready." He pecked her on the nose. "Though I may need a cold shower or a run around the block."

She laughed. "I didn't say we couldn't be creative. Just careful." At his big grin, she playfully slapped him on the arm. "You're so easy."

Adelaide's phone buzzed on her nightstand.

"I wonder who could that be?" he said mischievously.

"Why do you look like you know something?"

"Let's just say that Jasper has always been like a brother to me, and Henry and I bonded today over how to properly hang a piñata."

She patted her nightstand for her phone and brought it close to her face.

It was a text, from Regina:

Book club, now. Kitchen. SOS.

Seconds later, Sophie:

I'll be there.

Coming.

Adelaide sat up at a speed she hadn't accomplished since before surgery.

"Whoa. Don't hurt yourself, babe."

"It's an SOS. Book club."

He propped up on his elbows. "I haven't heard you say that in a long time."

"What?" She threw on a sweatshirt, slipped her feet into her slippers, and padded toward the stairs.

"Book club."

The point made it home quickly, and Adelaide paused. She perched on the bed. Matt wrapped an arm around her waist and rested his hand on her thigh. "I really messed up," she said.

"Adelaide. You did what you thought was right at the time. You can only be better. That's it. Go down there, and whatever they have to give, just take it, and learn from it."

She ran her fingers through his short hair. "Thank you." Leaning down, she planted a kiss on his forehead.

Adelaide left the dark room and descended the stairs. Voices sounded from the kitchen. The kitchen exhaust whirred. Her nose wiggled at the smell of something savory. *Oh my God. Bacon. Butter.* Which only meant . . .

"Breakfast?" Adelaide said, walking into the kitchen, squinting. Every single light was on. A pan filled with bacon cooked while the waffle maker dripped batter. On the table was an amber bottle of maple syrup and a powdered sugar shaker.

"I got hungry," Regina said. "And Henry had nothing in his kitchen, typical bachelor. You'd think he'd have a fridge full since he's a baker. But anyway, I still had your house key."

Adelaide sat at the table, where a pajama-clad Sophie already waited, eyebrows raised, which meant that she, too, didn't know what this was about, but was going with it.

"Here we go." Regina flipped a waffle onto a plate and set it in front of Sophie. "So, now that we're all together, I thought that maybe we should talk about the book, since you insisted we read it, Adelaide." She laughed. "Okay, okay, so I didn't really read all of the book, but I watched the movie the last couple of hours. And I get why you picked it. The story wasn't only about their relationships with men. It was also about their relationships with themselves and the friends that supported them."

Adelaide cleared her throat, tentative at Regina's sudden change in demeanor. But she responded with gusto, because she would take any kind of communication from her. "I really like how the author tackled four different strong personalities of women who were there for each other rather than to bring each other down."

"See? That's the thing . . . toward the end I was ready to just give up on the book—I mean, movie—because each one of the characters, despite their differences, was sometimes too stubborn for her own good. It was frustrating that they couldn't see what they could do to improve their situation."

"It's never that easy, though," Sophie said.

"I know. It isn't." Regina turned off the stove, and grabbed her plate, already piled with food. She joined them at the kitchen table. "Because it takes a while to really understand who and what the real problem is. Back then, it was Logan's affair—and now, my intent on blaming someone else for it."

"Regina," Adelaide started, because she had

more to say, too. "This is not on you. This was on me. It was my fault then and it's my fault now. I always so much want for things to be fine, when I should have allowed things to simply *be,* and accepted as such. I'm so sorry."

"No, no, no," Sophie said. "It was also on me. Back then, I should have gone to you immediately, Regina. But I wasn't sure if I should intrude. If it happened today, it would have been different. I would have called everything out right there and then at the festival. I wouldn't have hesitated."

Regina clasped her hands together. "Adelaide, I'm still mad. I still have feelings, lots of them. But I also moved on long ago, and after this week, as painful as it has been being with other type A–ers in this little house, I realized that I can't keep going without you both. Sophie, I know I said that I'd never forgiven you, but spending time here with you proved that not only was that not true, but I shouldn't have written you off. It was wrong, but I can't go back in time to fix things, though I wish I could. When it comes down to it, I missed you."

Sophie pressed her lips together. "I really missed you, too."

Adelaide's eyes filled with tears.

"I can't say it will be smooth from here on out, but I don't want to miss anyone anymore. I don't want to lose time," Regina said.

"Really?" Adelaide asked. Her chest heaved with relief, with gratitude.

"We have years to catch up on," Sophie said.

"Years together," Adelaide said, "but can we really try again?"

Regina nodded. "We can. Try."

Sophie sniffled. "Damn it. Why are you making me cry into my waffles?"

Regina put a hand in the middle of the table, and Adelaide clasped it. Sophie laid a hand on top of theirs.

It was their old tradition in a new age, tested by time, and strengthened by a book club far away.

EPILOGUE
Regina

One Year Later

Regina stepped down from her rented moving van and slipped the sunglasses off her face. The wind whipped with the start of spring, and she tightened her scarf around her neck. She stared at the red brick of an eight-hundred-square-foot town house in Old Town Alexandria.

The door on the passenger side opened, and Miko bounded out.

"Here she is," she said. "Home sweet home."

"It's like Baby Bear."

"It is." She tousled his hair, and laughed. The town house, a Georgian, was situated in between two taller town houses, like a Mama and Papa Bear. "It's perfect for the three of us. The school is two blocks down, and Ninang Adelaide is only three blocks South. Your dad is only two miles from here. And, bonus, parking spaces on this street are only for residents."

Speaking of. Regina turned and put a hand over her forehead to block the sun. Shortly, she detected the rumble of Baby and then the shine of her bumper as it crested the small cobblestone hill. It parked a street down, at an open spot. "Lola just parked, Miko."

They waited patiently for Gloria to walk up the street. She had a visor over her head, expansive so it shaded the sides of her face. Still, her smile was bright, matching her pink windbreaker and blue jean capris. "I can't wait to see your new house."

"Our house, Ma," she reminded her.

It had been a whirlwind since she returned to Columbus after her trip to Adelaide's last year. After a thorough review of her business, Regina indeed had had no choice but to close, but it wasn't going to be for long. "After all," Regina reminded her mother, "you helped with the deposit for this and for the new business. We have a bedroom with your name on it, and fully expect you to be here all the time."

"No more talk about money. What's mine is yours and Miko's. This is a good decision. New place, new opportunities. It's what I always hoped for you." She climbed the steps with them. "It's very cute. I can't wait to see inside."

"Wait till you see the kitchen." But when she jiggled the key into the door, it didn't work. "What the heck?" She inspected the key, then flipped to the other on the ring, and while the key slipped into the keyhole, it didn't turn.

"Maybe Missy gave you the wrong key?"

The red front door opened, and a rush of people

yelled. From around her, Regina felt the flutter of confetti. Henry swept her into his arms and kissed her. Adelaide and Matt and Genevieve followed, greeting Miko with a hug. Then came Sophie and Jasper, and Missy. They each had a plastic cup in their hand, filled with a pink bubbly drink.

A wave of nostalgia crashed over her so strong that she felt it deep in her chest. "Oh my goodness. What are you all doing here?"

"You think you're the only one who can throw a surprise party?" Adelaide said. "Actually it was Sophie who had the out-of-this-world idea to fill your fridge with food and make sure your bathroom's stocked. I only had the key."

"What can I say?" Sophie said. "Since we were visiting the girls in college, I thought, why not swing by to welcome you, since I suppose I owe you for all of those meals you cooked last year."

"Your girls go to school in North Carolina."

Sophie shrugged. "Like I said. I was in the neighborhood. Besides, I didn't want to miss out on meeting Lola Gloria. This is the woman who had to put up with Regina for at least eighteen years."

"Twenty-three now, because she was a boomerang." Her mother laughed.

"Hello. I am right here." Regina's face heated. "Seriously, I'm so surprised, and oh my God!" Regina walked through the living room, gawking

489

at the newly painted walls. She spun to face Adelaide. "You did this?"

"I did. It's the least I could do, for helping me last year. And because I know you like white on white. And to quote Sophie, what good am I as an interior decorator if I can't help the people I love?"

"Thank you. Thank you, everyone. I admit. It was tough leaving Georgia." She nodded toward Miko, who was now playing with Genevieve. He was showing her how to press the buttons on his handheld video game. "And I know we'll have some moments, but I'm excited to start anew. The Perfect Day personal chef, opening May 2022."

A round of applause ensued.

"Speaking of," Missy said, gesturing toward the rear of the home, "your documents and extra keys are on the kitchen counter, along with my phone number so you can add me to your friend list. I don't know what strings I have to pull, but I want in on this online book club you all started."

"Thank you, Missy, for finding this place for me."

"Of course!" Missy returned a stiff smile. Regina glanced at the others, and they, too, were silent.

"What's going on?" she asked.

"Go to the kitchen, iha," Gloria said.

"Okay."

Under everyone's watchful eye, Regina passed

through the darkened hallway, into the kitchen, which was brightly lit by the back windows. On the marble island was a little black box. Regina halted, stunned.

From behind her, hands on her shoulders gently nudged her forward. The sun through the window warmed her face, and along with it came energy and hope. She watched Henry get down on one knee.

Inside, she had expected this. Much like their kisses, their dates. Nothing was surprising or scary. Everything was tender and momentous. Like their conversations, their love flowed with ease, buoyed by trust the whole length of its journey.

His proposal was heartfelt. It was beautiful and tearful and perfect, and only made better that it was in the kitchen where she would, in the future, cook meals to show her love to her new husband, her growing son, and the new baby in her belly.

But today was for partying. After another round of applause, the wine flowed.

"Regina, Sophie! We need a selfie," Adelaide said, tipsy, cheeks pink.

"Yes!" Sophie said. "I have my phone right here."

"Soph, I've seen your selfies—might want Ad to do it," Regina teased.

"Listen, don't get all cocky just because it's your day."

"You don't know how to angle!"

"Hush, y'all! Dang." Adelaide extended her arm. On the phone screen, three women looked back, eleven years older, a little broken, a lot wiser, and inexplicably still surrounded by love.

"Say 'book club'!" Regina shouted, a spontaneous request at realizing what they had all overcome.

Their voices rang through the crowded kitchen. "Book club!"

ACKNOWLEDGMENTS

In a Book Club Far Away brewed inside me for so long that I wrote the first draft in about six weeks. But as with all first drafts (and even its consequent revisions), it didn't become a final book without being read and treated with care by an entire village of fantastic book people.

First, the inspiration: the military spouses and book club ladies (sometimes the combo of both depending on duty station) I've met during the last two-plus decades who have given me the foundation of friendship in my adult life. My life is richer because of your insight, love, laughter, and acceptance. You taught me to make friends quickly, to speak up, to help without reservation, to start anew with each fresh chapter. From you I nurtured my love of adventure, storytelling, and a glass of wine.

Sending thanks to these special readers (milspouses and avid book people) who have given me their points of view and who were brave enough to traverse my horrible typing skills in an earlier draft: Kim Cousins, Robin O'Sullivan, and Stephanie Winkelhake.

As always, many thanks to the #girlswritenight ladies, Annie Rains, Rachel Lacey, Sidney Halston, and April Hunt; #batsignal Mia Sosa,

Tracey Livesay, Priscilla Oliveras, Michele Arris, and Nina Crespo, who are truly beacons of positivity; the ever-vigilant and supportive Tall Poppy Writers, who I have the privilege of being a part of; #5amwritersclub, my everyday check-in, my early bird inspiration; and finally, innumerable and generous authors such as Julia Kelly, Amy Impellizzeri, Amy E. Reichert, and Camille Pagan.

Thank you to the team at Gallery Books! Erica Ferguson and Christine Masters for wrangling my words, Ella Laytham (once again!) for a gorgeous cover, and Jaime Putorti for the book's interior design. Bianca Salvant, Molly Gregory, and Michelle Podberezniak—sending thankful hearts your way!

LEO PR, thank you for your incredible work, most especially Kristin Dwyer, who is a reed amid rushing water.

Kate Dresser—we did it again! How did we do this? Thank you for intuitively knowing there was a book in my ramblings. You have a magical touch, but most of all, you are so patient with my process. Your belief in each book, in me, keeps me going when it gets tough.

Agent Rachel Brooks, the buffer of all of my thoughts, author whisperer. You are hereby dubbed Best Listener of All of Booklandia. You are incredible.

My loving parents, brothers, and sisters who

cheer me on from states away—I miss you all the time.

My children Greggy, Cooper, Ella, and Anna, resilient and loving Army brats—you all have experienced so much and you inspire every single one of my books.

To Greg, my husband and partner of over twenty years, all thus far entrenched in Army life, we've come so far from the lieutenants we once were, from the marriage we once had, from the tiny apartment we burned our first meals in. I love you.

Finally, to readers, bloggers, reviewers, book-sellers, and librarians: thank you for taking *In a Book Club Far Away* into your hearts! I hope you saw the love I have for military spouses and dependents, the joy of the Army life despite its challenges, my belief in friendship, and the wonder and magic a book club can bring to a community. I'm grateful for your support.

Books are
produced in the
United States
using U.S.-based
materials

Books are printed
using a revolutionary
new process called
THINKtech™ that
lowers energy usage
by 70% and increases
overall quality

Books are
durable and
flexible
because of
Smyth-sewing

Paper is
sourced using
environmentally
responsible
foresting methods
and the
paper is acid-free

Center Point Large Print
600 Brooks Road / PO Box 1
Thorndike, ME 04986-0001 USA

(207) 568-3717

US & Canada:
1 800 929-9108
www.centerpointlargeprint.com